# Praise for Christy Barritt and her novels

"These characters address the age-old question of whether it is possible to have a career and family, a sacrifice that's often made by members of our military. The pace is steady as the characters seek to find purpose through tragedy."

—*RT Book Reviews* on
*High-Stakes Holiday Reunion*

"At its core, this is a spy story that will keep readers on their toes. The two headstrong lead characters perfectly complement each other."

—*RT Book Reviews* on *Hidden Agenda*

"Unpredictability, action and a surprising perp add to this satisfying suspense."

—*RT Book Reviews* on *Dark Harbor*

# Praise for Sandra Robbins and her novels

"The gripping storyline pulls the reader along for a wild ride, while the characters demonstrate that God can bring peace amid chaos."

—*RT Book Reviews* on *Yuletide Jeopardy*

"The mystery is well done and loosely based on a real-life case."

—*RT Book Reviews* on *Trail of Secrets*

...............g peace from past

...... on *Shattered Identity*

**Christy Barritt**'s books have won a Daphne du Maurier Award for Excellence in Suspense and Mystery and have been twice nominated for an RT Reviewers' Choice Best Book Award. She's married to her Prince Charming, a man who thinks she's hilarious—but only when she's not trying to be. Christy's a self-proclaimed klutz, an avid music lover and a road-trip aficionado. For more information, visit her website at christybarritt.com.

An award-winning, multipublished author of Christian fiction, **Sandra Robbins** wrote seventeen titles for Love Inspired Suspense.

# High-Stakes Holiday Reunion

Christy Barritt

&

# Yuletide Jeopardy

Sandra Robbins

HARLEQUIN® LOVE INSPIRED® SUSPENSE

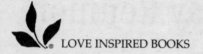

**LOVE INSPIRED BOOKS**

Recycling programs for this product may not exist in your area.

ISBN-13: 978-1-335-44816-3

High-Stakes Holiday Reunion and Yuletide Jeopardy

Copyright © 2018 by Harlequin Books S.A.

The publisher acknowledges the copyright holders of the individual works as follows:

High-Stakes Holiday Reunion
Copyright © 2013 by Christy Barritt

Yuletide Jeopardy
Copyright © 2013 by Sandra Robbins

www.Harlequin.com

**Printed in U.S.A.**

# CONTENTS

HIGH-STAKES HOLIDAY REUNION      7
Christy Barritt

YULETIDE JEOPARDY      239
Sandra Robbins

# HIGH-STAKES HOLIDAY REUNION

Christy Barritt

This book is dedicated to my readers.
Your friendship and notes of encouragement
mean the world to me and always brighten my day.

Peace I leave with you; my peace I give to you. Not as the world gives do I give to you. Let not your hearts be troubled, neither let them be afraid.
—*John* 14:27

# Chapter One

As Ashley Wilson rounded the corner, her foot slammed onto the brakes.

What…?

In the distance, her brother's house came into view. A commotion on the lawn caused her blood to freeze.

Three men in suits scuffled near the sidewalk. Her brother Josh's tall, lanky form jerked in the middle of the crowd as he struggled against the men. What were they doing to her brother? Who were these men?

Her gaze went to the two black sedans parked at the curb. The men were trying to…force her brother into one?

She yanked her gaze from the scene to her clock. David. Where was the eight-year-old? His bus hadn't come yet. It couldn't have. Ashley was on her way to meet him, but had arrived a good ten minutes early.

Still, panic raced through her.

She wanted to throw the car into Park, rush from her seat and intercede. But there was no way she could overtake all of those men.

Her gaze zoomed in on the black metal at one of the men's waistband. A gun. These men were armed.

Her heart stopped when she saw a tiny head bobbing in the crowd.

David. Her precious nephew, David. Her reason for waking up in the morning. Her reason for working at home as a web designer with flexible hours. Her heartbeat.

They had David. She covered her mouth as a guttural cry escaped.

How had they gotten David? He was supposed to be in school. Had Josh pulled him out early today?

Some of her logic returned, hitting her with the force of a lightning bolt. The police. She had to call the police. That was all there was to it.

She reached into her purse and fumbled with the cell phone, her hands trembling so badly she wasn't sure she could dial.

She glanced up just in time to see one of the men point her way and yell something.

Two of the men pulled their guns and began running toward her car.

Toward her.

She threw the car in Reverse. She had to get away. If they caught her then there'd be no way she could help. She slammed her foot onto the accelerator. Her neck snapped back with the force, but she didn't care. Adrenaline pumped through her veins.

That's when she heard the first pop. Her heart sped. They were shooting at her. She ducked just as the windshield shattered.

She screamed but kept going. Reaching the street

behind her, she pulled hard on the steering wheel, threw the car into Drive and squealed off. Another pop sounded behind her but didn't reach her car.

She glanced in her rearview mirror. The men had stopped running. She'd lost them. For now.

She craned her neck, trying to see beyond the eerie, spiderweb-like lines etched into her windshield. She could hardly see the road. Finally, she reached the street leading away from the neighborhood.

Her mind raced a million miles a minute. What had just happened? What should she do now?

The police, she remembered. She needed to call the police.

Grief crushed her heart. David. Poor David. She needed to help him, to soothe him and wipe his tears. Since Josh's wife had died, Ashley had filled in as a mother figure. Now her heart squeezed with a maternal grief.

No, the best thing she could do was to let the authorities know. There was no way her 120 pounds could take down all three of those men. Probably not even one of them.

Keeping one eye on the road, she grabbed the phone, which had fallen to the floor in her haste to escape. Her fingers trembled on the keypad. Before she could dial, the phone beeped with an incoming call.

She saw the number, and her heart raced—first with hope, then dread. Her brother?

She looked back at the road, swerving away from an oncoming car. Quickly, she answered. "Josh? What's going on?"

"You can't call the police, Ashley." His words tumbled into each other, and panic laced his voice, making its pitch rise.

"Josh, I'm scared."

"Ashley—"

Before he could finish, another voice came on the line. "We'll find you and kill you, Ashley Wilson. You weren't supposed to see that."

The words sent cold fear through her. "Who is this? What do you want with my brother?"

"Stay out of it," the man growled.

Even the sound of his voice conjured up images of evil, of a heartless man. "What about David? Can I just get David? Leave him out of this. Please. He's just a child."

Suddenly, the black sedan appeared in her rearview mirror—coming fast and closing the space between them too quickly. Memories of her accident began to crush her last shred of sanity. No, she couldn't let her mind go there. Not now.

She swerved onto a side road, the phone slipping from her hand as she gripped the wheel. She didn't have time to worry about it now. She accelerated. A glance behind her confirmed that the car turned down the same street. A man hung out the side window, a gun in hand.

She had to think, and quickly. She didn't have much time.

Just then, the back glass shattered. She screamed, trying to maintain her control of the car. Wind—cold and sharp—whipped around her. Pellets of glass rained down from her hair. She couldn't drive like this much longer. It wasn't safe—for her or anyone around her.

But her survival instinct was greater than her fear. She had to stay alive—not for her sake, but for David's.

A busy highway waited ahead. Before she reached it, she turned onto another side street. Immediately, she pulled into a parking lot. A shopping center shadowed her car as she drove full-speed in front of the structure. At the corner, she swerved around the building and slammed on the brakes.

Maybe they hadn't seen her. Hopefully, they'd assumed that she'd gone straight.

But just in case they didn't, she grabbed her purse and her phone and jumped out of the car.

Two delivery trucks were parked behind the strip mall, and their drivers were unloading boxes of product. Ashley picked the closest one and ran toward him. He looked up as she approached, his eyebrows furrowed in curiosity.

"I'm sorry," she mumbled, not stopping to ask permission. She ran through the propped-open door instead, darted through the back offices and break room and into a hardware store.

Her gaze fluttered wildly about the building. Where now? Where could she hide?

The black sedan flew past the front windows of the store. They knew she'd come this way. Now what did she do?

She crouched down, waiting until the car disappeared.

Then she sprinted out the front door and toward the opposite end of the row of shops. What store had that other delivery truck been stopped behind? She pictured the design on the truck. Pastries.

Taking a guess, she slipped inside a drug store, running until she reached the back.

"Hey, what are you doing?" A man in a cashier's smock held up a hand to stop her as she charged into the door marked "Employees Only."

"Sorry." She didn't stop to hear his response. She went straight to the back door. She paused there, slowly peeking around the edge of it.

She spotted the black sedan parked haphazardly beside her car. A man jumped from the vehicle and ran in through that same delivery door and into the hardware store. It was only a matter of moments before they found her and killed her. She couldn't let that happen.

The other delivery truck wasn't far away. Only a few feet. The driver had packed up and was climbing into the front. That truck seemed her only hope at the moment.

She crept outside, concealed behind a Dumpster. If she ran, she might make it onto the back of the truck before the driver realized what was happening. She had to. It was her only chance.

Staying low, she slunk toward the truck. The engine started. She didn't have much time. If she was going to make a move, it had to be now.

*Lord, help me.*

She lunged toward the back door. Her hand connected with the handle.

It opened. Praise God, it opened.

She swung into the back of the truck, colliding with a rack full of prepackaged donuts and cupcakes. She closed the door just as the man in black exited the hardware store.

She was going to get away, she realized.

But her heartbeat didn't slow as she wondered if her brother and nephew would be so fortunate.

Christopher Jordan ran a hand over his face, weariness from a long, hard week of work compounding until a pulsing headache thumped at the back of his head. He'd worked too late—again. Now darkness surrounded his car as he drove the hour back to his house.

He really should buy a place closer to work. But this house had lots of memories for him, and he couldn't give those up yet. He needed those memories now. He needed good memories to push out all of the bad ones.

He turned off the highway, and the streets became quieter, darker. Just like his soul, he thought. Ever since he returned from war, he hadn't felt like himself.

Just how was he going to remedy that?

Good memories, he thought. He just needed to hold on to the good. That, along with his faith in God, would help to pull him through his inner turmoil.

Finally, he turned onto his street. All he could think about was getting home for the weekend, being alone and not doing anything for as long as humanly possible—which meant until Monday came and it was back to work again.

He knew his stress was from more than just his work. He'd only been back from the Middle East for three months, and memories of the place still haunted him. Every night, nightmares jolted him awake. Too many images stained his mind. It seemed as if they'd been imprinted on his soul, and for the rest of his life he'd carry the burden of his time deployed.

He'd gotten out of the military, taken a job as a training specialist at the private security contracting firm Iron, Incorporated, also known as Eyes. He taught tactical training, such as sharpshooting and use of force to law-enforcement groups that came to Eyes for instruction. Eyes worked with both local law-enforcement communities, as well as the Department of Defense, in training personnel, developing programs and equipment, and for other special assignments.

He'd taken the job in hopes of repairing some of the damage his psyche had suffered. He'd thought he was stronger than all of this. But the deaths of those around him had begun to take their toll on him, and now he wondered if he'd ever be the same.

He'd poured himself into work at his new job, hoping to erase the pain. But it was always there, cold and achy and throbbing.

The two-story house that his grandfather had left to him came into view. The place was out in the middle of nowhere. Some would call it isolated. Christopher called it breathing room. He slowed as he turned into his driveway, his headlights skimming the front of the house.

His foot pressed on the brakes. Was that something on his porch? In his rocking chair?

In the dark, he could hardly tell. Something was out of place, but whatever was on the rocking chair only appeared to be a shadow.

He should have left the porch light on, he supposed, but he hadn't thought about it when he left home this morning. Now all of his instincts were on alert. Could it have to do with his SEAL team bringing down the leader of that terrorist group? Had their names been leaked? They'd all be logical targets in the aftermath of the terrorist group's demise.

But especially Christopher. He'd been the one to pull the trigger.

He reached under the front seat and pulled out the gun he kept there. He carried it with him at all times as a part of his job.

Slowly, cautiously, he got out of his car. Yes, there was definitely something on his porch. Or was it… someone?

He crept toward the steps. The bitter cold air filled his lungs, heightening his awareness even more. Who would be hanging out on his porch at night? Had one of the terrorists found him?

With his other hand, he fingered the phone in his pocket. Should he call for backup? No, not yet. They'd only think he was paranoid, only push him harder to get more counseling for PTSD. The last thing this soldier wanted to do was talk about his feelings, especially with a stranger.

He scanned the usually welcoming porch again. The railing still looked intact. Even the strands of evergreen that he'd draped there, complete with red Christmas bows, were in place. He didn't see anyone lurking behind the bushes or peeking around the corner of the house.

With the skill of a trained fighter, he climbed the steps, his gun pointed at the figure on his porch. He couldn't see a face. The person appeared to be hiding underneath a coat—arms, legs, face and all.

He cocked his gun, all of his instincts on alert, each

of his muscles poised for action. "You have three seconds to show yourself before I fire."

The figure flinched, and a mad fluttering of limbs ensued. Finally, a head popped up. Familiar eyes stared at him, wide with fear. The facts hit him one by one. Honey-blond hair. Oval face. Slim build. He couldn't see the color of her eyes, but he instinctively knew they were blue.

The woman raised a slender hand. "Please, don't shoot. It's me." Her voice sounded soft, lyrical—and desperate.

"Ashley?" He lowered his gun, disbelief washing over him. It couldn't be. No, not Ashley. Not his ex-fiancée, the woman whose heart he'd broken when he'd called off their engagement. Their parting had been one of the most painful conversations he'd ever had, and still when he thought about it today, an ache formed in his chest. He'd had to make a decision between his career or a family. His country had needed him, so he'd chosen his career. He tried to live without regret; he thought he was stronger than that. But whenever he allowed himself to think about Ashley, regret was the very emotion that tried to creep into his mind. He'd loved that woman at one time. Times had changed, though; he had changed.

She nodded slowly, raw emotion lining her eyes. She pulled the white, wool coat around her more tightly as the wind picked up again, sweeping dry leaves across the porch. The sound tightened his nerves.

"Christopher."

Instinctively, he stepped closer. He'd both dreamed and had nightmares about this moment for so long.

During those dark moments on the battlefield, he'd wondered what it would be like to see Ashley again.

And never had he imagined it like this. Not him with a gun in his hand and her with a look of absolute vulnerability straining each of her lovely features. No, in his moments when he'd faced death, he'd imagined Ashley forgiving him, smiling, picking up where they'd left off. He knew that would never happen. Even if there weren't any hard feelings between them, Christopher knew he was too broken and damaged to be in a relationship right now.

He remembered their last conversation and paused, unsure how to greet her. Not with a hug. Not with the way things had ended. A handshake seemed too formal when considering their past relationship. Instead, he settled for putting his gun away and making an effort to relax his shoulders.

He and Ashley had met at a mutual friend's house on New Year's Eve more than a decade ago, and it had been a textbook case of love at first sight. Not only had he instantly thought she was beautiful, but her smile, her love for life, her hope for the future had hooked him. She'd pulled him out of the shell he easily sucked himself into—most people didn't see it because he'd hidden it well with easygoing small talk. But Ashley had always seen right through him. She had a way about her that made him open up.

Their two years together were filled with easy, effortless moments. Relationships like that didn't happen often. Six months before the wedding, he'd called things off.

Ashley brushed a hair out of her face and licked

her lips. Her eyes implored him. "I'm sorry to show up here, but I didn't know where else to go." Her voice sounded tight and strained.

He reached toward her, compassion and concern pounding through his veins, but his hand dropped midway. "Are you okay?"

She hesitated and then shook her head. Those wide, pleading eyes met his again. "I need your help."

He stared at her another moment, thoughts and emotions colliding inside him. His help? What could he possibly help her with? Whatever it was, his gut told him it was serious. "Let's go inside. Get you out of the cold."

As she stepped closer, Christopher wanted to soak her in, to absorb all the changes in her over the past several years. But he couldn't do that. It was no longer his right.

He unlocked the door, noticing that she was shivering uncontrollably. From the cold? Or from something deeper?

He flipped the light on in the entryway and dust bunnies floated across the wooden floor. Perhaps he'd neglected housekeeping more than he should have. He offered an apologetic grin. "I wasn't expecting to see you. I would have straightened up some."

She stepped inside, her face grim with…sorrow? Fear? Grief? His grin slipped. With a hand on her back, he led her into the living room where boxes still waited along the walls for him to unpack.

She shivered again. "Believe me. I wasn't expecting to be here. I only came here because I was desperate."

The brutal honesty of her words stung. She'd made

it clear when they last talked that she never wanted to see him again. Christopher couldn't blame her. Things had ended badly. He'd made the best decision possible at the time. But in hindsight, he'd wondered if it was the worst decision ever.

He didn't have time to think about what could have been now. Instead, he led her to the couch, one that had been left here by his grandfather. This was probably the same sofa that had been here back when he and Ashley were dating, when they used to come over and play dominoes with his granddad. "Have a seat."

She lowered herself and folded her arms across her chest. Her legs were crossed at the ankles, and trembles still claimed her muscles. Her gaze pulled on his. "I'm in trouble, Christopher. I didn't know where else to go."

His jaw flexed under the weight of her words, but he nodded. "Go on."

"My brother and nephew have been kidnapped, and you're the only one who can help."

## Chapter Two

Ashley swallowed hard as she watched Christopher blink and tilt his head. It would take anyone some time to comprehend her words. She was still having a hard time comprehending them.

"Say that again?" His voice held a touch of disbelief and confusion.

She shook her head, emotion tightening her muscles. "Listen, I know it's a lot to take in. I'm still trying to take it all in. It just seems like a nightmare, but it's not." She closed her eyes, wishing this was all just a bad dream and that she'd wake up to find everyone safe and sound. Things like this didn't happen to ordinary people like Ashley. Only it *had* happened.

Christopher shifted in his seat and leaned toward her, his full attention on her. He'd always been such a good listener. At one time, it had been one of the many qualities she'd loved about him. Their breakup had devastated her, though. Now almost every memory of him caused hurt instead of joy. Those hurts had been compounding for nearly a decade. Only desperation would lead her back here.

"Why don't you start from the beginning?" Christopher urged.

She sucked in a deep breath before recounting the story, detail by detail. Christopher listened quietly, nodding on occasion. He murmured words of encouragement as he tried to grasp her story.

"You jumped on the back of a bakery truck to escape?" He squinted.

She nodded, knowing how crazy she sounded. It was amazing the things a person did while fighting to survive. She'd been there before—emotionally, at least. "I jumped off at the next stop."

"And how'd you end up here?"

"I ran into Karina about a month ago at the grocery store, and she told me that you were back in town." Karina was married to a SEAL and remained a distant but mutual friend. "I used my cell phone to find Karina's number and asked if she knew where you were living now. She said at your granddad's old place. I snuck off the truck, called a taxi and now I'm here."

He stared at her a moment, an unreadable expression on his face. "Ashley, if you don't mind me asking, why here? Why me?"

How could she tell him the truth about how Josh and David's disappearance affected him also? She couldn't. Not yet. She'd only tell him the secret she'd been carrying with her for years as a last, desperate measure.

For so long, she'd been bitter about Christopher walking out of her life. Now here she was, basically at his mercy. Where did she even start?

She held her hands in the air to show her confusion. The action also showed her surrender. She'd basically raised her white flag when she arrived here, an unspoken agreement to put the past behind them. But could she really do that? She let out her breath slowly. "I don't know where else to go. I can't go to the police. I think these men would kill Josh and David if I did." She glanced at her hands, now in her lap. "I thought maybe you could help."

Christopher leaned forward. He'd aged since Ashley had last seen him. He used to have the boy-next-door look about him. He'd been all-American with his tousled blond hair, easy smile and friendly green eyes. What had changed besides the fact that he was beefier now, more man and less boy? He was still chiseled and defined. He carried himself with his head raised high and his eyes wide and alert. He was confident, capable and tough.

But right now, whenever he looked at her, a strange emotion loomed in the depths of his eyes. Weariness? Hardness? Apathy? She didn't know.

"Why would someone abduct your brother and his little boy, Ashley? That's what doesn't make any sense to me."

She shook her head, grief clutching her heart again as their parting images filled her mind. "I don't know. Josh had been working on some big projects for his company. He never told me any details, though, as to what exactly he was doing."

He shifted but kept his gaze on her. "He's some kind of computer genius, right?"

She nodded. "He's absolutely brilliant when it comes

to anything to do with technology. There's nothing he can't do."

He rubbed his hands on his jeans and shook his head. "How about his wife? Have you talked to her? Does she know about any of this?"

"She died three years ago. Cancer." Her heart panged as she said the words aloud.

"I'm sorry, Ashley. You said they had a son? I knew they'd been trying."

Ashley's throat burned as she nodded. She remembered all of the Sunday brunches Christopher had shared with her family. He'd seemed to fit right in. That part of her life seemed so long ago. So much had changed since then. "David. He's eight, and he's a wonderful little boy." Her voice caught. "I'm so worried about him, Christopher."

Christopher stood and ran a hand over his face. "I'm not an expert at tracking down missing persons, Ashley. Terrorists, maybe. But this… I want to help. I really do. I just…"

"Please, Christopher. I don't know where else to go." She looked up at him, hoping her eyes conveyed her desperation. She would have never come to him unless she was desperate. He had to know that.

He was silent a moment before nodding. "Let me call some of my friends at Eyes. Maybe they can—"

"Eyes?"

He nodded. "They're a private security contracting firm."

"I've heard murmurs about them in the area. I didn't realize you worked for them now. Karina just said that you were a contractor for the Department of Defense."

"That's right. I'm a training specialist. It's a nice change from what I was doing. I'm sure someone there can help us. The men who run the operation have connections…well, everywhere. Local law enforcement, FBI, CIA, you name it."

"That sounds perfect. Thank you." A touch of hope filled her for the first time since all of this had happened.

He pointed outside. "In the meantime, the apartment over the garage isn't much, but you can stay there tonight, if you want."

She shook her head harder than intended and started to rise. "I can't even think about sleeping. I need to go find them, Christopher. Now. Don't you understand?"

His hand covered her arm, and he pulled her back down onto the sofa. "Ashley, I know you want to go out there and search, but we have no idea where to even look. We need a plan. We at least need a clue. If we go out there right now, all we'll be doing is driving around in circles. It's best if we get a good night's rest and start fresh tomorrow morning."

The truth of his words washed over her. It wasn't what she wanted to hear, but he did make sense. If they left tonight, where would they go? What exactly would they do? She had no idea.

Finally, she nodded. "You're right. I can call a taxi, though. Go to a hotel for the night."

"Don't be silly. You should stay close, just in case."

Just in case what? Her throat burned, but the question wouldn't leave her lips. Instead, she said, "Okay. I hate to impose, but I don't have a lot of choices right now."

Her cell phone buzzed in her pocket. She pulled it out and saw that she had a text message.

Tell anyone and the boy dies

She gasped and dropped the phone. They wouldn't really hurt little David, would they? She squeezed the skin between her eyes and began praying.

"What is it?" Christopher leaned down and picked up the phone. The words he read there made his blood go cold. He glanced up at Ashley and saw that her face was deathly pale. The woman looked as if she were on the brink of a breakdown. Who wouldn't be, in her shoes? Two of the people she loved most in the world had been snatched right in front of her, and she was sure to feel helpless about what to do.

A tear trickled down her face. She looked so alone with her arms pulled across her chest. Christopher put her phone on the table and impulsively pulled her into his arms in a feeble attempt to offer comfort.

She stiffened in his embrace. Bad idea, he realized. Really bad idea.

He released her, his throat tight with emotion. "I'm sorry, Ashley."

She sighed. "I am, too."

The way she said the words made him wonder about their meaning. What was she sorry about? That he was the only one who could help her?

Her eyes met his, and he could see the emotions pulling at her.

"I didn't come back to rekindle a romance, Christopher," she whispered. "You know that. Right?"

He nodded, picking up on the compassion and sensitivity in her words. "Of course."

Part of him had never forgotten about Ashley, but he knew she wouldn't forgive him for calling off their engagement. It was just as well that way. At least their rift would help them both keep their distance.

He pointed toward the back door, ready to end this conversation. "How about if I show you upstairs?"

Maybe some time away from each other would be just what they both needed. Put them in the same room for ten minutes and fireworks had begun exploding—and not the good kind of fireworks, either.

He grabbed some sheets and blankets before they stepped out the back door. Darkness surrounded them. Christopher reached back inside to flip on a small light, but nothing happened. "Must be burned out," he muttered. "Just watch your step."

The full force of winter was evident in the dried leaves along the wooden floorboards beneath them and the skeletal outline of trees in the distance. The entire back side of the house faced the beautiful and massive James River. The grass faded into marshland and then into glimmering blue water—when you could see it during the daytime hours, at least. Tonight, all that was visible was the blackness.

"Follow me." Christopher led her up a flight of wooden stairs, pulled out some keys and unlocked the door just as another breeze swept over the area. "I heard we might get some snow," he muttered, pushing the door open. Their conversation somehow seemed awkward, like they were strangers trying to fill the silence.

"Yeah, I heard that, too. It's been a while since we've had a good snowstorm in this area." Her cheeks flushed as she said the words.

Christopher remembered a snowstorm they'd had here nine years ago. He and Ashley had spent the whole weekend huddled inside together by the fire and talking about forever. They'd talked about marriage and children and how they were going to celebrate their 25th anniversary. Too many memories for his comfort.

They stepped into the apartment, which was located over a detached garage. He tried the light switch, but again, nothing happened. "Must be a breaker. I'll check on it in a second. Let me just put these sheets down."

As he placed the sheets on the bed in the darkened room, his gaze scanned the place quickly. He'd only been up here once since he'd been back, but the place appeared untouched. He turned back toward Ashley, who stood uncomfortably in the center of the room, her arms wrapped around herself again. His gaze latched on to her a moment. Was it even possible that she was more beautiful than before? She'd filled out more, but the extra weight looked good on her. She looked more naturally beautiful with only a little makeup on and her hair straight and long—fuss-free, if he had to guess.

She looked up at him, the strain in her eyes obvious. "I know this is awkward, and I'm sorry about that. I'll repay you for your help. I don't know how, but I will."

How did Christopher tell her that he was the one who needed to repay her for all of the heartache he'd caused? He bit down on his lip. He couldn't.

All he could do was to help her find her brother and nephew.

As much as Ashley resented the man in front of her, God had been trying to teach her a lesson in forgiveness lately. Yet she'd kept holding on. Now she would have no choice but to face her feelings of resentment and abandonment head-on.

Christopher stepped closer, the raw look in his eyes making her throat go dry. She wondered what had changed in him over the past several years since she'd seen him last. "I'm glad you came to me, Ashley. I want to help."

*Nothing will ever make up for your choosing your career over me.* She didn't say the words aloud. Instead, she reached for the sheets on the bed. "I'll be fine. If you don't mind hitting the breaker, I can take care of the rest in here."

He continued staring until finally he stepped back and nodded, his hands on his hips. "Good night, Ashley."

She hugged the sheets to her. "Good night, Christopher."

He took a step toward the door when gunfire exploded outside.

"Get down!" Christopher threw her to the floor, covering her body with his.

Her heart pounded louder than a drum in her ears as prickly fear took hold of her. What was going on? Had those men found her?

Her gaze skittered across the room. They had to hide—but where? There was only this room, a closet and a small bathroom. There was no other escape except the door they'd entered through, and stepping outside now would make them open targets.

The gunfire continued. Glass broke. A car alarm wailed. It sounded like a war outside.

She turned enough to see Christopher. She flinched when she saw the expression on his face. She'd seen a lot of expressions on him before, but never one like this. His face was tight, his eyes livid, his lips pulled into a rigid line. He looked like a cat ready to pounce.

The war. Karina had warned Ashley in their brief conversation earlier that the war had changed him. Was this what she meant?

Fear unlike anything she'd ever felt before today threatened to suffocate her. It was only a matter of time before the gunmen found them up here. It was only a matter of time before they killed her and Christopher.

Ashley scooted from beneath him and crouched by the wall. "Do you still have your gun?" she whispered.

Christopher pulled himself up and squatted beside her, alert and ready to spring into action. He shook his head. "I left it on the table inside. Wasn't planning on needing it."

"They're going to kill us." Her voice cracked as the gunfire continued. Was it her imagination or was the sound getting closer and closer?

He gripped her arm, his voice stern. "Don't say that. We'll get out of this somehow."

Was he in the same place she was? "We're sitting ducks. It's just a matter of time before they find us."

"Don't talk like that. I've gotten out of worse before." He nodded toward the bathroom. "Stay low and go into the bathroom. We'll buy ourselves as much time as possible."

Her hands trembled against the floor as she dragged herself toward the small space. He'd gotten out of worse than this? She couldn't imagine. Didn't want to imagine.

Nausea roiled in her gut. *Lord, help us. Help David and Josh.*

Just who were these men? Why did they want her

dead? How had they found her? The questions repeated themselves over and over.

Her hands connected with the cool tile of the bathroom floor. Gunshots continued to explode outside. They were trying to make sure Ashley was dead, weren't they? And out here in the country, there was no one else around to hear the commotion and come help.

Fear threatened to seize each of her muscles. Christopher jetted into the bathroom behind her and quietly shut the door. Ashley climbed into the bathtub—located against an interior wall—and Christopher sat beside her. She pulled her knees to her chest and tried to even out her breathing.

The cold air seemed to crackle with fear, with certainty of death.

Then everything went silent outside.

Ashley wasn't sure which was worse—the gunfire or the silence.

What were the gunmen doing? Had they gone inside the house to look for them, to make sure a bullet had pierced their flesh?

When they discovered Ashley wasn't there, would they come out to the garage to finish the job? She pressed herself harder into the cool tile.

Christopher leaned close enough that Ashley could feel his breath on her cheek. "Stay here. Understand?"

"Where are you going?" She grabbed his arm, desperate to keep her only known ally close—even if he had broken her heart at one time.

He locked gazes with her, that same confidence that had always made her feel safe shining in his eyes. "I'm going to find something to fight with."

"But they have guns!" She squeezed harder, her own fear creeping in.

"If I go down, I'm going to go down fighting, Ashley." His voice was steady, holding not even a hint of disbelief. "I want you to stay in here. Lock the door when I leave. Understand?"

She couldn't answer. She only stared at him silently. Despair threatened to bite deep.

"Understand?"

Finally, she nodded as reality set in.

He tried to stand but Ashley pulled him back down. "I came here for your help, not to get you killed." Her voice cracked with fear and regret. How had her life turned into this?

His eyes softened for a moment. "I know. Trust me. Okay?"

She didn't know if she could ever trust him again. But in this moment, she had no choice. She nodded. Her heart pounded in her ears as he pulled the door open. She held her breath, waiting for more gunfire to break out—only this time closer.

There was nothing.

He pointed to the lock before closing the door. Tears rolled down her face as she turned the button and heard the mechanism click in place.

*Lord, be with him. Please. He may have broken my heart, but I never wanted this.*

Something creaked outside.

The steps. Someone was coming up the steps.

Fear squeezed tighter as she braced herself for whatever was about to come.

## Chapter Three

All Christopher had been able to find in the closet was an old metal pipe that was probably leftover from some plumbing work. It wasn't a gun or a grenade, but it would work. He didn't have any other options.

He stood on the other side of the door frame, pressed into the wall and ready to swing into action. Adrenaline surged through him, intensifying his heart rate and causing sweat to dot his forehead. If he could catch the shooter off guard, maybe he had a chance.

The problem was that he'd estimated there to be at least three shooters. All of that gunfire had come from more than one weapon. These men carried semiautomatics, and they'd brought no shortage of ammunition. One man he might be able to take. But an unarmed man taking on three men with semiautomatic weapons?

Another round of gunshots cracked the air outside of his home. Flashbacks of the Middle East pounded his memories. Mortar shells, improvised explosive devices, enemy combatants. Men bleeding, women crying, children searching for their parents.

He ran a hand over his eyes. No, he was in Virginia now. Not a dusty village in Afghanistan. So why could he practically smell the burning of C-4? Why did his skin feel gritty with sand and dust?

He shook his head. *Snap out of it, Jordan.*

But the memories continued to batter him. He squeezed his eyes shut, wishing he could turn off his thoughts as easily as turning off a TV.

Another creak on the stairs pulled him back to reality, back to the here and now. Someone was definitely coming up. Christopher gripped the pipe tighter, bracing himself for the coming struggle.

Another creak. Then another. They were getting closer. They had to be only a few steps away.

Christopher would swing as soon as they opened the door. Best-case scenario, he'd knock the man out and grab his weapon. Worst-case scenario…well, he wouldn't go there.

All he knew was that he and Ashley might be the only hope for saving a little boy. That was worth fighting for.

A wooden step outside moaned under the weight of an intruder. Whoever the man was, he was right outside the door now. Christopher could practically hear him breathing, could almost feel his presence only inches away, separated by the door.

He tightened his grip on the cylinder in his hands. His muscles were wound tight enough to spring. Sweat trickled down from his temple. It was do or die.

Just then, a bullet pierced the air. His gaze darted across the dark room. Where had that gunshot come from? It was too far away to have come from the man outside the door. Even more concerning—had it pierced the garage? Was Ashley okay?

He stared at the door, waiting to see the handle jiggle. He anticipated more shots exploding. Something hit the landing outside the door with a loud thud. A moan followed, then a grunt.

He willed himself to remain still. Everything in him wanted to open the door and see what was happening. He had to remain silent, though. Patience could mean life or death; winning a battle or losing it. He'd learned that through experience.

Afghanistan flashed into his mind again. At once, he was transported back in time and pressed against the wall of an abandoned house. Rags—or were they clothes?—were strewn across the dirty floor. The air smelled like death.

Where was Liam? Why wasn't he answering his radio? The insurgents were—

Another thud sounded outside. Christopher snapped back to reality, shaking his head to dislodge his memories of war. The thud was followed by what sounded like something large being dragged away. What in the world was happening out there? The sounds repeated for a few minutes until finally there was silence again.

He waited. And waited.

Were these men planning something else? Or had their original plans been thwarted? By what, though?

Staying low, he crept back to the bathroom. He tapped on the door once. "Ashley. It's me."

The door opened so quickly that Christopher was certain her hand had been on the knob the whole time. She practically fell into the room, fell into him. Her limbs shook with fear.

"You're alive," she whispered. She started to reach for him but stopped.

He grabbed her elbow anyway, but only to help her stay upright. "I'm fine. You okay?"

Worry stained her gaze. "What's going on? I thought… I thought you'd been shot. I heard…" She didn't finish her thought.

His heart tugged with compassion, but he shoved those emotions aside. Right now there was only room for one thing—logic. Emotions would only lead him astray. "I don't know what happened out there. It's been quiet now for ten minutes. I don't want to take the chance that they're still out there trying to wait us out. We should lay low for a little while longer."

She nodded quickly. Christopher wanted to sit beside her, to offer her some comfort and put her mind at rest. He wished that he could distract her with chitchat—do something to keep her mind off the matters at hand. But he couldn't. Instead, he stood by the bathroom door, still gripping that pipe. The last thing he wanted was for someone to catch him off guard.

Ashley showing up today had already filled his quota on that for a lifetime.

Ashley pulled her knees to her chest, hating feeling so helpless, hating that she'd gotten Christopher into this mess. Her anxiety had her feeling nauseous and jittery. So she just kept praying the same prayers over and over again. *Lord, help us. Help David and Josh.*

Then there had been her crazy worry over Christopher. She'd heard that gunshot—it had sounded so close—and she was sure he'd been hit. All she could think about were the many unfinished conversations they needed to have. *She* needed to have.

Which caused another swell of anxiety to rise in her.

The strangest comfort filled her when she saw the pure determination on Christopher's face as he stood in the doorway. He'd always been tough and protective. They were two of the things she'd loved about him at one time. She couldn't imagine feeling safer around anyone. But feeling physically safe was entirely different from feeling emotionally safe.

Christopher had made it clear when he left that she wasn't important to him. She obviously hadn't captured his heart enough for him to try and make their relationship work. No, true love hadn't conquered all. Or they hadn't had true love. She wasn't sure which was worse.

She wondered if he'd found his perfect woman yet, the one he would do anything to be with. That person was not her. Despite that, she knew that Christopher would give his life for her, whether she was his fiancée or just someone from his past.

She understood what it was like to feel protective of someone. Without a second thought, she would take a bullet for her nephew. Whenever they were together, it seemed like she was trying to protect him from something—viruses, bullies, drivers who weren't paying attention. She tried to protect him from other things, too, things like the heartbreak of losing his mom and loneliness from a father who worked too much.

What she wouldn't give to be able to protect him now. Her heart squeezed with pain.

Minutes ticked by. Just what was going on outside? Had the shooters given up? That just didn't seem likely. But why else would they leave? Or had they?

She hugged her knees tighter.

*Lord, help us. Help David and Josh.*

"I'm going to go down and check things out." Christopher's voice pulled her from her heavy thoughts.

New alarm spread through her. She straightened, forcing herself not to grab him. "But what if they're still there?"

His jaw flexed. "I haven't heard a sound in a half hour."

"But—"

"I'll be careful, Ashley. I've been in hostile situations before. I can handle myself."

She stared at him a moment, knowing that his mind was equally as strong and tough as his well-defined muscles and quick reflexes. She had to trust him. What other choice did she have? Finally, she nodded.

She wanted to blurt out everything on her mind before he walked to his possible death.

*Just in case you never come back, I thought you should know that I found out a month after we broke up that I was pregnant with your child. My brother adopted the baby, and his name is David. I've been wanting to tell you for years...*

She sucked on her bottom lip.

*It's your son who was snatched today.*

How exactly did someone tell her ex-fiancé that?

How did she tell him that back when they'd been young and foolish, that one night of passion had turned into a baby? The sweetest little baby that Ashley had ever laid eyes on. Giving him up for adoption had been the most gut-wrenching thing she'd ever done. But she couldn't provide for a baby. Not only had she been in college and without a job or the ability to get a job that paid more than minimum wage, but then there was the car accident that happened when David was only two months old. Ashley had spent six months in the hospital, and she'd had months of physical therapy after that. Her brother and his wife had been so desperate for a child and she'd been unable to take care of little David. They'd adopted him before his first birthday.

That's why she knew Christopher was the only person who could help her right now. This was his son.

Everything that she'd tried so carefully to control was slipping away. She couldn't protect David. She couldn't keep Christopher at a distance. She would have to face her fears and eventually tell Christopher the truth. The walls she'd so carefully constructed were coming down fast.

She sucked in a long, deep breath. Silence surrounded her again. Was Christopher okay? She'd heard nothing since he left.

At least nothing meant no gunfire, either. Right?

How long did she wait before checking on him? She glanced at her watch. Ten more minutes. That was as long as she could possibly stand it. What if he was bleeding and hurt? What if he needed her help? She'd sent him into a battle that wasn't his to fight.

She let her head fall back against the cold tile wall. All was quiet. Suspiciously quiet. The silence was driving her mad.

She stood and began pacing the small space. Maybe she could go to the window and peer out. She could be quick and quiet.

It beat sitting here and doing nothing.

Before she could second-guess herself, she twisted the doorknob. Slowly, she pushed the door open. Her gaze roamed the space there. Everything looked the same. No figures lurked in the shadows…she didn't think, at least.

She took her first step out, every cell of her body

alert and ready to pounce into action. Slowly, she tip-toed across the floor to the window, not relaxing for even a second. Would someone jump out at her? Were they lying in wait?

She ducked low under the window and carefully raised her head to peer out. She flinched when she saw all of the windows in Christopher's house had been shattered. Christmas wreathes that had once graced the glass panes now lay like corpses on the deck and in the flower beds.

She watched for a sign of movement, but saw nothing. Where was Christopher? What was taking him so long?

She crawled across the floor to the closet. Was there anything left in here she could use as a weapon? She spotted a vacuum, some old coats and a wooden bar full of clothes hangers that stretched across the top. It would have to do. She stood and wedged the bar from its holders. It wasn't much, but at least it was something.

Doubt filled her as she crept toward the door. She shouldn't do this. But she had to. If they were going to shoot her, they would shoot her. But if they were gone and Christopher needed help, then she had to get downstairs.

Stark fear gripped her as she opened the door. She listened. Nothing except the wind blowing some stray leaves across the ground. Her heart leaped into her throat when she saw blood across the wooden landing at her feet.

Blood? Whose blood? What had happened? She followed the trail all the way to the bottom. Someone had been shot up here and then dragged back down. Terror rose in her.

She couldn't turn back now. If she let fear dictate

what she did, she might be in the bathroom for days, afraid to leave. But each step down the stairs felt like a step closer to her death.

*Be strong, Ashley. You can do this.* She'd never been a quitter. Not even when she gave David up for adoption. No, she'd simply been giving him the opportunity for a better life—a life that she could still be a part of.

But if she hadn't given him up for adoption, would he be in this situation now? Regret squeezed her heart again. She couldn't think like that. Not now.

She continued her descent. Everything remained silent. She gripped the wooden rod like a baseball bat, wishing it would protect her from bullets.

At the bottom of the stairs, she saw that the blood trail ended at the edge of the deck. Whoever had been shot had been dragged onto the grass. Into the woods? She couldn't be sure.

She swung her head back up, soaking in her surroundings. She had to pay attention. Her life depended on it.

The back door of Christopher's house was wide open. She paused at the corner of the garage and slowly peered around. Nothing. No one. As quickly as possible, she darted across the deck. She stopped at the doorway.

With baited breath, she raked her gaze across the inside. Lots of broken glass. A splintered coffee table. The Christmas tree lay wounded on its side.

But no one was in sight. Not even Christopher.

Certainly he hadn't abandoned her. Not again.

She shook her head. No, he wouldn't do that. Not in this situation.

Still, doubt trickled down her spine. Trust was such a fragile, fickle thing at times.

She stepped inside. Glass crunched at her feet. She froze, waiting for the telltale sound that someone had heard her.

Nothing.

Slowly, carefully, she crept forward. She kept her back to the wall. Her breathing sounded so heavy in her own ears that she wondered if she'd even hear someone sneak up on her.

When she heard a noise upstairs, she knew she would.

Someone was in the house. Had that person killed Christopher, dragged his body into the woods and gone back upstairs to check for her?

Just then, the stairs creaked. Someone was coming down. Coming toward her.

She glanced around, desperate for a place to hide. Instead, she pressed herself into the wall.

When the intruder got to the bottom of the steps, she would swing the stick and hit him.

And she'd pray that her hit would knock him out.

But before she had a chance to swing, a gun cocked behind her, and the fear that was becoming all too familiar froze her blood—again.

## Chapter Four

Christopher approached the intruder from behind, veering off the main staircase at the last minute and taking a second set of stairs on the other end of the house. There was still one person in the house. Just one, best he could tell.

It was dark, void of any light. The air was hazy, evidence of a smoke bomb. And the smell of ammunition hung heavy in the atmosphere.

The sounds, the smells…they all reminded him of another time, another place.

A time and place he was trying to forget.

He rounded the corner and spotted someone crouching beneath the first staircase. Crouching, ready to attack?

He cocked his gun, drawing on all of his training. It was time to get some answers.

"Don't move," he commanded. "Or I'll shoot."

The figure twirled around, a stick in hand. Wide, familiar eyes met his. Fear stretched across their depths.

His muscles relaxed a moment, but the relief was

quickly replaced with agitation. "Ashley? Are you crazy? I told you stay in the garage!"

"Christopher?" Ashley blinked, her stick still hoisted over her shoulder as if she might swing.

He lowered his gun and glared at the woman in front of him. Even in the dark, Christopher could tell that her face was void of any color or life. "Yes, it's me. It's a good thing I didn't shoot you. I heard the glass crunching downstairs and thought the men were back to finish the job."

"I saw the blood on the stairs. I thought you were… dead. I…"

He raised an eyebrow. "You were coming to defeat the bad guys with a dowel rod?"

She shrugged. "I had to do something. I couldn't stay up there forever."

He stepped closer so she would be sure to see the irritation in his gaze. "I told you I'd be back."

She didn't look away. She was still as stubborn as ever. "You've been gone for hours."

"Twenty minutes." He sliced his hand through the air. "Twenty minutes is all."

She frowned and lowered her stick before jutting out her chin again. "It felt like hours."

He scowled again and ran a hand over his face as he dragged in a ragged breath. Images of war continued to beat at him. They tried to transport him back in time. He wouldn't let them. Still, Ashley coming up on him like that could have been ugly. Really ugly. That was the second time he'd pulled a gun on her in less than four hours. "Are you okay?"

She nodded, strain pulling at each of her features. "I'm fine. Are the men gone?"

"Best I can tell. They messed this place up, didn't they?" His gaze roamed around them. It looked like a massacre, only thankfully, the only casualties were his furniture, belongings and the house itself.

"I'm sorry," she blurted. "I should have never come."

"Don't be ridiculous. This is just stuff. It can be fixed. Besides, you weren't the one with the gun."

Big, luminous eyes looked up to meet his. "Who was? Who were those men?"

He looked away before he got lost in the depths of those baby blues and shook his head. "I have no idea. But they mean serious business."

"Why'd they leave?"

"That's what I want to know, also. They didn't do all of this damage just to send a message. They used a smoke bomb and everything. They came here to kill us. I want to know why they left before finishing the job."

"And where did the blood come from by the garage?"

"Another great question." He put his hand on her back. "I know one thing. We're getting out of here before they decide to come back. I called Eyes and they're sending some men out. They should be here any minute, but we're not waiting around."

"Where are we going?"

"I have an idea." He led her toward the front door.

She reached back. "My phone. It was in the living room."

"Forget about it. That's probably how they traced you here. All those new-fangled phones have built-in GPSs. You're better off without it." He grabbed his jacket—surprisingly still intact—from the back of a chair.

"But what if Josh or David try to call?"

"If you're dead, it will do no good."

They stepped out of the front door—which had been ripped from its hinges—and onto the front porch. His truck had bullet holes in the window also, but the tires looked fine. "I'm glad you're wearing a coat. It might be a cold ride."

He opened the door and, using the thick sleeve of his jacket, he brushed broken glass shards from the seat. Then he ushered Ashley inside, instructing her to be careful. They didn't have much time. Every minute counted.

He cranked the engine—and the heat—and turned around in the driveway. The cold wind hit his face as he took off down the road. Ashley sat beside him, seat belt strapped across her chest, and her arms wrapped over her. He wished he had a blanket to offer her. Instead, he pulled off his coat and draped it over her.

"You're going to freeze," she muttered.

"You're always cold, even without thirty-degree wind hitting you in the face. I'll be fine."

He remembered that about her. He remembered a lot about her. Now wasn't the time to think about those things. Now he had to think about staying alive.

This was not what he needed right now. No, right now he needed time to enjoy a quieter pace. He needed time to let his soul heal.

But instead, God had brought Ashley Wilson back into his life.

As if that wasn't more of an emotional storm than

he could handle, throw in the fact that someone was trying to kill her and, in effect, him also.

This was not the relaxing, healing time he'd anticipated when he'd come home and taken this new job.

When he'd last spoken to Ashley, she'd been finishing up her degree at a local college. She'd been working two jobs, trying to make ends meet. He'd always said that she was one of the hardest workers he'd ever met. She'd been focused, at the top of her class in academics and determined to do things on her own. Her dad had retired on disability after an injury at work, and money had been tight with her family. She'd even had the opportunity to play volleyball on a partial scholarship for a college down in North Carolina, but she'd turned it down to be close to her mom, dad and brother.

Guilt plagued him about that decision. He knew part of the reason she'd said no to that scholarship was because of him. They'd been planning their future together. She'd wanted to stick close by both for her family and because she felt it was important to give their relationship the time and effort it required.

Was she angry still? He couldn't blame her if she was. He'd broken her heart.

"I can't believe this is happening," Ashley muttered.

"It feels surreal to me, too, if it makes you feel better."

She shook her head. "I just want to wake up and discover this is all a bad dream."

He wondered if by *all* she included him? Probably.

His eyes watered from the wind. Thankfully, he didn't see anyone behind him. A glance at his watch told him it was past midnight now. There wasn't usually much traffic out on these back roads, especially not at this time of night.

From the corner of his eye, he saw Ashley shivering in the seat beside him. If he'd had another vehicle, he would have driven it. But desperate times called for desperate measures. Wasn't that how the saying went?

He took back roads, all the way from Isle of Wight where he lived, through the neighboring Suffolk into Chesapeake and finally to Virginia Beach. Nearly an hour after he left, he pulled up to a guardhouse, showed his ID, had his truck searched as standard procedure and pulled through the gates.

"Where are we?" Ashley asked.

"We're at Iron, Incorporated's headquarters. You'll be safe here for the night. I promise."

Ashley stared at the huge, lodgelike building in front of her. So this was the prestigious paramilitary contracting firm she'd heard hints about. They were secretive in what they did, but people around town always whispered about them with pride. Rumors had it that they'd guarded ambassadors in the Middle East and developed cutting-edge technology that was soon to be released to help keep soldiers safer. They were said to be the best of the best.

She didn't feel like soaking in the awe of the Eyes' campus, though. She couldn't even feel her skin anymore, not after the brutal wind had frozen it on the way here. All she wanted was to get off this roller-coaster ride for a moment and clear her head.

When they pulled to a stop, she didn't wait for Christopher to get her door. Instead, she opened it, watching as some leftover glass rained to the ground below. She slid out, landing with a bounce on the asphalt.

They started walking toward the door when Christopher called her name and stopped her. He reached for her hair. Just the feeling of his fingers tangled in her tresses caused a shiver to race down her spine. It was like her body was betraying her. It should know better than to get warm fuzzies about Christopher, especially after all that had happened.

He held up a shiny speck. "Just some glass."

She nodded, stuffed her hands in her pockets and kept walking. Christopher hurried ahead to the door and pulled it open for her. She gladly stepped inside the quiet and warm space. Her gaze swept the area—the ceiling stretched more than two stories high. Fireplaces flanked either side of the large lobby, which was also filled with leather couches and plush rugs. A majestic Christmas tree stretched high in the corner, filled with ornaments that looked like they'd been made by schoolchildren. She didn't have time to dwell on that now. She walked over to the fireplace and knelt in front of it, letting the heat melt her frozen limbs.

"I'm going to get coffee," Christopher called. "You still like yours black?"

She nodded, holding her hands up to the flames. He remembered. What did she expect? That he'd totally forgotten about their time together? That he'd erased it from his memory?

He returned a moment later with a steaming mug. She remained in front of the fire and took a sip. The liquid burned her mouth, but she didn't care. Warmth was more important now. Maybe it would cause her shivers to finally stop.

"I've got to make a phone call, Ashley. Are you going to be okay here for a moment?"

She nodded again, wishing he wasn't acting so concerned. It was easier not to like him if he acted mean and nasty. But when had he ever been mean and nasty?—unless you counted when he broke up with her. But even then, he'd been compassionate. His eyes had even welled with tears at one point.

The day flashed back into her memory. She could tell that something was wrong when he'd called her by phone. His voice had sounded too serious, too strained.

*He's going to tell me he's going to the Middle East again,* she'd thought.

She'd braced herself for the conversation, fluctuating between wanting to be supportive and wanting to beg him to stay.

*Be a good fiancée. Accept that this is his job. Let him go, even if it means postponing the wedding.*

He'd asked if they could meet down at the Virginia Beach boardwalk—one of their favorite places. She'd bundled up—it was cold outside—and waited for him on their favorite bench. Die-hard joggers had paced past, seagulls had complained overhead, salty air had filled her nostrils.

As soon as she'd seen Christopher walking toward her, she could tell something was wrong.

Her spine had stiffened. *This is about more than Afghanistan, isn't it?* But what? In their two years together, they'd never even had a major fight. That's how easy and natural their relationship had been.

Those expressive green eyes had held torn emotions as he sat beside her. His shoulders even looked burdened. "I can't be with you, Ashley," he'd told her.

"What do you mean?"

"I've realized that I can't be a good SEAL and a good husband."

"What are you talking about?" She'd blinked back her confusion, certain that she hadn't heard him correctly. What he said didn't make sense.

He'd grabbed her hand. "You're the only person I want to be with, Ashley. But that's not fair to my country. I promised them I would protect our freedoms. I'm not doing that when I'm thinking about you. Being a SEAL…it's almost like being married. And I've already made that commitment."

"You're breaking up with me?" Her voice had cracked in disbelief. How had things gone from perfect to this?

Water had filled his eyes. "I'm sorry, Ashley. I've been pretending I could do both, but it's become clear that I can't."

She snapped back to the present and the blazing fire in front of her. Funny, she hadn't thought about Christopher's tear-filled eyes in a long time. Oh, she'd thought about the breakup, but somehow she'd blocked out memories of how anguished he'd looked during their conversation. Christopher was the last person she wanted to be thinking about right now.

She dragged her mind from one bad thought to another—David. Where was he right now? Was he warm? Comfortable? Had they fed him?

She took another sip of coffee, her hands still trembling as her heart ached.

*Please, Lord, don't let him be scared.*

As anxiety squeezed her, she nearly dropped her coffee when a hand reached out and grabbed it. She looked up and saw Christopher there. Just in the nick of time. Again. Like always.

Except when he'd left her.

She had to stop thinking about that and start concentrating solely on the matters at hand. Her heart was just in such a fragile state right now that it kept going other places. Christopher helped her into a plush chair. She set her coffee on the table, unsure if her hands could hold it any longer.

"Two of the guys from Eyes are coming down. Jack and Denton. They're still here, working on a big project for the Department of Defense. They're the best. They'll be able to help."

"Thank you," she mumbled. After a few minutes of silence stretched between them, she asked, "How'd you end up here, Christopher? I never thought you'd leave the military. I thought you'd be a career guy."

A new somberness seemed to come over him. "So did I. But life changes sometimes. It was time."

"How long have you been back?"

"Three months." He changed the subject. "How about you? You still a web designer?"

She nodded. "Started my own business about five years ago."

"You're a business owner now?"

"I was working for a corporation, but I was miserable. Great benefits, great pay, but no fulfillment, you know what I mean? So I took a leap of faith and started my own company. I design websites for some major companies, all while working in the luxury of my own home. I've been really blessed."

A smile spread over his face. "I know that's what you always wanted to do. I'm glad you were able to."

"Yeah, at least some things worked out according to plan." She clamped her mouth shut. Now why had she gone and said that? It wasn't very mature of her. She glanced at her hands. "I'm sorry."

"I deserved it."

"No, you didn't. I don't know what's gotten into me."

"All of this is a lot to handle. I think you're doing just fine."

Her gaze connected with his. "It's only by God's grace we're alive, isn't it?"

"I couldn't agree more."

She stared at him. He meant those words, didn't he? When they'd known each other before, neither had been Christians. She must have stared at him long enough that he felt obligated to give an explanation.

"When you've seen some of the things that I saw over in the Middle East, you start believing there's a God pretty quickly."

"I'd imagine." *When you have to give your child up for adoption, you start believing pretty quickly, too.* She kept that part to herself.

Just then, two men tromped down the stairs. She drew in a deep breath, ready to formulate a plan to get her brother and son back.

Jack Sergeant, the CEO of Eyes, and Mark Denton, his second in command, came to a stop in front of them. Both looked like they'd been working long hours. They'd abandoned their ties and coats. The top button of Denton's white shirt was open and the shadow of a beard had already formed on his cheeks.

Mark—who went by Denton—had helped to train Christopher as a SEAL before going to work for the CIA. He'd been Christopher's contact in getting a job here and, for that, Christopher was grateful.

Christopher trusted Jack and Denton more than if they'd been brothers. Both had been SEALs and had earned reputations as being trustworthy and loyal, as well as innovative and at the top of their game in the paramilitary contracting world. He'd jumped at the chance to come work for them.

They introduced themselves to Ashley. Jack put his hands on his hips, his brow furrowed with concern. "What's going on?"

Ashley glanced at Christopher before sucking in a deep breath and telling her story. Even though she had to be exhausted and scared, she maintained a calm demeanor that he could appreciate. Except for her voice cracking a few times, she stuck to the facts.

Denton stepped forward. "Is there anything you can remember about the car?"

She nodded. "The license plate number."

Christopher raised his eyebrows. "You can?"

She nodded again. "I thought the police were the only ones who could do something with that information, though. I figured it would do us no good."

Jack shook his head. "We'll look into it. You have no idea who these men are?"

Ashley shook her head. "No, I have no idea. We're

just simple, everyday people. Things like this don't happen to us."

Jack grunted. Christopher knew that he understood what it was like when simple, everyday people got mixed up in things bigger than they seemed equipped to handle. That was how Jack had met the woman who was now his wife, for that matter. At least that reminded Christopher of how good things could come from bad situations, similar to the flower garden he'd stumbled upon in the middle of a military base. Some soldiers had decided to make the place feel like home and planted roses and hollyhocks and other varieties he couldn't identify. How they'd made those flowers grow in that soil, he'd never know. But they had, and they'd proven to him that from the dust something beautiful could grow.

"You're both welcome to stay here for as long as you need to," Jack started. "Christopher, the men are at your place now, checking things out and boarding up your windows. You did the right thing by leaving immediately. In the meantime, we'll look into that license plate number and see what we can find out." He glanced at Ashley. "Why don't you give us your address and a house key? We'll search your place also, just to make sure there's nothing we're missing."

"I appreciate it." Her gaze met each person's in the circle while her hand clutched the necklace at her throat. "I appreciate all of your help. I have no idea what I'm doing."

Jack patted her arm. "We're glad you're here. Let us know if you need anything else." He offered a curt wave before he headed back up the stairs.

Denton lingered, his gaze meeting Christopher's. "Christopher, can I speak with you for a moment?"

Christopher nodded and followed him to a corner. He glanced back at Ashley and saw that she'd already gravitated back toward the fire again. By the set of her shoulders, she looked like she was carrying a weight far heavier than she should bear.

He turned back to Denton. "What is it?"

Denton lowered his voice. "Are you sure you can handle this?" His eyes showed that he was dead serious.

"Of course." Christopher wasn't sure what his superior was getting at.

Denton crossed his arms and shifted, his voice still low and conspirative. "You took this job to recover from war. You're being thrown right back into a battle, though."

Christopher straightened. "I can handle it."

"I know you think you're tough. You are tough. But even the toughest soldiers have to step away from the battle sometimes."

"Sometimes a soldier has no choice but to go back into the fight. They have to reach down inside and find strength, even when they don't think they have it. That's what one of the men who once trained me said, at least." He kept his chin raised and stood at full attention, though he knew Denton would tell him to be at ease.

Denton stared at him a moment before nodding. A smile stretched across his face and he gripped his arm. Denton had been that man who said those words. "I'm here for you if you need me."

"You always have been. I appreciate that, sir."

Denton leaned closer. "Listen, I don't know what your past relationship is with Ashley, but I get the feeling you two were more than friends."

"Yes, we were. We were engaged, to be exact."

His eyes widened a moment. "This was the girl you were crazy about while you were in training, huh? I remember the way you talked about her like she was the best thing to ever happen to you."

"She was the best thing to ever happen to me." His heart squeezed as he said the words. They were true. Walking away from Ashley had felt like walking away from his heart.

"Don't let your past get in the way of doing what you have to do."

"Yes, sir." He glanced back over at Ashley. Those words would be the hardest to follow through on. Remembering their time together was so bittersweet.

Somehow, he had to ignore the fact that she hated him and realize that God had brought her back into his life for some reason…maybe even just forgiveness and closure? He didn't know.

But he did know that, in Christ, all things worked together for His good.

Somehow, someway, something good was going to come out of all of this.

The question was…what?

## Chapter Five

Christopher stared at the alarm clock on the night-stand beside his bed. The red numbers stared back at him. Six-twenty, and he was wide awake.

He'd been wide-awake for a long time.

For most of the night, for that matter.

He tossed toward the other side of his bed, trying to grab a few more minutes of rest. Back at home, there was a bottle of sleeping pills lying on his night-stand. He'd refused to take them, despite his doctor's encouragement. He liked to think he was strong enough to weather the storms of life without the help of any medication.

Even if he'd had the pills with him now, he wouldn't have taken any last night. He wanted to be on guard.

Between his return home, the unexpected reappearance of Ashley in his life, and the danger surrounding her, sleep had just been a dream.

He should be used to it. He hadn't had a good night's rest in months. Too many images from Afghanistan haunted him.

He'd gone to counseling all of four times, and it hadn't done him any good. All the counselor had wanted to do was talk about things. He was tired of talking about things. He just wanted to move on.

Being back in the States was an entirely different kind of battleground.

*Hang on to the good memories,* he reminded himself, punching his pillow with his fist.

He was thankful that Jack had given him a job at Eyes as a Training Specialist. He hoped his soul would have time to heal away from the battleground. But now he'd been thrust into the face of danger again, it seemed. But how could he turn Ashley away? He couldn't.

Ashley's face drifted into his mind. They'd had some good times together—some really good times, actually. Their relationship had been so simple, filled with long walks, road trips and movie marathons.

Then things had ended. No, make that, then *he'd* ended things.

He never thought he'd see her again. Or if he did see her again, he expected her to be married with kids in tow. She was the kind of woman who'd make a great mother and wife. He knew that's all she'd dreamed of for so long. She had everything a guy could want. So why was she still single? And why had she come to him of all people? Was there something she wasn't telling him? He couldn't even begin to fathom what that thing might be.

Finally, after tossing and turning for thirty more minutes, he dragged himself out of bed and hopped in the shower. Someone had left some clothes outside his door. He quickly put on the jeans and sweatshirt, making a mental note that he needed to run to the store and buy a few things today.

He stepped outside his room and stared at the door beside his. Ashley's room. It was only 7:00 a.m. Was Ashley awake yet? She'd always been an early riser. She liked to go jogging or biking before starting her day. He remembered many mornings when they'd met at the beach to run together on the boardwalk. Those memories seemed like an entirely different lifetime ago.

He raised his hand to knock at her door but stopped. He would let her sleep, or at the very least, have some privacy. When she was ready, she'd come downstairs. He needed some coffee and a bite to eat. Maybe that would wake him up. At the end of the hallway, he peered out the window and saw at least two inches of snow piled on top of everything, cloaking the landscape in innocence.

The weather forecaster had gotten it right for once. What did you know?

A blazing fire greeted him downstairs as he made his way toward the kitchen. The space was already filled with a group of law-enforcement trainees. He recognized several and waved hello. He'd been one of their instructors and had been teaching them about use of force. That responsibility had been passed on to someone else until this ordeal with Ashley subsided.

He began pouring himself a cup of coffee when he heard someone behind him.

"Christopher."

He turned away from the coffeepot at the sound of

Ashley's voice, making sure any sign of his exhaustion disappeared from his face.

She stood in front of him, her eyes wide and crystal clear and as breathtaking as ever. Man, she was beautiful with that oval face, pert nose and glossy hair. If anything, the years had only made her more attractive. He could stare at her all day, and it would never get old.

"Morning, Ashley." He raised his mug. "Care for some coffee?"

She nodded and crossed her arms over her chest. He had the crazy desire to pull her into a hug, to stroke her hair and tell her everything would be okay. But he couldn't do that. Ashley Wilson was off-limits. She was now, and she should have been ten years ago.

He forced his thoughts to go in another direction. He focused on the here and the now. He knew he couldn't forget the past—and that he shouldn't—but right now he just couldn't deal with it. "Grab a plate. Breakfast is on the house."

She hesitated, but only for a moment, before putting some eggs and fruit on her plate. They sat down together at a table by the window. She thanked him before closing her eyes. Was she praying?

She pulled her eyes open, her gaze dull as it met his. "I wish they'd taken me and not David," she blurted.

"It doesn't sound like they want to kill him, Ashley. They could have already killed them both, but they haven't. Instead, they're just using that threat as leverage for you not to tell. No, I think they want your brother and David for another reason."

She nodded. "That makes sense, I guess. I just wish they'd left David out of it. He's so young and innocent. He always tries to be so tough, though. He's a real soldier—or trouper, I suppose." Her gaze met his. What was that emotion in her eyes? Regret, it almost seemed. But why?

Christopher looked up as Mark Denton approached the table with that cocky swagger he was known for. He pulled back a chair. "Mind if I sit down?"

Using his foot, Christopher pushed a chair out for him. "Please do."

Denton pulled the seat to the end of the table and straddled it. His gaze met Ashley's. "We got a trace on that license plate."

Her eyes brightened. "What did you discover?"

"It turns out the man who owns the car is named Gil Travis. Have you ever heard of him?"

Ashley shook her head. "Gil Travis? The name doesn't sound familiar."

Denton's lips pulled into a tight, grim line. "He's on the FBI's most-wanted list."

She blinked, as if trying to process his words. "What?"

Denton nodded. "He's affiliated with a terrorist organization called His People. Do you remember the bombing of that federal building up in Richmond several years ago?"

Christopher was well aware of who the group was. That particular story had made national news after five people had died.

Ashley nodded also. "Yeah, I remember that. It was all over the news."

"His People were behind it. They're determined to take down the America we know and love. They're some dangerous men, and Gil is their second in command—more of a tactical commander who plans their attacks against targets here in the U.S., as well as at embassies overseas."

"Why? Why does this group hate America so much?" Ashley asked.

Denton grimaced. "The organization formed in the 1970s under the leadership of Abar Numair—"

"He's the man who was killed several months ago, right? By some of the U.S. special forces?"

Denton briefly glanced at Christopher before nodding. "That's correct. This organization has cells all over the world, including some here in the U.S. Most of the people who join the organization have some kind of ties to the Middle East."

"Are they Islamic extremists?" Ashley asked.

Denton shook his head again. "No, that's the surprising part. Probably twenty percent of their membership is Muslim. The real reason these men have come together is that they have some kind of bone to pick with the U.S. Gil, for example. His dad was killed in a drone attack over in Iraq. His mother remarried and moved to the United States, making him a citizen—a citizen with a huge grudge."

"People with grudges can do terrible things," Ashley mumbled.

"Authorities are still trying to figure out who provides their funding for them. That's what makes them scary—there are some unknown members who stay secret." Denton pulled out a photo. "Do you recognize him?"

Ashley studied the photo for a minute. Christopher

immediately recognized the tall man with a head full of dark hair, cold, black eyes and sunken cheeks. "He looks vaguely familiar, but no."

"That's Gil Travis," Denton said.

Ashley's gaze met Denton's. "I still don't understand. What does my brother have to do with this? It just doesn't make sense."

Denton drew in a deep breath. "We're still trying to figure that out. What did you say your brother did for a living again?"

"He programs computers. He's one of the best—" Her eyes widened as she stopped midsentence. "He's one of the best in the country," she finished softly. She turned toward Christopher, licking her lips. "He could hack into almost any system."

"Including the government's," Denton filled in.

"He wouldn't do that." She swung her head back and forth. "He's too ethical. Especially now that he's a dad…."

Christopher seemed to remember that Josh had gotten into trouble in high school for doing some hacking, but that was a long time ago. People changed, especially when they became parents. Certainly Josh wouldn't do anything to put his son in jeopardy.

"If he had a gun to his head, he might." Denton leaned toward her. "We're going to need to find out some information from you, Ashley."

"Sure. I'll share anything." She grimaced after she said the words. What was that about, Christopher wondered?

Denton leaned toward her. "Tell me about your brother."

"He's the classic computer nerd. He's an absolute whiz at anything computer-related. TechShare recruited him to work for them four or five years ago."

"TechShare?" Denton questioned.

"They're some computer company. I hadn't heard of them, either, before Josh got a job with them. Apparently, they design some of the processors that the bigger companies buy. I don't know. He doesn't really like to talk about his work. He says it's boring."

Denton watched her closely, almost as if he were a human lie detector. "How about his family? Tell me about them."

"His wife died a few years ago from cancer. I'm his only sibling. My mom passed away nearly a decade ago, and my dad is living in a retirement community down in South Carolina now."

"Just one child?" Denton continued. He took a sip of coffee, his gaze never leaving hers.

She licked her lips again. "Just one. A son named David. He's eight."

"Anything we need to know about him?"

Her cheeks flushed. "He…he's, um…he's adopted. You don't think that has anything to do with this, do you?"

Denton shrugged. "Who knows? Anything's a possibility now. Was it an open or closed adoption?"

"Open."

"Do you know the birth mother's name?" Christopher turned toward Ashley, feeling like they could be onto something. "Maybe we could start there. We could find her and see if she has anything to do with this."

"I can… I can try to get her name for you. I doubt

it would do any good. I think you're looking in the wrong direction."

Christopher stared at her another moment, wondering why she was acting so strangely. Earlier, she'd seemed so anxious to do whatever was necessary. Now hesitancy seemed to lace each movement. "We need to explore every possibility, Ashley."

"I agree." She rubbed her temples before finally pointing behind her. "Do you mind if I run to the restroom for a moment?"

Denton leaned back and crossed his arms over his chest. "Not at all."

She fled so quickly that she nearly knocked over a chair. Why had she reacted so strangely to that question? Perhaps it was just the stress of everything that was getting to her. So what if David had been adopted? He knew that Josh and his wife were having trouble getting pregnant. Many couples turned to adoption. So why was Ashley acting so flustered by the question?

He turned toward Denton. "This whole situation doesn't look good, does it?"

Denton shook his head grimly, tapping his pen against the side of the coffee mug. "No, not at all. These are some serious men we're dealing with. They're ruthless, cold and will stop at nothing to get what they want."

Hearing Denton say the words aloud made cold fear course through Christopher. Ashley was somehow caught up in the middle of this, and he didn't like that one bit. "Where's this leave Ashley?"

"As soon as they figure out where she is, they'll try to kill her. I don't recommend staying in one place for very long. These men have a lot of resources. They'll close in eventually. I just can't tell you when."

Christopher nodded. Yep, it was even worse than he'd ever imagined.

Ashley splashed some water on her face, trying to calm herself down. She let the water drop from the tip of her nose into the basin of the porcelain sink. Her hands, white-knuckled, gripped the edges of the counter like a life preserver. Fitting, since she felt like she was hanging on for every last breath.

They might have to look into David's adoption records, just to rule out the idea that his birth mom had nothing to do with this? Now that was something she hadn't expected to hear. How was she going to get around this? Or would she?

She had to pull herself together. She'd do whatever she had to do to get her son back. And that was that. If that meant that she had to face the mistakes of her past head-on, then that's what she'd do. But she wouldn't like it.

She grabbed a paper towel and blotted her face before pausing to stare at herself in the mirror. She looked like she'd aged ten years overnight. How things could change in the blink of an eye.

John 14:27 slipped into her mind. *Peace I leave with you; my peace I give to you. Not as the world gives do I give to you. Let not your hearts be troubled, neither let them be afraid.*

Yet all her heart felt was troubled and afraid.

*Please, Lord, help me to trust that everything is in Your hands. Give me the wisdom to know what to do next. Give me the courage to have conversations that might rock Christopher's world.*

For good measure, she wiped one more paper towel over her face and glanced at her reflection once more. Hollow eyes, pale skin and dull hair. She'd imagined running into Christopher again after their breakup and looking fabulous, making him want to eat his heart out. Instead, he was probably glad he'd gotten away while he could. If only that worry was her biggest problem right now.

She pushed the door open and trudged back through the lobby and into the cafeteria. Denton was gone and it was just Christopher sipping his coffee. She slid into the chair across from him and stared at her eggs, which were now cold and unappealing. Instead, she stabbed a piece of pineapple with her fork.

She could feel Christopher's gaze on her. Surprisingly, she didn't feel shaken by his scrutiny. Some intrinsic part of her still seemed to trust the man and find strength from him.

Which made no sense whatsoever.

"You okay?"

"Just feeling a little shaken." She took a bite of the fruit. "Denton's gone?"

"He had to take a phone call."

She put her fork back on her plate, her appetite totally gone. Even the pineapple, one of her favorite foods, couldn't whet her appetite. "What's next?"

Christopher's green eyes studied her a moment. "It would really help if there was anything you could remember about David's birth parents. There might be a connection there that will help us find him now."

She nodded, her throat burning. Did he suspect that he was connected to David at all? She didn't think so. "I don't know what to say."

His gaze pierced hers. "Did you ever meet her?"

"In a vague sort of way, I suppose you could say that." Nausea roiled in her gut. Should she simply tell him the truth? Just drop the news on him here and now and get all of her secrets out in the open? The words wouldn't leave her throat.

Christopher pressed his palms into the table and leaned toward her, his eyes narrowed in confusion. "What does that mean, Ashley? Is something wrong?"

*Tell him. Just tell him.*

She opened her mouth, ready to share the truth. But instead, she blurted, "I'm just not feeling that great. I'm sorry." She ran a hand over her face before straightening. Maybe she could ease into the information. Fear threatened to strangle her, and she couldn't seem to take a hold of the emotion. "Okay. Let's see. I think she was young. Maybe 19 or 20. She was single. Any other information you'd have to get from the court files. I can't help you. But I can say that I think we're looking in the wrong direction. Nothing about his birth mother screamed terrorist."

"How about his dad? Did you ever meet his dad?"

Her throat burned again. "He seemed perfectly… normal. You know, I really think we should look in other directions." Fear won. Ashley couldn't tell him. Not now. All of these years, she'd made Christopher out to be the bad guy when, in truth, what she'd done had probably been worse.

It was going to be heartbreaking for her to come to terms with that truth.

Christopher stared at her for a moment before nodding. "I see."

Their gazes met and tension stretched between them.

"Bad news, guys." They both turned toward Denton as he strode into the room. He stopped in front of them, his expression grim. He turned toward Ashley. "I sent someone to check on your car this morning. You said you left it behind that shopping center off Military Highway?"

She nodded.

He slapped a picture onto the table. "It's demolished."

She blinked, her face growing even paler, as she stared at the unrecognizable piece of charred metal in the picture. "Demolished?"

"Someone set it on fire." Denton shifted. "We also sent someone to your apartment. Your desk has been cleared. I can only assume there was a computer there at one time."

She nodded. "That's right. I do all of my web design on that computer."

"I'm sorry to tell you this, but it's gone now."

She couldn't pull her eyes from the image of her charred car in front of her. "Why would they do that to my car? Why would they take my computer?"

Christopher put his hand on her arm, pulling her back to reality. "Because they want to send a message, Ashley. They want to let you know they're not done with you yet."

## Chapter Six

Ashley huddled beneath her coat in an SUV that Denton had let them use. They needed to go and buy some items to use until this whole nightmare ended. Clothes, toiletries, shoes—they only had what they'd fled with. It wasn't safe to go to either of their places to retrieve anything.

Wind swept in from the open door in the driver's seat as Christopher climbed in beside her. He slammed the door and cranked the engine. Christmas music blared on the radio, and cool air gusted at full power through the vents.

He blew on his fingers, his breath forming frosty puffs that matched the sky around them. "It will take a few minutes for this to heat up." That apologetic look appeared in Christopher's eyes again.

Ashley nodded, pulling her coat tighter and staring out the window at the white surrounding them. The frigid weather seemed to match the chill that started at her core and spread through her veins every time she thought about Josh and David.

"It's going to be okay, Ashley." Christopher's voice broke through her brittle thoughts, pulling her back to the present.

She cleared her throat, pushing away the emotions that came upon hearing the genuine concern in his voice. "I have no idea what's going on or what we're going to do. Nothing feels okay."

He stared at her a moment. She could feel his eyes on her, but she didn't look up, didn't want him to see the fear in her gaze. She already knew what his eyes looked like—big and green and warm. She studied them a million times in the past, absorbing their every fleck and every emotion they conveyed.

"You're right, Ashley. Nothing does feel okay. All of this is crazy. We're just going to take it step by step."

There he went again. He had a way of making her feel like everything would be fine. At one time he'd been her rock, her best friend and the man who made her heart do cartwheels. Now he was going to be her bodyguard—and that was it. She needed boundaries unless she wanted to get her heart broken again. There had always been something unseen between them, some force that pulled them together that made them forget about the rest of the world. They'd had that elusive, ever-desired "it" factor that so many love songs had been written about. She'd thought they were soul mates.

It was obvious that the invisible pull between them could easily draw them together again if she let it. This time, she wasn't a little girl. She was a grown woman, not one given to whims or flights of fancy or delusions of romance. No, next time she fell in love, she'd do it using her brain. And her brain constantly reminded her of how wrong Christopher was for her, despite how her heart might protest.

Somehow her life had turned into something fit for a movie—a terribly frightening movie. Just two days ago her biggest worry had been whether she should go to the gym or watch her favorite Christmas movie. What she wouldn't give for life to be like that again. "I just want to find Josh and David."

"If you find them, then you find the men who want to kill you. Not a good idea. Let Jack and Denton handle it. They're good at what they do."

She shook her head, the answers becoming clear in her mind. "No, that's the thing. I need to find my brother and nephew *before* the men who snatched them find me. I just can't sit around and do nothing. It's not an option. I need to be proactive. I'll rent a car—"

"If you use a credit card, they'll be able to trace you."

"I'll borrow a car, then. Certainly one of the families at church has an extra one I could use."

"You risk pulling them into the middle of this mess. And, even if you find a car, then what?"

She mulled over his words. It was true. She couldn't risk pulling anyone else into the middle of this. But if she could find a car, somehow and someway, maybe she could form a plan. "If I can find a car, I'll drive until an answer smacks me in the face." She sighed and rubbed her temples as the futility of her plan hit her. "They make this look so easy in the movies."

"Life isn't a movie. Movies are nice and tidy bundles with everything resolved at the end. Life is messy and tangled with very few certainties. Our next breath isn't promised, no matter who we are."

"That sounds like a fact you know all too well." She'd heard through a couple of mutual acquaintances that they'd lost a member of their SEAL team during one of their raids. Christopher hadn't mentioned it yet in their brief time together, but Ashley knew his world had been turned upside down when that happened. The brotherhood of the SEAL teams was amazing, a fact she'd seen firsthand when she and Christopher were engaged. Losing someone on your team was like losing a family member.

His lips pulled into a tight line. "Unfortunately, I do."

Grim reality set in around her. How would all of this turn out? She had to believe for the best. Otherwise, hopelessness would paralyze her.

They needed to search for answers at Ground Zero, she realized.

"I know where to start," she muttered.

"Where's that?" He stared at her, tension stretching between them. She knew him well enough to know that one of his biggest stressors had always been worrying about her safety. His laidback attitude always disappeared if he thought she might be in danger—physically, emotionally, mentally—whatever the case. At least, that's the way it used to be.

She raised her chin. It wasn't his job to worry about her anymore. She could take care of herself. "My brother's house."

"I don't know if that's a good idea." His lips pulled into a tight, grim line.

"Do you have any others?" She tried to keep the

edge from her voice, but emotion threatened to burst through. She couldn't sit idly by while David and Josh were in danger.

"Yeah, keep you safe. Tuck you away somewhere until this storm has passed." Somewhere in his voice she heard a touch of that protectiveness that she'd always loved. But he had no reason to be protective of her now. They were two estranged friends who'd been thrown together again after years apart. In those years, they'd changed; they'd become new people. And once this was over, they'd go back to the way things had been.

"You know I'm not a sit back and stay quiet kind of girl, Christopher." Outside the window, the landscape morphed from back roads into suburban housing developments and shopping centers.

He smiled. "Yeah, I know."

She crossed her arms over her chest. "There is a back way to get into Josh's house."

He looked into the distance and sighed. "I'm stating for the record that I have reservations about this."

"You know I'm going to do it with or without you."

"Exactly."

She stared at him, waiting for his response. Finally, he nodded. "I'm calling some men from Eyes in to check things out first. And we're not making any moves until it gets dark outside."

Christopher watched as Ashley picked up a blue sweater and raised it in the air. Her eyes narrowed as if she was imagining herself in it before she draped it over her arm and continued looking.

That method of determining what she wanted would have to do for now. They didn't have time to try on any clothes. They had to get what they needed and keep moving.

Christopher had decided to come to a local mall to do their shopping. What better place to blend in than the throngs of people out looking for last-minute Christmas gifts. How far away was Christmas again? A week?

He hadn't been looking forward to the holiday. His mom was out of town. His dad had been out of his life for two decades. His grandfather was dead. Christopher had planned on spending the day alone, reflecting on life—the past, the future, his failures, his successes, his regrets, his victories. Then he'd pray he could leave all of those things at the feet of a God who'd been born in a stable, but had grown to be the Savior of the world and his reason for hope.

He'd convinced himself that being alone was what he wanted, though he knew it wasn't the truth. He'd made his choices. He'd traded a family for his career.

And now his career was over, and he was left with what felt like nothing.

He glanced around him once more, as he'd been doing since they arrived. He might actually enjoy a day like this, if it wasn't for the circumstances that had brought them there. Garlands and evergreens decorated the countertops and columns and displays. "We Wish You a Merry Christmas" rang out through the speakers. Excitement seemed to zing through the air. The holiday rush—wasn't that what people called it?

As Ashley stepped away, Christopher remained

close. Anyone watching would think they were a couple out shopping together. No one would guess their history. It wasn't every day that God brought you the chance to make things right. The most he could hope for was Ashley's forgiveness. He'd ruined any possibility of a second chance, of Ashley being in his life again. But it didn't matter. He was too messed up from the war. He feared too much that he'd let Ashley down again, just like his own father had let Christopher down when he walked away from their family.

Despite that, there was so much he and Ashley needed to talk about, but now wasn't the time. Now they just had to concentrate on staying alive.

Christopher's mind raced back in time to trips they had made together a decade ago. Even doing simple things like grocery shopping together had been fun with Ashley. She had a way of offering commentary on the most mundane things, making routines seem entertaining.

Back then, they'd wanted to be together as much as possible.

She'd always said it wasn't the big things in life that you remembered. It was the small, everyday things that were important.

When he thought back to their time together, it was the simple things about their relationship that made him smile—things like jogging together, picking out the perfect apple, watching the sunrise and searching for seashells along the bay.

He shook his head, snapping back to the present. His gaze scanned the store. Two men walked in together and immediately separated. Christopher saw the way they glanced at each other, as if communicating in some unspoken way. Both perused shirts at opposite sides of the store. Funny, because the trendy clothes here looked nothing like what the suited men would wear.

Christopher gripped Ashley's arm. "We need to go."

She looked up, startled. "What do you mean?"

"I mean, they've found us."

She dropped the sweater as Christopher pulled her toward the back of the store. They slipped past the dressing rooms and into the office. All the employees were on the sales floor, busy helping with the Christmas rush, so there was no one to stop them.

He pushed through a back entrance that led to a hallway that ran behind the stores—usually reserved only for employees. As soon as their feet hit the tile there, he grabbed Ashley's hand and began running. "We've got to get out of here!"

Just as they rounded a corner, someone else emerged from the doorway. Shots rang out, echoing in the small space.

In a mall? These men were shooting at them in a mall? They meant serious business.

"Come on!" He pulled her into a store. Would those men be as brazen as to shoot at them in plain sight?

*Please, Lord, keep everyone safe, not just us.*

He sucked in a breath when he realized they'd stepped into a hair salon. The minimally decorated store offered no cover. As they emerged from the back, all the customers and stylists inside stared at them from their booths.

Christopher kept a tight hold of Ashley's hand,

pulling her through the space until they reached the crowded mall. He skidded to a halt after stepping into the ocean of people toting shopping bags and over-size coats.

Where were those men? It was only a matter of time before they found them again. They had to hide.

Now.

To their right was a "pictures with Santa" area. He had to lead the shooters away from that display, just in case the men started shooting again. He pulled Ashley toward the food court instead. He plunged into the middle of the crowd, hoping to stay concealed.

From behind them, he heard a yell.

Then more gunfire erupted.

Screams scattered throughout the crowd. People ducked or ran or cried out or did all three.

Christopher and Ashley burst into a sprint. They were on the second floor. They had to get downstairs and out to the car. Two mall-security officers ran past, radios in hand.

But the two gunmen kept shooting.

Who were they?

And if they were desperate to kill Ashley so they wouldn't be discovered, then why were they shooting at her in a mall where they would be discovered? There had to be more to this than either of them realized.

He'd think about that later. Right now, they had to stay alive.

The escalators were just ahead. Going downstairs would be risky, but what other choice did they have?

A bullet grazed past his arm, and he pulled tighter on Ashley's hand. "Stay with me here!"

Just before he got on the escalator, he pulled a trash can down behind him and created an obstacle that would hopefully gain them a few extra seconds. He took the steps by two, slowing only enough to keep his balance. Another shot was fired.

When they reached the bottom, he grabbed the emergency off switch. The escalator came to a halt, and the two men tumbled downward at the loss of motion.

He used their stumble as an opportunity to pull Ashley into a department store.

He glanced back in time to see a mall cop grab one of the men. The man swung his gun around and aimed it right at the security officer. Then Christopher heard the blast of another bullet being fired.

*Oh, Lord, help us all.*

Ashley let out a small cry behind him. She'd seen it also.

Shoppers huddled behind displays of toasters and blenders. Others ran toward the doors.

They weren't going to be able to outrun the gunmen, Christopher realized. They were too close on their heels. Even if they made it outside, they'd be goners in the empty stretch of parking lot between the mall and the cars. The men would catch them.

"This way." He pulled Ashley toward the housewares section, looping around and hopefully throwing the men off their trail for a moment. He had to find a place to hide. Now.

Finally, he saw something that might conceal them—for a moment, at least. He eased a display mattress off its frame. "Get in. Quick."

Ashley climbed into the wood frame and ducked

down. He quickly crawled in beside her and pulled the mattress back over.

He prayed that the outside of the bedding display was straight enough that no one would notice he'd moved it. He'd tried to be careful.

"What are we doing?" Fear strained Ashley's voice. He could only see her outline as faint slivers of light crept through small gaps in the wood frame.

"We can't outrun them, Ashley. We've got to lose their trail and then take off."

He scooted closer to one of those gaps and peered out. It was hard to make out anything, but he saw policemen running past. Good. The police had been called in. That might make the men run. He could hope.

"How'd they find us?" Ashley whispered.

"Good question. I have no idea."

Footsteps came their way. Was that…?

His pulse raced. It was one of the men. And he was walking right toward them.

Ashley's heartbeat pounded in her ears. Her blood raced through her veins, hot and urgent. What was going on? Why were these men being so brazen?

Christopher stiffened beside her. Had he spotted one of them? She dared not speak, just in case he had. She dared not move or do anything that might give away their whereabouts.

Christopher turned toward her. Even in the dim light, she could sense the urgency in his eyes as he put a finger over his lips to motion "quiet."

"Do you see them?" someone yelled nearby.

"I lost them. They can't be far," another man replied.

"The police are looking for us. We don't have much time."

The second voice got closer. "We shouldn't need much time. They have to be around here somewhere."

"Make it quick."

One of the men muttered profanities under his breath. Ashley could see their legs. The men were right beside the comforter display. Right beside them.

Ashley closed her eyes, lifting up fervent prayers. *Lord, keep us invisible.*

"The police are coming. We've got to go. We'll find them later!"

The men took off in a run.

Her heart stilled…but only for a moment.

They waited what was probably another ten minutes—it felt like hours, though. Finally, when the area was clear of both the shooters and the cops, Christopher nudged the mattress from above them. He stepped out and grabbed her hand, pulling her to her feet.

"Look calm and collected," he whispered.

She nodded, and they casually began walking toward the door. Her gaze scanned the area again. Two officers hovered near the store's mall entrance.

They probably didn't know to look for Christopher and Ashley—yet. All of their efforts were focused on the gunmen. When they reviewed the security tapes later, they'd see Christopher and Ashley fleeing. They'd want to bring them in for questioning.

Still, Christopher grabbed a coat from a rack and handed it to her. "Put this on."

She didn't argue. She slipped the blue coat on over

her white one. Christopher grabbed another coat from across the aisle and did the same.

Smart thinking, just in case anyone was looking for them. They'd be able to slip outside and get away—hopefully.

Christopher dropped some money on the register as they passed.

Finally, they reached the outside doors and stepped into the parking lot. Bright sunlight hit them. Police cars swarmed the building.

An officer reached for them. "You need to get out of the way. There are shooters in the building!"

They nodded and ran toward their SUV. As they passed a police cruiser, a radio crackled inside. "We're looking for a man and a woman also. The woman is wearing a white coat…"

Ashley willed herself to keep her steps casual, to not draw attention to themselves. The SUV was just within sight. Only a few more steps…

When she was within arm's reach, she broke into a jog and climbed inside. Each of her limbs shook with fear, with the mounting pressure of how serious this situation was. Christopher cranked the engine and they took off down the road. At last, they were safe.

For a moment, at least.

# Chapter Seven

Christopher's thoughts raced as he started down the road. How had those men found them? Christopher's only guess was that they realized Ashley was with him, and that he worked for Eyes. Perhaps they'd had men stationed near the Eyes' headquarters, just waiting for them to leave. But that would take a lot of planning and manpower. Why would they put so many resources toward tracking down and killing Ashley?

"That was a nightmare. A dark, horrific nightmare." Ashley slunk down in the seat and rubbed her temples. "I hope that poor security guard is okay. I hope no one else was hurt."

"Me, too," he muttered.

"I can't even comprehend how someone could do that."

No, she couldn't. That's because she was sweet and innocent. He wouldn't want her to be any other way. But he had to be honest with her.

"Ashley, this is going to be all over the news."

She nodded and nibbled on her thumbnail. "I know."

"The police—maybe even the FBI—are going to pore over all of the security-camera footage from the mall. That could eventually lead them to us. I don't know how long we're going to be able to keep your brother and nephew's disappearance under wraps."

"I'll just push as hard as I can until they track us down. At least I have a head start."

What was she thinking? That if she found her brother and nephew, she'd be able to burst through the doors to save them single-handedly? He was trying to leave the decisions in her hands, for the most part, at least. After all, it was her family that was on the line.

But how far should he let her go? He didn't know. He only knew that he'd be by her side and try to protect her from any danger that came her way. She *was* going to do this with or without him.

He sighed and they headed toward a more upscale area of Virginia Beach, careful to avoid the icy patches on the road. They traveled back toward her brother's house. They had to remain low and not draw any attention to themselves. These men had found them at the mall. Certainly they could find them at her brother's house, an obvious choice for where they might go.

At Ashley's direction, he pulled into a subdivision, a place where no doubt many doctors and lawyers lived—people who earned a nice paycheck. The homes were all brick and large with expansive yards. Each lawn was neatly manicured. Her brother had done well for himself.

"Park here." Ashley pointed to a section of trees.

"On the street?"

She nodded. "Trust me."

The thing was, he did trust her. She had a great head on her shoulders. But this situation…it was hard to know exactly what to do when thrust into an unknown circumstance like this one.

He pulled up along the curb to an area on the edge of the neighborhood. A large cluster of trees stood to one side. Snow and ice frosted the tree limbs and blanketed most of the ground. From the look of those dark clouds in the distance, they'd be getting some more snow soon.

"Did the guys from Eyes check out the place?" she asked.

Christopher nodded. "Yeah, there are two guys stationed outside of the house now. They haven't seen any signs that someone's there. Despite that, we need to play it safe."

Ashley nibbled on her lip as she stared at the woods. "If we cut through those trees, we'll get to my brother's house. His neighbor is out of town for the next week. They're down in Disney World. If we can get into their backyard, they have a massive tree house that offers a bird's-eye view of my brother's yard. We can watch from there to see if anyone is at the house." She glanced at him. "What do you think?"

"It sounds like a place to start. Let me check in with the guys first." He dialed their number. The men were stationed in cars at opposite ends of the house, and there were no new updates since they'd spoken earlier. Christopher told them that they were headed over. Those guards would offer a second set of eyes, but they'd still need to take precautions.

He popped his door open. "Let's go."

She gripped his arm, her touch causing warmth

to spread through his veins. In all these years, Ashley hadn't lost her ability to affect him like that. "But they'll see our footprints in the snow."

"We'll see theirs also. That's the good news. I'll find a branch to try and cover up our tracks. The snow didn't make it through all of those tree limbs in the wooded area, though, so that will help."

She stared at him another moment, apprehension knotting between her eyes, before finally nodding and opening her door. He grabbed a branch and began wiping away evidence of their path. His kept his gaze attuned to passing cars or anyone suspicious. He saw no one. Still, he remained on guard. Things weren't always as they seemed. He had firsthand knowledge of that.

They traveled quickly through the patch of trees until finally they reached a privacy fence. He motioned for Ashley to stay back as he crept forward. A gate waited along the back of the barrier.

He tugged at the handle. It was locked. He nodded at Ashley before scaling the fence and unlatching the gate for her. She slipped inside, her breaths coming out in raspy, icy puffs. She pressed herself into the wooden pickets, her wide-eyed gaze soaking in everything around her.

The good news was that he hadn't seen any other footprints or signs that anyone was around. The bad news was that it was biting-cold outside and would only get colder as the sun began to sink farther on the horizon.

He spotted the tree house in the distance. They crept toward the massive, hand-built structure. Ashley climbed the ladder to the top, Christopher right behind her. His gaze continued to scan the area as they moved, waiting for a sign that they had been spotted.

So far, so good.

They scrambled inside. The walls of the tree house blocked the bitter wind that swept over the area—at least a little.

Christopher peered out the window. Ashley was right. This tree house did offer the perfect view of her brother's house and yard. "How'd you know about this tree house? That the family was out of town?"

"I bring David over here to play sometimes."

"You're really close to him, aren't you?"

"Yeah, I love him…like he's my own."

"He's lucky to have you."

She nodded. Why did she look like the motion was painful, though? Why did her gaze look so strained?

He didn't have time to ponder that now. Instead, he watched the backyard. When he'd known Josh, he'd lived in a townhouse in an older part of town. So much had changed in the years since he'd talked to Ashley last.

"It looks like your brother has done well for himself." He kept his gaze on the backyard.

"With a better job and more money, unfortunately, has come less time for the family."

"Nothing's worth sacrificing family." Even as he said the words, he realized how Ashley would probably take them. After all, wasn't that why he'd broken up with her?

She said nothing, so he continued to watch silently. The sun began to sink, cloaking the area in dusky gray, until finally the night was on them.

He'd seen no signs of movement. If they were going to check out the house, now was the time. He looked back at Ashley. "You ready?"

"Ready as I'll ever be."

He reached for her hand. "Let's go, then."

Now, why did he have to reach for her hand? Ashley had been doing just fine sitting huddled in the corner by herself, trying to get his words out of her mind.

*Nothing's worth sacrificing family.*

Nothing except his career, Ashley supposed.

She couldn't let those thoughts linger in her mind, though. They'd only make her weak. Right now, she had to concentrate on finding Josh and David. That was all there was to it.

Christopher pulled her along, his hand warm and strong and way too familiar. Relief filled her when he released his grip in order to help her jump the fence. A moment later, he landed beside her and they ran toward Josh's house. Christopher covered their tracks again as they moved, making sure no one could easily trace them.

As they climbed onto the deck, Ashley pulled her keys from her pocket. The metal was cold on her already numb fingers—apparently they weren't completely numb, though. She could still feel the bitter cold. Christopher took them from her, calmly inserted them into the back door, and they slipped inside.

They both paused, listening in the dark room. All Ashley could hear was her heartbeat in her ears. Christopher held up a finger to his lips, signaling her to stay quiet and to stay where she was. He crept around the edge of the house and upstairs, making sure everything was clear. Ashley could barely breathe. Around every corner, she waited, expecting someone to jump out.

But there was nothing.

Christopher returned and shoved a flashlight into her hand. Turning on the lights would be too risky, be too obvious of a sign that they were here.

"Where should we start?"

"Let's look on Josh's desk," she whispered. "Maybe there's a clue there." She started toward the corner room on the first floor. Christopher stuck close by. Just having him near calmed her spirit, made her feel like she could face giants.

"You have any idea what we should look for?"

She shook her head, shining her light across the wooden floorboards. "No, but I'm assuming we'll know when we see it."

"Sounds like a good theory to me."

She stepped into the office and scanned the room. Josh's computer was gone. All three of them. But otherwise, everything appeared in place.

Strange.

She hurried across the room to her brother's desk and shoved some papers aside. There were bills, hand-scribbled notes and piles of paper for his work. There was nothing, however, that gave her any idea of what was going on.

She grabbed his calendar and began flipping through it while Christopher paced the perimeter. "Anything?"

"Not yet," she mumbled. She flipped through the pages. There, on the month of December, was an address. Who's address was that? It was for a place about an hour north of here in Williamsburg.

It might not be anything, but right now it was all she had to go on.

She stuffed his calendar and some other random papers into a backpack. Then she turned toward Christopher. "I think this is as good as it's going to get."

"Come on. Let's get out of here before we test our luck."

Ashley grabbed his arm and pointed to the window. A shadow lingered there. "We may be too late."

Christopher pulled Ashley back, tucking her behind a wall and out of the line of sight for any windows on that side of the house. His gaze darted about the house, looking for signs that anyone else was outside. He saw nothing, but still didn't let down his guard.

Slowly, he pulled out his cell phone. One of the guards outside answered. "Are you both still in your car?" Christopher asked.

"We're still here. Haven't seen any signs of movement out here."

"We think someone is at the back door. It's not one of you?"

"No, sir. We can go check it out."

Christopher clenched his teeth. "Be careful." He hung up and turned back toward Ashley. "How do you feel about guns?"

"If using one is what I have to do, I'll do it."

"Good, because as soon as we get out of here, I'm getting you one."

"My brother has one upstairs under his bed," she whispered.

He raised his eyebrows. "He does?"

She nodded. "I always worried about him having it with David in the house."

"Why would your brother have a gun?"

She shrugged. "I don't know. He said something about everyone having the right to defend their home or something."

"You okay with going up there to get it?" His gaze flickered up the stairs. He hated to separate, but he had to go into this potential battle with every resource possible.

Fear glimmered in her eyes for a moment, but she nodded, anyway. "If it means staying alive to find David then absolutely."

"I'll keep an eye on things down here. Just stay low and stay quiet. No lights."

"Got it."

His throat tightened as he watched her creep toward the staircase. *Please, Lord, watch over her.* He knew there was only one staircase in the home. He'd already checked the upstairs once and found it safe. She should be okay running up there to get the gun and back.

In the meantime, he had to keep his eyes open for the man he'd seen outside the home. Where had he gone? What exactly was he doing?

The men yesterday had annihilated Christopher's house without hesitation. The person outside the house now was quiet, almost stealthlike in whatever they were doing. Why the change?

Ashley crept back down the stairs. Relief filled him. So far, so good.

She handed him a metal-sided case. Carefully, he opened the box, pulled out the handgun and shoved the magazine in place. "Only put your finger on the trigger when you're ready to shoot," he whispered.

Her hands trembled beneath his, but she nodded. "Got it."

"I want you to stay right here. If someone comes into the house, shoot them."

Her eyes were wide as she nodded.

"I'm going to check out the perimeter. I'll be right back." He locked gazes with her. "Don't come looking for me."

She nodded again.

He stayed low around the edges of the house. He peered out windows but saw no one. Still, his heart pounded in his ears.

His People. They weren't a group to be messed with. How had Josh gotten himself entangled with them? And why did he really have a gun in the house? Josh had never seemed like the gun type, more like the intellectual pacifist. Had something spooked him recently?

After he went around the entire house, he found Ashley again, still pressed against the wall and standing at full attention. "Did you hear anything?"

"Only you." Ashley shivered. "Did they leave?"

"The guys are checking it out right now."

Just then, someone knocked at the door. "Agent Jordan, it's me."

He opened the door, and a rosy-cheeked guard came inside. "There were definitely footprints on the deck.

Three sets. We can assume one belonged to you, another to Ms. Wilson and the third to an unknown person. All three sets led through the snow and out the back gate. We didn't catch anyone."

So someone had been here, most likely seen Christopher and Ashley inside, and left. But why?

He leveled his gaze with Ashley. "We've got to go."

She didn't argue. The guard drove them back to their SUV. Christopher checked it out for signs of tampering before they climbed in and locked the doors. A brief moment of relief filled the air. They'd made it this far.

Ashley turned toward him, concern lacing her gaze. "What now?"

He cranked the engine and pulled onto the street. "Now you go back to the Eyes headquarters."

She shook her head. "I have another idea. I want to go to the address I found on my brother's calendar." She glanced at her watch. "It's only six-thirty. It's not too late to show up somewhere unannounced."

"That's not a good idea." It sounded like a terrible idea, for that matter. Best-case scenario, the address was nothing except a random location that had nothing to do with this fiasco. Worst-case scenario, they were walking right into the hands of the men who were trying to kill them.

"Do you have a better one?"

He nodded, his jaw firmly set. "Yeah, I do. Taking you somewhere safe. That's my idea."

She straightened beside him. He couldn't see her gaze, but he imagined the indignation there. "Christopher, this is my problem, not yours. And it doesn't matter where I am. I don't feel safe anywhere right now. I can't just sit around and be passive. I've got to find answers."

"The deeper into this we get, the lesser the chance I can keep you safe."

"I don't want you to keep me safe, Christopher." Her words came out faster and faster.

"Then why did you come to me?" It was a fair question and one that he'd been tossing around since last night.

"Because I need help."

"Why me?" He glanced over to catch a glimpse of her eyes.

Her cheeks flushed and she looked away. "It's complicated."

"I'd say we have time."

She squeezed her lips together and stared in the distance. "I really just want to concentrate on finding Josh and David now. You don't have to come. You can walk away right now if you want to."

He shook his head resolutely. "I'm not walking away." He was in too far. Plus, they still didn't have that closure he'd hoped for.

"Don't say I didn't offer."

"By the end of this, I want an answer from you. I want an explanation, Ashley, on why you came to me, of all people. I think I at least deserve that."

She nodded, her features strained.

He started driving toward the address.

# Chapter Eight

As they continued down the road, Ashley's chest felt like a gigantic brick pressed on it. She had to tell Christopher the truth sometime. But she dreaded how he would take the news.

In her mind, she'd tried to remember Christopher as someone who was so career-focused that he was heartless. But seeing him again, she knew that wasn't true. He would have been a great father—loving in discipline, gentle in teaching and active in life.

Guilt pressed in on her.

If only things had been different. A million times she had questioned her decision on giving up David for adoption. Maybe she should have kept him, gotten some kind of job that didn't take a college degree and become a single mom.

But she'd wanted her boy to have a stable home life, one with a mom and a dad. She didn't want him to face the uncertainty of whether or not they'd have electricity or groceries. Nor had she wanted to depend on the government or her parents.

Then she'd been in the car accident and had spent six months in the hospital trying to recover. Her brother had taken care of her baby in the process. When she saw how her brother and his wife had bonded with David, she knew what she had to do. She'd prayed about the decision and had peace when she decided to see if her brother wanted to adopt. Right now that choice seemed like the worst idea ever, though.

"What are you thinking about?"

Christopher's voice pulled her out of her churning thoughts. She shrugged. "Not much." Yet the truth was that she'd been thinking about everything.

Did Christopher need to know about David? Did he *really* need to know? Maybe it would be better if she spared him the truth. But could she live with herself if she did?

The lines used to seem so clear to her, but they no longer were.

"My GPS is saying we're almost there. This look familiar to you at all?"

They'd headed north from Virginia Beach toward Williamsburg. They'd pulled off the interstate thirty minutes ago and were now traveling on the dark, snow-slicked back roads of the community. Occasionally they passed a store or a house, but mostly they passed trees.

"No, this doesn't seem familiar."

Finally, they pulled into a neighborhood full of large, brick townhomes. Ashley looked at the address again and pointed. "Right there."

Christopher pulled to a stop in front of the house. Two windows were lit, making it appear that someone was home. Ashley's hand went to the door handle, but

Christopher's kept her in the car. She looked back at him. He'd gone from casual to all business in a matter of seconds. His eyes left no room for argument.

"Be careful. If anything happens to me, run."

His words caused an ominous dread to form in her gut. Despite that, she opened her door. Her feet hit the crunchy snow that had been packed down by passing cars. She shook off any fear that threatened to grasp her and fell into step beside Christopher.

She paused by the car parked in the short driveway as they passed it. Why did the vehicle look familiar? It was a burgundy luxury sedan. She shook her head, unable to place it at the moment.

They reached the porch. Christopher directed her to stand to the side as he knocked. Ashley could see the tension in his shoulders, in the set of his jaw. Would this be another ambush attack? Would the next sound they heard be that of gunfire?

*Lord, watch over us.*

She'd been praying that prayer a lot lately. John 14:27 flittered through her mind. "Let not your hearts be troubled, neither let them be afraid."

*Lord, I'm failing at that command. Forgive me. Help me.*

A moment later, someone pulled the door open. Quiet stretched for a moment. Ashley would take that over the sound of an automatic weapon. Still, she willed herself to remain to the side, out of the line of sight.

"Can I help you?" A masculine voice came from inside the house. Why did it sound familiar, like she'd heard it before?

"We'd like to ask you a few questions," Christopher started.

"Me? Why would you want to ask me any questions? And who are you?"

She dared to glance over and satisfy her curiosity. She blinked at the figure she saw there. "Wally?" She stepped from the shadows.

Wally Stancil's eyes widened beneath his oversize glasses. He stood only a few inches taller than her five feet, six inches. His thinness only added to his small demeanor. "Ashley Wilson? What are you doing here? It's been a while."

She shook her head, disbelief filling her. "I had no idea this was your house."

"And I had no idea you'd show up here."

"You guys know each other?" Christopher asked, slight annoyance across his face. "Can someone fill me in?"

Ashley pointed to the man at the door. "Wally is one of my brother's coworkers."

"Don't forget to mention that we did go out on a date once also," he added, his eyes sparkling as he pushed his glasses up higher on his nose.

Ashley forced a smile. It had been one of the worst dates of her life. They'd had absolutely no chemistry, but she couldn't quite convince Wally of that. Her lips twisted in a half smile. "Wally, this is an old friend, Christopher Jordan."

"Nice to meet you." He waved his hand toward the inside of the house. "Get out of the cold. Come in and tell me what I can do to help you."

Ashley stepped inside, Christopher close behind.

Wally led them to a living room off the entryway and offered them some coffee, which they both refused. Finally, they all settled across from each other on couches that faced each other. Wally flipped off the TV, where news coverage of the mall shooting was on.

Wally pointed to the screen. "Did you hear about that? Some rough stuff. Not sure what's happening in this world."

Ashley's throat burned. "I heard. It's just terrible. Did they catch the guys who did it yet?"

He shook his head. "Not yet. They're not sure how they disappeared. I guess there are four persons of interest all together. Three men and one woman. That's all they're saying."

"Scary," Ashley muttered. She knew firsthand just how scary it was.

"Now, to what do I owe the pleasure of this visit?" Wally leaned toward them, curiosity showing in his eyes. "I don't suppose you're here to beg me to go out with you again?"

Ashley smiled apologetically. "I'm actually trying to find out some information on my brother."

His eyebrows shot up. "Your brother? Josh? What about him?"

She licked her lips, trying to figure out how to approach the subject delicately. "I know the two of you work together. I was hoping you could tell me if he's been acting strangely lately."

Wally shrugged. "Not that I can think of. Is he okay? I noticed he didn't come into work yesterday. I assumed he wasn't feeling well."

"That's what we're trying to figure out," Christopher said. "Anything you might know would be helpful."

Wally's gaze flickered back and forth momentarily before he shook his head. "I'm afraid I can't help. I know he's been busy lately. We haven't had much time to talk."

Ashley wasn't ready to give up. "I saw your address was on his calendar. It looked like you'd gotten together recently."

Wally shifted in his seat but remained composed and calm. "We talked about getting together, but he canceled on me at the last minute. He said there was something he wanted to discuss, something about work. I never found out what it was."

Ashley leaned closer. "And you have no idea?"

He shook his head again. "No, I have no idea."

"Exactly what kind of project was he working on at TechShare?" Christopher asked.

"What kind of project?" He drew in a deep breath. "We were just doing some programming for a new computer processor the company is trying to develop. Nothing exciting."

"Is the new processor something that other companies were trying to get their hands on?" Christopher asked.

Wally shrugged. "I suppose the product was competitive. I mean, technology changes so fast. Every company wants to be at the top of their game. Tech-Share is no different. We hadn't been warned about any direct threats, however."

"Is there someone at the job who could speak directly to the matter?" Christopher asked.

Wally's bony shoulders again reached toward the

ceiling. "I guess you could call our boss." He grabbed some paper from the table and jotted something down. "Here's his number."

Ashley took the paper and slipped it into her pocket as another thought formed in her mind. She raised her chin and glanced at Wally. "I have a better idea. Maybe I'll visit him in the office."

He shook his head. "They don't really smile on unexpected visitors."

"We'll handle that. In the meantime, what's the address?" Christopher pressed.

Wally's gaze moved back and forth between the two of them. Finally, he snatched the paper back and jotted down something else. "Don't say I didn't warn you."

Ashley didn't know what that meant, but she nodded, anyway. They all stood, and Wally walked them toward the door. She wished she'd found more answers, but at least they had somewhere to go from here.

Streetlights flickered by, momentarily lighting the interior of the SUV, as they left the dark neighborhood. Ashley's thoughts turned over and over, trying to make sense of things, trying to find answers that were just out of her reach.

"So you really went on a date with that guy?"

She pulled her lips into a tight line. "I did. There was a lot of pressure from my family. They kept spouting something about me having expectations that are too high."

"So they wanted you to settle?"

"Exactly." She'd grumbled about that very thing on many occasions, but no one seemed to understand her.

"I went out with Wally just to appease them. But it was a horrible date. We had nothing to talk about. Nothing in common. And I couldn't even fake being interested in our conversation or our food or anything, really." The truth was: no one could compare to Christopher. She'd been on a lot of dates, but no one measured up.

"He certainly seemed happy to see you."

Her lips pulled tighter.

"And he's certainly the opposite of me. Maybe you should give him another chance. Maybe he's exactly what you need."

She scowled at him. "You're funny. At least you think you are."

"Come on, Ashley—"

She softened her voice. "I'm not the same person I used to be, Christopher. Life happens. You change. Things you used to like, you don't like anymore." Things like tough military men with soft hearts. *Like you.*

His expression sobered. "You're right. People do change."

And with people changing, relationships changed. *Like us, for example. Why did I ever think we would work together?* The idea was crazy.

At one time, she'd thought they were perfect together. But now she realized that she craved someone who'd be home every night, someone with a job that didn't put his life on the line. Most of all, she craved being with someone who'd make her feel loved. All Christopher had done was make her realize that she hadn't been worth it to him.

She crossed her arms over her chest. "So what now? Talking to Wally didn't give us any more answers. I still have no idea why my brother and nephew would be snatched or where they might be or what to do next."

"You've got to give it more time."

"I don't have more time! With every minute that passes, I feel like my brother and nephew are that much farther out of reach." She hated that her voice rose with each word; she hated the despair that crept into her inflection.

Christopher's gaze landed on her. "Maybe we should call the authorities in, Ashley. They are more well-equipped to handle these things. Besides, they're probably looking for us after that debacle at the mall."

She shook her head. "I can't. They made it clear that they'd kill David and Josh if I reported what happened."

"That doesn't make sense. They're keeping them alive for a reason. Otherwise, they would have just shot them on the spot. They've got to know the authorities are going to find out at some point. Josh won't show up for work. His mail won't be collected. David won't be at school. Whether you tell them or not, eventually the police are going to figure out something is wrong."

Ashley bit down on her lip. He was right. So why had they threatened her not to tell? Was it because she could describe them? Had they been trying to buy more time?

They did want her brother and nephew alive, she realized. That was the good news.

The bad news was that they wanted her dead. Or were they trying to abduct her also? Nothing made sense.

Was it possible that this nightmare had only taken place over two days' time? It felt like weeks had passed since she saw Josh and David abducted.

He pulled into a parking lot. "Here's the office." He glanced at the address again. "It's a bit smaller than I imagined. You ever been here before?"

Ashley shook her head. "No, I haven't. I doubt anyone's here. All the lights are off."

"We might as well knock since we're here." He glanced at her. "You stay here in the SUV. Lock the doors behind me. And keep that gun handy. Got it?"

She nodded.

She watched as Christopher approached the dark glass door. She realized probably no one was here, but they had to try, anyway. At least it was something.

He knocked at the door, his gaze constantly roving the area. The darkness surrounding them made Ashley shiver. A lone light lit the parking lot and the blue letters from TechShare offered a slight glow. But regardless, she felt so isolated out here, like anyone could get to them.

Just like they'd done today at the mall.

She shivered again as she thought about it.

Christopher climbed back into the SUV. "No one's there. We'll have to try again on Monday. Maybe we can figure out something then."

The long day was beginning to pull at her. She was tired, both physically and emotionally.

"I say we go back to Eyes and report to Jack and Denton everything that's happened today."

She nodded and put her head into the seat.

*Let not your hearts be troubled, neither let them be afraid.*

That verse was going to be harder to implement than she'd like.

## Chapter Nine

As soon as they arrived back at the Eyes headquarters, Christopher suggested they grab a bite to eat since food had been the last thing on either of their minds throughout the day. The cafeteria employees were gone, but he was able to pull together some leftovers from an earlier meal.

They sat across from each other in the cafeteria with stewed beef served in crusty bread bowls. Both ate silently for several minutes. Outside, darkness stared at them. It reminded him a bit of his past and his future. His past was filled with bad memories; the future was filled with uncertainties.

He watched Ashley a moment, wondering what was going through her mind. He wished he could reach out to her more, but he couldn't. It wasn't his place. He'd simply help her to work through this whole ordeal on her own time. What else could he do?

"What would you be doing now if I hadn't shown up at your doorstep?" Ashley asked, tearing off a piece of bread.

"I'd be working around the house probably." Trying to touch that ever-elusive thing called peace. He took another bite of his stew, savoring the warmth, as well as the quiet around him. "As you could probably tell by the boxes scattered around everywhere, it was a work in progress."

She frowned. "I'll pay you back for any damages there. I know it's a mess."

He waved her off. "I'm not worried about it." He wiped his mouth. "How about you, Ashley? What would you be doing on an ordinary weekend?"

She looked off into the distance, as if entering a different world for a moment. "I would have probably stopped by to see if David wanted to play in the snow with me." A faint smile brushed her lips. "He loves the snow, and we don't always get a lot of it around here."

"It sounds like you're really close to him." Every time she said his name, her voice became warmer and her eyes softer.

She nodded. "I am. Josh's job consumes him sometimes, so I spend a lot of time with David. It's especially nice because I work at home, so my schedule is flexible. I even have a bedroom set up for David at my condo."

"I always knew you'd be a great mom."

Her face lost its color. "What?"

He shrugged. "You know, you're great with kids. I know you don't have any of your own, but you'd probably get the award for being Super Aunt or something."

She laughed weakly and muttered, "Thanks."

"You live in Virginia Beach?"

She shook her head. "Portsmouth. Only a block from

the Elizabeth River, close to the downtown area. It's kind of fun to be able to walk places."

She'd always been idealistic, wanting to live in a small town where everyone knew everyone. They'd talked about moving out to the mountains one day, out toward where there was a slower pace of life. "And your dad?"

"He's down in South Carolina now, living in one of those retirement communities. He plays golf every day. He loves it. I even think he might be *dating* a widow he met there."

"I heard about your mom's passing. I'm sorry about that." A mutual friend had shared the news, but he hadn't wanted to complicate anything by calling Ashley to offer his sympathy. They'd only been broken up a few months at the time.

"It was a shock to all of us. It's amazing how life can change in the blink of an eye. First it was my mom from a heart attack. Six years later, Lena died of cancer. Now Josh and David have been abducted. It seems surreal." She shook her head in disbelief before clearing her throat. "How about you? How's your family?"

"My granddad passed away three years ago. You probably figured that out when we were at his house." He'd left the place to Christopher, but it wasn't the same without his granddad there. Still, he'd hold those memories close, and being at the house was the easiest place to do that.

"He was a good man."

"He was," Christopher agreed. "My mom got remarried and moved to Maine. She seems really happy.

I haven't talked to my dad in years. I think I was ten the last time he popped into my life. Then there's me."

"You've been back for three months you said?"

He nodded. "That's right. I'm still trying to adjust to life back here in the commonwealth." He was trying to adjust to life, period. Everything about his psyche felt so rocky right now. Would he ever be in a place where he was ready for a relationship, where he felt capable of opening himself up? Sometimes—most of the time—he felt like the answer was clearly a "no." Some of his friends had returned from war without an arm or a leg. Christopher had returned with what felt like part of his soul missing, forever lost on those deadly battlegrounds and amidst the horror of war.

"I thought for sure that you'd be career military. I just can't get over the fact that you're back here."

"As someone told me earlier today, people change."

Her eyes quickly lit with amusement before fading into a dull shimmer. "Yes, they do."

He leaned toward her, hungry to find out what she was concealing behind those beautiful eyes of hers. "But the core of a person stays the same, don't you think?"

She shrugged, her gaze fluttering up to meet his. "Maybe."

"Take you, for example. You're still Ashley Wilson. You still have a great smile. You're still smart and athletic and you care about others. Maybe your experiences have changed. Maybe your views have changed. But you're still Ashley."

"Life is always a process, isn't it? If I stayed the same and stayed sheltered from all the storms, I wouldn't appreciate life nearly as much as I do today." She leaned closer. "How about you? You're obviously still tough and protective. What's changed about you?"

Himself. Now that was a topic he wasn't ready to talk about. He leaned back as memories began to crowd in again. "War's changed me, Ashley. I've seen too many things. Too much death. Too much hurt."

War had damaged him too much, so much that he knew he'd been broken beyond repair. His future seemed bleak, like any possibility of a healthy relationship was gone. He'd seen and experienced a great deal of tragedy.

She leaned back and bit her lip for a moment, sweet compassion staining her gaze. "I can't imagine being in your shoes."

"I'm glad you've never been in my shoes. They haven't always been fun shoes to wear." His footsteps included dragging the lifeless body of his best friend back to the Humvee, rushing him back to camp in the hope the medics there could save him.

They couldn't.

There had been too much death. Too much pain. Too much loss.

She cleared her throat and whispered, "For what it's worth, I appreciate everyone who's served the country like you have."

Her words did warm his heart for a moment. It had taken her a lot of strength to say that, especially since his service to the country had led him away from her. "Thank you."

She nodded. "No, thank you." She stared at her half-eaten food for a moment before letting out a long sigh. "If it's okay, I'm going to turn in for the night."

"There's a church service here on the campus tomorrow morning at nine. You interested?"

"Yeah, that sounds great. I'll meet you in the hallway at 8:45? Does that work?"

"Sounds great. See you then." He watched her walk away.

Maybe they were making some progress in mending the divides in their relationship. Sometimes, out of the most devastating circumstances, the most beautiful things could grow. He remembered that flower garden on the base in Afghanistan again.

He hoped forgiveness might bloom out of the horrific circumstances surrounding them now.

Good memories, he reminded himself. Out of all the bad, he was going to walk away from this with something good.

The church service the next morning had been held in a small chapel located on the lower level of the Eyes' main building or "The Lodge" as Ashley had heard it called. According to Christopher, they'd hired a chaplain and began services there a few months ago. Some of their trainees stayed at the facilities for a couple of weeks at a time. They'd found the chapel to be an optimal place of comfort and spiritual "training."

The service had been nice and brought back some of Ashley's focus. She could always tell when her faith began to waver because her life felt scattered, her worries felt greater and regrets haunted her. But when she read God's word and focused on trusting Him, all the little stuff in life seemed to fall into place. Even if it didn't, she felt like she had the strength to handle it.

And her brother and David's abduction was no small thing, but she was still praying for wisdom.

After the service, she and Christopher had lunch in the cafeteria with Jack and his wife, as well as several other people who worked at Eyes. The cook had whipped up spaghetti and meatballs, and the savory scent filled her with a yearning for home. Instead, she tried to enjoy the people around her.

Jack's wife, Rachel, ran a nonprofit called 26 Letters, which set up volunteers to write letters to members of the military stationed overseas. She had a son named Aidan who looked around seven years old and the bump on her abdomen hinted that a new baby might be coming in a few months.

Every time Ashley looked at the boy, she was reminded of David, and sadness pressed on her heart.

She wished she could enjoy the conversation, that she could forget about the problems at hand and simply focus on being social.

But she couldn't do it.

First her thoughts drifted to how nice it would be to be a part of such a group. Then she thought about how nice it would be just to be a part of a couple. What would it be like to have someone to share her secrets with? Someone to help her carry her burdens? Someone to tell her everything would be okay?

But all those thoughts weren't getting her any closer to finding two of the people she loved the most in this world.

Finally, she leaned over and whispered to Christopher, "Do you think it would be okay if I used a computer?"

He wiped his mouth before nodding. "I can arrange that. We have secure lines up in my office. Even your brother couldn't hack into their systems."

"You don't think so? He's brilliant."

He stood and placed his napkin in his seat. "Didn't he get in trouble in high school for that?"

Her cheeks reddened as she also stood. "Yeah, he got bored and hacked into the school system's servers and changed some grades," she whispered, hoping no one else heard. "That doesn't mean anything."

He raised his hands. "I wasn't accusing anyone. I'm just trying to put the pieces together."

She forced a smile at the crowd of people at the table now staring at them. She offered a small wave. "Nice to meet all of you. Thanks for letting me eat with you."

They all called out their goodbyes. They really were a nice group. What would it be like to chat with them outside of this situation? It didn't matter because that was never going to happen.

Christopher led her upstairs to his office, a plain space with no decorations or personal touches. The room could have been anyone's office. She shook her head for a moment. "You need to put up a few pictures or something in here. It looks depressing."

He grinned at her. "Decorating isn't exactly my first priority, but I'll keep that in mind."

Yes, he could use a woman's touch. But not her touch. Someone else's. Maybe one of those nice women downstairs had a friend they could set him up with.

Despite how Ashley tried to be nonchalant with her

thoughts, her heart still tugged with…something. What was that? Longing? Attraction?

Those were emotions she needed to shove way, way down until they disappeared, never to be found again.

He glanced up at her, his eyes twinkling for a moment, as he pulled up the computer screen. Perhaps she'd overstepped her boundaries and been too personal with him. She should have kept things simple and professional.

He stepped back. "The computer's all yours."

She settled in the chair and typed in the web address for her email server. She wanted to make sure her brother hadn't tried to contact her. Christopher continued to stand beside her, his arms crossed as if he was on guard against her doing something stupid.

She glanced up at him. "I just want to check my email."

"Do you really think your brother emailed you?"

She shook her head. "No, but if anyone's trying to contact me, this is how they'll do it. I'm constantly on my computer emailing people, both for personal and professional purposes. I have some design jobs I'm working on."

"Who hires you?"

She shrugged. "It varies. But my brother helped me develop this security system for my websites. Because of that system, some big companies have hired me instead of doing their websites in house. I've had credit unions, stores, even a pharmaceutical company hire me to do their sites."

"So you're pretty good at this computer stuff yourself."

She shrugged again. "To an extent. Not like my brother. I really like the creative side of it. He likes the technical side."

She glanced up and saw Christopher's eyes were shining with…what was that? Admiration?

Her cheeks flushed, and she looked away. She had to concentrate on the task at hand. Why was she tempted, just for a moment, to concentrate on Christopher, instead?

Because concentrating on Christopher was a bad, bad idea.

Christopher couldn't help but feel a surge of respect for Ashley. She'd risen above some challenging circumstances and been able to achieve her dreams. She'd always been a whiz at graphic design. Not only had she found a career in the field, but she'd excelled. Who wouldn't admire that?

What he still couldn't figure out was why she'd come to him. Of all the people in the world she could have looked to for help, he had no idea why she'd chosen him.

Not that he was complaining. He saw this as a second chance to make things right and not in a "get back together" kind of way. No, he knew there was no chance of that. Even if Ashley could forgive him, the war had left him too broken. But maybe he could make it so she didn't hate him anymore.

He'd given up trying to explain himself and his decisions. He'd given up thinking that she might understand. They'd been young and in love. They'd never had any disagreements or arguments. They were perfect together. So he could understand that she was hurt over his decision, even if he was trying to do what was best for his country.

"Interesting…" She leaned toward the computer, a wrinkle forming on the skin between her eyes.

He scooted his seat around beside her. "What is it?"

She pointed to an email on the screen. "I don't recognize this email address. The subject line says, 'Urgent.' Normally I'd delete something like that, but with everything that's happened…"

He reached over and clicked on the email for her. A video message popped onto the screen. A boy with light brown hair, freckles and a defined jawline stared at the camera for a moment. Something about the boy seemed familiar…but what?

Ashley gasped beside him. "It's David. That's David."

"Hi, Ashley," his voice rang out. He smiled and did a quick little wave at the camera. A white wall made up the background and nothing else was visible. "My dad's friends told me to make this video for you. They said I should tell you to be quiet. I told them that didn't sound very nice, but they told me to say it, anyway. I miss you. I wish you could come visit—"

Someone cut him off and his image froze on the screen.

Ashley let out a small cry. Christopher squeezed her shoulder, knowing he could never fully comprehend all of the emotions she must be feeling. That boy was like a son to her.

"The good news is that he's okay," he murmured. "He doesn't even look scared."

She nodded, rubbing her lips with her fingers and staring at David's frozen picture on the screen. "That is good news. Why did he say *my dad's friends,* though?"

"That's probably what they told him to say." He leaned closer, squinting at the image on the screen. It looked pretty clean; it was unlikely they'd find clues there. "We need to have this video analyzed, see if technicians can pick up anything."

She nodded, her hand now in a fist over her mouth. She tore her eyes away from the screen long enough to glance at him. "He's so precious, Christopher."

"He looks like one tough, smart kid. Polite, too."

Unreadable emotion flooded her gaze. "You would love him, Christopher. He's great. Adventurous. He's got a bit of a daredevil in him."

He smiled. "It sounds like I would like him. I can't wait to meet him one day."

Tears glimmered in her eyes as she looked away. "I hope you can."

He squeezed her shoulder again. "I will. We're going to get David and your brother back."

She closed her eyes as if trying to conceal her pain. "Thanks."

"I'm going to go get one of our technicians. You stay put here for a moment. Okay?"

"Got it."

Christopher jogged down the hall and grabbed two of the guys who worked IT for them. Adrenaline pumped through his blood as he hurried back toward Ashley. He stepped inside his office in time to see her running her finger down the computer screen. The image made his heart lurch.

She dropped her hand and scooted out of the way as the IT guys surrounded the computer.

"I feel like if I look away then I'm abandoning him," she whispered. "That video's all I have to hold on to right now."

"At least you know he's okay. That's important."

She nodded.

"Let's see what we can find out," one of the technicians started. He pulled his seat closer to the table. "Maybe we can isolate some background noises that will give us some kind of indication as to where they are."

He began typing furiously on the computer's mainframe. He hit a few more keys and scrunched his eyebrows together before sitting back and letting out a grunt.

"What's going on?" Christopher stepped closer and saw that the computer screen had become pixelated.

"Unplug it!" Ashley yelled.

The technician's hands scrambled around the computer until he reached the back and jerked out a wire. He muttered under his breath as the screen finally went black.

Christopher didn't have to ask. He knew what had just happened. A virus. There had been a virus in that email.

These men were trying to get at them at whatever angle they could. He had a feeling Ashley's heart had just been ripped out from her, similar to that computer cable. He had to get to the bottom of this before these people became like a virus to Ashley's soul.

## *Chapter Ten*

Ashley should have known. So much for getting clues there.

But where did that leave them?

She sat on the floor, leaning against the wall of Christopher's office. Her head felt like it weighed a hundred pounds—a hundred throbbing pounds.

When would they ever catch a break? What was she missing?

A hand clamped down on her shoulder. "There will be more clues. Just wait." She looked up and saw Christopher looking down on her.

"That just seemed to be our best one."

With his fingers gently pressing on her arm, he pulled her up. "Come on. Let's let these guys work. There's something I want to do with you."

They started walking toward the other end of the building. "Where are we going?"

He smiled. "You'll see. Grab your coat and gun."

She stopped by her room and did just that before

meeting Christopher in the hallway. They walked outside, across the lawn and to another building.

Once she stepped inside, the smell of smoke hit her—only it wasn't the smell of burning wood or metal. This was different, unique in and of itself.

It smelled like the inside of Christopher's house after those men had destroyed it.

It smelled like gunpowder.

She glanced up at Christopher. He grinned, all lopsided and boylike, an image that sent her back in time. "A shooting range," he explained. "It's time to teach you how to handle a gun."

"Is this really necessary?" Certainly, she wouldn't need to use a gun. Except that she knew she might, whether she wanted to or not.

"It could mean the difference of getting your nephew back or not."

She nodded, the decision firmly made up in her mind. "Let's do it then."

The range was empty of anyone but them. He led her to a lane and handed her some earplugs and protective glasses. Then he put the gun she'd retrieved from her room in her hands. The metal felt cold and foreign. But she was willing to take on something new. She didn't have much of a choice.

"Hold you arms out like this," he said, adjusting her reach. "Don't lock your elbows in place."

She loosened her arms, which was the opposite of what she wanted to do. "Got it."

He patted her hip. "Keep your legs shoulder-width apart. There's a bit of a kickback after you fire. Having a steady stance will give you more stability. Just be aware that it's going to happen, though, okay?"

She nodded, wishing he wasn't so close. But he stood right beside her, his arms easily wrapping around her. Not in a romantic way, simply as an instructor and student. That didn't stop every inch of her skin from becoming alive, however.

"Now, just take your time and aim at the target. Use your dominant eye."

The gun shook in her hands as she held it and pointed toward the target at the end of the berm.

"When you've got your target in sight, press the trigger, don't pull it. That motion keeps you in control."

She could hardly do anything with Christopher standing this close. Nonetheless, she tried to concentrate on what he was saying. Even after all of these years, he still had that effect on her. It was a good thing she'd realized that warm, happy feelings didn't equate into lasting love—even temporary infatuation, for that matter. They usually translated into heartbreak.

Her heart leaped into her throat as she stared down the barrel of the gun. Finally, she pressed the trigger. The kickback took her breath away for a moment, causing a surge of adrenaline. She pulled up her protective eyewear and looked at the target at the end.

Christopher pushed a button and the punctured paper traveled down the ceiling toward them. He studied it a moment before nodding beside her. "Not bad."

She hit a couple of inches north of the center. "What do you know? Maybe I should consider a career change."

He offered a wry grin. "I don't know about that. We

need people in the world who have big hearts, and we need people in the world who are ready to jump into battle."

"Didn't you always say that a good SEAL had both of those things?"

He glanced down for a moment. "I might have said that. It takes all kinds of people to make the world go round, right?"

"Sure enough."

His face lost the moment of vulnerability it had presented briefly. He motioned toward the target and his lips pulled tight. "Let's keep working."

What was that about? If Ashley asked, she had a feeling he wouldn't tell her.

They continued to shoot, each round getting better and better. The gun was beginning to feel less foreign and more familiar. Still, she prayed she never had to use it.

Finally, she handed the weapon to him. "Let's see what you can do."

He took the gun from her and began firing. Every shot hit the target dead-on. She was stunned by his accuracy. "I'm impressed."

"You should be. He was the best shooter the military had," someone said behind them.

Ashley looked up as Denton walked into the range. It seemed like every time she saw the man, he brought bad news. Still, she nodded hello.

He stopped in front of her. "Could I chat with you a moment, Ashley?"

Dread filled her. "Of course."

He dipped his head toward the front door. "How about we take a walk? The sidewalks have been cleared enough that they shouldn't be slick."

"Sure thing." She grabbed her coat and pulled it on as she walked toward the exit. As they stepped outside, lemonade-colored sunshine hit them—it felt more like frozen lemonade with the brisk chill in the air, though. Thankfully, the day was warmer than yesterday, even though snow still lingered on the ground.

They began walking silently down the sidewalk. Anticipation built in her as she waited for what Denton had to say. His hands were shoved down into the pockets of his black leather coat, and he walked with slow, purposeful steps.

Finally, he broke the silence. "So I did some research on the boy your brother adopted."

Her cheeks heated, even though she willed them to stop. "Did you?"

"I saw your name listed as the boy's mother."

She dragged her steps for a moment. Did she deny it? Own up to it? More of her carefully controlled life began to crumble. Finally, she nodded. "It's true. I was young and in college—I couldn't support a child. My brother wanted a baby, so he adopted mine. It just all made sense."

Denton glanced over at her. "And the boy's father? Is he in the picture?"

Her throat burned. "I didn't tell him so, no, he's not involved."

His eyebrows shot up. "You didn't tell him?"

Did Denton know? Ashley couldn't be sure. She only knew her heart squeezed with anxiety. "It's a long story. But let's just say when the boy's father left, he made it clear that he wasn't a family man. This was the best choice for all of us."

He nodded. "I see. That's pretty harsh." They took a few more ambling steps. "I guess this is all a secret?"

"You could say that."

"Is there anybody in your past who could want to hurt the boy?"

She pointed her finger at herself. "In *my* past? No, I have nothing to do with this."

"Are you sure?"

"I'm positive. No one knows…"

"You're sure the dad's not a part of this?"

She stopped. "Of course he's not. His name isn't even on the birth certificate."

"I'm asking because if his dad just happened to be on some specially trained team that, let's say, took down terrorists, then that might be another possibility as to why Josh and David were abducted. It could help us to track down the men behind this."

Her cheeks burned as dreadful possibilities filled her. "I don't know what you're talking about." But her mind raced…could that be the connection they were missing?

"Really? Because that boy had the greenest eyes. They almost looked like…" He stopped and shook his head purposefully. "No, I don't know what I'm thinking."

She said nothing. She couldn't say it, couldn't admit it. Or could she? No, this had nothing to do with Christopher. The idea was crazy.

They started walking silently together again. Finally, Denton spoke. "Did Christopher ever tell you what his nickname was as a SEAL?"

She shook her head. She had no idea, and, at the moment, she couldn't even say she really cared.

"They called him Captain America."

Her gaze flicked up toward Denton. "Like the superhero?"

Denton nodded. "Yeah, like the superhero. He was selfless, always trying to look out for everyone else, always talking about how our country was worth fighting for. He was a real inspiration."

"Selfless?" she practically stuttered. A selfless person didn't leave his fiancée six months before the wedding so he could be a better soldier. She bit down and said nothing else.

Denton stared at her a moment before nodding toward the inside. "I guess it's time to get out of the cold."

He started walking away when Ashley grabbed his arm. "You can't tell anyone about what you found out, Denton. Please. It's…important to me."

Perceptive, compassionate eyes met hers. "It's yours to tell, Ashley. Not mine. But if there's anything else you can tell me that might shine some more light on your brother and nephew's disappearance, please let me know. Nothing is insignificant."

Anxiety and dread pooled in her stomach as she nodded. "Got it."

She stood outside and raised her head toward the wind, letting it hit her skin until she couldn't feel her face anymore. This discomfort beat that of breaking the news to Christopher.

She had to tell him, didn't she? She couldn't put it off any longer.

Christopher shot a few more rounds after Ashley and Denton left the range. Each pull of the trigger seemed to be a release of emotion as doubt and suspicion rose in him.

He lowered his gun and shook his head. What had that been about? What could Denton have wanted to talk privately with Ashley about? He'd put his life on hold to help her, and now she was keeping secrets?

He pulled off his protective eyewear and his earplugs, his thoughts still churning. If he was supposed to know about their conversation, Denton or Ashley would tell him. They wouldn't keep something from him that could be pivotal to their search.

Why didn't that realization make him feel better, though? What was so secretive that he couldn't know, especially when considering everything they'd already been through together? That was the reason he was so up in arms, wasn't it? It had nothing to do with the sparks of electricity he'd felt when he'd taught Ashley to shoot. It had nothing to do with the way her smile was beginning to occupy his thoughts. Because those things, while enjoyable, were off-limits on so many levels.

He tried to brush off those thoughts as he began cleaning his gun. His work here was done. He'd go check on the IT guys and see if they'd found out anything else. At least that quest for information would keep his mind occupied.

As he stepped outside to go back to the main building, he made a mental list of what they needed to do. They needed to visit TechShare again. And then what? Did they have any other leads?

Here in the States, working as a civilian, they didn't have satellite surveillance or intelligence like he'd had when he was a SEAL. Here, he had to rely on good old-fashioned investigating if he wanted to find any answers.

He paused when he saw Ashley standing on the sidewalk, her face raised to the wind and eyes squeezed shut as if in agony. What was going on?

And why did she have to look so beautiful, even in her distressed state? She still had the ability to take his breath away. There wasn't a single thing about her that wasn't lovely and loveable, all the way from her pert nose and glossy hair to her fiercely loyal spirit and warm gaze.

She opened her eyes and caught him staring at her. She quickly straightened but didn't even attempt a smile. "Christopher."

"I didn't mean to intrude." And he had intruded. He wasn't sure on what, but Ashley's thoughts looked heavy enough to crush her.

"No, you're just the person I was hoping to talk to." She sucked in a deep, long breath. The agonized look remained in her eyes. "You want to take a walk? The fresh air is nice."

"Absolutely."

They fell in step beside each other. He gave her the space and time she needed to pull together her thoughts. Whatever she had to say, it seemed to be a burden. He braced himself for her words. Had she secretly befriended a terrorist? He just couldn't even begin to fathom what had her so tense.

She shoved her hands deep into the pockets of her blue coat. Her steps seemed slow, uncertain almost.

"So there's something I've been meaning to talk to you about."

"You can tell me anything, Ashley."

She licked her lips. "It's a little complicated, Christopher. Actually, it's a lot complicated, at least when it comes to my heart."

When it comes to her heart? Had she been mixed up with someone shady who was bad news? Fire rushed through his veins at the thought. He'd always imagined her marrying someone stable and secure, someone who'd take good care of her.

Who was he kidding? He'd always imagined her marrying him. Only that couldn't happen. War had left him warped and incapable of a committed, healthy relationship. Ashley deserved someone better, someone who wasn't consumed with the tragedies he'd faced.

She paced a few more steps, her face tight. Whatever she had to say, she was struggling.

Finally, she stopped and licked her lips again. When she looked at him, the emotion in her eyes broke his heart. "Christopher, when you left me…" She paused, her eyes wavering in thought. "When you left, I was angry."

"You had every right to be."

She heaved in a deep breath. "I didn't ever want anything to do with you again. I told myself that you'd made your choice, and that I had to get on with my life. That's what you told me you wanted."

"I did." He clearly remembered saying those words. Each one had made his heart feel like it was crumbling away, bit by bit.

"You told me that you'd chosen to be career military instead of going the family-man route, right?"

He nodded, wondering where she was going with this. "I think I did say something like that."

She squeezed her lips together and shook her head. "Look, Christopher, this is really hard for me. There's no easy way to say it."

"I'm a big boy. Don't worry about me. Just say it."

She swallowed hard. "Christopher, I— We—"

Before she could finish her sentence, an explosion sounded behind them. They glanced back to see a huge ball of fire rising up from the guardhouse at the Eyes' entrance.

## Chapter Eleven

"We've got to leave. We can't stay anywhere too long, or they'll find us."

Ashley nodded as she absorbed Christopher's words. She was still in shock over the car bomb that had killed the guard at the gate, as well as the driver of the vehicle who'd pulled up to the entrance with a bomb in his trunk.

They'd spent the last four hours dealing with the aftermath of the attack. Looking for survivors, calling the authorities, picking up the pieces.

Not Ashley, of course. They'd tucked her away, afraid there might be another attack. So she'd sat at the window and watched the devastation around her. Wasn't that what her life had turned into? Ground Zero after an attack?

The FBI had come in and she'd given them a statement. She'd told them about Josh and David, praying in the process that she wasn't getting them killed. Guilt had filled her when one of the agents had looked outraged over her not reporting their abduction sooner.

A rock and a hard place. She'd been there before, and it wasn't a fun place to be.

She stared out the window again, trying to find even a sprig of hope in the barrenness of her soul at the moment. "That poor guard. He looked so young."

Christopher's lips pulled into a tight line. "I know. These men are clearly trying to send a message. We've got to get you out of here. Grab your things."

She felt numb as Christopher led her back upstairs and into her room. In a trancelike state, she stuffed her few measly belongings into one of the shopping bags she'd picked up on their trip Saturday before meeting him in the hallway.

Christopher's eyes glowed with compassion as he looked down at her. She tried not to let his sensitivity to her emotions clutch at her heart. She was already feeling so vulnerable.

"You ready?"

She nodded, even though she felt anything but ready. If the terrorists could get to her inside the Eyes' headquarters, just what was waiting for her outside of these gates? She had to be strong, though, for David's sake if no one else's.

Christopher led her outside and to a waiting SUV. A moment later, they took off through an alternate exit out of the Eyes' headquarters. She remained silent as they wove through the dark streets. The sun had set at least three hours ago. In the distance, the lights from emergency vehicles still flashed, a reminder of the tragedy that had occurred.

Ashley said nothing. There was nothing to say.

Miles and miles of road passed and she stared out the window, lost in her thoughts.

Finally, they pulled down a long, winding lane surrounded by woods. A cabin, complete with the front porch light on, waited for them at the end. She sat up straighter, curiosity driving away the doldrums. "Where are we?"

Christopher put the car in park and stared at her for a moment. "It's a safe house."

"A safe house?" She blinked. She'd heard about safe houses before. She never thought she would need one, though. They were for…people in danger. That now included her. She never thought *Ashley Wilson* and *danger* would be in the same sentence.

"We'll be out of danger here tonight. We won't stay anywhere more than one night, though, just as a precaution." He opened the door and grabbed their bags from the back.

Still numb, she followed him through the darkness and toward the house. A man stood at the door, waiting for them. Christopher introduced him as a guard who'd been assigned to stay there and keep an eye on the place for them.

Ashley stepped inside. The space was small, but homey. Someone had even taken the time to light a fire and warm the air for them. It wasn't quite home sweet home, but it would do.

She couldn't let the coziness of the place allow her to let down her guard, however. She might be safe for the moment, but the moment would soon pass.

Christopher's hands went to her shoulders. She looked up at him, sucking in a breath at his closeness.

Firelight danced on his face, the amber hues softening his features. For a moment—and just a moment—she felt like she was nineteen again, and young and in love. She snapped out of it and took a step back. Christopher's hands still remained on her shoulders, but she realized his touch was meant to ground her and not as a romantic advance.

"Did you want to finish having that conversation now?" he asked.

That conversation? It took her a moment to even remember what that conversation was. David. Being his son. The devastation that would follow. No, there'd been enough devastation for one day.

She shook her head. "No, not now. I just need to rest now." She was too tired. Too much had happened and she didn't want to muddy the waters any more than they already had been.

He nodded. Was that disappointment in his eyes? His hands slipped from her shoulders, and he scooted back a step. "Okay."

She turned toward one of the bedrooms down the hall, realizing just how out of control her emotions were tonight. Because for another moment there she'd felt some of her attraction to Christopher return.

Things between them would never work out. Never. Hadn't she learned that already? And when she shared her secret, their rift would become even greater. "I just need to get some shut-eye."

She fled before he could ask any more questions.

The next morning, Christopher sat at the kitchen table and stared outside. The snow still covered the ground, though it had started to melt. On the edge of the woods that surrounded the cabin, two deer found a patch of grass and nibbled there, occasionally glancing around for any signs of danger.

They reminded him, for a moment, of Ashley. She was so innocent, but she'd become like prey to the men who were hunting her. Everywhere she went, she couldn't let down her guard, not even for a second. She was graceful, beautiful…and in danger.

He sipped his coffee. He hadn't been able to sleep for most of the evening as his mind replayed what had happened over and over again. Each time he closed his eyes, that explosion rocked his world.

It sent him back to Afghanistan. Sent him back to that final raid. Sent him back to finding Liam outside, shot down by combatants' gunfire.

He closed his eyes as the memories came again. At once, he was back on the ground beside his friend.

*"Stay with me! I'm going to get you help."*

*Liam shook his head. "No, get out of here. It's too late for me. I'll only slow you down."*

*"I'm not leaving here without you."*

*"Christopher, go! Don't let them take another life."*

*Gunfire exploded in the distance. Yells and shouts crept over the hill. The insurgents were getting closer. It was just a matter of time.*

*Before Liam could argue, he hoisted his friend over his shoulder. Then, as gunfire rained behind him, he ran toward the Humvee. He ran and ran. His lungs burned. His—*

He shook his head. He was in Virginia. So why did

his mind so easily travel back to Kabul? How long would it be until the nightmares stopped?

*Lord, I know You make all things work together for our good. Even when we can't see it. I definitely can't see it now, but I pray that Your hand would be on all of this.*

A moment later, Ashley came padding down the hallway. She looked like she hadn't slept any better than he did. She pulled up a seat across from him and plopped down. "Morning."

He stood. "Coffee?"

"Please."

He brought her a cup. She took a slow, long sip and closed her eyes. "Thank you."

"How'd you sleep?"

She frowned. "I didn't. Everything just kept replaying in my head."

"Yeah, I know what that's like."

She took another sip. "Please tell me that you don't expect me to stay here with only my thoughts for company? I will lose my mind if I'm expected to sit around and twiddle my thumbs."

"I didn't take you hostage, Ashley. Even though I would prefer it if you did just hunker down. I'd feel better." Keeping her under lock and key was tempting, just for safety's sake.

She shook her head. "I've got to find Josh and David. I've got to track every lead. I've got to do something."

He nodded. Her answer hadn't surprised him, not in the least. "I know."

"I was hoping we might visit TechShare and see if Josh's boss is in."

"We can do that."

"And I never did check my voice mail yesterday. I just want to make sure there are no messages...you know, from my brother or something. Would you mind?"

He grabbed his phone from the counter. "The line is secure. Go ahead."

She began tapping in some numbers. A moment later, her lips twisted in confusion. Finally, she put the phone down and stared at him.

"This message is from one of the companies that hired me."

"What's going on?" He set his mug down.

"It's strange. He said information from his website has been compromised."

"Don't hackers do stuff like that all the time?"

She shook her head. "No, it's strange because I have multiple layers of security set up on my sites. They've never been compromised. He sounds livid. He wants to meet with me about it—with his lawyers."

"That doesn't sound good." He leaned closer. "You should consider that this could be a setup, Ashley. This could be a way that someone's trying to lure you out of hiding. They knew putting your professional reputation on the line would draw you out."

She squinted. "You think?"

"Maybe. You never know."

"The man who called wasn't my original contact. His name is Damian Maro. He said the previous communications director left the company."

"How about if I call Denton and let him run his name through the system?"

"Might not be a bad idea."

Christopher came back into the room a few minutes later with a piece of paper in his hands. "Denton did a quick scan of his name. He said he can't find a connection with the company he claims to be with. Of course, if he's new, it could take a while to show up."

Ashley shrugged. "Maybe."

Christopher held up the paper. "Denton did find an address for a Damian Maro. Why don't we go pay him a visit?"

"Now?"

He nodded. "Yeah, when he's not expecting us."

"Let's do it."

Ashley's fingers dug into the seat as they headed down the road. What would today hold? Hopefully, she'd get some answers. She couldn't hope for all of the answers, but at least one would do. For now.

Christopher glanced over at her, his grip tight on the steering wheel. "We're near TechShare. Do you want to swing by there before going to visit this Damian guy who left that message?"

Ashley nodded. "That sounds like a plan. Maybe Josh's boss will be willing to talk to us."

Christopher pulled off the road, and a few minutes later they drove into the same parking lot where they'd stopped this past weekend. The difference was that now it was daylight and cars filled each of the spaces there. Hopefully, Josh's boss would be in and might have some answers.

Christopher put the car in park and turned toward her. "Let's go see what they have to say."

She nodded and climbed out of the car. They walked

to the nondescript gray building. TechShare. She'd never heard of the company before her brother started working for them, but apparently they were responsible for a lot of the computer programs and parts that were used today.

A plain reception area greeted them as they stepped inside out of the cold. A young brunette sat behind a desk with a professional smile on her face. "How can I help you today?"

"We're here to see Garland Evans," Christopher said. He strode up to the desk, looking every bit as self-assured and in charge as he ever had. At one time, Ashley had loved that about him. If she let herself, she could easily love it again.

The receptionist's smile slipped some. "Mr. Evans? Do you have an appointment?"

Christopher shook his head. "No, but it's important that we speak with him."

The brunette quirked an eyebrow. "And you are?"

Ashley stepped forward. "Josh Wilson's sister."

Her eyes widened but only for a split second. "Let me see if Mr. Evans is available. He's a very busy man." She punched some numbers into her phone and whispered a few things into the device before hanging up and turning to them. "I just talked to his secretary. He's in meetings all day, unfortunately, but we can set up an appointment for you."

Ashley shook her head. If Mr. Evans was in this building, she had to talk to him before she left. "We drove up here just to see him. It's extremely important. It's about my brother."

"I understand, but—"

"We're not leaving until we speak with him," Christopher said. His voice sounded authoritative and sent shivers down Ashley's spine.

The receptionist's eyes widened. "One more minute."

This time, she slipped out a door leading to some offices in the back. The minutes ticked by. Finally, she came out. A distinguished-looking, gray-haired man followed behind her. He extended his hand to Ashley. "I'm Garland."

"I'm Ashley Wilson, and this is my friend Christopher Jordan."

He nodded curtly. His blue eyes looked perceptive but tired. "What can I do for you?"

"Is there a place we could talk in private?" Ashley asked.

"Of course. Let's go in the meeting room we have right here." He led them to a room off the reception area. They sat down at a gray table. Mr. Evans remained the picture of a professional with his crisp sleeves perched atop the table.

Ashley decided not to waste any more time. She locked gazes with Mr. Evans. "I'll just get down to business. I'm worried about my brother, and I wondered if there was anyone you know of who was trying to steal information on the plans he was working on for the company?"

His gaze traveled perceptively from Ashley to Christopher and then back. "Steal the information on the plans?"

Ashley shook her head, unwilling to back down— not when the lives of people she loved were on the line.

"I don't know exactly what my brother was working on. But I do know how competitive the technology field can be. Whatever project he was handling, was there any chance someone else wanted it?"

He remained silent for a moment before nodding slowly. "I suppose there's always that chance. We haven't received any direct threats, however, if that's what you're asking. May I ask why you're questioning me about this? Is your brother in some sort of trouble? I thought he was on vacation."

Ashley licked her lips. How did she answer that without giving away too much about her brother?

Christopher spoke up. "We believe someone is threatening him. We're just trying to get to the bottom of things while he's away, using his vacation time."

Garland nodded slowly, thoughtfully. "I see. I'm sorry to hear there's been a threat, but I don't believe it has anything to do with his work here. Yes, he's developing some cutting-edge technology, but I don't think it would put his life at risk."

Ashley wasn't ready to give up yet. "Is there anything else you can tell us about his work here? Anything that might give us an idea of what's going on?"

"I wish I could tell you something, but I can't. There's nothing to tell. He seems to get along with everyone here and be well respected. I wish I could help you. I really do."

Christopher cleared his throat. "So there's nothing going on here at work that you think would be the cause for any conflict?"

"As I've already said, no, there's nothing here that's cause for alarm—just a bunch of computer techies doing their job and helping technology to run a little more smoothly."

Ashley nodded, her gut roiling with disappointment. She'd hoped for so much more from their visit. "Thanks for your help."

He stood and straightened his sleeves before handing her a card. "If you need anything, let me know."

As Ashley stepped outside, all she could think was that they'd just hit another dead end.

## Chapter Twelve

Their next stop was at Damian's house. As they sat across the street from his home, Christopher was grateful that the SUV's windows had a slight tint to them, which made it harder for anyone to see they were there. A car sat in the driveway, making it appear someone was inside the two-story, stucco-sided house.

He glanced in his rearview mirror again. Why couldn't he shake the feeling that he was being followed? He'd felt like that ever since Ashley had shown up on his doorstep. As he scanned the area around him, he saw nothing out of place. Still, he didn't let down his guard.

Beside him, Ashley hung up the phone and shook her head. "You'll never believe this. My brother called David's school on Friday and told them he was going to be out sick for a while. Why would he do that?"

Did Josh have something to do with all of this? The evidence was beginning to point to a "yes." Christopher knew it was a possibility that Ashley didn't want to consider. He settled on saying, "That surprises me."

"I also called one of Josh's neighbors about picking up his mail. While I was on the phone, the post officer came by and said that the mail had been stopped at my brother's house for two weeks. That doesn't even make any sense."

Christopher tried to find some words of comfort. "Maybe his captors made him do those things so the police wouldn't be alerted."

She shook her head. "I just don't even know what to think."

"The answers will come to light. Just give it time."

She shook her head again. "I don't have time. That's the problem. With each second, I feel like Josh and David are slipping further and further away."

He stared at the house, trying to steer the conversation away from the obscure and onto the tangible. "Tell me more about this company whose website was hacked."

"The company is local, but this website was for an online store that would complement their physical locations. I helped them set up all of their sales pages, as well as a check-out system with security verifications."

"What kind of store?"

"They sell holistic products—you know, vitamins, supplements, all natural stuff. They're a growing company. If I remember correctly, they have thirty stores, mostly here in Virginia but they're about to expand to other states."

"You said something about layers of security?"

She nodded. "It's my brother's theory. He said you need multiple layers from multiple sources in order to keep your sites safe. He helped me with that aspect of each site. That's why I have such a hard time believing that anything could have been compromised. It doesn't make any sense. My sites have never been hacked. Even Koury Pharmaceuticals hired me."

He recognized the name. "That is impressive."

"They hired me based on my record. A pharmaceutical company can't risk being hacked. People's lives are on the line if they are because the hacker could change vital information about their products. That's why this is so unbelievable to me."

He sat up and nodded toward the door. "Look, someone's leaving now. Do you recognize him?" A man, probably in his late forties with a stout build, walked toward the sedan in the driveway. His gaze shifted around him, but he kept going.

Ashley shook her head. "No, I've never met him. Like I said, his name isn't even familiar. He definitely wasn't my contact at the company."

There was a good chance that this man wasn't even with the company. As the man got into his car and started down road, Christopher eased out behind him. They followed a comfortable distance behind. Finally, he pulled in front of a restaurant in downtown Norfolk.

Good. Somewhere public. That would be the perfect place to talk to the man and find out what was really going on.

Christopher found a parking spot along the street. Once the man disappeared inside, they climbed from their vehicle, crossed the road and stepped into the neo-Southern restaurant. As Ashley started forward, Christopher pulled her back into the waiting area. The hostess stared at them suspiciously from behind her stand while patrons cast curious glances their way.

He leaned in close enough to Ashley that her hair tickled his cheek. "Easy," he muttered.

He peered around the corner and spotted the man—Damian—being seated at a corner table with two other men.

"What are you doing?" Ashley whispered.

Christopher leaned in close again, this time getting a whiff of her flowery scent. Something about the smell brought him a good measure of comfort. He nodded toward the distance. "You recognize any of them?"

She shook her head, pulling her coat closer. "Not a single one."

"If there's any place to talk to them, this would be it. It's nice and public." He glanced around the crowded space, one that was decorated with oversize roosters and sprouts of cotton stalks in milk jugs.

Ashley's eyes remained on the men. "If those are the same men who tried to shoot us in a mall, I doubt they'll blink an eye at pulling their guns here."

"They're not expecting us here. That's the difference." Still, he was well aware of the gun at his waist. He hoped more than anything that he didn't have to use it.

Ashley finally glanced up at him, a new determination in her gaze. "You should let me do the talking, just in case there is any validity in what he's saying and he actually does work for the company who hired me."

He raised his hands. "I'm just here for moral support. And protection." Of all the people he'd saved in his life, he could think of no one he desired to watch over more than Ashley. That realization caused Christopher to feel slightly off balance.

She nodded, seriousness staining her gaze. "I appreciate it."

She started toward their table, and he trailed behind. From the way she held her shoulders, he could hardly tell she was nervous. "Mr. Maro?"

The man looked up, his cool gaze accessing her. He had more bald spots than hair and wore a suit that looked expensive. Two men sat on either side of him. Both were large—both in frame and in weight—and one had an ugly scar across his forehead. What looked like tea, presumably sweet, waited in condensation-covered pickling jars in front of them, and fried green tomatoes sat in the center of the table.

Damian's eyebrows flickered up. "Yes?"

"I got a message from you about your company's website."

He squinted. "And you are?"

"Ashley Wilson."

His eyes lit and he shifted in his seat. "Ms. Wilson. How unexpected. How did you know to find me here?"

She raised her chin. "I just had to make a few phone calls."

His gaze moved back toward Christopher. "You brought police protection, I see? Off duty, I assume? Was that necessary? Perhaps it's protocol. That's what I'll believe. Better that than to be insulted." His eyes flickered. "Have a seat."

She shook her head. "I'd rather not. I can't really stay and talk very long. I'm in town so I thought I should try to meet with you during this very short window of time."

His eyes seemed to darken. "I see."

"As you can imagine, I'm anxious to resolve any issues you might be having with the site. I was concerned because in all of the conference calls with your company, your name never came up. I was surprised you were the one who contacted me."

Christopher glanced behind him. Was someone lingering outside the front door? The same shadow that he'd sensed following them since this all began? His muscles tightened as he felt danger closing in.

Damian chuckled. "As I said in my voice mail, I'm new with the company and I've been assigned to oversee this massive glitch that has us all on edge, especially since you promised a better product than what's been delivered."

Her hands went to her hips and a new fire lit her voice. "My websites have firewalls that hackers can't get past. So why did you really want to see me?"

"I can understand why you're leery." He glanced at the two men on either side of him. "I'm also a little on edge, especially since you've confronted me here at a restaurant of all places. Why don't we talk about this back at my office?"

She shook her head. "Have you talked to Joey Anderson about any of this?"

"Mr. Anderson is the one who approached me."

Ashley's lips curled in a small smile. "Was he? That's funny, because Joey is a woman."

The man smirked. "You're a smart one. I'll hand that to you. There are many things a computer expert can do for you. Clarifying whether someone with a unisex name is a male or female is apparently not one of them."

"My brother is not involved with this." She took a step closer, looking ready to jab him in the chest to drive home her point. Christopher's hand encircled her arm and held her back.

"How about you, Ashley? Are you involved?" The man's voice remained ice cold, absent of any emotion.

"Where's my brother?"

He shrugged. "I don't know what you're talking about."

"If you hurt that little boy, so help me…" She lunged toward him again, but Christopher held her back.

Damian only smiled with that blank look in his eyes.

Christopher tugged at her, the feeling of danger closing in becoming tighter and more urgent. "Come on, Ashley. Let's get out of here."

"Going so soon? I thought the fun was just beginning."

She pulled away, back toward Damian, and sneered. "What fun would that be that you're talking about?"

"The fun where you die."

Warning alarms were sounding in Christopher's head. They had to get out of here. Now.

"Come on, Ashley. We've got to go." He pulled her toward the door.

"Tell me where David is!"

Damian smiled, that same self-satisfied smirk that made Christopher want to lunge at him also. "You'll have to find him yourself. Unless we kill you first."

The two men seated on either side of him stood.

Too late. Christopher's muscles tightened. This didn't look good. Not good at all. He pulled Ashley closer.

"Why don't you two go for a little ride with my friends here? I call them Bruno and Babyface," Damian said. "They'll take good care of you."

"We're not going anywhere with you," Christopher muttered.

"Fine. We can do the dirty work here, if we must. But you'll be making more work for us, cleaning up. I suppose it will be worth it."

Christopher was all-too aware of his gun tucked into his waistband. He just had to get a hold of it somehow without drawing attention to himself. Still, even with his gun, could he take down these guys? He wasn't sure.

Another man appeared at the front door, blocking their exit.

Not this again.

Not another game of chase.

But apparently, that was exactly what they were playing right now.

He mentally counted to three and then took off toward an emergency exit door to the side. He pulled Ashley with him. Alarms wailed as soon as he opened the door, but he kept charging forward. The men trailed not too far behind.

They burst into the chilly air and darted toward their SUV. Shots fired behind them, coming dangerously close.

He hit a button on his key chain and the lights flashed on the vehicle, unlocking the doors. With the men still at their heels, they dove inside the car. Keeping his head low, Christopher jammed the keys in the ignition, cranked it, and threw the car into Drive.

"Stay down!" he yelled.

Ashley crouched on the floor. Glass showered around her as a bullet hit the windshield. Christopher squealed into traffic, narrowly missing an oncoming car.

A bullet hit their wheel. The car lurched. Ashley screamed.

He gripped the steering wheel, desperate to maintain control of the vehicle. The wheel pulled to the right, thumping along the road on the deflated tire.

He glanced in his rearview mirror and saw the men standing on the street corner, staring after the vehicle.

They were going to get away. Barely, but Christopher would take whatever victories he could.


As Ashley pulled herself back up into the seat, she glanced down at her biceps and saw the blood there. She'd been hit. In her haste to stay alive, she hadn't even noticed the injury.

But even in her haste to stay alive she couldn't outrun her memories. Her heart still pounded erratically from the drive. She instantly remembered the sound of crushing metal, the feeling of broken limbs, the panic over feeling herself begin to die.

It had been a long time since those memories had consumed her. But feeling so close to being in another accident had triggered the thoughts and sent her toppling back in time. She gripped the armrest and took a few deep breaths.

She was going to get through this. She had to. Moving forward was the only option.

From the driver's seat, Christopher touched her arm, his eyes wrinkling as he stared at her wound. "You're hurt."

She touched the cut, squinting with sudden discomfort. "I'll be okay." And she would be. Things could have turned out far, far worse.

"A bullet must have grazed you. We need to get you help." His grip on the steering wheel tightened as he frowned.

She shook her head, unwilling to stop—yet. They needed to get farther away. Those men could still find them. "It's not that bad. A bandage and some ointment will do the trick."

The SUV continued to bump down the road. They'd made it out of Norfolk and now headed north on the interstate. Ashley knew enough to realize they wouldn't make it much farther on this tire. She wasn't sure how much longer her nerves would let her continue to travel. Each bump of the tires seemed to nudge her thoughts back into the past.

Ashley stared out the window and took a deep breath. She had to focus on the present. What had that meeting been about? Just who was that man? And why were these men so brazen, so determined to get to Ashley at any cost?

Christopher pulled off the interstate. "This is the end of the road for us right now, Ashley. I'll call Denton and he'll send someone out here to help us. This SUV just isn't going to make it anymore."

A small community came into view in front of

them. A river graced one side of the town and a strip of shops nestled into a cliff on the other. It looked familiar, like she'd been here before, but she couldn't place it. "Where are we?"

"Historic Yorktown."

"Nice." She pointed to a restaurant in the distance, The Revolutionary Grill. "It looks like it's open. Can we grab a bite to eat and I'll get cleaned up?" Ever since she'd smelled those fried green tomatoes, her stomach had been rumbling.

"Absolutely."

Relief filled her when they pulled into a parking space. Finally. The car ride had nearly done her in. It brought back too many memories of the accident that had nearly claimed her life.

Christopher gripped her elbow and helped her from the car and into the grill. They stepped inside the restaurant, pleasantly surprised by the warm decor. Patrons scattered the dining area, chatting quietly to each other. The place had an old-world charm about it.

A petite woman with long, brown hair greeted them at the door, a baby on her hip and an apologetic smile on her lips. "We're short-staffed tonight so I'm working with one less arm. We usually try to be a little more professional than this. Table for two?"

"Don't apologize. He's adorable." Ashley smiled. "And, yes, please. A table for two."

The woman stepped closer and pointed to Ashley's arm. "That's a nasty cut. Do you want me to get my first-aid kit for you?"

"Would you?" A bandage sounded really nice. The cut throbbed, though she didn't want to admit it.

"Absolutely." She extended her hand. "I'm Kylie, by the way. This is my and my husband, Nate's restaurant."

Ashley glanced around again, liking the place already. "It's lovely."

She grinned. "Thank you." She led them to a corner table, placed the menus in front of them, and then hurried to the back.

Ashley watched in the distance as Kylie talked to a man in the kitchen. He kissed her forehead and affectionately tousled the boy's hair before grabbing something from the cabinet. Ashley's heart lurched at the sight of the happy little family.

Having a happy little family apparently wasn't in store for her. The sooner she accepted that, the better. Seeing Christopher had stirred up those old hopes, but she had to let them go.

The man from the back approached their table. "My wife tells me you need the first-aid kit?"

Christopher nodded. "We had a little accident. If you have a bandage, that would be much appreciated."

The man put a plastic box on the table. "Here you go. Use whatever you need. If we can do anything for you, let us know, otherwise we'll leave you be." He took a step away before looking back. "And welcome to The Revolutionary Grill."

Christopher came around to her side of the booth and pulled Ashley's sleeve up. The feeling of his fingers against her skin caused shivers to shimmy up her arm.

"They seem nice," he muttered. "Nothing like a small town."

"I still love small towns," Ashley said as Christopher dabbed some ointment on her wound. She tried not to flinch. She'd never been a very good patient.

"You always did."

"One day, that's where I'll move." She tried to keep her thoughts focused on anything but her wound. It stung as Christopher sprayed something on it.

"Why not now?"

"I wanted to stay close to David." *Because he's my son.* She kept those words to herself.

He glanced up at her, his green eyes making her heart do an unwilling flip. "You really love him, don't you?"

She nodded, refusing to let the tears escape from her eyes. "More than life."

"He's lucky to have you." Christopher pressed a bandage over the cut and pulled her sleeve back down. Ashley could finally breathe again when he slipped back over to his side of the booth. He could *not* have this effect on her. It just wasn't healthy.

She licked her lips, changing the subject. "That was close back there."

He nodded and his eyes clouded. "Too close. Every lead we follow hasn't brought us any answers, just more questions. There's something we're missing."

"I wish I knew what." She felt practically willing to give her life to find out. Without answers, she was no good to anyone.

Another waitress appeared. Ashley's stomach growled, so she didn't waste any time perusing the menu. She ordered salmon served over fettuccine. Christopher picked the catfish with fries.

She glanced out the window and saw fat flakes of snow had begun to fall again. The overhead music began a soft rendition of "It's Beginning to Look a Lot Like Christmas." "Two snowfalls in four days? That's gotta be a record around here."

Christopher followed her gaze out the window. "Maybe people will have their white Christmas after all."

She twirled the ice in her glass of water. "I keep forgetting that it's only a few days away." Her gaze focused on Christopher. Maybe this would be a good time to talk about him, to at least find out some answers to the haunting questions about him. "Do you miss being a SEAL, Christopher?"

His gaze darkened, but he didn't look away. "At times."

"Why do you always get that pained look in your eyes whenever you talk about being a SEAL?"

She expected him to deny it. Instead, he shrugged and pushed his water away. "There were some rough times, Ashley. My days over there were filled with purpose and adrenaline-pumping adventure. But I've seen things that you don't ever forget."

She couldn't even imagine the things that he'd experienced. "Have you tried counseling?"

"A few times. All they want to talk about is PTSD. I don't see how that helps anything."

She cleared her throat, venturing into ground she wasn't sure she wanted to cover. Some little voice inside seemed to nag at her to take the leap, anyway. "People told me I had PTSD after my car accident."

His eyes widened. "Your car accident?"

She nodded. She didn't like to talk about it, but sometimes she knew she had to. She knew her story could help other people. "Yeah, I was hit head-on by a drunk driver."

He blinked and leaned toward her. "Really? Why didn't I hear about this?"

"I told people not to tell you." It was the truth. At least she'd gotten that much out. Maybe she'd take baby steps closer and closer toward the total and complete truth of the situation.

"Why would you do that?" A touch of hurt stained his voice.

"I didn't want you coming back to check on me out of sympathy. Besides, I didn't feel like I could handle seeing you emotionally. I already had enough other things on my plate at that point." She twirled her ice around again.

He frowned. "Tell me about what happened."

She closed her eyes a moment, hating to relive any part of the tragic ordeal. Most people were blessed enough to block out those painful moments. She'd been wide awake during the accident and even afterward when the EMTs pulled her broken body from the car. Thankfully, David hadn't been with her. "I shattered my pelvic bone, broke two ribs, my collarbone, and my leg basically snapped."

He grimaced. "I had no idea."

She nodded tightly. "I have all kinds of screws holding me together now. It was rough, to say the least. Doctors put me in a medically induced coma for a while. After that, I had months of therapy. Every time

I got in a car, I had panic attacks. I kept remembering the accident. I kept waiting for another one to happen."

"You seem to do well now." The way he looked at her made her feel like he didn't see anything or anyone else besides her.

She swallowed hard and looked down at her hands. "Physically, it took a lot of therapy, but for the most part I feel like my old self. Emotionally, it took a lot of talking."

"Talking?" His head tilted.

She locked gazes with him. "I found a support group. Whenever I would feel that panic rising up in me, I'd find someone to talk to. I prayed a lot. I tried to look for the good around me."

"What do you mean?"

"I found that some of the best therapy involved simply being positive. I clung to the good instead of the pain. I could have been killed. I could have ended up in a vegetative state. I had to remember to be thankful."

Their food came, and they lifted up a brief prayer before digging in.

Christopher's eyes met hers from across the table. "I'm sorry you went through that, Ashley."

She nodded and swallowed her bite of pasta. "I don't talk about it a lot. It was a rough time in my life. But I believe that good can come from the worst situations."

A smile crept across his lips. "I've been thinking that exact same thing recently. God seems to keep sending me those reminders."

"I've realized that He doesn't always let us see the entire game plan, but He gives us the next step at just the right moment. He gives us enough to keep us going and to keep us trusting Him. I think it helps to find purpose in our tragedies, to find a way to use them for good."

His smile widened. "You're absolutely right. I couldn't agree more." He pointed to her food. "Do you remember that time we tried to make that gourmet meal?"

The remembrance was bittersweet. This was the first time they'd reminisced about what used to be between them. She nodded. "It was awful. I knew when we—if we—got married, that one of us was going to have to learn to cook or we'd be getting lots of takeout."

Silence passed between them. *Tell him,* an inner voice seemed to say.

What better time than now? What better place than here in public where he was sure to keep his emotions under control. He had to know the other part about how the accident had affected her.

She opened her mouth, determined to push the words out.

But a glance out the window showed her that Denton had shown up with another vehicle for them.

She shook her head. She'd have to wait. Again.

Eventually, she wouldn't be able to put off telling him the truth.

## *Chapter Thirteen*

Ashley threw her head back into the pillow, trying to adjust to being in another new safe house. She didn't even know where this one was. She hadn't asked.

Her mind raced and sleep eluded her. There were too many thoughts demanding her attention. Thoughts about Christopher. Thoughts about Josh. Thoughts about David. With each breath, the stark reality of each situation deepened; it became darker and more confusing.

She turned over again, wishing she could escape the painful reflections, when a sound caught her ear.

She stiffened as she listened. What was that? Had someone gotten into the house?

Another yell zipped through the air, this clearly with the word, "Stop! What do you think you're doing?"

That was Christopher. He was in trouble.

She grabbed the gun on her nightstand and threw a sweatshirt on over her yoga pants and T-shirt.

The gun trembled in her hands as she got closer to

the door. She couldn't just stay in the bedroom while her friend could be in danger.

"Get back! Everyone get back!"

Her spine stiffened again. What was going on? His words weren't making sense.

Her throat dry, she pulled the door open. A dark hallway greeted her. Despite Christopher's yells, the house was surprisingly absent of any movement. She took her first step, staying close to the wall. Sweat sprinkled across her forehead.

She could do this. Whatever situation she met with in the living room, she could handle it. She just had to think with a clear head and remain calm.

"Liam!"

She took another step when a shadow appeared at the end of the hallway. She raised her gun.

"Don't shoot," a voice urged. "It's me. Agent Johnson."

The guard, she realized.

She relaxed her arms, but only for a moment. "What's going on?"

He stepped closer and nodded toward the living room. "He's having a nightmare."

Some unknown emotion clutched at her heart. "A nightmare? That's what all that yelling was for?"

He nodded. "I'm trying to figure out if I should wake him."

She fully lowered her gun. "Let me."

Her heart panged with compassion. The war had played games with Christopher's mind, hadn't it? These were more than nightmares. These were night terrors. He hadn't come back from the war unscathed after all.

She crept into the living room. The lights were off, but her eyes had adjusted to the darkness enough that she could make out the furniture. She walked to the couch and knelt there.

She watched Christopher for a moment. His muscles twitched like he was fighting some kind of invisible battle. His breathing was heavier than normal. The blanket had been kicked off.

She knew she needed to be careful. When she woke him, she had no idea what kind of mental state he might be in.

Gently, she put a hand on his shoulder. His arm was hard and solid beneath her. She gave a little shake. "Christopher. You need to wake up."

"No! It's going to blow!"

She closed her eyes, but only for a moment. "Christopher, you're having a nightmare."

"Get down!" His entire body jerked under the weight of his dreams.

She shook harder. "Christopher, wake up."

Suddenly, he sat up on the couch. He grabbed a gun—where had that been?—and pointed it directly at her. "I said get down!"

His eyes were wide, his breathing heavy.

Ashley stared at the gun, how it was aimed directly at her face. Her throat went dry and time turned into gel. "It's Ashley, Christopher. You're having a bad dream. You need to wake up."

"I said get down!"

"Christopher, it's me! Snap out of it." Cold fear sprinkled over her forehead.

At once, the trancelike state cleared from his eyes. He

put his gun down and lowered his head into his hands and let out a moan. "What are you doing?" he mumbled.

She wasn't sure who he was talking to—himself or her. She put her hand on his knee and stared at him. "You were having a terrible dream."

He rubbed his face. "Yeah, I was."

She sat beside him on the couch. "Do you want to talk about it?"

He shook his head. "I never want to talk about it."

"Maybe I should have said, do you *need* to talk about it?"

He was quiet, and she let him have his moment. She rested her hand on his back. She could feel his racing heart pulsating throughout his body.

He rubbed his face again. "Every time I close my eyes, I go back to Afghanistan."

"You go back to the war." Grief clutched her heart. Life could be so hard sometimes; certain moments were so difficult to get through. The even harder part sometimes was when you didn't know what to do to help.

He rested his face in his hands, the burden he was carrying evident in his every movement. "I wait for another explosion. I wait to find another body or to hear another cry of despair from someone who's lost a loved one."

"That wears on you after a while, Christopher."

"I can't get the images out of my head. I can still hear it, smell it, feel it."

"You know you're back here now. You're safe." She wanted more than anything to be able to comfort him, to help take away some of his pain.

He nodded before leaning back on the couch, still

staring straight ahead. "On a conscious level, I do. On a subconscious level…that's a different story."

"I'm sure being here in this situation with me hasn't helped anything." As she said the words, her heart sank with realization. She'd burdened him with too much by asking for his help.

He reached over and cupped her cheek. Some of the heaviness left his gaze, replaced with a tantalizing swirl of emotion that threatened to lure her in. "I want to be there for you. I've always wanted to be there for you, Ashley."

Her throat tightened. Christopher had no idea what he was saying. He was still groggy from sleep and nightmares. And it didn't matter, anyway. His actions had spoken louder than his words. Now wasn't the time Ashley wanted to talk about it, though. Now she just wanted to help him get through this moment.

Her hand covered Christopher's. Despite her logic, she fought the emotions that wanted to rise to the surface. What would it be like to give him another chance—to give them another chance?

No, she couldn't do it. Her heart wasn't ready for it.

She pulled his hand down but didn't release her grip on it. "You should rest, Christopher." She pulled the pillow onto her lap. "I'll stay with you."

Surprisingly, he didn't argue. He settled back down into the couch. She ran her hands through his hair, trying in some way to comfort him.

After a while, his breathing evened out, and he went back to sleep.

Christopher awoke feeling better rested than he had in weeks—maybe even months or years. He sat up, trying to gather his surroundings. Had he really been sleeping that hard?

Finally, the room came into focus. The safe house.

Last night flashed into his memory. The nightmare. Ashley being there. Mumbling things he wouldn't have said in his normally guarded state.

All of that confirmed to him that he was in no place to pursue a relationship—with anyone. He'd pulled a gun on her, for goodness' sake. His mind was messed up. Would it ever recover?

He glanced over. Ashley was cuddled against the side of the couch, sleeping soundly. Her hand rested on his shoulder, and his pillow was in her lap.

That's why he'd slept so well last night—because it had been so comforting having someone else there for him. He'd been so alone for so long. Having someone else actually watch out for him for a change was a nice feeling.

But he couldn't get used to it.

He'd really appreciated the way she'd opened up to him last night about her accident. He felt like they'd taken a major step forward in their relationship. Even when he'd brought up their past, she hadn't gotten all teary eyed, but she'd actually smiled.

God made all things work together for our good. He was working in this situation, too, wasn't He? Maybe He'd never restore their relationship to what it was, but maybe they could actually be friends again. Maybe God had brought them together, each to help the other heal.

Was the accident the big secret that she'd kept from him? He didn't know. The news had come as a shock. He wished he'd been able to be there for her. He couldn't even imagine how tough those months of recovery must have been....

Ashley's eyes fluttered open and a sleepy smile crossed her face as she pushed herself upright. "Is it morning?"

He nodded. "Yeah, it sure is."

The haze cleared from her eyes, and she squeezed his shoulder. "How are you feeling?"

"Good. Terrible. I'm not sure." He sat up straighter and raked his hands through his hair. "Sorry you had to see that."

"Don't apologize." Her focus remained on him. "You have nightmares like that a lot, don't you?"

He nodded. "I wish I could say no, but I do have terrible dreams. Even if I'm not in Afghanistan physically, I just can't seem to leave mentally."

"That's a big burden to carry."

"I can handle it."

"Someone else could help you carry that burden, you know. It might not seem quite as heavy."

He glanced at her. "You mean a shrink? No, thanks."

"Talking to someone isn't a sign of weakness."

"I know you're trying to help, Ashley, but I'm fine." He stood and ran his hands through his hair again.

"Well, I just wanted to let you know that I'm there for you, if you need me. Like I told you last night, talking to other people about what I was feeling really helped me to heal. That, and a lot of prayer."

His heart lurched. Talking to Ashley sounded like a really good idea, at the moment, at least. But did he really want to go there? To open himself up like that?

Some of the wounds he had were deep; some of the memories seemed permanently painful.

"Thanks," he muttered, his throat burning. He stood. When it came to fight or flight, he almost always chose fight. But when it came to his heart, flight seemed to be his go-to choice. "I need to call Denton and see if he's heard anything."

There he went, putting off what he needed to do again. Delaying getting any help. Embracing denial that he truly needed a listening ear.

Wasn't that what a SEAL was about? Being tough? Self-reliant? All this talky-talky stuff seemed so wimpy. Yet, at the same time, the idea was tempting.

The little bit that he'd already revealed to Ashley made his burden seem lighter.

He shook his head and started down the hall to call Denton. His conversation with him caused him to put his earlier thoughts aside.

They had a lead on Josh and David's location.

Ashley stared at the warehouse from the window of the SUV. Wet drops of snow fell from the sky and slid down the window, only slightly obscuring her view of the law-enforcement vehicles parked haphazardly around the building.

"You ready for this?" Christopher asked beside her.

He'd called Denton, who'd told them the FBI had caught a break in the case. It had led them to a warehouse where they suspected Josh and David had been held. Denton had asked if Ashley and Christopher could come down to the site and identify a couple of items.

The thought made the pit in Ashley's stomach grow deeper and hollower.

Finally, she nodded. "Let's go."

They walked through slushy snow and met Denton. He stood among police officers and other men in suits—FBI agents, Ashley assumed. Denton reintroduced them to FBI agents Franco and Smith again. They'd already met after the Eyes bombing.

"We're hoping you can confirm whether or not your brother and nephew have been here," Denton said, walking with them toward the warehouse. "You'll also need to give a statement to Agents Franco and Smith. This is beyond our scope, Ashley. Other people are getting hurt."

"Not to mention the fiasco at the mall," Agent Franco said. He raised bushy eyebrows, showing his disapproval that they hadn't come forward as being involved in the entire mess.

She nodded, resigning herself to give up control of the situation.

She nearly snorted at the thought.

Control? She had no control of the situation. If she had control of it, her brother and David wouldn't be held captive somewhere right now while people around continually died or were injured. She had to let go of this.

They led her inside. Christopher stayed by her side, and, despite their past, she was grateful for his presence. A table had been set up in the center of the large room they entered. Various boxes and wires and other items Ashley couldn't identify were scattered about.

"Bombs," Christopher muttered. "They were building bombs here."

A cold chill shivered through her. These men were heartless. And they had Josh and David.

She paused by a computer. Had these men forced her brother to work on this computer? Her heart sank at the thought of what they might be going through.

"Over here is where I really want you to look." The FBI agent directed her down a hallway. Her feet scraped the cement floor. This place was so cold and impersonal. It was no place for a child.

The agent paused by a room and extended his hand as an invitation for her to go inside. She drew in a deep breath before stepping into the space. Her eyes assessed her surroundings. Some blankets lay rumpled in the corner. Some junk-food wrappers scattered the floor. An empty bottle of juice sat abandoned by the door.

She walked over toward the blankets and kneeled down. She pictured David lying there. Was this where he'd slept? Physical pain stabbed through her heart at the thought. What she wouldn't give to hold him, to give him a hug.

"We found this. Look familiar?" Agent Franco held up a piece of paper.

Ashley took it and studied it a moment. It was a hand-drawn picture of a woman beside a little boy. From the blond hair, she clearly recognized the woman as herself and the boy as David.

"Is that your nephew's?" Agent Franco asked.

She nodded. "Yeah, that's his." Her voice cracked as she said the words.

She ran her hand over the blanket. The soft folds gave her a little comfort.

Her hand hit something hard. She moved the material out of the way, trying to uncover what was lost in the heap. Finally, her fingers squeezed around the object, and she pulled it out.

Christopher leaned closer. "A pen? That's a bit of a letdown."

She sucked in a breath and shook her head. She knew exactly what it was. She'd given it to David. "No, this is a special pen. David went through a phase where he wanted to be a spy. This is a recording pen. If you press this button here—" she pointed to it "—you can record a message or a conversation."

She glanced at the men around her. Agent Franco gave her a nod, and she pressed the button.

Her brother's voice rang out. "Ashley, don't believe everything you hear. Don't trust everyone you meet. You're our only hope."

## Chapter Fourteen

Christopher squeezed Ashley's shoulder again. It seemed so impersonal, but what else could he do? She'd made it clear that she wanted him to keep his distance. Yet, at the same time, she obviously needed some comfort. "You did a good job, Ashley."

She nodded. She'd pulled her sleeves down over her hands and stood with her arms crossed, a faraway look in her eyes. He could only imagine what she might be thinking about. They stood in the middle of the warehouse, a cold, brittle space, probably even when the heat worked. Law-enforcement officials swarmed the building. Bomb-sniffing dogs pulled their handlers. Radios crackled.

They'd both just spent the last three hours being interrogated by the FBI and police. Ashley had told them what had happened, sticking only to the facts. She'd carried herself amazingly well, all things considered.

Right now, she stared off into the distance. Christopher remembered well how much she liked to have her own space when she was dealing with anything overwhelming, so he gave that to her now. Her eyes flickered, as if she was having some kind of internal conversation with herself…or perhaps rehashing everything that had already happened.

Finally, she turned to Christopher, pure determination shining in her eyes. "I want to visit Wally again."

"Your brother's friend?"

She nodded and nibbled on her bottom lip for a moment. "I have a feeling there's something he's not telling me. I need to ask him some more questions."

"What brought that on?"

Ashley shook her head slowly, thoughtfully. "I'm just retracing our steps. I think he's our best choice for finding out more information."

He glanced at his watch. "Let me check with Denton and Agent Franco and see if it's okay if we leave."

He hesitated before stepping away. Both men said it was fine if they left, and that they'd be in touch. The ride was silent as they made their way north to Wally's house. Ashley was usually such a chatterbox. She could talk to anyone, anywhere. But either she'd changed since they'd last known each other or this situation was nearly unbearable. Maybe both.

They waited outside Wally's house. Finally, at seven o'clock, a car pulled into the driveway. Wally got out. He looked around him as he walked to the door, almost as if he could feel their eyes on him.

Christopher put his hand on the door handle. "Let's go."

They broke free from the car and charged up the sidewalk toward Wally. The man turned around, his eyes wide with fear. "What do you want—?" He paused when he recognized them and lowered his hands. "Ashley. What are you doing here?"

Ashley tried to step forward, but Christopher tugged her back. He didn't know who to trust right now, which made nearly everyone a suspect.

"I need to talk to you, Wally," Ashley said.

"I thought we already talked." His voice sounded tense, high-pitched.

Ashley's eyes looked pleading and earnest as she stared at her brother's friend. "I have more questions."

He started walking toward the door, shaking his head as he went. "I don't know what else I can tell you."

She grabbed his arm, pulling him to a halt on the walkway in front of the steps leading to his porch. "Please, Wally. It's important."

He stared at her a moment before finally nodding. His gaze searched around him again, the action pulling Christopher's muscles tighter. "Okay, but I don't have long."

"What aren't you telling me about my brother? I know you're hiding something. I just don't know what. His life…" She swallowed. "His life is in danger."

"In danger?" He pushed his glasses up higher and shifted awkwardly. "What do you mean?"

She shook her head. "I can't tell you anything else. I only know he's in trouble. I'm trying to find some answers, and I'm afraid you're the only one who has them."

His gaze flickered once more before finally settled back on Ashley. "I shouldn't say anything. I promised on my life that I wouldn't."

"Please." The tone of voice rang of desperation, of being on the fringe of hopelessness.

He let out a short sigh and ran his hand through his hair. He paced back and forth in three-step increments before jerking to a stop and staring at Ashley. "Your brother was being investigated."

Ashley's eyes widened. "Investigated?"

He nodded. "The higher-ups at the company thought he could be selling industry secrets. That's all rumor, mind you."

"Selling industry secrets to whom?" Ashley demanded. "Another company?"

He shook his head. "No. To terrorists."

Her mouth gaped open. "Someone thought my brother was helping the other side? He would never do that."

Wally shrugged as if he wasn't quite that sure. "There's one other thing."

"What's that?" The words seemed to tumble from her mouth. Her hands gripped her arms, reminding him of someone holding on for dear life.

"Someone at TechShare apparently hacked into the federal government's computer system. Everyone thinks it was your brother. He was looking at jail time if they found him guilty."

Ashley shook her head. "You've got to be kidding me. My brother would never do that."

He raised his hands. "I'm just telling you what I heard."

Christopher stepped closer. "Why are you acting scared? Are you being watched?"

"I'm Josh's friend. Don't you think I look guilty, too? I've been on edge for the past couple of weeks. I've felt like someone was watching me. There. Are you happy now?"

"This is serious, Wally." Ashley's voice contained a touch of exasperation.

He raised his chin. "I'm well aware."

Christopher held his frustration at bay, knowing the importance of keeping a level head in the situation. But the pit in his stomach grew. And with each new sinking depth, he realized that his concern for Ashley was continuing to widen—widening enough for him to know that his heart was beginning to get involved far beyond a mere friendship level.

He stared at Wally a moment, watching the man with his nervous twitches. Why was he nervous? He felt sure the man was hiding something else. "Is there anything else you need to tell us?"

"That's all I know. I hope your brother is okay. I really do." He paused long enough to push up his glasses and glance over at Christopher. An unreadable emotion lingered in his eyes. "And I hope he hasn't gotten himself into trouble."

Christopher had been quiet for most of the way to whatever new safe house they were traveling to for the night. Ashley had a feeling that he was mulling over some thoughts, so she let him. But from the way he gripped the steering wheel, those thoughts were heavy and intense.

Her gut told her that she wouldn't like what Christopher had to say whenever he spoke again. She wasn't sure why she was so concerned about what he was thinking, when her own thoughts were a mess.

Her brother? Being investigated? She just couldn't believe it. Did Christopher?

They pulled up onto a new property for the evening. Same routine. Different guard. This time, the place was an actual log cabin, nestled away in the foothills of Virginia. If Ashley weren't so upset—and if she wasn't with Christopher—she actually might enjoy a stay here.

As soon as they stepped inside, Christopher began pacing the living room. She sank onto the couch, her gut twisting as tension filled the room.

Finally, he stopped pacing and turned toward her. "We need to talk."

Her throat burned. She remembered starting a conversation with those very words. They hadn't had a chance to finish it yet, though. She'd been delaying the inevitable. She nodded. "Okay."

He lowered himself beside her. Concern furrowed his brows as he stared at her. "You've got to give this up, Ashley. We're in over our heads. If your brother is guilty, you could become an accomplice in all of this by trying to help him now. Leave it to the authorities."

She blinked, trying to comprehend his words. "I can't give up."

He grabbed her hand. "Don't you see we're dealing with some dangerous men here? This is above me and it's above you. We need the entire Special Forces to win this war, and all we've got is me and you. We're not enough. I can't protect you from a court of law, if that's what it comes down to. This could get ugly on so many levels."

"I can't give up." Her throat burned as she said the words.

He shook his head. "Why not? Why can't you leave this to the authorities?"

"I just can't." She could hardly breathe as she realized she'd have to tell him the truth. Reality became clear to her. She'd put it off again and again.

"Ashley, the deeper we get into this, the more I worry about you and your safety. We're talking about His People, about terrorism, about bombings. I can't understand why you won't leave this to the authorities and just concentrate on keeping yourself safe."

Her heart leaped into her throat. There was so much pressure building inside her chest that she thought she might pass out. Passing out would be too easy, though. She had to tell him the truth, and telling him the truth would be the hardest thing of all. "Christopher…"

He leaned closer. He cared about her, didn't he? She could see in his eyes, and that realization made her confession that much harder.

"Yes?" he mumbled.

Adrenaline charged through the air. "There's something I need to tell you." Her voice cracked every other syllable.

"Go ahead."

Shakes overcame her. She sat back on the couch and jammed her hands underneath her legs to quell the trembles. Nausea roiled in her gut.

*I can't do this.*

But she had to. This was the only thing that would make him realize the seriousness of the situation. Plus, Christopher just plain needed to know. It was the right thing. She'd been denying that for a long time, but lately the truth had been smacking her in the face with absolute clarity.

"Whatever it is, you can tell me, Ashley." Christopher's voice sounded soothing and sure.

Her gaze flickered up to his, and she licked her lips. She was going to get through this without throwing up. "Christopher, I don't know how to say this. So I'm just going to say it."

"Okay."

"I need to start by saying I'm sorry." Moisture filled her eyes.

His eyebrows twitched together. "About what?"

She licked her lips again, pulling back the tears that wanted to rise up. "Christopher, about a month after we broke up, I started feeling ill. I blamed it on the stress from the breakup." She glanced at her lap. "As you know, it was hard on me."

"I know, Ashley." Compassion and sorrow stained his voice.

"I finally went to the doctor to make sure everything was okay. I'd lost some weight. I felt nauseous all the time. I didn't want to get out of bed." She rubbed her hands on her jeans, praying for the courage to say what she had to say next. "I found out I was pregnant, Christopher." Her gaze rose up to meet his.

His eyes widened. "Pregnant? You were pregnant?" Waves of emotion flashed through his eyes. Disbelief. Surprise. Realization.

"What…what happened? Did you miscarry? You should have told me."

She shook her head. "I carried the baby to term. He was a beautiful boy."

"A boy?"

She nodded. "Yes, a boy. I named him David. He's your son, Christopher."

The war in the Middle East felt like a walk in the park compared to this bombshell.

Christopher stood and began pacing and running his hands through his hair. He couldn't have heard Ashley correctly. No, this couldn't be happening.

Ashley was suddenly at his side, her hands on his arm. Her eyes pleaded with him. "I'm sorry, Christopher."

He shook his head and kept pacing, moving out of her touch. "I don't understand."

Nothing made sense. That couldn't be possible. No, no, no.

Ashley's sweet voice broke into his thoughts. "I know it's a lot to soak in."

A lot to soak in? He had a son. A *son.*

Whom he'd never met.

Who could have changed his world. Given him another reason to get up in the morning. Given him another reason to fight for the future.

"How could you keep this from me?" Anger tinged his voice as he whirled around to face her.

To her credit, she didn't back down. "You were gone. You were in Afghanistan. You'd made it clear you didn't want a family or any commitments back here at home that would distract you from your role as a SEAL. What was I supposed to do?"

"You were supposed to tell me and let me decide!"

Her hands went to her hips. "You did decide when you left me!"

He shook his head and began pacing again. "This is different, Ashley. A boy needs a father."

"He has a father. Josh adopted him."

"If I had known…" How things would have been different if he'd known. Majorly different. Entirely different.

"What would you have done, Christopher? Would you have gotten out of the military? Would you have changed your mind and married me, anyway? What would you have done?" Her voice rose in pitch.

He raked his hand through his hair. "Maybe. Maybe I would have."

She shook her head. "I wouldn't have let you marry me out of obligation. You didn't love me enough to try to make it work before. No way would I marry you because you felt guilty."

"Obligation?" His eyes felt like they might pop out of their sockets. "Ashley, marrying you was the only thing I wanted to do, and that was the problem. Your heart can't be in two places. I couldn't be fair to you and to the military."

"And you made your decision. You were going to be a military man. That was your first love."

"It wasn't like that, Ashley." He tried not to let defeat enter his voice, but with each word, he found his fight fading. Could he ever make her understand?

"I've tried for nine years to figure out exactly what it was like, Christopher, and if I haven't figured it out yet, I probably won't."

He drew in a deep breath. He didn't want to turn

the conversation away from his son. *Their* son. "You should have told me, Ashley. It would have been the right thing."

She raised her chin. "I got in my accident when he was only two months old. Josh and his wife took care of him for me for all of those months. When I looked at them together—" she sucked in a deep breath "—I knew what I had to do. I knew I couldn't give him what he needed without a job, with my physical therapy, without a spouse. You have no idea how hard that pill was to swallow. I only wanted what was best for him."

He jammed his finger into his chest. "Me. I would have been best for him."

"You weren't here, Christopher." She shook her head and closed her eyes.

He sank back into the couch and buried his face in his hands. He'd been on the verge of confessing how much he cared about her. Then she'd dropped this bombshell. Any hope of rekindling what they'd had dissolved like yesterday's snow. "I just don't know what to say."

"I realize you're upset with me. I don't blame you. As much as I tried to justify what I did, I've realized I made the wrong choice and I regret that." Her voice cracked. "I'm going to give you some time to process everything."

With that, she stood and crept away. He heard the click of her bedroom door a few seconds later.

Women. Would he ever understand them? He doubted it.

He wouldn't even try right now.

Right now, he had to let the truth sink in. He was a father.

# Chapter Fifteen

Ashley pressed her forehead against the door. In all of her self-righteousness, she'd hurt Christopher. He'd hurt her, too, so she'd thought it was okay. But that's who she used to be. As soon as she became a Christian she should have called him and told him the truth. But she couldn't undo the past now.

The conversation replayed in her head and made the pounding there even worse. How had she expected it to go? Had she expected that he'd be delighted and smiling the whole time?

How would she feel in Christopher's shoes?

She didn't know. She just didn't know right now.

Her hand went to her stomach. All throughout her pregnancy with David she'd wondered what it would have been like to have a spouse by her side, someone who would delight in each kick and movement. Then she'd remembered that her fiancé had abandoned her, and eventually she resigned to the fact that she was alone.

A couple of people had suggested she terminate the

pregnancy. She knew she could never do that. This was a baby inside her. Her baby.

Christopher's baby.

If circumstances had been different, they would have had a wonderful life together as a family. It would have been filled with sweet evenings playing blocks and making cookies and exploring the backyard. But she'd never been a "what if" kind of girl. That wasn't the way life had worked out. Everyone made their choices and you had to keep moving forward.

So why did her heart twist with regret?

Something moved across the moonlight shining in her window.

Her lungs tightened.

A shadow.

A shadow had passed her window.

She pulled herself up straight and stared at the window. Was that a person passing by? Had the men found them? Or was that the guard just making his rounds?

Funny, she'd never noticed him walking the perimeter before.

She wanted to peer out the window, to confirm that everything was okay.

But then the image of someone seeing her, the picture of a gun aimed right at her, filled her mind, and she remained frozen.

No, she had to get a grip. She could have just been seeing things, but before she went to sound the warning bells, she needed to look.

Drawing in all of her courage, she crawled toward the wall. Remaining low, she paused beneath the sill.

It was nothing. Her imagination.

If that was true, why were her limbs shaking so badly?

Her throat burned as she swallowed. Slowly, carefully, she rose up. At the corner of the window, she leaned toward the glass.

*Please, just let me see woods and darkness. No men with guns. No leering figures.*

The outside came into view. Trees. Darkness.

Her gaze continued to scan the area.

The movement she'd thought she'd seen was just a bird. Nothing to be worried about. Those men hadn't found them. Again.

Her gaze reached the far side of its scope. So far, so good.

A slight movement at the side of the window caught her eye. She sucked in a scream. A man was pressed there, right against the side of the house next to her window.

And he was staring directly at her.

Christopher was still fuming mad. He couldn't sleep, which was nothing unusual. Instead, he paced the living room, hoping the movement would help to sort out his thoughts.

How could she? *How could she?* That was the question that kept replaying in his mind. He'd thought more of Ashley, never that she'd be one to pull a stunt like this. She was always so well thought out and planned. She always put other people's needs above her own. She was—

"Christopher, someone's outside."

He jerked his head toward the hallway and saw

Ashley standing there with wide, panic-filled eyes. He stopped pacing, adrenaline crackling through the air. "What do you mean?"

She pointed with her thumb over her shoulder. "I mean, there's a man outside my window." Her voice cracked as her words tumbled out.

His senses instantly went on alert, and he put his emotions aside. "Just one?"

"I only saw one." Her gaze darted around the room. "Where's Bruce?"

"He should be at the front door." He paced over to the area, but there was no one there. He took a few steps closer, his hand going to the gun at his waist. "Maybe he stepped outside for a moment." Even as he said the words, cold reality hit him. Christopher was never one to be blissfully optimistic. If Bruce wasn't inside, there was a good chance he was in trouble.

She shook her head. "I hope not."

"Stay back." He walked toward the front door, bracing himself for battle.

"You're not going out there, are you?" Ashley's voice held a hint of desperation, of fear.

He didn't want his heart to soften, but it did, anyway. He paused and lowered his voice. "We can't sit here and wait for whatever's going to happen. I've got to see what's going on."

"But if you walk outside you're an open target." Her fingers dug into his arm.

He stepped closer, keeping his voice even. "I'm trained. I'll be fine. Besides, I'm not going down until I meet my son."

Her cheeks flushed. At least she had the decency

to look halfway embarrassed. He cast those thoughts aside. There would be time for them later.

Ashley swallowed, her throat muscles looking tight and rigid as her hand slipped away from his arm, and she stepped back. "Be careful, Christopher," she muttered, her voice barely above a whisper.

Apprehension stretched across his shoulders as he put his hand on the doorknob. On the mental count of three, he pulled the door open. An empty porch waited for him.

He listened carefully for a sign of something—someone.

Nothing. He heard nothing.

The woods beyond the house appeared empty, but the dark spaces there could easily conceal someone.

But what if Ashley had simply been seeing things? What if it was just Bruce pacing the perimeter of the house? Still, her fear had been genuine.

He had to check things out.

He took his first step outside, his senses attuned to every movement, every sound. He held his gun, his muscles rigid and ready to fight. The cold air was no match for the beads of sweat that formed across his forehead.

A son. His son. He had to stay alive to meet him.

He had to find him to meet him.

He stayed close to the wall of the house as he crept around the building. His footsteps were light, not making a sound. Stealthlike, just as he'd been trained.

He paused at the corner then peered around.

Still nothing. No one.

Then a stick cracked in the distance.

Tension ratcheted his muscles. Someone was out there.

He raised his gun. Just what were they planning? How many people were out there exactly?

*Lord, some supernatural help might be nice right about now.*

Another stick cracked until a figure appeared from the woods. The man raised his hands in surrender as he approached. "We need to talk."

Christopher still aimed his gun directly at the man's chest. Adrenaline pumped through him. Images of Afghanistan flashed back. Insurgents. Suicide bombers—

No, this wasn't Afghanistan. But these men might be just as deadly.

"Who are you?" Christopher growled.

The man's hands remained raised in the air. As he came closer, Christopher noted that the man was probably in his late twenties with dark hair and he wore all black. "It's a long story. I'd like to explain."

Christopher didn't trust *that* easily. "Where's Bruce?"

"He's okay. I just had to get him away for a few minutes so we could talk alone. With Ashley."

"I'm not letting you get anywhere near her." Christopher examined the man more closely. Why did he seem familiar? Like he'd seen his face in the crowds before? "You're the man who's been following us, aren't you?"

"I can explain. If you'll let me." The man's eyes looked honest. But the best of them could fool anyone.

Christopher kept his gun raised. "You better start explaining now before I pull this trigger."

The man shook his head. "Listen, you don't want to do that. I'm on your side."

His muscles slacked—but just for a moment. "I'm not so sure about that."

"Please, I'm with the CIA. I was assigned to track Ashley Wilson, to make sure she wasn't working for His People. Like her brother."

Ashley stared at the dark-haired man sitting across from them. Christopher had his cell to his ear and his gun aimed at the man. The CIA? Could the man's story get any bigger or more glorified? There was no way she was caught up in some real-life spy mission. No way.

Christopher lowered his phone and sat down beside her. "Denton confirmed that he's legit," Christopher muttered.

The man—Ed Carter, he'd said his name was—nodded. "We worked together for two years. Mark Denton is a good man."

Ashley wasn't in the mood for chitchat. "Tell us where Bruce is," Ashley demanded.

The man raised his hands and patted the air as if to say "calm down." "I will, but only after you listen to me. I'm on a need-to-know basis. You're not even supposed to know who I am, let alone your guard. Trust me. He's fine."

Fire ignited in her veins. "Trust you? I don't even know you. Why would I trust you?"

He reached into the pocket of his coat and pulled out his badge. "I'm with the CIA. My name is Ed Carter. I'm twenty-nine years old, and I've been trailing you for the past four days."

"Why are you here? Why are you talking to us?" Christopher asked. "I want some answers. Now."

The man raised his hands again. "I know. I know. And I'm going to give them to you." He turned toward Ashley. "Maybe I should start with this explanation. TechShare is just a cover name for a CIA office."

She blinked, trying to comprehend what he was saying. "A CIA office? What are you talking about?" There her mind went again, feeling like she was in the middle of some spy movie. Only this wasn't a movie. This was her life—her upside-down, crazy, how-had-she-gotten-here life.

Ed Carter didn't blink as his gaze connected with hers. "Ashley, your brother didn't work for a corporation that was developing new computer software. He was recruited by the CIA to work in our cyberterrorism division. Your brother was not only proficient in hacking into systems, but he was also quite talented at developing viruses. He was, quite frankly, a genius."

Where was he going with this? "So he was abducted by His People for his knowledge?"

Ed's face remained grim as he shook his head. "Not quite. We think he was working for His People all along. We think he's giving them information, for a price."

She stood. "For a price? What are you talking about? My brother would never do that!"

Christopher pulled her back down. "Just hear him out, Ashley."

Fury warmed her blood, though. How could this man think that? What proof did he have?

"Ashley, we found a large deposit that had been made into your brother's checking account. We traced the money back to His People. There have been other signs that he's been doing some illegal things. We think he started playing hardball with them and that's when they snatched him."

She shook her head. "I don't believe you."

"I'm telling the truth, Ashley."

"Don't you guys always lie? Isn't that what you do? Twist things around to get what you want?"

He stared at her, not bothering to repeat what he'd already said. Which made her even madder.

She heaved in a deep breath, trying to maintain her control. "Why have you been following me?"

Ed leaned on his elbows, looking casual and as if he did this sort of thing every day. "We suspected your brother may have been working with someone. We thought it could be you. I was hoping you would lead us to your brother."

"You were the person who was outside his house that evening while Christopher and I were searching through his things," Ashley said.

He nodded. "I was. I was there when the men demolished your house, Christopher. I've pretty much been your shadow since we realized Josh had disappeared."

Ashley shook her head, trying to comprehend everything he was saying. "Why didn't you just follow those men in order to find my brother? Wouldn't that make more sense?"

"They're all just henchmen. They won't lead us to the person we need to find."

Christopher shook his head. "What do you mean?"

"I mean, if we cut off their funding, then we essentially cut them off. But no one knows who's giving these people all of their money. He's guarded like a treasure. But someone, somewhere has got to be able to lead us to him."

"You thought I was that person?" Ashley pointed to herself.

"It was our best guess. I've realized you're looking for him yourself. That's become obvious. It's also become obvious that with the two of you being together, they can kill two birds with one stone."

"What are you getting at?" Christopher asked.

Ed stared at Christopher. "I think you know what I'm getting at. Someone took down Abar Numair, the man who started His People. They may have restructured since then, but they don't easily forget. Having you involved in this case is like a bonus to them. If they can kill Ashley and one of the SEALs who helped bring their leader down, then they're twice as happy."

Christopher straightened beside her. "No one knows I was on that team."

"No, but if they had a computer hacker working for them, they might be able to find out highly classified information like that." He raised an eyebrow as his words settled over them.

A chill spread through Ashley. This was getting worse by the minute. Maybe she didn't want to know the truth. Maybe she should just find David and Josh, and not worry about any of the details.

But she knew she couldn't do that.

"Let's say all of that is true. How about me? I don't understand why they're trying to kill me. Why don't they just let me fade into obscurity?"

"My theory, once I realized you weren't working for them, is this. You saw your brother being abducted, and they wanted to make a statement that no one could get in their way. You could identify them and possibly even offer clues that would lead authorities to them— at least lead them closer. They don't want anything or anyone to get in the way with their plan."

She shook her head. "This is all crazy."

"I know."

Christopher shifted beside her. "Why come out tonight and let us know who you are?"

"It was time. I realized you weren't working for the other side. I'm going to be in and out, but I'll help you when I can."

"Is there something you know that you want to tell us?" Ashley asked.

"Your brother and nephew are on the move. They don't stay anywhere for very long. Those men want you, for some reason. You need to be careful. Very careful."

Ashley nodded, her shivers intensifying.

Death was chasing her.

The question was: Would it ever catch her?

# Chapter Sixteen

After Ed left, Christopher found Bruce tied up in the shed. Apparently, he'd been knocked unconscious but unharmed. Christopher had welcomed the chance to be away from Ashley and the whirlwind of emotions she always brought with her, even for just a moment.

How could she?

He couldn't stop asking himself that question. But at the same time, he had to focus on the bigger picture right now. How was he going to find his son and keep him safe?

He walked back into the cabin and spotted Ashley sitting on the couch, her knees pulled to her chest, and a far-off look in her eyes.

He didn't want to feel sorry for her. He really didn't.

But his heart couldn't help but pang with compassion.

"If I had my way, I wouldn't be around you right now," he started. "It's going to take me some time to process everything that's happened."

She blanched. "I deserve that."

"But we don't have any choice but to work together. Not if we want what's best for David. My son."

"Our son." Her features looked strained as she said the words. Suddenly, she sat up straighter, a new light in her eyes. "Maybe we can switch roles with these men. Maybe we can chase them for a change."

Her words caused him to freeze. "How? And what would that prove?"

She shrugged. "Lure them out and then follow them. Maybe they'd lead us to David. Maybe they'd at least lead us to someone who could tell us where David is."

He shook his head, thinking that sounded like the worst idea ever. "I don't know if we'd be able to lure them out, Ash. As soon as they spotted us, they would just shoot."

"Not if they didn't know it was us. Not if we were hard to recognize. I know we still wouldn't have much time. But it's better than nothing, isn't it?"

He shook his head. It was true. It was something. But so many things could go wrong. "I don't know…"

"Think about it, at least." She stood. "In the meantime, can I use the computer? I want to think through a few ideas."

"The less you're on the computer, the better. Whoever these guys are, they seem to know their way around the web. Even with the firewalls I have, I worry that they'll somehow trace you."

"I'll be quick. Only a few minutes."

He stared at her another moment before finally nodding. "Please, be quick. Until these guys are behind bars, we need to take every precaution possible."

He grabbed the laptop from his room and handed it

to Ashley. Then he kept himself busy by making some coffee. There was no more sleeping for him tonight. His adrenaline was pumping too hard.

They did need another plan of action. But what? Was Ashley's idea one worth considering? Or would it just get them killed?

He didn't know.

"What…?" Ashley gasped.

That familiar tension returned to his shoulders. He strode up behind Ashley, wondering what was wrong.

"This can't be right," she muttered.

"What?"

"Someone drained all the money from my bank account."

He peered closer. Sure enough, all the money was gone. Not only that, but someone had overdrafted by hundreds of dollars.

"With the right technology and know-how, you can do anything. Someone obviously hacked into the bank's system and stole your identity." The question was: Had her very own brother done that? Even the CIA was investigating him.

But he knew Josh, and couldn't imagine him ever doing anything that might harm his sister. Perhaps someone had put the deposit in Josh's bank account in the same way they'd taken money from Ashley's. Maybe someone had set him up.

"I've got to see if there are any messages from David again."

"Don't click on them if there are. That's the only computer I've got."

She nodded and began tapping away. She leaned toward the screen. "I don't believe it."

Did he want to know? "What now?"

"It's an email from Damian. He said there's more to come if I don't give up the information."

"What information?"

"I have no idea." She glanced up at him. "But this could be just the bait I need."

Ashley shifted nervously as the wind hit her. She leaned against the railing of the outdoor ice skating rink, trying to look casual.

Only a few feet away stood Christopher. He wore a baseball cap and an oversize coat. He stood close enough to help her, need be, but far enough away that it didn't look like they were together. All around the rink, there were undercover law-enforcement officials, each looking casual and unassuming.

The plan had been set in motion. It had taken a lot of prodding and some quick planning, but here they were. The FBI, the local police, and Eyes had all gotten involved.

This was a gamble. Ashley knew that. But she was running out of options.

So many things could go wrong. Christopher had said that much.

Even as mad as he was at her, Ashley knew that he didn't want any harm to come to her.

Her breath came out in a frosty puff in front of her as Ashley watched, from across the way, a woman approach the rink. She wore Ashley's coat, was approximately her height, and had a wig on. She also wore a bulletproof vest under all of her other layers.

Ashley's stomach twisted with anxiety. Would this actually work?

It felt like her last hope. She desperately wanted to take this game of chase into her own hands. She'd never find her son if all she did was run from the bad guys.

Her gaze scanned the area again, looking for a sign of something suspicious. A man in a black overcoat approached the opposite side of the rink. Was this man one of His People?

Christopher peered over the top of his newspaper. Ashley attempted to take another sip of her coffee, but her hands trembled so badly she feared they'd give her away.

So many things could go wrong.

But they wouldn't. She had to stay positive.

There were various agents waiting in cars around the complex. As soon as the men took off, they'd follow them. Hopefully, they'd get some answers.

She'd had to beg Christopher to even let her come at all. She knew it was a risky move being here, but she'd never been very good at being passive. Being passive would not lead her back to David.

A few more people joined the skating rink fun. Most of them went directly to the ice. Ashley noticed another man, this one wearing a black leather jacket, who sat on a bench not too far away.

Was he one of the men who'd chased them at the mall? One of the men the police were looking for? Perhaps it was Babyface or Bruno. She couldn't tell from where she stood.

Her throat burned as she swallowed. Luckily, most children were in school right now. But there were still enough innocent bystanders around that things could turn ugly.

*Please protect everyone,* she prayed silently. *And please forgive me for not telling Christopher sooner. Please help me to forgive myself.*

After seeing the look in Christopher's eyes—the utter devastation—she'd had a moment of 20/20 hindsight. She should have told him from the start.

What if he never got to meet his son?

There she went again. She had to think positive.

Two men approached the decoy.

This was the moment, Ashley realized, when they'd find out if their plan worked or not.

The men closed in around the woman in the distance. Around them, people skated, totally clueless as to what was going on. Clueless about the danger that could erupt.

Ashley's gaze focused on another man who'd joined the area. He wore a blue coat and a ball cap. He didn't look familiar.

So why did Ashley have a feeling he was a part of all of this somehow? She kept her gaze on him.

He pulled out a cell phone and began talking to someone. His gaze was on the two decoys. Was he an Eyes agent? FBI? Or His People?

The other two men moved closer and closer. With the utmost professionalism, the men from Eyes blended in, not showing a sign that they were actually soldiers and law enforcement.

Her gaze went back to the man in the blue coat. She

tried to make eye contact with Christopher, but his hat was pulled down low. He was attuned to everything happening with the setup.

It worked. They'd lured the men out of hiding.

But now what? Her hands shook harder until finally she threw away her coffee, put her phone in her pocket, and shoved her hands in after it.

Something shiny gleamed from beneath one of the men in black's jacket. A gun. He was going to shoot.

"Everybody down!" someone yelled.

Nervous gasps and screams spread through the crowd. One of the men raised his gun, no longer hiding its presence. He aimed at one of the decoys and fired.

Screams from the crowd became louder as people scrambled away.

Her gaze went back to the man in the blue jacket. He remained there, unmoving. Just what was his role in all of this?

The Eyes agents drew their weapons.

The man in blue took a step away.

Ashley hurried toward Christopher. "Come on."

"What are you doing?"

"We've got to follow him!"

"Who?"

"Just trust me!"

Christopher began jogging beside her. The man in blue spotted them and took off in a sprint. Ashley's legs burned as they chased him through the streets of downtown Norfolk. He darted across an intersection. Ashley looked both ways. It would be tight, but…

Drivers leaned on their horns, letting them know

their displeasure at being stopped. But Ashley and Christopher kept going.

As they ran, Christopher pulled out his phone and explained to someone what they were doing. Ashley heard him muttering something about needing a car.

The man turned the corner, out of sight for a moment. Christopher grabbed her hand. His legs were longer than hers, but he pulled her along, not letting her slow down.

She didn't want to lose any momentum, even though her lungs screamed and her muscles ached. They had to follow this man.

Sirens sounded from across town. What was going on at the skating rink? She'd have to wait to find out.

The man came into sight again. This time, he had a gun in his hand. A bullet fired past them.

"Get down!" Christopher pulled her behind a car as another spray of bullets flew past them. She huddled behind a tire, her hands covering her head. Her heart beat furiously and she could hardly take a deep enough breath to fill her lungs.

Christopher peered up.

"He's getting into a car," Christopher muttered. "He's going to get away."

Christopher's heart pounded in his chest. The man couldn't get away. He might be their only link to finding his son.

Above them, the windshield of the car shattered as another bullet pierced the air. But his gun remained in his holster. The last thing Christopher wanted was to open fire in a busy metropolitan area. There was too much risk for casualties.

Ashley gasped beside him as another bullet flew past them. People ran screaming from the area. They scattered with fear.

The entire downtown seemed to be holding its breath, waiting for whatever would happen next.

They had to chase that vehicle. Now.

Just then, a car squealed around the corner and stopped beside them. Denton peered out the driver's-side window. "Get in!"

They hopped into the backseat just as Denton peeled off down the street. The car in front of them swerved before weaving in and out of traffic. Denton stayed on their trail.

Beside him, Ashley gripped the seat with terror, each turn tossing her across the car. Quickly, Christopher reached across her and strapped her seat belt over her. He then pulled on his own. This was going to be a wild ride.

Denton was capable, but they had to take every precaution.

The car in front of them turned sharply onto a street and gunned the engine. Cars swerved out of the way to miss the oncoming vehicle.

Denton threw on brakes, turning quickly to keep up with the car. The car fishtailed before righting itself. Ashley gripped his arm with white knuckles, her eyes as big as full moons.

Certainly she had to be reliving the accident that had nearly killed her. He gripped her hand, trying to bring her back to reality. He knew what it was like to get sucked into bad memories.

Denton gained on the car. A glance at the dash showed he was traveling at ninety miles an hour to catch up. Dangerously high speeds for the middle of a metropolitan area. Dangerously high speeds for anywhere.

Christopher's eyes widened when he saw a train coming in the distance. The car in front of them kept speeding forward. He held his breath, anticipating what would happen next.

The gunman was going to try and beat the locomotive across the tracks.

He clutched the armrest.

The train barreled forward.

The car in front of them didn't slow.

Their collision appeared more and more imminent.

Denton pressed on the brakes. "No way. I can't do it."

The car in front of them reached the tracks. Just as the front wheels began to cross, the locomotive engine collided with the vehicle. Metal screeched. Glass shattered. Flames exploded.

Christopher pulled Ashley's head into his chest as a small cry escaped her. Denton's car came to a complete stop, and they all stared at the tragedy in front of them.

A tragedy on so many levels, he couldn't help but think. So many levels.

Ashley leaned against the car, watching the destruction around her. The scene seemed too familiar. The burning of melted metal and plastic. The loss of life. The hopelessness of feeling like she'd never find Josh and David.

It brought back fresh memories of her accident and the agonizing decisions she'd made afterward. Life was full of unexpected turns and twists. Some of those changes were good; some knocked you off balance; some seemed to seep into your soul.

Every time she looked at the mangled metal in front of her, she was pulled back in time to that horrible night when she'd been driving home from the store. She'd seen the oncoming car traveling down the two-lane road. She'd been headed to pick up David from her father's house. Thank goodness her baby hadn't been with her. At the last minute, the oncoming car had swerved into her lane going 45 miles an hour.

She hadn't had the blessing of unconsciousness. No, she'd felt all the tear-inducing pain. Seen every agonizing moment as passersby tried in vain to help. She'd smelled the burning metal, tasted the blood in her mouth, heard the urgency in people's voices.

Staring at the scene now, each limb trembled. Her breaths came too quickly. Each sound made her jump.

Christopher's hand clamped down on her shoulder. "Are you okay?"

She shrugged. "Trying to push away the bad memories—the old ones and the new ones."

He squeezed tighter. "I understand."

They shared a smile. If anyone understood, Christopher certainly did. "I know." Despite the strain between them, he still acted out of integrity to help her. That meant a lot to her.

Emergency-management personnel continued to clean up the scene. No one had imagined it happening like this. That man had to have known he would die when he pulled in front of that train. He'd rather die than betray his loyalties. That was dedication. Or insanity, depending on how one wanted to look at it.

"It was a good try, Ash. We almost had them," Christopher muttered.

Ashley shook her head. "Almost doesn't get me any closer to Josh or David."

"We'll get there eventually."

She dared to look at him. "What if it's too late?"

"It won't be." He pulled her toward his chest again. She didn't fight him. If he wanted to hold her up, then so be it. She needed something to help her stand. She had her faith, but even that was starting to feel fragile. She knew God didn't always answer prayers in the way she wanted, but that He still had a plan regardless. Right now, she was having a hard time trusting that plan.

She stepped back and cleared her throat, trying to focus her thoughts. She turned toward Denton. "What happened at the rink?"

Christopher's hand slipped away, and she instantly missed it. Why did her heart and her mind so constantly clash?

"The FBI took one of the men into custody, but he's not talking."

A worse thought slammed into her mind. "Was anyone hurt?" *Please, no more people hurt. There's been too many already.*

Denton shook his head. "No. Thank goodness."

Relief washed over her heart but just for a moment. They had a man in custody, she rationalized. Maybe they'd get some information from him.

But why did she have a feeling they wouldn't?

## Chapter Seventeen

Four hours later, they were at another safe house in another location in another town. Christopher was in the shower, and Ashley was curled on the sofa, trying to make sense of her thoughts. Finding any logic in this mess seemed impossible.

She'd already taken a shower and towel-dried her hair before she pulled on some yoga pants and a long-sleeve T-shirt. She'd tried to let the steam evaporate the memories that flashed through her every time she closed her eyes. If only it was that easy.

Where did they even go from here? She wouldn't give up—she couldn't. She'd keep fighting until she found David and Josh, even if she had to go at it alone.

She glanced across the room. Christopher's computer was on the kitchen table. He'd warned her to stay away from it, warned her that her every keystroke could be traceable. Even with the firewalls and precautions Eyes had made, these His People cronies were good enough that nothing was safe. Still, the laptop seemed to call to her, to beckon her to investigate.

The computer, technology, the internet…that's where the answers were, she realized. And that may be the only place she was going to find any answers about her brother, any of that help that her brother had alluded to when he said she was *their only hope.*

She could still hear the water pounding in the bathroom. Christopher probably had a good five minutes before coming out. She could do a lot in five minutes, and certainly she couldn't be traced in such a short amount of time.

Quickly, she scrambled over to the table. She opened the laptop and booted up the system. A moment later, she pulled up her websites. Her brother had helped her develop the security layers for each site. Had he somehow manipulated the security variants on her site? Why would he do that?

She went to the website of her biggest client—Koury Pharmaceuticals—and pulled up the site's interface. She stared at the administration page. Was there anything different? She searched through the different levels, looking for something—anything—before shaking her head. Everything appeared to be normal.

So what was wrong? Anything? Or was she looking too hard for something that wasn't there?

Most of the site was static, and the only thing that ever changed was the "comments" section. As a last resort, she clicked on that page to see the new feedback people had left. She scanned through each statement. Nothing.

The only place she had left to look was in the spam folder. She knew there would mostly be advertisements there from other online businesses, but she clicked there, anyway. Just as she thought—it was just junk.

Except one made her freeze.

There was a comment from Charlie Brown. She used to call her brother that when they were young. Her fingers trembled as she clicked the comments. The first line read, "Home for the Holidays."

Had her brother found a way to email her? Or was this a virus? Or a trick?

She read the rest of the message. "I can't wait to see you at home for Christmas. I wonder if the old tree house is still standing?"

The old tree house?

Was he talking about the house where they'd grown up? They'd had a tree house outside where she and her brother used to play. One year, they'd even reenacted *A Charlie Brown Christmas* with their friends.

"What are you doing?" a voice boomed behind her. "Are you trying to lure blood-hungry terrorists right to our doorstep?"

She nearly jumped out of her seat. She twirled around to see Christopher standing there, water still dripping from his hair. Fire flamed in his eyes.

"I'm following a hunch. I think I found a message from my brother."

His eyes narrowed. "Are you sure?"

"Of course I can't be sure. But this one spam message mentioned things that only he would know about."

"But you're not sure, and that's the point. I asked you to stay away. Every time we get on the computer, something seems to go wrong. I thought we agreed?"

She stood, not ready to back down. "The computer is the key here! I don't know why or how or what, but somehow this all ties back into technology. I'm not going to find my brother without a computer. I'm sure of it."

He stepped closer and glared down at her. "And I'm sure that if you don't stop using that computer, then you're going to die."

"Why do you even care?"

His hands flew in the air. "Of course I care! I've always cared."

"You could have fooled me!" What was he talking about? He'd made it clear that he didn't care. How could he deny that?

"Ashley—"

"No, don't Ashley me." She shook her head and jabbed her finger into her chest. "At least I owned up to my mistake. At least I showed some regret."

His face softened. "Ashley, there hasn't been a day that's gone by that I haven't regretted breaking up with you."

His words felt like ice water in her face. She backed up as disbelief filled her. "You don't mean that."

"Of course I do. I questioned myself a million times. I missed you. For almost a decade, I've missed you."

Her throat squeezed with emotion. "You never told me any of that."

"Of course not. I didn't expect you to wait around. That wouldn't be fair. You were supposed to meet a great guy and have all the happiness you deserved."

"You were the only *happiness* I wanted."

"I'm ruined, Ashley. War has messed me up. I can't ever see myself in a healthy relationship again."

"You can't see it or you're afraid to see it?"

They stared at each other a moment, something unspoken between them. Christopher's hands reached for her arms, and he pulled her closer. Something unseen—and strong—seemed to draw them closer. For a moment, Ashley felt young and infatuated again. Christopher raised his hand and stroked her cheek.

"Ashley—"

A loud knock sounded at the door. They both jumped back from each other. Christopher ran a hand through his wet hair and strode across the room. The guard stood there. "Denton just radioed me. Said you're not answering your phone."

Christopher stomped away. "My phone's in my room. Let me call him."

She still had to tell him about Charlie Brown.

Christopher's head swam in confusion. Could Ashley still have feelings for him? Was that even possible? But for a moment—and just a moment—he thought he saw that old, familiar affection in her gaze.

Then the knock on the door had sounded. It was just as well. All of their emotions were heightened right now. The last thing either of them needed was to do something they regretted.

He escaped to his room and dialed Denton's number. "What's going on?"

"The guy the FBI took into custody today gave us an address."

His hands went to his hips, something sounding way too easy about that discovery. "Why'd he give that up?"

"Plea deal. We're headed there now."

He grabbed a piece of scrap paper and a pen from the nightstand. "Where?"

"1020 Lindsey Lane in Chesterfield."

"Got it."

He ran a towel through his hair again and then threw his clothes in the bag. He was going to watch the raid. He needed to be there and see this for himself.

He paced back into the hallway to tell Ashley that he had to step away for a while. He wanted to be there if they did find Josh and David. Ashley would want him to be there.

Ashley's eyes widened when she saw him. "Where are you going?"

"They got a lead. I want to be there and see how it pans out."

"You're not leaving me."

He shook his head. "It's not safe for you to be there."

"You better believe I'm going to be there." Her jaw set in that familiar, determined way.

But he shook his head again. "Not a good idea."

"Where are you going?"

"Chesterfield."

Her eyes widened. "1020 Lindsey Lane, by chance?"

He paused. "How'd you know?"

"Because that's the house where Josh and I lived through elementary school before we moved down to Virginia Beach. That's what I was trying to tell you."

He let her revelation sink in. Maybe the information was legit. But if it was, then why did his gut still twist like something was wrong? "I don't like this. It just seems too easy."

"I'd say the same thing if I hadn't seen that email."

"Someone could have faked it, known about the nickname."

She shook her head. "I was never allowed to call Josh that except around family. No one else knows the nickname. If someone knows it, it's because Josh told them and he wouldn't do that."

He nodded toward the door. "I've gotta go."

"Take me with you. Please."

"What if it's a trap?"

"I'll be careful. I'll stay in the car if I have to. I just want to be there."

He paused, feeling his resolve crumbling. Finally, he nodded. "But only if you promise to stay on the perimeter. No sneaking off to check computers or do any investigating on your own. We don't know if this email is legitimate or not."

She nodded. "It's a deal. I promise."

He waved for her to follow. "Let's go, then."

Ashley stood on the edge of the property, close to a line of police cars and other unmarked sedans. Apparently, the FBI had been called in. She'd also seen Ed Carter. This bust was a big deal.

She prayed her brother and David would be discovered safe and sound.

Denton swaggered over to her, a walkie-talkie of some sort in his hands. She waited for him to give an update, but he shook his head. "Nothing yet. They're still testing out the place, making sure it's safe."

She nodded, her throat dry. That's where Christopher was. In the line of duty. Ever the soldier.

"Can I tell you something?"

She glanced up at Denton. "Sure." Tension squeezed her neck muscles as she said the word.

"Christopher wore the reality of his decision to break up with you every day. He did a great job covering it up and putting on his soldier's face when he was working. But I knew him well enough to see his struggle."

She shook her head, unable to accept what he said. "I realized it was hard for him. It was hard for me, too. Maybe I should be more compassionate and understanding. But all I feel is hurt. Every woman wants to be the 'one' a man would do anything to be with. No woman wants to be second place."

He shifted his weight. The overhead streetlight cast shadows across his eyes. "Let me explain it to you like this, then. Christopher is practically legendary in the Special Ops community. He's the one who took the shot and brought down Abar Numair."

"The leader of the terrorist group? The one who was all over the news?" Her eyes widened. "He was the sniper?"

Denton nodded. "Yeah, it was Christopher. It was a hard shot to make. His life was in danger. If he'd been caught, he would have been tortured long and hard. Death would have been a welcome relief."

She shivered at the thought.

"Ashley, do you realize what the sacrifice of his personal happiness means? It means that thousands of people aren't going to die at the hands of Abar Numair. It means Americans are safer, that there's less threat of a terrorist attack. His decision may have broken your heart, but his decision has saved thousands of lives."

Reality washed over her. Christopher's decision to dedicate himself to the military really had been self-sacrificing. Ashley had always known that his service was important—even if he only saved one person. But the entire scope of what he'd done became clear.

She closed her eyes as guilt began pounding at her temples. She really had been selfish, hadn't she? She hadn't been able to see any of that before now, though. She'd only been able to see her own pain and feelings of rejection.

Guilt filled her, but was immediately replaced with…love? Could that be what that emotion was? Love and pride and the biggest desire she'd ever had to reconcile with someone?

She had to talk to Christopher. She had to tell him finally that she understood. That she was wrong. She had to ask for a new start. For forgiveness.

Her gaze latched on to the house in the distance. That's where he was now.

She turned back to Denton. "Thank you, Denton. I needed to hear that. I needed to hear it eight years ago, I suppose."

"Everything happens in God's timing. Right now is the time for understanding."

She nodded and grabbed his arm before he started to walk away. "Thanks again."

She nibbled on her nail as her thoughts crashed together inside. How could she not have seen this before? How could her focus have been so narrow? How would things have been different if she hadn't been so stubborn and prideful when Christopher had broken up with her? If she'd actually told him she was pregnant?

But if she'd told him she was pregnant, would he still have made the world a better place?

God's timing was perfect. Maybe this really would all work together for good.

But the time when she was able to speak to Christopher wouldn't come soon enough. All of these years... certainly she could wait another hour or two.

Denton wandered back over to the line of law-enforcement personnel who served as the second line of defense. Her heart beat so fast it seemed to stutter a few beats while trying to keep up. The truth had never seemed clearer before.

"Hey, there," someone said beside her.

She looked up and saw Wally. "I heard about Tech-Share. They called you in, too, huh? I'm surprised they didn't call in the army."

He nodded. "Yeah, they'd called in almost everyone for this one."

"You think it's a setup?"

He shrugged. "You never know. You've got to be careful, though."

"I just hope it's all over soon. I want my old life back." Her old life back, only with Christopher this time.

"You might have to wait on that for a while."

"What do you mean—?" She looked down and saw the gun protruding from his jacket. Her second moment of truth for the day hit her.

Wally was the one working for the other side, not her brother.

Wally.

She knew her brother couldn't work for people who hated this country. She'd known he was better than that. Thank goodness he was better than that.

But right now, a gun was aimed right at her.

## *Chapter Eighteen*

Christopher took a step back from the house as the SWAT team entered. A winter wind whipped around, its bitter chill almost feeling like an ominous hint of the future.

His gut churned. Something was wrong. He felt sure of it.

Was this a setup? Exactly what was going on here? What was that nagging feeling that told him he was missing something?

He glanced back, expecting to see Ashley standing there in the distance, leaning against the car and watching them just as she'd been doing since they arrived. Staying back a safe distance. Away from harm. Away from danger.

He blinked.

Ashley was gone.

But where?

All of his senses went on alert. Any doubt that something was off disappeared, replaced with complete clarity. Ashley was in trouble, and he had to do something about it. Now.

He jogged back toward the line of police officers and found Denton. "Where's Ashley?"

"She's right over..." He turned and looked over his shoulder. "She was right there."

Christopher kept jogging. He reached the road just in time to see a car pulling away, two heads bobbing inside. He instantly recognized the sedan.

Wally. Wally had Ashley. Wally was one of the bad guys.

He burst into a sprint until he reached his SUV. He threw himself inside, shoved the keys in the ignition and jammed the gears into Drive. Then his foot hit the accelerator. No way was he letting that car out of his sight.

No, the woman he loved was inside. Despite all of the ups and downs of their relationship, their love was the real thing. They'd both made mistakes, both had regrets, but the fact that their paths had led back to each other was no coincidence. This was their second chance and he wasn't going to let it slip away.

Wally's car remained in the distance. Christopher wanted to stay close, but not enough to alert Wally that he was being followed. He had to make sure his timing was flawless—otherwise he might lose them. Tension stretched across his shoulders at the thought.

His phone rang, and he grabbed it out of his pocket. It was Denton.

"Which way are you headed?"

Christopher told him his approximate coordinates.

"Keep me updated. I'm sending backup."

"Just make sure they stay a safe distance behind. I don't want to clue them in that we're on to them,"

Christopher muttered. Wally merged onto the interstate ahead. Good, it would be easier to remain concealed in the flow of traffic there.

"You know it."

A loud blast filled the phone line. "Denton? What was that? Are you okay?"

Yells and screams sounded in his ear. He could hear Denton shouting orders to people before coming back on the line. "The house just exploded."

"It exploded?" His muscles stiffened harder.

"Yeah, the whole place was wired. As soon as the door opened, it went up in flames."

"So it was just a trap..." He should have known. These guys had been one—if not more—steps ahead of them this whole time. But that was going to change, and soon.

"Someone knew that email would get Ashley out here. We've been playing their game."

The car ahead of him weaved in and out of traffic. Christopher stayed a safe distance behind them. His heartbeat fast but steady. He wasn't going to let someone else down. He'd had to carry the body of his best friend from the battlefield. He refused to do the same for the woman he loved.

Finally, the sedan pulled off the interstate. It merged into highway traffic and through side streets, remaining in a heavily populated area. Best Christopher could tell, Wally didn't suspect he was being followed.

The sedan finally pulled to a stop in front of a business park. Christopher looked at the sign atop the building... Koury Pharmaceuticals?

The company Ashley had worked for, designing

their website? This must be their U.S. production facility.

A car door opened and, a moment later, Wally began dragging Ashley toward the building. The man looked around, as if searching for any onlookers. He never looked Christopher's way, though. Christopher stayed where he was, hidden behind some cars in an adjacent parking lot.

Christopher wanted to jump out and stop him, but he knew the distance between them was too great. He'd have to wait until they got inside, and then pray that he could get inside also. He had to plan his moves carefully. Darkness had fallen, and the blackness would work to his advantage.

He called Denton and let him know where he was. Then he approached the building, searching for security cameras that might clue someone in that he was here. He spotted one at the corner of the building. He had to be fast.

He darted toward the front door. A quick tug told him it was locked. Of course. That didn't surprise him. He pressed himself against the side of the building, hoping that the cameras wouldn't pick up on him there.

He crept around the perimeter of the facility, looking for a crack—a place where he might gain entry. All of the windows were locked, as was a service door in the back. He leaned against the rough bricks, desperate to think of a plan B.

Voices drifted outside. They were muted and impossible to understand. But they were close—on the other side of the window, he guessed.

Slowly, he raised himself up. Blinds covered the

glass, but in between the slats he could see inside. Ashley. His heart raced at the sight of her.

She sat at a computer with a gun to her head. Wally stood on one side of her and Gil Travis on the other. Another man—this one with white, thinning hair and a designer business suit on, stood behind them. The man's hands were on his hips as he watched everything unfold, almost appearing like a king looking over his domain.

Everything began to click in his mind.

The unseen head honcho and financial backer behind His People was the president of Koury Pharmaceuticals, wasn't he? He would have the money to fund all of their crazy schemes. And he was influential enough that he'd want to keep his affiliation quiet. If word leaked to the public, his stocks would drop. His company—and the money he was funneling into the terrorist organization—would be destroyed. If Christopher remembered correctly, the pharmaceutical company's headquarters was over in France. And based on the man's olive complexion, he was probably from the Middle East.

Christopher glanced to the other side of the room.

His heart lurched when he spotted a little boy beside Josh in the corner. That had to be David. Now that he knew who David really was, he couldn't miss how much the boy looked just like a perfect mix of him and Ashley.

And that boy didn't look like he was scared. He looked ticked, for that matter. Josh had a hand on his arm, as if he had to hold the boy back from running over to help Ashley. Christopher smiled. The boy had a fighting spirit. Just like he did.

Yes, that night so many years ago was a mistake. But this little boy wasn't, and Christopher couldn't wait to get to know him.

But first he had to get inside and save him. And Ashley. More than anything, he wanted to finish their earlier conversation. He wanted to find out if they ever had another chance together.

Good memories.

That's what he'd make with Ashley and David. That's what he needed to drive away all of the bad memories that wanted to haunt him. They'd be better than any therapy.

For the first time in a long time, he felt his first touch of hope.

An emergency exit door was only a few windows down.

An idea grew in his mind.

He went to the woods and found a rock. He threw it at the window, then pressed himself into the building on the other side of the exit door.

Shouts sounded from inside. He drew his gun. He'd fought for his country for long enough. Now it was time to fight for his family.

As soon as the door opened, he brought the butt of his gun down on the man's head. He sank to the ground. Christopher grabbed the man's gun, stuck it in his waistband and crept inside.

The hallway was clear.

He darted into an empty room. He looked around. A supply closet. At least this would give him a chance to gather his bearings. He couldn't exactly walk into the other room and shoot Wally and Erol Koury in front of David.

No, he needed a plan. And fast.

"Give us the information!" Wally growled.

Ashley's fingers were unsteady on the keyboard. All she could feel was the gun at her temple. All she could think about was how one slip of the finger could end her life—right in front of her son. Sweat sprinkled her forehead, yet her throat remained amazingly dry and sore. "I don't know what you're talking about!"

His other hand pinched her neck. "There are codes embedded into your websites. I need them."

"I didn't put any codes there." Her voice rose in pitch with each word.

Gil Travis—she recognized him from the picture—sneered from the other side. "No, but your brother did."

She craned her neck around. "Josh?"

He shrugged on the floor across the room. He looked pale and tired. But he was alive. So was David. "I had to hide them somewhere. I set up the firewall for you so hackers couldn't get into your sites, but you set up the passcodes."

Yes, she had. They involved several layers of security. Her clients trusted her with their companies' reputations. She tried to be as careful as possible. Wally pinched at her neck again until she cried out.

"Don't hurt her!" David tried to leap to his feet, but Josh pulled him back down.

She held up a hand. "I'm fine, honey. Don't worry about me."

The boy's eyes held pure determination—just like his father's did. Her heart was comforted, but only for a moment, when she realized he wasn't scared. He was ready to fight.

She looked back over at Erol Koury, the president of Koury Pharmaceuticals. She had no idea he was involved with all of this. But now she understood why he'd hired her—not just for her web expertise but as another way of having a connection with her brother. Nothing was a coincidence when it came to these men.

Wally squeezed her neck again until she gasped with pain. "I don't have any of those codes with me," she insisted.

Erol stormed toward her. "What do you mean you don't have them with you? You don't have them online anywhere?"

She looked up and shook her head. "That wouldn't be very secure, and I promised my clients only the best."

Erol's eyes looked empty as he stared at her, his nostrils flaring. "Where are they, then?"

"They're in my condo, at the bottom of a vase, where hackers can't get to them." After the words tumbled out, she licked her lips, wondering how the men would react.

"At the bottom of a vase?" Erol screamed.

She shrugged. "I figured no one could find them there. I was right. You didn't find them, did you? Even my brilliant brother didn't think to look there."

Erol sighed and ran a hand down his face. "We've worked too hard to get to this point to let everything fall apart now. None of this was supposed to happen."

He swiveled toward Josh. "All you had to do was come work for me, Josh. But no, you had to stand on your principles."

"I love my country more than I love a big paycheck, Erol. Unlike some people." Josh glared at Wally.

Wally narrowed his eyes. "If you had just cooperated, we wouldn't be in this mess right now."

"If you had just had integrity, then so many people wouldn't be dead!" Josh snarled back.

"Quiet! All of you!" Erol paced the room. "Leave the boy here with his dad. Take her and go back to her apartment. Get those passcodes. Now."

As Wally jerked her to her feet, she looked back at Josh. "What kind of codes are embedded on my sites?"

He frowned. "Codes that can destroy the entire infrastructure of the United States—on all levels. Economic, national security...nuclear."

Erol chuckled. "Wouldn't that teach this haughty country not to be so arrogant?"

Wally tried to push her forward, but she dug her heels in and turned back toward her brother again. "Josh, why would you have those kind of codes? I don't understand."

"I had to develop them as a part of my work. Wally worked on the project with me, but my gut told me he wasn't who he claimed." Josh scowled at his former coworker. "I knew I had to hide the technology I'd developed before the wrong person got their hands on it."

"Why my website?"

"Because I knew they'd be unreachable. You know what I always say. Have layers of security to get through. You were one of my layers. I'm sorry."

Wally jerked her toward the door again. "Come on. We've got another trip to make. We've got to hurry before you little boyfriend finds us. He's been a real pain."

She glanced back at David. She didn't want to leave him again. But would this buy her more time? More time so that people—that Christopher—could find them? She could only pray that would be the case.

Gun still in hand, Christopher cracked the door open. Two guards stood outside of the office where Ashley was. He'd have to take them down. He could only guess how many other people might be around. When would Denton and his men be here?

He needed backup.

But he might not have time for backup.

He heard the door open, and his back muscles went rigid.

Ashley tumbled out, Wally right behind her. A gun dug into her back. Tears rushed down her cheeks, and her lip bled as if she'd been punched. Anger surged through him.

There was no time to lose, he realized. If he was going to act, it had to be now.

In the shadows of the supply closet, he raised his gun.

Images of his last night in Afghanistan tried to flash back, but he refused to let the memories come. Not now. He couldn't afford to relive the past, not when the future was on the line. He'd saved a country from a terrorist. Certainly he could save the woman he loved.

With the precision of the sharpshooter he'd been, he aimed at Wally. He waited, making sure no one else stepped out behind them. The door closed, and Wally shoved Ashley again.

That's when Christopher pulled the trigger.

Wally went down, moaning in pain. The guards flanking him scrambled in a panic. In the mad flurry of activity, he didn't have a clean shot.

"Right there!" One of the guards spotted him and raised his gun.

Christopher shot the man's shoulder. Quickly, he got the other guard in his crosshairs and fired. He went down with a cry. He hadn't shot to kill, only to maim.

Ashley's eyes widened as she looked down the hallway. Was there someone else? Someone he couldn't see because of the door beside him?

Ashley reached behind her and pulled out her own gun. She'd brought her gun, just like he encouraged her to do. Good girl.

With trembling hands, she pressed the trigger. Christopher heard a grunt outside his door and the crash of someone hitting the floor. Ashley may have just saved his life.

Ashley waved him over, her head swerving from side to side as she checked to see if the coast was clear. He pushed open the door and ran toward her, knowing that they didn't have much time before more men came running. He grabbed the guards' guns and dropped them in a trash can out of their reach.

His eyes quickly soaked Ashley in when he reached her. She appeared shaken but otherwise fine. "You okay?"

She nodded, gratitude filling her gaze. "Better now that you're here."

Christopher reached for the door. They had to get David and Josh. Now.

Just as they stepped in, Erol had David in a choke-hold. "Not so fast," he muttered. "You're not as smart as you think you are. Put down your guns or the boy gets hurt."

"No one needs to get hurt," Christopher muttered. His eyes were on David. His son. His sweet son. The boy's perceptive gaze flickered from Ashley to Christopher, keen intelligence flashing in his eyes.

"Put your guns down," Erol ordered.

Christopher began lowering his gun to the floor when David suddenly bit Erol's arm. The man howled with pain.

It was just the break they needed. Christopher swooped up his gun again. In three quick strokes, he'd pulled David away from Erol, kicked the gun out of his hand, and snapped the man's arms behind him.

Lights flashed outside. Feet trampled close by. Shouts ensued.

Help was here.

They were safe.

Finally, they were safe.

After everyone had been successfully taken into custody and as the feds scurried about the building collecting evidence, Christopher squatted down next to David. His son. His heart stuttered at the mere thought of it. As he glanced in the boy's eyes for the first time, an indescribable love filled him.

*Take it easy, Jordan,* he reminded himself. *That boy has no idea who you are.*

He smiled, trying to look more relaxed than he felt. "That was an awfully brave thing you did there."

The boy raised his chin—just like Ashley always did. He had Ashley's oval face and chin, but his hair and eye color. Pure determination filled his gaze. "I don't like to see people bullied. It's not right."

Christopher grinned. He already liked David, and he couldn't wait to get to know him better. He still had so much to learn, so much he'd like to teach him—if Ashley and Josh would let him be a part of the boy's life. They hadn't gotten that far in their conversations. But he hoped to be a part of Ashley's life also. He glanced over at her, saw how much she loved the boy, and he suddenly understood why she wanted to protect him so much. It didn't justify what she'd done, but he knew forgiveness was a powerful tool and one that he was more than willing to employ right now.

For the sake of his family. Hope like he hadn't felt in a long time filled him.

Ashley hadn't stopped hugging David since Erol had been apprehended. Josh had been led away to be debriefed. But he paused for long enough to mutter a "thank you" and "sorry."

Ashley pulled away from David and looked at the boy, her eyes full of warmth. She looked beautiful, even with blood trickling down her forehead and the start of a bruise at the side of her eye.

She glanced at Christopher and sucked in a deep breath. "David, this is my friend, Christopher. He's been looking forward to meeting you."

Christopher continued to soak in the boy in front of him. He looked like he'd been well taken care of, even in his captivity. Even if he hadn't been, Christopher had a feeling that the boy wasn't the type to be a victim. He was the type to stay strong and resilient. "You're a little trouper, just like your aunt said."

Their eyes met, and Ashley smiled before muttering, "The apple doesn't fall far from the tree."

David's voice cut into their moment, the time when unspoken promises were made, but no one knew except the two of them. "What does that mean? Who has apples?"

"I'll explain later." She studied his face. "Are you okay? Are you really okay? I was worried about you."

He shrugged and pushed out his lips as if bored. "I guess. I missed you, Ashley."

Ashley's arms seemed to squeeze him tighter. "I missed you, too. More than you can ever know."

"I want to build a snowman with you. Those men wouldn't let me go outside and play. They weren't very nice, but they did feed me cheese puffs. Lots and lots of cheese puffs."

Christopher smiled this time. "I'm sure we can arrange something, as soon as we're cleared to leave here."

"You know what tomorrow is?" David's eyes lit with excitement. He didn't let them answer. "It's Christmas Eve!"

Christopher and Ashley shared another glance. He'd all but forgotten just how close the holiday was. With everything else that had been going on, they'd all been a little distracted.

David frowned. "My dad said he probably wasn't going to be able to spend it with me. He said he might have to go away for a while, but that I could stay with you, Ashley."

Ashley squeezed his arm. "You're always welcome to stay with me."

"He told me your secret." David's eyes glowed as he stared up at her.

Ashley's face went white. "What secret?"

"He told me that you're my mom."

Ashley blinked, as if uncertain whether or not to believe him. "He…he told you that?"

"It's okay, Ashley. You've always been like my mom. I think Dad was afraid something would happen to him. He said I'd never be alone, that my family was bigger than I realized."

Ashley looked up at Christopher, bewilderment across her features. They needed to talk. There was so much they needed to discuss. He could see it in Ashley's eyes that she felt the same way about him as Christopher did about her.

Medics rushed into the room. "We need to check you all over for injuries," one of them said.

They'd have to put off a conversation they should have had nearly a decade ago. But this time he wasn't going to let Ashley slip away from him again.

They reached another safe house, this one a cozy bungalow located on a lake in the foothills of the Blue Ridge Mountains. Ashley had helped David get ready for bed, read him a bedtime story, and then tucked him into bed.

Her throat ached as she walked into the living room.

Christopher stoked the fire. He rose to his feet when he spotted her.

She rubbed her hands on her jeans. They'd had a lot of tough conversations already. But this one required not only owning up to the past but presenting an offer for the future.

She hooked a hair behind her ear as she reached him. "Can I talk to you a minute, Christopher?"

His gaze was steady on hers…steady and warm. "Of course."

A shiver raced through her when she heard the huskiness in his voice. She pointed to the couch. "We should sit."

They sat across from each other, close enough that their knees touched.

She rubbed her hands on her jeans again as her gaze reached up to meet his. "Look, I know we've been through a lot. I know you're angry with me, and I deserve it. I should have pushed through my emotions and realized that telling you about David was the right thing. Sometimes it's easier to realize these things in retrospect."

"That's true for all of us, Ashley."

She rested her hand on his knee. "I just wanted to say that I understand. Finally. I talked to Denton and after our conversation it just clicked in my mind, and I understand now why you had to go to Afghanistan."

"You do?" Light gleamed in his eyes.

She nodded, her emotions squeezing her. "I feel like I was actually the one being selfish throughout the whole thing. I can see that now."

His hand covered hers. "That's not true. It was an

agonizing decision, no matter how you looked at it. There were no real winners."

"Except maybe the world." She offered a small smile.

Christopher gave her one in return. It quickly disappeared, replaced with a firm-set jaw and serious eyes. "I'd like to think the world is a better place, that my sacrifices weren't for nothing."

"No, the world is a better place."

He scooted closer. "I wish you didn't have to get hurt in the process." He cupped her cheek with one hand. "Ashley, you've always been the only one for me. No one else has even remotely caught my eye. My heart's always been with you."

Her spirit seemed to breathe with new life, lifting with hope inside her. "Even as mad as I was, I've always loved you, Christopher. Always."

His other arm snaked around her waist and he pulled her close. Their lips met, sweetly, tenderly.

After the heartbreak of the past week, Ashley realized one thing: all things do work together for the good of those who love Christ. Sometimes it just might take years to realize it, though.

# *Epilogue*

$A$shley straightened the white slacks and snow-white sweater she wore. It wasn't exactly a wedding dress, but there would be time for a big wedding later—if that's what she and Christopher decided on. Really, the wedding was so unimportant to her. It was the marriage that mattered.

Instead of planning and waiting for a future date, she and Christopher had decided to get married in a small ceremony at the Eyes' headquarters. They'd had eight long years of being apart. Neither wanted to waste any more time.

In five minutes, it would be the New Year and they would officially become husband and wife. Mr. and Mrs. Christopher Jordan. It had a nice ring to it. It always had.

She stood before a chaplain with a small audience gathered around her in the massive lobby area at Eyes. David was at her side, holding their rings, and looking handsome in some khakis, an olive-green sweater and a Navy ball cap that Christopher had given him. The boy hadn't wanted to take it off.

The two of them bonded quickly, and David already looked up at Christopher with a glimmer of admiration in his eyes. Christopher had told his son stories—happy, adventurous ones—about being a SEAL, about training, about toughening up. David held on to each word and asked questions. They'd talked about fishing and hiking and playing football.

Josh, in the meantime, had been sent into hiding for a while, at least until some of this storm passed. He knew too much, had seen too much. He'd asked Ashley and Christopher if they'd watch out for David. He'd told them he'd had moments of clarity while in captivity, and that's why he'd told David that Ashley was really his mom. David had taken it all in stride, something that Ashley was immensely thankful for.

They hadn't yet told him that Christopher was his real daddy, but they would with time. When the right moment came, they'd know it. They didn't want to give the boy too much to handle at once.

Christopher stood in front of her, wearing jeans and a Kelly-green sweater that made his eyes pop. A fire blazed in the background. The Christmas tree stood in the corner still, and some of Christopher's friends—and the very people who'd kept them both alive during this whole ordeal—sat around them.

Ashley hardly saw anyone except for Christopher and David. Her soon-to-be husband squeezed her hands, never taking his eyes off her since the start of the ceremony. She was so glad that their paths had led them back to each other. She praised God for truly working all things together for their good.

"Ashley, do you take this man, Christopher Jordan,

to be your lawfully wedded husband?" the chaplain asked. "To have and to hold from this day forward."

Ashley's heart glowed with warmth as she looked up at Christopher. This was the moment she'd been dreaming about for so long. It almost seemed surreal, as if she'd wake up and he'd be gone. He squeezed her hands again, as if reading her thoughts, and reminding her that this was no dream.

She smiled. "I do."

"Christopher, do you take this woman, Ashley Wilson, to be your lawfully wedded wife?"

"You better believe it." The look in his eyes was pure affection, unmasked and unbridled and out there for everyone to see.

"I now pronounce you man and wife. You may—" the chaplain glanced at his watch and paused for a second before looking up with a grin "—kiss the bride."

Just as Christopher's lips came down on hers, balloons and confetti rained down on them from above.

"Happy New Year!" everyone around them yelled.

Laughing, they stepped back. Ashley put her arm around David's shoulders and pulled him into a group hug with Christopher as everyone cheered.

Her family. Together at last.

It truly was going to be a happy new year.

A happy lifetime for that matter, as long as Christopher and David were by her side.

\* \* \* \* \*

Dear Reader,

As I was listening to a radio interview with a former Navy SEAL not long ago, I found myself fascinated with what he had to say. He talked about how hard it was to be a Navy SEAL and to have a family, saying that it was extremely difficult to be committed to both.

That interview made me start thinking about the sacrifices our military personnel make, especially those who are in the Special Forces. Long deployments, stress from the battlefield and trouble adjusting to life back at home are only a few of the challenges these families face. Not long after listening to that interview, this book was born.

I hope you enjoyed Ashley and Christopher's story, along with the reminder that God can work everything—even our mistakes—together for our good.

# YULETIDE JEOPARDY

Sandra Robbins

To Kathy

A Great Friend and Critique Partner

Let all bitterness, and wrath, and anger,
and clamour, and evil speaking,
be put away from you, with all malice:
And be ye kind one to another, tenderhearted,
forgiving one another, even as God for Christ's sake
hath forgiven you.
—*Ephesians* 4:31–32

# Chapter One

The WKIZ-TV van skidded to a stop near the police cars blocking the entrance to the Memphis-Arkansas Bridge, and Grace Kincaid jumped from the vehicle before her cameraman had time to turn off the engine. The blue lights on the cruisers flashed in the cold December morning fog that drifted up from the Mississippi River below.

She held up her identification badge, which hung from a lanyard around her neck as she ran toward the officers who stood beside the cars. "Grace Kincaid, WKIZ. I had an urgent message that a man who's threatening to jump from the bridge wants to talk to me."

Captain Wilson, who she had interviewed once, pointed toward the middle of the bridge. "His name is Timothy Mitchell. Do you know him?"

Grace's eyes widened, and she nodded. "His son was a friend of mine in high school. He committed suicide on this bridge when we were seniors."

"We found that out," he said.

Grace's mind raced at the possibilities of this story.

The father of her high school boyfriend was threatening suicide on the same bridge where his son had died, and he'd asked for her. Stories like this came along maybe once in a career. If she handled this right, the video would make a good addition to her application when she decided to apply to the networks again. She had to handle this carefully if she was to have a happy ending to this story by getting Mr. Mitchell safely off the bridge.

She turned to Captain Wilson. "Has he asked for anything else?"

"Mr. Mitchell asked for you and Detective Alex Crowne, but he's not here yet. You can wait here until he arrives," Captain Wilson said.

Grace groaned inwardly. Just what she needed. This story had just gotten a lot more complicated. She hadn't seen Alex since the wedding of their best friends Laura Webber and Brad Austin six months ago, and he'd ignored her then. He would probably do the same thing when he arrived at the bridge because he still couldn't stand to be near her. Instead of accepting his part in their failed romance, he had chosen to blame her, and she supposed he always would.

Grace shook her head. No way was he going to ignore her today and let this story slip through her fingers. She didn't need Alex Crowne to help her with a man she'd known well once upon a time. With any luck she could have Mr. Mitchell down and be gone before Alex arrived.

"No, thanks. He can join me when he gets here." A cold gust of wind whipped her coat around her knees, and she shivered at the early-morning chill. She pulled her gloves from her coat pocket, tugged them on and nodded to her cameraman Derek. "Let's go. Be sure you keep that camera on. This will be our lead-in story on the noon and six o'clock news."

Derek nodded. "Gotcha."

Grace hurried toward the two officers who stood up ahead in the roadway next to the knee-high concrete barrier that separated it from the pedestrian walkway. As she came closer, her heart sank at the sight of the man who straddled the walkway railing on the river side of the bridge. His eyes were closed, and he swayed back and forth on the handrail as his long, white hair blew about his face.

The years had taken a toll on the once-handsome man. She'd heard that after his son's death he had spiraled into a deep depression and had spent time in and out of mental institutions. Tears filled Grace's eyes. The man balancing on the railing just feet away from her looked nothing like the wealthy businessman she'd once known.

One of the officers glanced from her to Mr. Mitchell as she approached. "Just let him talk and tell you what's on his mind. Maybe you can distract him long enough for us to get him off that railing."

Grace glanced around to make sure Derek had the camera rolling and nodded. "I'll try."

She cleared her throat. "Mr. Mitchell," she called out.

Another gust of wind blew across the bridge, and the man wobbled as he struggled to maintain his balance. For a moment it looked as if he might fall to the river below, but he steadied himself. "Is that you, Grace?"

Chills rippled up her spine at the sight of the gaunt figure perched on the railing. She took a deep breath and stepped closer. "Yes. I understand you wanted to see me. What can I do to help you?"

The man didn't speak for a moment. His eyes narrowed, and his gaze raked Grace. Her skin burned as his intense stare bored into her very soul. "You can find out who murdered my son."

Grace didn't know if it was the force of Mr. Mitchell's words or the veins that stood out in his neck and face that frightened her the most. "Mr. Mitchell, Landon committed suicide. Don't you remember? His car was found parked on this bridge. The door was open, and the keys were still in the ignition. There was a note on the seat that said he was sorry."

His eyes blazed with fury. "He didn't commit suicide. The note was printed off a computer. Landon hated typing on the computer. He would have left a handwritten note. Everybody was too quick to decide it was suicide."

She shook her head and frowned. "Mr. Mitchell, I noticed changes in Landon during the two years before he died. He started skipping school, his grades dropped and he cut himself off from his old friends. I thought he was going through some kind of depression, so I wasn't surprised when he killed himself."

The man closed his eyes and yelled at the top of his voice. "He didn't kill himself! He was murdered. It was that secret group he joined that killed him. You knew about it and didn't tell anybody."

Grace's eyes grew wide, and she held up her hand. "Mr. Mitchell, please be careful. You're going to fall."

The words were no sooner out of her mouth than another wind gust whipped across the bridge. The loose-fitting, unbuttoned coat he wore flapped around his body. He grabbed the bar he straddled and clamped his legs around the base of the railing as he wobbled from side to side. Grace drew in a sharp breath and released it when he steadied himself.

She waited until he'd regained his balance before she spoke. "I understand how hard his death must have been for you. I wish I could have done something to help him, but he shut me out of his life. He never told me he joined a secret group. What makes you think he did?"

"Because after his death I found money hidden everywhere in his room. And I also found his journal. It was filled with all kinds of rambling entries about his successful deals and how much money he and his partners had made. There was a wolf's head drawn on every page."

"I never heard him say anything about wolves. Maybe it was just his way of doodling on the page."

Mr. Mitchell shook his head. "No, it was more than that. One night I went into his room when he was sleeping to cover him with an extra blanket, and I saw a wolf's head tattooed on his shoulder. So don't tell me there wasn't a secret group. I know there was. They were evil, and they killed my son." The last words ended in a sob.

"If you're right about this, I would like to help prove it. You say there was a journal that told about this group. Where is it now?"

He reached in his coat pocket and pulled out a

leather book. "Here it is. I've read it over and over ever since he died."

"Would you let me look at it?" Grace inched forward and stepped over the low barrier onto the pedestrian walkway.

"Grace, stop right there. Don't get too close." Her heart thudded at the voice that came from behind her. It didn't matter how long it had been since she'd heard it. She'd know it anywhere. Alex Crowne had arrived on the bridge, and his command reminded her of the tone he'd used when cautioning her about something when they were children.

She frowned and shook her head. They weren't children anymore, and he'd long ago given up the right to be concerned about her safety. She arched an eyebrow and glanced over her shoulder. "It's all right, Alex. I just want to see the journal."

Mr. Mitchell tilted his head back and laughed before he glared at Alex. "So Detective Crowne who supposedly solves cold cases came, too." He leaned forward. "When I read in the paper you had been picked to help head up the new Cold Case Unit with the police, I begged you to solve my son's murder. When are you going to do it?"

"I looked into the case like I said I would do," Alex said, "and I told you I wasn't able to find any new evidence that his death was anything but a suicide."

Grace inched closer. "Mr. Mitchell, I'm sure Alex will be glad to look into Landon's death again." She turned her head and glanced at Alex over her shoulder. "You'll do that, won't you?"

Alex looked at her, then to Mr. Mitchell. "Of course I will."

Grace smiled and turned her gaze back to Landon's father. "We'll both see what we can find out. Now why don't you give me the journal and come down from the railing?"

Alex stepped over the barrier and came to a stop behind her. "No, Grace. Don't get any closer."

Without looking around, she waved Alex off. "It's okay." She moved closer to the railing and stretched out her hand. "I'm a reporter. If I see anything that makes me think Landon was murdered, I'll find out who did it."

Mr. Mitchell started to hold out the book but pulled it back. "Do you promise you'll find out who killed him?"

"I promise I'll look into his death, and Alex said he would also."

Hesitantly, he sat up straight and held out the book. Another strong gust of wind swept across the bridge, but it wasn't the sudden breeze that chilled Grace. Her skin prickled at the change in Mr. Mitchell's face. Whereas moments ago he had looked like a grieving father, his eyes now held a maniacal glare, and he stared at her as if seeing her for the first time.

"Grace, be careful!" Alex's warning came too late.

Grace reached out to take the journal. Before she could touch it, Landon's father hurled the book into the air and grabbed her by the wrist. "You can look at it with me at the bottom of the river."

Grace slammed against the bridge railing and gaped in horror as the book sailed downward toward the river.

She looked up into Mr. Mitchell's crazed eyes and tried to break free, but it was no use. He held her in a vise-like grip. "You know who killed my son."

"Grace!" Alex's panicked yell reached her, and she struggled to twist free.

Mr. Mitchell's hold on her tightened, and with a loud scream he fell backward off the railing but managed to clamp his free hand around the handrail. With one hand circling her wrist and the other clutching the railing, he dangled in midair and pulled her toward him.

Grace clawed for a hold on the railing with her free hand and watched in horror as he uncurled one finger from his grip on the handrail. He grinned and lifted another finger. Her feet lifted from the walkway, and she screamed at the excruciating pain radiating up her arm. She tried to wedge her feet between the metal rods that supported the railing, but she couldn't grab a foothold as his weight pulled her closer and closer to the top of the railing. In a few seconds she would be pulled from the bridge to a watery grave below.

Just when she thought all hope was lost, Alex's left arm encircled her waist, and he stretched his right one over the railing in an effort to reach Mr. Mitchell. The two uniformed officers appeared on either side of her to help Alex. Before they could catch hold of Mr. Mitchell, he released his hold on Grace's wrist and the railing, but Alex grabbed him by the sleeve of his open coat before he could fall.

"Help me pull him up," Alex yelled as he tightened his grip on Mr. Mitchell's coat. The officers reached down to assist.

Before they could pull him to safety, Mr. Mitchell

threw back his head, released a bone-chilling laugh, and wriggled out of the coat. Grace had a split-second glance of the surprised look that flashed across his face before he plummeted toward the murky waters below. With them free of Mr. Mitchell's weight, she and Alex tumbled backward and landed on the walkway pavement with his arms wrapped around her.

She only had a moment to realize she was safe before Alex was on his feet and rushing back to the railing. She sat up and watched him lean over the railing and scan the river below. He turned to the officer next to him. "I don't see him. Notify harbor patrol where he went into the water. If we're lucky, we may be able to recover his body before the current carries it downstream."

Alex's shoulders sagged as he continued to look down at the water. After a moment, he turned and glared at her. Grace tried to rise, but her shaking legs wouldn't cooperate. Alex strode back to her, grabbed her uninjured arm and lifted her to stand next to him. She pushed a lock of hair out of her face and struggled to keep from bursting into tears. "Thank you, Alex. If it wasn't for you, I'd be dead right now."

The muscle in his jaw twitched, and his eyebrows drew down across his nose. He released a long breath and shook his head. "I've seen you do a lot of crazy things, but nothing can top what you did today."

She started to answer, but she noticed Derek still held the camera. "Derek, you can stop now. Go on back to the van and wait for me."

He lowered the camera and glanced from her to Alex. "Are you sure you're all right?"

"I'm fine. I'll be with you in a few minutes." Her wrist throbbed, and she massaged it as she watched Derek walk away. Then she turned back to Alex. Anger boiled up in her, and she took a step closer to Alex and stared up into his angry eyes. "May I ask what your problem is, Detective Crowne?" she hissed.

He didn't back away from her. Instead, he leaned toward her until they were face-to-face. "My problem? It was your problem. You almost got yourself killed. Why didn't you wait for me to get here? I might have been able to talk him down off that railing."

Grace straightened her back and stared at him. "I had no idea when you'd get here, and I wanted to get Mr. Mitchell down as quickly as possible."

"And you wanted to be the main rescuer in the story, didn't you? You forget I know you too well, Grace. Your story on the noon news would sure look a lot better if you'd saved a man from a watery grave without the help of the police."

Her face grew warm, and she shook her head. "I think he was determined to end his life no matter who was here."

"Maybe," Alex said. "But we might have avoided the attempt on your life. I told you not to go any closer, and you didn't pay any attention to me. That shouldn't surprise me since you've never listened to me about anything."

His words cut deep, and she struggled to keep from bursting into tears. "What do you mean? Have you forgotten I'm the girl who followed you everywhere from the time we were ten years old? And that I'm also the girl who loved you and you threw my love away as if it was nothing? I'd say you're the one who never listened."

He shook his head and gave a sarcastic chuckle. "I guess it's true. Two people can see a situation and interpret it in an entirely different way. If I remember correctly, it was you who walked away from me without caring how I felt."

She took a step back from Alex and tried to stem the tears welling in her eyes. She'd never been able to make him understand her side of their breakup, and she probably never would. It saddened her to think their once close friendship had come to this.

She lifted her chin and took a deep breath. "Who are you to talk about caring? You haven't even asked me how I'm feeling after almost taking a hundred-foot dive into the river. For your information I didn't ask to come here today, and I sure didn't ask to almost get killed. I was trying to save a man's life." Her battle to stop her tears failed, and she wiped at one that slipped down her cheek. "It turns out I didn't help, and your attitude has turned a bad day into an even worse one. I'd like to say it was nice seeing you again, but it wasn't."

Alex raked his fingers through his hair. "Grace, don't you understand—"

She held up her hand. "I think you've made your feelings very clear, Alex. Now I need to get back to work."

Clutching her fists at her side, she whirled and stormed down the walkway in the direction of the station's van. She'd failed to get the story of stopping a man from committing suicide that she'd first visualized when she set foot on the bridge. Instead of a piece to add to her résumé, she'd ended up with the last tragic moments of a man's life.

She didn't think she would ever forget the look on Mr. Mitchell's face right before he plunged to the river. She needed to get back to the station and decide how she would use the footage on the noon newscast, but at the moment she couldn't bear to think about the sad events on the bridge this morning. Maybe when she had calmed down, she could reflect on all that happened on the bridge today, but right now she needed to get as far away from it as possible.

Alex watched Grace stride away from him. Her blond hair glistened in the sunlight that had chased off the early-morning fog. She held her back erect, and anger oozed from every pore in her body. That was his doing. He should never have attacked her like that. After all she'd just had the scare of a lifetime, and he hadn't helped any with his harsh words.

He'd spoken before he had time to think. But he'd been so scared when he saw Mitchell grab her arm and go over the side of the bridge. At first he couldn't move, and then instinct kicked in. He had his arm around her and was pulling her backward before he realized what was happening.

He raised a shaking hand and brushed it across his eyes. Regret that he hadn't been able to save Timothy Mitchell hit him like a kick in the stomach, and he knew it would be a long time before he could forget the look on the man's face when he'd truly realized at that last moment he was about to die. But he had to keep reminding himself Grace had lived. If he'd been a second later, she would be at the bottom of the Mississippi River with Mr. Mitchell right now. He almost groaned aloud at the thought. As usual, their meeting today had ended like many others in the past, but this one was his fault.

His eyes followed Grace, who had stopped to talk with Captain Wilson, and he wished he could take back the harsh words he'd spoken earlier. He couldn't, though, just like he couldn't undo the past.

He'd had many tense moments since he'd joined the force, but today had to be the worst he'd ever experienced. At the moment he'd thought she was going over the bridge, he didn't think of her as the woman who had broken his heart. He remembered her as the little girl who had shared his childhood with him. He had to make her understand how scared he'd been.

Alex turned to the officers who'd gathered at the railing and now watched the rolling water. "Do you need me for anything else?"

One of the officers who had tried to reach Mitchell shook his head. "There's not much more to do here. Thanks for the help."

Grace turned away from Captain Wilson and headed toward her van. Alex took a deep breath and jogged to catch up with her. She'd opened the door and was about to climb into the van when he called out to her. "Grace, wait. I want to talk with you."

She closed the van's door and glared at him as he approached. Her eyes flashed with anger when he stopped in front of her. "Do you want to berate me further for my bad judgment?"

Alex swallowed. "No. I wanted to make sure you're

all right and apologize for the way I spoke to you on the bridge. You'd just seen a man die, and you were almost killed yourself. After all you became a victim, too, when Mitchell tried to kill you. I shouldn't have spoken to you the way I did. I'm sorry."

She frowned and shook her head. "So after all these years, your only concern for my welfare is because you saw me as a victim on that bridge."

He gritted his teeth and leaned closer. "You know that's not true, Grace."

"You still hate me, don't you?" She tilted her head to one side. "It's sad to think that after all these years we find it difficult to be around each other."

He took a deep breath. "Yeah, but every time we're together, it ends with angry words like it did on the bridge this morning. I don't want it to end that way this time."

She looked at him for a moment before she spoke. "Neither do I. I'm always sad afterward when that happens."

He sighed. "Me, too, but it doesn't change anything. There's too much history between us, Grace."

She opened her mouth to speak but didn't say anything. After a moment her shoulders sagged, and she nodded. "There is, and there's no way to undo the past. All we can do is try to make the best of it. I'd like for us to at least be civil when we run into each other, though."

"I hope we can in time," he said.

"Maybe we'll have time to make it happen while we're trying to find out the truth about Landon's death."

For a moment he thought he'd misunderstood her,

but the determined look in her eye told him she knew exactly what she had said. "You can't be serious."

"Oh, but I am." She glanced around as if checking to see if anyone could overhear them before she lowered her voice. "What if his father was right and he was murdered?"

Alex shook his head. "Just because Mr. Mitchell says so doesn't make it true. The police did a thorough investigation, and they believed it was suicide."

"But still…"

"Suicide, Grace. That's all there is to it."

She arched an eyebrow. "So are you saying you won't help me find out the truth? We both promised him we would find out about Landon's death."

Alex stepped closer and frowned. "That was before the man tried to kill you. I think that canceled all promises."

"No, it doesn't. What if he was right and Landon was murdered? Did you ever hear anybody talk about a secret society at school?"

Alex thought for a moment before he responded. "I suppose I did. There was always talk about some mysterious group who lurked in the shadows. But I thought it was just gossip."

"What if it wasn't? What if there was a secret group and they killed Landon?"

Alex glanced at his watch. "I don't have time for this, Grace. I have real unsolved crimes I'm working on. Landon's death was a suicide. I have better things to do than go chasing after some silly rumor that circulated in our high school twelve years ago."

He started to turn away, but she grabbed his arm.

"No, I'm not going to let you ignore this. We made a promise to a man right before he died. We may find it hard to be around each other, but that doesn't release us from doing what is right. We have to find out the truth, Alex."

He stared at her a moment before he pulled loose from her grip. "Although Landon's body was recovered, the medical examiner couldn't establish for certain the cause of death. So the case was never officially closed. Since it's a cold case, I'll look into it again. If I find out anything, I'll let you know."

She shook her head. "If it's a cold case, you have a responsibility to investigate it. And I have an obligation to my station. I'm not about to let this story go."

Understanding dawned, and he chuckled. "Oh, I get it. All your talk about doing what's right was just a ploy to get me to help you with a big story. What do you want, Grace? Are you tired of being back in Memphis and you need something that can get you back to the major networks?"

Her face flushed, and she shook her head. "No, Alex. I want the truth, and I'm not going to give up until I find it. I worked as an investigative reporter before I went to the anchor desk, and I can do it again. It would help to have the police involved with this, too. But if you don't help me, I'll just have to do it on my own."

"You're still as headstrong as ever." He studied her for a moment. "I don't believe you want the truth, but it so happens I do. You're right about one thing. It is my job to work a cold case, so I'll help you investigate Landon's death."

She swallowed. "How can you work with me on an investigation if you hate me so much?"

His shoulders sagged, and he shook his head. "I don't hate you, Grace. I don't trust you."

Tears sparkled in her eyes, but he didn't blink. He'd seen enough of her tears through the years to know it was her way of getting what she wanted. He cleared his throat and glanced down at her arm. "I need to get back to work, and you need to go to a hospital and get that arm checked."

She nodded. "Derek is going to take me by the hospital before we go back to the station." She started to climb in the van but turned back to face Alex. "You're right about a lot of things about me, Alex. I made some mistakes in the past, but you did, too. And you're wrong about my reasons for wanting to find out the truth about Landon's death. I hope you can come to see that."

He didn't know how to answer her, so he shook his head and stepped back from the van. He watched it drive away before he walked to where he'd parked his car.

When he'd gotten out of bed this morning, he'd expected a routine day at work. So far there had been nothing routine about it. He'd seen a man fall to his death, and he'd prevented Grace from following him into the Mississippi River. Now he was about to take another look at a cold case that hadn't produced a lead in twelve years.

The most troubling thing, however, was the fact Grace wanted to be involved. He didn't know if he'd be able to cope with that or not. Being around her stirred up too many painful memories. She'd broken his heart, and it had taken him years to get to the place where he was now. All he could do was protect himself so it didn't happen again. He didn't intend to ever let anyone hurt him again the way she had.

## Chapter Two

Even with the bright lights on the set, a chill rippled through Grace's body as she watched the footage from the bridge play on the monitor. She and Derek had reviewed the final cut several times, but her heart still hammered every time she watched her struggle to keep from going over the railing.

When the footage ended, the camera focused back on the WKIZ News anchor desk. Her coanchor Todd Livingston turned to her and flashed his trademark toothy smile. "Wow, Grace. You had quite a morning. Thank goodness that detective was there to keep you from being pulled over the railing."

Grace returned his smile. "Yes, Todd. It was touch-and-go there for a few minutes, but thanks to Detective Crowne, I wasn't hurt."

His gaze dropped to the elastic bandage around her wrist. "What did the doctor say about your arm?"

She held up her arm. "It's just a sprain. It should be okay in a few days. I really am lucky."

Todd looked into the camera and broadened his

smile. "Knowing you, I doubt if you'll let a little thing like a sprained wrist slow you down."

She chuckled. "No, I won't. Before Mr. Mitchell plunged to his death, I promised him I would look into his son's death and see what I could find."

Todd turned back to her, his eyes wide. "But I thought you said his son committed suicide."

"The police suspect suicide, but they can't be sure. There was blood on the front seat. Mr. Mitchell believed his son was murdered and that the scene was staged to look like a suicide."

"So, what happens if you find something that suggests it might have been murder?"

"That's a matter for the police, of course. I've already talked with Detective Alex Crowne of the Cold Case Unit, and he's agreed to investigate the case with me." She looked into the camera. "If there's anyone who has information about Landon Mitchell's death or a high school secret society that he might have been a member of, you can contact me here at the station. Even if it's something that seems inconsequential, get in touch with me. You never can tell what detail might help to solve a crime."

Todd picked up the papers in front of him and shuffled them into a neat stack. "Well, that's all the time we have for today." He glanced at Grace and gave an exaggerated shiver. "Suicide on the Memphis-Arkansas Bridge? A secret society in one of our high schools? A twelve-year-old unsolved death? It sounds like my busy bee coanchor has enough to keep the newsroom buzzing for a while. Tune in tomorrow and see what she has for us next."

Grace plastered a smile on her face and held it until the camera shut down. Then she turned to Todd. "Were you trying to embarrass me on air?"

His eyes grew wide. "Why should I do that? You do it quite well without any help from me."

Her skin warmed, and she scooped up the papers on the desk in front of her. "What is that supposed to mean?"

Todd pushed to his feet. "Nothing. I just can't imagine a story about a secret society of high school kids in the most prestigious school in the city going on a killing spree. I have better stories to focus on than something like that."

Grace rose and faced him. She tilted her head to one side and smiled. "You know, Todd, I figured out a long time ago what the difference was between the two of us. We both love to report the news. But all I want is to keep the public informed about what's going on in the world. You, on the other hand, only care how you can use your reports to propel you to a network job."

Anger flashed across his face, but it disappeared when he noticed the cameramen were listening to their conversation. He took a deep breath and flashed his smile again. "And maybe it will, Grace. You might have blown your chance with the networks, but I haven't yet."

Grace watched Todd walk away before she turned to leave the set. Derek shook his head and pointed to Todd's retreating figure. "Don't let that guy get under your skin, Grace. He's jealous that you get more fan mail than he does. Everybody here at the station knows the reason you left your job in New York, and they admire you for coming back to help take care of your father after he was wounded in that drive-by shooting. We really respect you for that, Grace."

Her heart thudded as it did every time she thought of her active father confined to a wheelchair for the rest of his life. "Thanks, Derek. My family means a lot to me."

"I know that, but you need to watch your back. Todd made life miserable for his last coanchor before you came. He wants to anchor alone, and he wants to be in a bigger market." He stuck his hands in his pockets, observed Todd as he walked away and chuckled. "I sure do wish he would get a job at another station. Everybody here would be a lot happier."

Grace laughed. "Me, too, but I don't have time to worry about Todd today. We have an interview with the mayor this afternoon. Are you ready to go?"

"Yeah, do you want to grab a bite of lunch and head on downtown to his office?"

"I'm going to get my hair cut on my lunch hour today. I'll meet you there at two. Okay?"

"Sounds good to me. I'll see you then."

Grace hurried back to her office and had just grabbed her purse when her cell phone rang. Caller ID identified it as a private number, and she frowned. She sat down behind her desk and pulled the phone to her ear. "Hello."

"Grace, I saw your broadcast on the noon news. I thought we needed to talk."

Although the voice sounded familiar, she couldn't identify it. The thought crossed her mind that the caller was using some sort of voice distortion. "Who is this?"

"For personal reasons I'd like my identity to remain

a secret. I'm sure you have anonymous callers a lot in your work. Just think of me that way—a nameless caller who wants to help you."

Grace took a deep breath. "Okay, but how did you get my private cell phone number?"

"It really doesn't matter. I called because I think you need to be careful."

Grace's hand tightened on the phone. "What's that supposed to mean?"

"It means that there are people who don't want you to get too close to the truth. Leave the past alone. You'll only end up getting hurt if you dig into Landon's death."

Grace gasped. "That sounds like a threat. Are you trying to scare me?"

"No, I'm warning you."

"Do you have some information about Landon's death?"

"Yes."

Grace sat up straighter in her chair and pressed her cell phone harder against her ear. "Was he murdered?"

"Please, Grace, for your own good, let it go."

"I can't let it go. Landon was my friend, and from the way you're talking, he was your friend, too. Don't you want people to know the truth?" He didn't answer for a moment, and she feared he'd disconnected the call. "Are you still there?"

She heard a heavy sigh. "All right. I tried to persuade you, but you haven't listened. If you're determined to continue, I see there's nothing I can do to discourage you. I have something I want to give you."

Grace's eyes grew wide. "I'll meet with you. Just tell me where and when."

"No, I don't want to do that."

"Then mail it to me."

"I suppose I could…." His voice trailed off. Then he inhaled. "No, I'll leave it for you somewhere."

She frowned. "Where?"

"I—I don't know. Somewhere that no one else would find it unless they were specifically looking for it. I'll think about it and let you know where to look. I'll call you again."

Grace's heart beat faster. She couldn't let him hang up before he'd agreed to give her his information. "Wait, don't go yet. Tell me where to look, and I'll do it."

He was quiet for a moment. "I remember hearing you say once that you are a geocacher."

"Yes, I am."

"And you said you like puzzle clues that lead to the hidden cache."

Grace frowned. "Yes, but I don't understand what that—"

"Has to do with finding Landon's killer?" Grace's skin prickled at the sudden change in the caller's voice. Moments ago it had been soft and reassuring. Suddenly it had become harsh and demanding. "You don't understand a lot of things, Miss Kincaid. If you want to find Landon's killer, you're going to have to solve much more than a geocache puzzle. I'm looking forward to seeing how smart you really are."

Grace stood up and gripped the phone tighter. "Don't threaten me, Mr. Anonymous. You may find out I'm a lot smarter than you thought."

"I doubt it."

Grace chuckled. "I get it now. You didn't call to warn me off. You wanted me more intrigued with this investigation than ever. If that was your plan, it seems to have worked. No way am I going to give up until I find out the truth."

He laughed, and the piercing tone chilled her. "Aren't you a little afraid of me?"

Her breath hitched in her throat, and her hand holding the phone shook. "N-no."

A laugh echoed in her ear. "Yes, you are. I can hear it in your voice. You'd be wise to be very afraid of me. You have no idea what's about to come down on you. Look for my instructions. Game on, Miss Kincaid."

Before she could ask another question, the call disconnected. She stared at her phone for a moment and debated whether or not she should call Alex. He'd asked her to let him know if she found out anything. So far the only thing she knew was that someone wanted to play some kind of game with evidence he claimed to have about Landon's death and he wanted her scared of him.

If her shaking legs were any indication, being afraid of him wasn't going to be a problem, but she couldn't give up now. She might have just talked to Landon's killer. Alex probably wouldn't agree, though. He would more likely think she'd received a call from some prankster who pretended to have information, but she wasn't so sure.

A cold chill ran up her arm at the memory of the voice on the phone. He said he heard her on the broadcast. Maybe she shouldn't talk about the investigation on the air. From now on, she'd be careful what she said.

There were a lot of crazy people in the world, and the last thing she needed was to become the target of one.

Alex tossed the file he'd been studying down in front of him, propped his arms on his desk and buried his face in his hands. What was the matter with him? He'd been tense ever since he came into the office. Maybe he hadn't gotten over watching a man jump to his death, but in his heart he knew that wasn't true.

The main reason he'd been distracted all morning was because he couldn't quit thinking about Grace. He'd put their past behind him years ago, and now she wanted them to work together to investigate Landon Mitchell's death. Even though he'd agreed, he wasn't sure he was ready to do that. They would have to see each other from time to time, and that could stir up a lot of old memories that needed to be forgotten.

He pushed to his feet, let out a ragged breath and ran his hand through his hair. Maybe some lunch would make him feel better. Before he could turn and leave the office, the door opened, and his partners, Brad Austin and Seth Dawtry, walked into the room. Brad held a sack with the name of Alex's favorite fast food place printed on the side.

"Seth and I were downtown and had lunch. We stopped and picked something up for you since you were holding the office down."

Alex grinned, reached for the sack and sank back into his chair. "Thanks. I was about to go get something. Now I can eat at my desk."

Brad nodded. "We thought you might not be in the mood to go out. You've had a tough morning."

Alex sighed. "Yeah, it's never easy seeing someone commit suicide."

Brad and Seth exchanged glances. "Well, if you need to talk, buddy, we're here for you."

"Thanks, guys, I appreciate it, but I'm okay."

Brad opened his mouth to say something but shook his head, walked to his desk and dropped down in his chair. Seth considered Alex for a moment before he ambled over to his desk. When his partners appeared engrossed in what they were doing, Alex relaxed in his chair and pulled the burger and fries from the bag. He picked up a French fry, dredged it in catsup and shoved it in his mouth.

The thought of the look on Mr. Mitchell's face as he plummeted toward the river flashed in Alex's mind, and he frowned. He tried to chew the French fry he'd just put in his mouth, but he might as well have been eating sawdust for all the taste he got out of the piece of potato. He swallowed the fry, picked up the remainder of his lunch and put it back in the bag for later. There was no point in forcing himself to eat when his stomach churned. Maybe he needed to stop by the drugstore on his way home this afternoon and get something for a queasy stomach.

The problem was he'd had this feeling for years. It recurred every time he saw Grace, and he'd never found any medicine that could cure what ailed him. All he had to do was keep his distance from her, and after a few days he'd feel better.

After a few minutes he pushed to his feet. "I'm going to the break room for a cup of coffee. Anybody want anything?"

Brad and Seth shook their heads, and he strode from the room. He'd only taken a few steps down the hall when he heard music drifting from the break room. He stopped, glanced down at his watch and grimaced. Just his luck. It was time for the WKIZ noon news. He hesitated at the door, unsure if he should enter or turn and walk back to his office. He rubbed his hand over his eyes, took a deep breath and walked inside.

Several officers sat on the couch that faced the television, and their gazes were locked on the picture that filled the screen. Grace sat behind the anchor desk and in her usual professional manner related the events of the morning as she looked into the camera.

He couldn't move as she switched to the video the cameraman had filmed on the bridge. He shoved his hands into his pockets, leaned up against the door frame and watched in fascination as she reported the lead-in story for the newscast. His throat tightened, and his heart thudded as he relived each terrifying moment. Perspiration dotted his forehead, and he reached up to wipe it away.

One of the officers glanced up and saw him standing in the doorway. "Hey, Crowne. That was some rescue you pulled off. I didn't know you could move that fast." The officers looked at each other and chuckled.

Alex pushed to his full height and managed a weak smile. "I just wish I could have saved Mitchell, but at least Grace Kincaid didn't go over the side, too."

He glanced back at the screen as the camera focused on Grace's face again. Behind her he could see red poinsettias arranged on shelves. As he studied her sitting among the holiday decorations on the set, he was reminded of Christmas their senior year in college. He couldn't wait for her to get back to Memphis from Philadelphia that year, but it hadn't turned out to be the happy time he'd anticipated. Instead, it had ended with his heart broken. Every Christmas since then had held little interest for him.

After a moment he stepped into the room and dropped down in a chair. He sat through the rest of Grace's newscast, but he didn't leave when the program was over and the other officers had returned to their desks.

Suddenly he felt tired. Maybe the morning's events were just catching up with him. He leaned his head back, closed his eyes and drifted on the edge of sleep. The ringing of his phone jerked him awake, and he sat up straight. He had no idea how long he'd been in the break room.

He sat up and pulled his phone from his pocket. "Hello."

"Alex, this is Grace. Are you all right? You sound groggy."

He closed his eyes and rubbed his hand over them. "I'm alone in the break room, and I must have nodded off. The phone woke me. Why are you calling?"

She hesitated a moment. "I don't know if it means anything or not, but I just had a strange phone call."

He sat up straighter. "What do you mean?"

"Someone called and wouldn't tell me who it was. He said he has something he wants me to see."

"So you think he must have some information about Landon's death?"

"I do, but as the conversation progressed, he became sinister."

Alex rubbed the back of his neck. "Did he say he would call again?"

"No. He said he was going to hide whatever it is he has and he'll send me a clue where it is. I thought you should know."

He nodded. "I'm glad you called. Did he say anything else?"

She hesitated a moment. "He said I should be afraid of him."

Alex exhaled and shook his head. "I don't like the sound of that. Be careful, Grace. Don't go to the parking lot alone when you leave work, and watch for anybody following you. Let me know if you hear from him again or if you receive anything from him."

"I will. I'll talk to you later."

He disconnected the call and sighed. This was what he'd been afraid would happen. The calls were already beginning to come. Whether or not this one was legitimate remained to be seen. But no matter, Grace's first thought had been to call him, and she'd probably do the same the next time something occurred that might affect the investigation.

The last thing he needed in his life was to spend time with Grace Kincaid, but it seemed that's where he'd been headed ever since Timothy Mitchell decided to jump off the bridge. All he could do now was guard against renewing any kind of friendship with Grace. He was determined that wasn't going to happen.

## Chapter Three

Grace pulled her car into her reserved parking spot at the television station and turned off the engine, but for some reason, she couldn't make herself get out. She didn't know if it was driving through the heavy morning traffic or her lack of sleep the night before that had left her feeling exhausted. She rubbed her hands over her eyes and tried to blot out the picture that had flashed in her mind during her sleepless night. Every time she'd closed her eyes, the scene on the bridge had popped into her mind. She saw herself grasping the bridge railing and staring down into Mr. Mitchell's wild eyes.

Her wrist throbbed, and she massaged it. A shiver went up her spine. No matter how hard she'd tried, she couldn't dispel the fear that flowed through her every time she thought of that moment.

She shook her head, took a deep breath and climbed out of the car. Thinking about what might have been was doing her no good. Today she would be thankful she was alive. She said a quick prayer of thanks as she headed into the building and down the hallway to her small office.

The minute she walked in the door she spotted the small box wrapped in brown paper on her desk. Her name and the address of the station were on the mailing label, but there were no stamps on the package. This had not come through the mail.

She was about to pick it up when a voice at the door startled her. "I see you found your delivery."

Grace whirled to see Julie Colter, a new employee, standing in the doorway. "Good morning, Julie. Did you see who delivered this?"

"Yes, it was a private messenger service. The guy asked if I would give it to you and I said I would."

Grace frowned. "Did you sign that you'd received the delivery?"

Julie shook her head. "No, he was gone before I had a chance to ask him."

Grace sighed. "Do you know the name of the messenger service?"

Julie thought for a moment before she shook her head again. "No, he just said it was a special delivery for you. I guess I assumed he was from a service." Julie's eyebrows rose, and her face turned red. "Did I do something wrong, Miss Kincaid?"

Grace hesitated before she answered. "Sometimes our newscasts can upset some people. We don't know who might send something harmful to us. We just need to be careful when accepting deliveries."

Tears welled in Julie's eyes, and she bit down on her lip. "Oh, Miss Kincaid, please don't tell the station manager I did anything wrong. I need this job. If he fired me, I don't know what I'd do."

Grace reached out and patted Julie's arm. "Now, now. Don't get upset. Nobody's going to get fired. You just need to be more careful in the future."

Julie nodded. "I will. I promise. Now, is there anything I can do for you?"

"No, thank you."

Julie eased toward the door. "Then I'll get back to work, and I promise I won't make that mistake again."

Grace nodded and didn't speak as the girl left the room. How many mistakes had Julie made since she was hired? It seemed the subject of Julie and her mishaps came up in the conversation no matter who you talked to at the station. She probably wouldn't make it much longer if her work didn't improve.

After a moment Grace turned her attention back to the package on her desk. Did it contain the clue her anonymous caller had told her about the day before? She leaned closer and studied the name and address on the mailing label. They had been typed, not handwritten, and there were no strings tied around the box, just tape to hold the paper.

Should she open it or not? Only a year ago a Memphis accountant had been injured when he opened an package that contained a bomb. Perhaps she should have Alex take a look at it or even dust it for fingerprints, but she would feel foolish if there was nothing threatening inside the envelope.

She pulled the tape loose and stepped back, then chuckled. If the box contained a bomb, a few steps away from the desk wouldn't be enough distance to

offer any protection. She eased back to the desk and
loosened the package's paper. It fell away to reveal
a square box that looked to be about eight inches on
each side.

Her heart pounded as she lifted the top of the box
and peered inside. A folded piece of paper lay atop
something wrapped in tissue paper. Frowning, she
pulled the note out and unfolded it.

Dear Miss Kincaid,
I enjoyed our chat yesterday, and I have done
as I promised. I have enclosed directions inside
this box for the first stop on your journey. For
a knowledgeable geocacher like you the puzzle
should be no problem. Solve it, and you will find
what I have left for you somewhere in the city. I
will be watching to see if you are successful. I'm
looking forward to our journey together as you
find out the truth about Landon's death.
Your Anonymous Friend

The words made Grace's skin prickle, and she read
the note several times before she reached in the box
and pulled out the tissue-wrapped object. She tore the
paper away and blinked her eyes in surprise at the
six-sided puzzle cube she held. She slowly turned it
and studied the twisty puzzle's mixture of white, red,
blue, orange, green and yellow squares. Someone had
turned the faces many times to make sure the colors
were thoroughly mixed over every surface.

Something written on one of the white squares
caught her eye, and she stared closer at it. Her breath

hitched in her throat. A quick glance over the other surfaces told her that more white squares had markings. GPS coordinates! Her caller had just sent her a challenge. Solve the puzzle by arranging all the white cubes on one side and she would have a location where she would find a clue about Landon's killer.

She dropped down in her desk chair and began to twist the faces of the puzzle in an attempt to get all the white-colored surfaces on one side. After twenty minutes she was ready to throw the toy in the trash can. She'd played with these puzzles when she was growing up and never had mastered the art of getting all the sides back in order. She doubted if she could do it now.

"What are you doing?" Todd stood in the doorway to her office. A smirk pulled at his lips, and he let his gaze drift back and forth from her face to the puzzle in her hand. "Don't you have anything better to do than play with toys? We do have a noon newscast to do, you know."

Grace opened her desk drawer, shoved the puzzle inside and stood. "I like to keep my mind sharp, Todd. You might try doing that sometime yourself."

He glared at her and took a step forward. "Someday you're going to go too far with me, Grace."

She ignored the remark and crossed her arms. "Do you need something?"

Todd shook his head. "No, I just thought I'd check and see if you'd had any response to your plea on yesterday's newscast for information about Landon Mitchell's death."

"I haven't had anything concrete yet."

He cocked one eyebrow. "But you have had something?"

She shook her head. "Nothing I can talk about."

He pursed his lips and frowned. "Okay. Let me know if I can help you with anything."

"I will."

She waited until he'd left before she sank back in her chair. Nothing would please Todd better than to scoop her on the story of Landon's death. She would have to be more careful in the future.

Grace pulled the drawer open and looked down at the puzzle. She should call Alex. She'd promised to let him know if she heard anything from her mysterious caller. She jumped up, hurried to the door and closed it before she returned to her desk and dialed Alex's cell phone. He answered on the first ring.

"Hello, Grace."

The abrupt tone of his voice startled her, and she winced. "My, my. Don't you sound grouchy this morning?"

"I'm sorry. It's already been a busy morning." His voice softened. "How are you feeling?"

"Better today."

"Good."

"I don't know if it means anything or not…" Her office door rattled as if someone was about to open it. She paused in speaking. "Hold on a minute."

She rose, walked to the door and pulled it open, but there was no one there. She stepped into the hallway and caught a glimpse of Todd just as he disappeared around the corner at the end of the hall. Had he been listening outside her door?

Frowning, she stepped back into her office and closed the door. "I'm sorry. I thought someone was at the door, but I was wrong. But the reason I called was to let you know I received a message from my caller this morning."

"Really?"

He remained silent as she related the details of her delivery this morning and her inability to solve the puzzle. "He told me this wasn't going to be easy, and he was right. So, I'm at a standstill. I don't know where to go until I get the GPS coordinates arranged on one side of the puzzle."

"This sounds weird to me, Grace. But then I've never done any geocaching. I've heard about it, and I know it's like an internet scavenger hunt. But I really don't know how it works."

She chuckled. "It doesn't seem like something you'd be interested in, but I love it. Like you said, it's an international internet scavenger hunt that's run from a website. A cache is usually a small item that can be placed along with a log book in a box or some other container and hidden aboveground. Then the person who's hidden the cache logs the coordinates on a geocaching website, and hunters enter the coordinates in a GPS to search for them."

"So the searcher gets to keep the treasure when he finds it?"

"Not necessarily. The geocacher signs the log book that's been left at the cache site and may take the item inside or leave it. If they choose to take the item, they are required to leave something of equal value for the next hunter to find. When they return home, they log into the website and report the date they found the cache. It's not about what's found in the box. It's all about the hunt. I spend a lot of my weekends looking for caches. It tests your mind, and you get a lot of exercise, too."

Alex was silent for a moment. "So whoever sent you this puzzle is familiar with geocaching, and he knows you are, too. He's left you a clue to Landon's death, and the only way you can find it is to solve the puzzle and get the coordinates. Then you'll know where to look."

"That's right. I told you I would call if I found out anything, but I have no idea whether or not I'll ever be able to get the puzzle faces turned so that all the whites are on one side."

"I was never much good at working those things, either. If you solve it, give me a call, and I'll go with you to the location. I don't want you going by yourself."

Grace sighed. "Okay, I'll let you know, but don't hold your breath. This may be a hopeless task."

"Thanks for calling, Grace, and keep in touch."

"I will."

Grace opened her desk drawer, picked up the puzzle, and twisted the surfaces. The longer she worked the more hopeless the task appeared. After about twenty minutes, she tossed the cube on her desk and rose to her feet. She might as well give up.

She placed her hands on her hips and looked down at the innocent-looking toy on her desk. Hidden on its surfaces were directions to a place that might reveal an answer to how Landon died. She had to get those coordinates lined up.

An idea hit her, and she smiled. There was more

than one way to find what she needed to know. She sat down at her computer and pulled up the internet. Within minutes she had the information she needed.

She rushed to the hallway and hurried to the small closet near the staff restroom where the custodian kept his tools. She grabbed a screwdriver, took it to her office, and sat down at her desk. Smiling to herself, she picked up the cube and followed the instructions she'd found on the internet. First she rotated the top layer by 45 degrees, and pried one of its edge cubes away from the other two layers. The piece fell to her desk.

One by one she pulled the small cubes away from the center axis of the toy and watched them tumble to her desk in a pile of colors. When they were all stripped from the cube, she laid the white stickered sides out as if they were one surface on the cube and studied them. Frowning, she rearranged the pieces until she was satisfied she'd finally gotten the correct latitude and longitude. Then she leaned forward, folded her arms on top of her desk and smiled.

The coordinates stood out from the white surfaces. All she had to do now was enter them in her GPS and she would be on her way to finding out the truth about Landon Mitchell's death. Smiling, she picked up her cell phone and punched in Alex's number. He answered on the first ring.

"Hi, Grace."

"I've figured out the coordinates."

"Already?"

She laughed. "Well, to tell the truth I took a short cut. I tore the cube apart and laid the white sides out until I had the numbers in the right order."

"That was smart. When do you want to go take a look at the cache site?"

She glanced at her watch. "It's almost time for the noon news. What if I pick you up at the police station about one-thirty?"

"Sounds good. See you then."

Grace disconnected the call and sat there a few minutes. Ever since she'd been back in Memphis, she'd tried to avoid seeing or talking with Alex. Then yesterday they'd been reunited by a man who wanted them to bring out the truth about his son's death. Although she wanted to uncover the facts, she still wasn't sure working with Alex was a good idea. Once she'd trusted Alex with all her heart, but when she'd needed him to have faith in her, he had failed her.

Her skin warmed at the thought of what Alex had said when he'd accused her the day before of wanting a story that would get her back to the networks. Although she'd denied it to Todd, in her heart she knew she hadn't really left that life behind.

Her primary reason for returning to Memphis had been to help her mother with her invalid father, but he was getting stronger every day. Maybe she could go back sometime in the future. That's why she couldn't let herself get sidetracked by old memories about Alex Crowne.

She glanced up at the clock on the wall and gasped. Thinking about what the future held for her would have to wait. Right now she had the noon broadcast to do. She picked up a pen and wrote the coordinates on a piece of paper, stuck it in an envelope and along with the puzzle pieces dropped it in her desk drawer.

\* \* \*

Alex consulted the GPS unit Grace had handed to him when he got into her car and then looked at the traffic in the lane beside them as they drove along East Parkway. "You need to change lanes. We're going to turn left onto the road that leads down to the Overton Park Pavilion up ahead."

Grace nodded and glanced in her mirrors before she eased into the left lane and put on her turn signal. "Thanks."

She hadn't said much since she'd picked him up. He wondered if it was because she was intent on finding the clue her caller said he'd left or if it was because he was with her. He shook the thought from his head and sat silent as she turned onto the road leading into the park and drove toward the parking lot at the pavilion.

When she pulled to a stop in the deserted parking lot, she glanced around. "Not many people out today."

He let his gaze drift over the pavilion and nodded. "It's almost Christmas, Grace, and the temperature is in the thirties. Not a good day to be having a picnic in the park."

Her face flushed, and she smiled. "Yeah, I guess I'm so excited about finding the cache that I wasn't thinking." She took a deep breath and reached for the door handle. "I guess there's no use waiting. Let's go."

They climbed from the car, and Alex waited until she had joined him. He held the GPS unit so that she could see it and pointed toward the line of trees at the back of the pavilion. "It looks like we need to go there. I hope your caller thought it was too cold to get very far away from the pavilion."

She smiled and pulled her coat tighter. "You should have been born in the tropics. You never did like the Memphis winters."

The memory of the two of them building a snowman in the yard of her home when they were about ten years old crossed his mind, and he smiled. "That's not true. I like some things about winter. Low temperatures don't happen to be one of them."

"Then let's get this hike over with as quickly as we can."

Together they set off toward the trees in the distance. They didn't speak as they entered the Old Forest State Natural Area of the park and ducked under some low-hanging bare tree branches. Within minutes they'd walked so far they could no longer see the pavilion. Alex plodded along, his feet growing colder by the moment, and kept his eyes on their coordinates.

Finally, he held up his hand. "This is it."

Grace stopped, propped her hands on her hips and looked around. "It has to be around here somewhere. It could be at the base of one of the trees or partially hidden under a rock. It can't be underground but somewhere that can be easily found."

Alex pointed to the right of where they stood. "I'll take the area over here, and you take the opposite side."

She nodded and turned away from him. For the next few minutes they inched their way around the area as they inspected the trunks and bases of the trees. Alex turned rocks over and inspected each low-hanging branch to see if anything was perched there. He had just finished replacing a large rock he'd picked up when Grace called out. "I have something here."

He jumped to his feet and arrived at her side just as she pulled a small box out of a hole that had rotted away at the base of a tree trunk. She stood and held up the small container. "Here it is."

"It's not a very big box."

She shrugged. "It's not always about the size. It's about what's inside."

Grace loosened the string tied around the box, pulled the top off and found a small sealed envelope lying on top of a folded piece of paper. She slid her finger beneath the flap to unseal it and shook the contents into her hand. Her eyes grew wide, and she gasped at the sterling-silver ring that fell into her palm.

Alex leaned closer and frowned. "What is it?"

Grace swallowed and struggled to speak. She held it up for him to see. "It's a friendship ring."

"Does this have some special meaning for you?"

She nodded. "Yes, Landon gave it to me for my sixteenth birthday." She pointed to the top of the ring. "He picked it out because it was designed with the infinity symbol across the top with our two birthstones set in it. He said it would always make me think of him."

Alex looked at the ring again, then back to her. "Then what's it doing here?"

"I don't know. When Landon and I quit dating, I gave him the ring back. He had changed so much I didn't want anything to remind me of him. He told me someday I would want to come back to him, and until then he was going to wear the ring on his pinkie finger. Every time I saw him in the hall at school he would have it on and would hold up his hand for me to see."

Alex frowned. "Do you think he might have been wearing it when he died?"

"After his body washed ashore, I asked his father if he was wearing the ring. I wanted to keep it to remember him by, but his father said it wasn't on his body. Do you think the killer could have taken the ring off his finger and kept it all these years?"

Alex shrugged. "It's possible. Some killers like to keep some item from their victims. But why would he want you to know he had this ring?" He glanced at the box she still held. "What is that in the bottom of the box?"

She pulled the paper out and unfolded it. "It's a note."

Alex eased closer. "What does it say?"

"'Good afternoon, Miss Kincaid. Congratulations on solving the puzzle and finding the first clue in your quest to discover how Landon really died. I thought you might like to have the ring I've kept all these years. As you know, it meant a lot to Landon. Now you must decide if you want to find out how I got it. If you want to know, then you must solve the next clue in hopes it will bring you the answers you desire. Does your search end here, or are you tempted to continue? The next move is yours, but be prepared for whatever may come.'"

Alex pulled the note from her hand and scanned it before he looked at her. "Is there nothing else inside?"

She glanced back in the box and pulled out another folded sheet of paper. "Here's something." She opened it and rolled her eyes in disgust. "It's a Sudoku puzzle."

"What? Let me see that." He glanced over the printed grid. "I see he's left the instructions for you at the bottom. Once you've solved the puzzle, you'll find the coordinates to the next clue in the sixth line across." He scanned the page for a moment before he looked back at Grace. "He's giving you clues instead of telling you what you want to know. I don't like this. He's taunting you, Grace. You need to stop this right now."

She shook her head. "But we have to keep looking into this, Alex. This guy knows something, or he wouldn't have this ring. He has to be the killer."

Alex shook his head. "Not we, Grace. This is getting out of hand. First he gives you an anonymous call, then he sends you a puzzle to find his hidden message, and when you do, there's another clue that threatens you. This guy is setting you up for something bad, and I don't like it. This is a matter for the police."

She glared at him. "No, I'm not giving up. I've been trained to follow a story wherever it goes. I'll keep working on this whether you help me or not."

"Grace, you're not listening to me. This is for your own good. I don't want to see you get hurt."

She snatched the note out of his hand and whirled. "I'm not going to get hurt. And I'm not giving up." She glanced over her shoulder as she stormed back through the forest.

He watched her go and shook his head in dismay. Yesterday Grace had accused him of being stubborn, but when she set her mind to something, she wouldn't give up. He kicked at a clump of dirt on the ground and took a deep breath.

She was determined to follow through on this, and he knew he'd do what he'd done ever since they were children. He'd be right there with her looking out for her. How could she still have a hold on him after all these years and after all they'd gone through? But she did, and he couldn't deny it. Maybe if he helped her with this case he could finally close the chapter on Grace Kincaid and put her out of his life permanently.

He jogged back through the forest to tell her he'd help her. When he emerged from the forest, he caught sight of her already in the parking lot. She stood next to her car, her cell phone to her ear. His skin prickled. Something wasn't right. As he got closer, he realized what it was. All four tires of her car had been slashed.

"Yes, the pavilion in Overton Park. I'm standing beside the car." She disconnected the call and turned as he came to a stop next to her. "I called the garage that I use. They'll take care of this and check to make sure no other damage was done before they deliver the car to my home later today."

"Good." He glanced around at the deserted parking lot. "I didn't see anybody when I came out of the forest. Did you?"

She nodded. "Just as I stepped out of the tree line, a car pulled out of the parking lot. At that distance I couldn't tell who was driving."

A gust of wind blew across the parking lot, and Alex shivered. "It's getting colder. I'll call Brad to come pick us up. Why don't we get in the car and wait for him there?"

She nodded. "That sounds good to me."

He walked over and opened the driver's door for her to step inside. Before she could move, the sharp crack of a gun split the quiet air, and a bullet slammed into the open car door. Alex lunged for Grace and knocked her to the ground as the second shot screamed over their heads.

"Get to the other side of the car," he yelled as he pulled his phone from the clip on his belt with one hand and his gun with the other. The shots appeared to have come from the forest. He fired in that direction, but he had no idea where the shooter was.

Grace scooted on her stomach to the far side of the car as shots continued to hit the side of her car. Alex crawled behind, his phone pressed to his ear as he fired off two more shots. "Officer under fire," he shouted into the phone. "Picnic pavilion at Overton Park. Need backup now!"

"Officers on their way." The 911 operator's voice crackled over the phone.

He grit his teeth and hoped they weren't too late as another bullet shattered the car's headlight. Fragments from the shattered headlight rained down on them as they scrambled to the far side of the car.

Alex sat up with his back pressed against the fender of the car and tried to peer around the front, but another bullet plowed into the front bumper. The gunfire seemed to be coming from a different direction. Maybe the shooter was working his way around so he had a clear shot at them now huddled beside the car.

Grace started to push up from the ground, but Alex shoved her back down and fell on top of her to shield her body as another bullet ripped past their heads. He was about to urge Grace to crawl to the back of the car when three police cruisers roared into the parking lot.

Before he could sit up, the officers, one of them holding a dog, jumped out of the cars, fanned out across the parking lot and headed toward the trees at the edge of the forest. Alex sat up and pulled Grace into a sitting position.

The lieutenant in charge of the officers squatted down beside them. "What happened here?"

Alex stood up and pulled Grace to her feet. "Thanks for getting here so quickly," he said as he began to relate the events in the park to the officer.

After about fifteen minutes one of the officers emerged from the forest and jogged to where they waited. "We searched the woods, sir. The dog hit on several places where the shooter had stood when he fired, but he was gone. He must have had his escape route planned well."

Alex nodded. "I could tell he was moving, trying to get a better shot."

"We're glad neither of you were hurt," the lieutenant said. His gaze traveled over the bullet-marked car and shook his head. "Too bad about the car. We're going to take another look in the woods before we go, but we'll be glad to give you a ride when we leave."

Alex shook his head. "No need for that. I'll call my partner." He pulled out his cell phone and punched in Brad's number.

Brad answered right away. "Hello."

"Brad, it's Alex. Grace and I are at the Overton Park Pavilion, and we need a ride. Can you come pick us up?"

"Sure, I'll be there right away."

"Thanks."

He disconnected the call and shoved the phone back in his pocket. "Brad should be here shortly. He can take you back to the television station. Would you like for me to give you a ride home this evening?"

"I'd appreciate it. I'll be ready as soon as the six o'clock news is over." A cold wind blew across the parking lot, and she drew her coat closer around her. She bit down on her lip and pointed to her car. "This doesn't change anything, Alex. I'm still going to pursue this story."

He gritted his teeth. "What's the matter with you? Are you crazy? Somebody just tried to kill us, and you want to keep going with this investigation? This is something for the police to address, not you."

"I don't understand why he waited until we got back to the car to shoot at us. He could have done that while we were in the forest."

Alex nodded. "I was wondering the same thing."

"What if he didn't intend to kill us? What if he only wanted to scare us?" She pulled the note from her pocket. "I think he wants us to find the next clue."

"We could offer what-ifs all day long and not be any closer to the truth than we are now," Alex said. "The facts are that someone lured you to a deserted place then shot at you. Whether or not he meant to kill you doesn't matter. Any one of those bullets could have found their mark. This is where your involvement with this investigation has to end."

"No, it doesn't." Tears sparkled in her eyes, and she pulled Landon's friendship ring from her pocket and slipped it on her finger. "I'm convinced that whoever shot at us took this ring off Landon's finger after he killed him. I promised his father I would find out the truth, and I'm not giving up until I know what it is."

"Grace, please…"

"No! I won't give up even if I have to do this on my own."

He exhaled and shook his head. It would do no good to argue with her, and he'd come to the decision about what he should do while he was still in the forest. "I know I'm wasting my breath trying to get you to see reason, Grace. If you're determined, I'm not going to let you do this alone." He sighed and reached for the paper she still held. "I work these puzzles all the time. I'll get started on it tonight."

"Thank you, Alex." She hesitated a moment, and he knew she was about to ask him to do something else.

He groaned inwardly. "I know that look, Grace. What else do you want me to do?"

"When you take me home, I'd like for you to come inside and be with me when I tell my parents what happened today."

He shook his head. "I don't know, Grace. Your father never did like me. To him I'll always be the gardener's son. I doubt if my presence will make any difference."

"You're wrong. My father is very different from when you knew him, and I want you to see for yourself. Please do this."

He wanted to tell her no, but her eyes begged him to do this. After a moment, he nodded. "Okay, I'll come in for a few minutes."

She smiled. "Thank you, Alex."

She crossed her arms and leaned back against the car. Alex turned and stared into the woods where the officers continued to search. He glanced down at the broken headlights and the bullet holes in the car. They had barely missed being killed today.

Cold fear washed over him, and he rubbed the hair on the back of his neck. Grace had opened a Pandora's box with her announcement on air that she was going to look into Landon Mitchell's death. There was nothing he could do to stop what might come, but one thing he could do was be there to make sure nothing happened to Grace.

# Chapter Four

Grace gazed out the window of Alex's car as he drove toward her home on the outskirts of Memphis. Usually she enjoyed the ride home from work, but not today. She had tried all afternoon to push her brush with death from her mind, but she couldn't. She didn't know if she would ever forget how those bullets had sounded as they hit her car. Thankfully, neither she nor Alex had been hurt, but the experience wasn't one she would soon forget.

Now she had to get through another troubling time. She had to tell her parents. If she didn't, they might read about it in the paper or hear it on the news. With her father's condition, she didn't want him upset, but she didn't see any way around it.

She straightened in her seat as they approached the edge of her family's property. Alex pulled into the driveway of the house, stopped at the gate and swiveled in his seat to face her. "Is the security code same or has it been changed?"

She smiled. "It's still the same."

Alex punched in the code and drove through the gates onto the grounds of the home where she and Alex had played as children while his father was working there. He drove forward and stopped in front of the sprawling house. "Here we are. Are you sure you want me to come in?"

"I am." She glanced down at her watch and opened the car door. "My parents may not be home yet. Dad had an appointment scheduled with a physical therapist for late this afternoon. I'm sure the cook has something for us to munch on while we're waiting for them. Come on inside."

Fifteen minutes later Grace and Alex sat on the sofa in the den and watched the blue gas flames flickering around the logs in the fireplace across the room. Grace set her coffee cup on the table at the end of the couch and turned to face Alex who sat at the other end. "I'm glad we have this time together before my parents get home. Everything has happened so fast for the past two days that we haven't had time to talk."

He set his cup down and exhaled. "Talk about what, Grace? I think we've probably said it all at one time or another."

"There are several things I'd like to say. First of all, I want to tell you about my father."

"What about him?"

She took a deep breath. "I want you to know what he's gone through in the past year. After the drive-by shooting he was in bed for a long time before he reached the point where he could be in a wheelchair. During that time the pastor of the church nearby visited him a lot and shared with him the things in life that are really important and how God can get you through the bad times. After a lot of Bible study and prayer, Dad turned his life over to God. Now he's trying to reach out to those he may have hurt in the past and apologize."

"B-but this is so unlike him. You're telling me that your father has become a believer?"

"I am. My mother and I are, too. My father's shooting has changed everyone in the Kincaid household. For the first time since I can remember, we're a real family. We also attend church every Sunday."

"Wow. I can't believe I'm hearing this."

She smiled. "It's true. Because I've put my trust in God, I've been able to get through a lot this past year, but there's one thing I know I have to do. I want to be friends with you again. I want you to forgive me for all the mistakes I made. I'm praying you can do that, and I think this is the time to try. I don't want us to go on saying and doing things that hurt each other. I think it's time we called a truce, especially since you've saved my life twice since yesterday morning."

He shook his head. "I don't know if we can ever be friends again, Grace. I'm glad I was there to save your life, but I was only doing my job."

She blinked to keep the tears from filling her eyes. "I'd like to think it was a bit more personal than that. But even if it's not, we can't keep going through life pretending the other one doesn't exist."

He took a deep breath. "Now that you're back in Memphis, it's hard to pretend you don't exist. I see you on television nearly every day or I see your picture in the paper. I saw you on the society page not too long ago at a dinner at your country club, and also at a swanky party for the Cotton Carnival. You looked like you were surrounded by your friends."

She looked at him for a moment before she spoke. "I have lots of friends that I enjoy being with. I'd like for us to be friends again."

He pulled his gaze away from her and looked into the fireplace flames again. As she took in his profile, the muscle in his jaw twitched. "I don't think that's going to happen. There's too much history between us, Grace."

She swallowed the lump in her throat and leaned forward. "We can try." She closed her eyes for a moment and bit down on her lip. When she opened her eyes, he was staring at her again. "I don't expect us to ever go back to where we were that summer before our senior year in college. I want to go back to the children we were when I followed you everywhere."

He let his gaze drift around the room. His eyes locked on the Christmas tree with the presents piled underneath and shook his head. "I've never seen that many presents under one tree in my life. It's just one more reminder of the differences in our lives. We may have been childhood friends, but you were the daughter of the rich banker and I was the son of his gardener. It wasn't okay with your father for you to be my friend then, and it certainly wasn't when I got that scholarship to attend the same private school as you."

"You know I didn't care what my father thought. I was thrilled when you got that athletic scholarship and we got to see each other at school."

A snort of disgust rumbled in Alex's throat. "Yeah,

we went to the same school, but I was never one of the guys." He grimaced. "Landon Mitchell and his friends never let me forget it."

Grace sank back against her chair. "I tried to tell you none of that mattered. Not to me, at least."

He shrugged. "Well, being accepted by the group matters to a high school kid, and it did to me. When I look back on it now, I see it from an adult's perspective, but it hurt back then."

"Did I ever make you feel like you weren't accepted?"

"No, but everything changed when you left for University of Pennsylvania and I stayed here at the University of Memphis. It was like I was free of all those childhood feelings and I was moving on with my life."

Grace sighed. "And then we ran into each other on Beale Street the summer before our senior years in college."

His eyebrows drew together, and he scowled. "There's no need for us to rehash all our history, Grace. To you it was a summer romance. To me it was more."

She clenched her fists in her lap and shook her head. "It was more to me, too. I really missed you that fall when I went back to school."

He rolled his eyes and glanced back at the blinking lights of the decorated tree. "Yeah, I sure had a merry Christmas that year when I found out you'd been making plans for us. You had the rest of our lives all planned out."

Her anger flared, but she tried to extinguish it. She would never be able to make Alex see the truth if she argued with him. "I didn't. I only wanted to take the chance to turn my internship at the Philadelphia television station into my first real job. They had offered me a good opportunity, one a new college graduate couldn't get anywhere else. You could be a cop anywhere."

His lips thinned, and he gritted his teeth. "I didn't want to be a cop anywhere. I wanted to be one right here in Memphis. I thought if you really loved me, you'd want me to work where I'd be the happiest."

"Ever since we were children, you'd done everything you could to make me happy. I thought if you could see what a great opportunity it was for me, you would give in and come to Philadelphia to work."

He shook his head. "You never understood how I love Memphis. It's where I was born and where I want to spend my life. In my job I've come to know the streets, the back alleys and the people who inhabit those places. I feel the music of Beale Street in my soul, and I love to watch the Mississippi River roll by. I could never feel that way about another place. I didn't want Philadelphia."

"So you made me choose."

He rubbed the back of his neck and sneered. "Yeah, and we both know which you chose—Philadelphia and all it offered for you. The boy who had loved you since he was ten years old was left behind without a second thought."

She shook her head. "No, you're wrong about that. I thought you'd change your mind after a while and come join me."

"And I thought you'd come back home. I waited a year for you, but you stayed in Philadelphia. Of course

I found out it wasn't just the job. It was Richard Champion the news anchor that was so appealing to you."

Grace almost flinched from the anger in Alex's eyes. Could she ever make him understand what it had been like for her alone in Philadelphia? "All right. Let's talk about Richard. He was my mentor at the TV station when I was doing my internship, nothing more. When I started my job there after graduation, he was kind to me. He knew we had broken up, and he offered me a shoulder to cry on. Before I knew it, we were going out to dinner, taking in movies or just hanging out and talking. He was my friend."

Alex's eyebrows arched. "How long did the *friendship* last?"

"I waited a year for you, Alex, but you didn't come. By that time I had a job, and I liked it. When Richard asked me to marry him, I couldn't think of a reason to say no. We got along well, and we understood what the other one went through in our jobs. There was just one thing lacking, although I didn't realize it at the time."

"What was that?"

"I didn't love him."

He leaned forward and gazed at her. "You can't imagine what I went through thinking about you married to that guy. But what happened? That's part of the story I've always wanted to know. Why didn't you marry him?"

Grace swallowed hard and met his gaze. "Because two weeks before the wedding I caught him with the weather girl at the station. As it turns out, she was only one of the women he was having an affair with."

A look of surprise flashed on Alex's face, and he

slumped back in his seat. "So that's why you went to New York to work instead of staying in Philadelphia."

"Yes."

"And now? Why did you really come home, Grace?"

"I'll be honest with you, Alex. I didn't want to quit my job in New York, but I did because I love my family. My father may be rich, but his money didn't help him any when he was shot. He's lucky to be alive even if he is confined to wheelchair for the rest of his life."

His features softened, and he nodded. "I was sorry to hear about that. I looked into the case after I joined the Cold Case Unit, but there weren't any leads. I wish I could have solved the case for you."

"I wish you could have, too." She took a deep breath. "When I first came back, Laura and I shared a house. After she and Brad married, my mother was having a difficult time, and I decided to move home. It was the best for all of us. I like my job at the station, and I come home to my family every night. It's not a very exciting life, but it's the one I have."

He didn't say anything for a moment, then he smiled. "Well, after what's happened the past two days, I'd say your life has just gotten a lot more exciting."

She laughed. "You can say that again." Her smile faded. "Do you think we can ever be friends again?"

He exhaled a long breath. "I don't know, Grace. I've spent the past five years angry at you for dismissing my feelings so easily. When I told you I loved you, I thought I could trust you with my heart. But you broke it, and I don't know if I can ever get the trust back I felt for you."

She nodded. "I understand. Now I know I was selfish and self-centered. I only thought of what I wanted. I never tried to come up with a compromise that could make us both happy. But then, neither did you."

"I guess we both failed. I guess we should chalk our romance up to one of those things that was never meant to be and go from there."

It surprised her to think that he might be right. She didn't know if her life would have been different if she'd never fallen in love with Alex, but at least she wouldn't have spent years getting over him. "I think it's time we put the past behind us and concentrate on what we're doing now. Maybe in discovering the truth about Landon's death, we can find our way back to being the friends we were when we were children."

He shook his head. "I don't know, Grace. Going back may be too difficult. But maybe we can at least be cordial to each other while we're working together."

She smiled. "Maybe so."

"Excuse me, Miss Kincaid."

Grace looked over her shoulder to see the maid standing in the doorway. "What is it, Nancy?"

"Your mother's car just drove into the garage. You said you wanted to know when she arrived so you could help her get your father inside."

Grace jumped to her feet. "Thank you, Nancy. Tell her I'll be right there."

She turned back to Alex. "I'm glad we had this talk today." She glanced at her watch and frowned. "They're later than usual. I'm sure my father will be hungry and will want to eat right away. Why don't you stay for dinner?"

Alex rose from the sofa and shook his head. "No, I really should go."

Grace waved her hand in dismissal. "Don't be silly. My parents will be glad to see you. Besides, I really do need you with me when I tell them about today."

She held her breath as he appeared to debate whether or not to stay. After a moment, he nodded. "Okay, if you're sure it will be all right."

"Of course it is. Now sit back down and wait until I help get my father in the house. I'll be back in a few minutes."

Grace hurried from the room before Alex had time to think up another reason to leave. She dreaded telling her parents about the incident in the park, but it had to be done. Her father didn't need something else to worry about right now. He needed to concentrate on the therapy that was restoring some movement to his legs.

Her prayer every night was that someday her father would be able to stand again. She hadn't dared pray yet that he could walk, just stand. If he could do that, it would make walking possible.

She glanced down at the friendship ring on her finger and said a quick prayer that God would lead her to the person who had kept Landon's ring for the past twelve years. If she and Alex could find him, they might find that he and Landon's killer were one and the same.

Dinner was drawing to a close, and Alex hoped he could soon make his exit. All during the meal Grace had tried to downplay the events of the past two days as best she could. He couldn't believe how her account of their experience in the park had lacked certain details. To hear her tell it, someone had slashed her tires and shot up her car. She'd left out the part where she and Alex had been present and cowering beside the car as bullets whizzed past them. He had arched his eyebrows as she related her version of the story, and she had frowned and given a slight shake of her head.

Her father's piercing blue eyes bored into him. "Thank you, Alex, for what you did yesterday at the bridge and taking care of her car in the park. Our family is indebted to you."

A frown pulled at Alex's forehead, and he rubbed his hand across his face. He could hardly believe Grace's father was speaking to him like this. In the past he'd always treated Alex like someone beneath the social level of his family and had ignored him when they met. Now there was a warm tone to his words, and Alex found it difficult to associate it with the man he had once known.

"There's no need to thank me, sir. I was just doing my job. Of course, since it was Grace, I was especially thankful I was successful."

"And so are her mother and I." He hesitated a moment. "I know your father must be very proud of your rise through the ranks in the police department."

"He is, sir."

"Well, I'm happy for you, too, but I do miss your father since he retired to Florida. When you speak to him, tell him hello for me."

"I'll do that. He'll be glad to know you miss him."

As the maid removed the dessert plates, Mr. Kincaid pushed the controls on his wheelchair and backed away from the table. "Let's have coffee in the den."

Alex moved to the back of Mrs. Kincaid's chair, assisted her as she rose to her feet and smiled. "Thank you for a wonderful dinner, Mrs. Kincaid."

She patted his arm and looked up into his eyes. "It was a pleasure having you, Alex, and please call us Martha and Harrison."

He darted a quick glance in Grace's direction before he swallowed and nodded. "Thank you. I'd like that."

Harrison led the way as they left the dining room and headed toward the den. When they entered the den, the coffee service sat on the table in front of the sofa. Martha pointed to it as she sank into a chair next to her husband's wheelchair. "Grace, would you serve the coffee?"

Grace nodded, sat down on the sofa and picked up the silver coffeepot. Her hand trembled a bit when Alex settled next to her. She smiled and handed him the first cup. "Black, just the way you like it."

A small smile pulled at his lips as he took the cup. "I see you can remember some things better than others."

Grace ducked her head and nodded before she poured two cups for her parents. When they were finally served, Alex glanced at Grace's father. "You seem to be doing well handling your wheelchair, Mr. Kin— I mean Harrison."

He nodded and set his cup on the tray of the wheelchair. "Yes. It took a while to get used to the controls of this motorized contraption, but I think I have it mastered now. It's not like walking, but it gets me around."

"I'm glad to see you're doing so well."

Harrison pursed his lips before he spoke. "I don't think I'd be doing so well today if you hadn't been there to help Grace yesterday and today. I want you to know how grateful we are to you."

Alex set his cup down and shook his head. "You've already thanked me for what I did, but I'm glad I was there, too. I'm sure any other policeman would have done the same."

"They might have done the same, but it wouldn't have meant as much to me. Especially with our history."

Alex shook his head. "Please, there's no need…"

He held up and hand and interrupted him. "Oh, but there is. I've had a lot of time to think this past year, and some of the things I've remembered have troubled me a great deal. One of those things is how I acted toward you in the past. I never liked your coming here with your father, but I tolerated it because he was the best gardener I'd ever had and because I knew he didn't want to leave you home alone after your mother passed away. I'm afraid I wasn't very gracious to you, and I said things that must have cut deeply into a child's heart."

Grace stilled and glanced at Alex. A slight flush covered her cheeks. He took a deep breath. "You're right about that, but it's in the past."

"Then when Grace told me the two of you were in love," her father continued, "I behaved even worse. I'm saying all this tonight, Alex, because I now realize how wrong I was to judge you because of my misguided ideas about social position. I've wanted to tell you this for some time, and I'm glad you're here tonight so I can. I want to ask you to forgive me for how I've treated you in the past. I hope you can find it in your heart to do so."

After a moment, Alex swallowed. "I forgive you,

Mr. Kincaid, and I thank you for telling me this. It means a lot to me."

Her father smiled. "Harrison, Alex. No more Mr. Kincaid."

A slow grin pulled at Alex's lips. "That may take some time, but I'll try."

Harrison let out a big breath. "Good. Now that's all taken care of, we can finish our coffee."

A rustling sound at the door alerted them that some-one had entered, and Alex glanced over his shoulder at Nancy, the maid, who stood just inside the room. She looked at Grace. "Excuse me, Miss Grace, a man from Hammonds Garage is on the phone. He says he needs to talk to you about all the damage to your car."

Grace set her cup on the coffee table and jumped to her feet. "Thanks, Nancy."

Her father glanced at Grace. "All the damage? I thought you said it was just a few bullet holes."

She cast a frantic look at Alex who had also risen be-fore she responded. "I'll, uh, go see what he has to say."

Her father shook his head. "No. I can tell you're hid-ing something from me. What's going on?" He moved his chair closer and glared at her. "I may be in a wheel-chair, but I still have my mental faculties. Are you not telling me something?"

Grace glanced over at the maid. "Nancy, please tell Mr. Hammonds I'll call him later." She turned back to her father. "Please, Dad, the doctor has told us it's not good for you to get upset. I was only trying to spare you the details."

Her father grasped the arms of his wheelchair and gritted his teeth. "Grace, tell me what's going on."

Even in his present condition, Grace's father could still create a commanding presence. Alex had seen it many times, and tonight was no exception. Grace turned to him, a pleading look on her face. "Alex, help me out here…."

Alex took a deep breath. "I'm sure Grace didn't want to worry you by not telling you everything that happened in the park today. The truth is her car was bombarded with gunfire today while we were huddled behind it." His voice seemed to echo in the now-quiet room.

Her father's face paled, and his mouth hung open. Her mother bolted out of her chair. "What did you say?"

Alex glanced at Grace and sighed. "I'm sorry, Grace, but they deserve to know what happened."

"What are you talking about?" Mr. Kincaid's voice thundered across the room.

Grace started to protest, but Alex held up his hand. "No, Grace. They need to know the truth." Before she could protest again, he began to speak and didn't quit until he had told them everything that had happened since the incident on the bridge. "So," he concluded, "I think Grace needs to back away from this story and let the police handle it."

"And I think you're right," her father said.

"So do I," her mother added.

Grace clasped her hands in her lap and stared down at them for a few moments before she took a deep breath, rose slowly to her feet and looked at her parents. "I understand your concern, but I can't back down from this. You knew when I entered this type of work that I might be called on to report stories that would put me in danger, but that's one of the things that drew me to journalism. I love the excitement of following a story, and I want to find out what happened to Landon. He was my friend, and I think I owe it to him to find out the truth about his death."

Her mother's eyes filled with tears. "Even at the expense of worrying your parents?"

Grace hurried to her mother's side and grasped her hands. "I don't want to worry you and Dad, but this is something I have to do." She glanced back at Alex. "Besides, I'll be safe. Alex has agreed to help me."

Her father studied them for a moment before he shook his head. "Don't you understand? Sometimes we have no control over what happens to us. Look at me. I'm a prime example of that. I never thought I'd end up in a wheelchair, but here I am."

Grace stared down at her clutched hands in her lap. "Dad, please, don't get upset."

"No," he said. "You have to understand how quickly something can happen that will change your life forever. Nothing seemed out of the ordinary when I left my office the day I was shot. People were leaving their workplaces, and the street was filled with traffic. All of a sudden I heard the roar of a car and gunshots. It took a few seconds for me to realize I was on the ground and bleeding. Even with so many potential witnesses around, nobody could describe the car or the shooter. The police thought someone shot into the crowd, and I was the unlucky one hit. I don't want this or even something worse for you."

"Please, Dad, try to understand. This means a lot to me."

"Grace, your mother and I think—"

Alex stepped forward and interrupted. "I think you're wasting your breath. I've already tried to talk Grace out of this. But I promise you, I'll stick close to her and make sure nothing happens to her."

Grace mouthed the words *thank you* before she turned to her father. "See, Dad? Alex will be with me."

Her father exhaled a deep breath and nodded. "Very well then. I don't like it, but I'll feel better if Alex is with you. Please be careful. I don't think your mother and I could stand it if anything happened to you."

Grace bent over her father and kissed his cheek, then stepped beside her mother and did the same thing. "Thank you. I love you both so much. I promise I'll be careful."

Tears flooded her father's eyes, and he glanced at Alex. "Promise me you'll take care of my daughter, Alex."

Alex nodded. "I'll do everything in my power to keep her safe, sir."

"Good." He cleared his throat and glanced at her mother. "Now why don't you help me to my room, and we can leave these two young people alone?"

"You don't have to do that," Alex protested.

Her father shook his head. "No, I'm tired. I had a rough day with my therapist. I'm ready to go to bed." He smiled at them. "Good night, Alex. It was good to have you in our home, and, Grace, I'll see you in the morning."

Alex stood next to Grace as her mother followed the slowly moving wheelchair from the room. When the door closed, she turned back to Alex. "Thank you for supporting me."

He rubbed the back of his neck and shook his head.

"I don't think I did you any favors. I'd feel better if you'd do what your father wanted and forget all about Landon Mitchell's death."

"I can't do that."

He studied her for a moment. "No, I guess you can't. You always went after what you wanted, and it didn't matter what anybody else said or if they got hurt as long as you got your way. You'd think after all these years I would have learned my lesson, but I guess I haven't." He exhaled and pulled the Sudoku puzzle from his pocket. "Why don't we work on this now?"

Before she could answer, he strode across the room, grabbed a chair and carried it to the desk by the window. After a moment she followed, and they sank down in the two chairs now at the desk.

Neither of them spoke. Then Alex laid the paper he held on the desk, pulled a pencil from a cup that held a variety of writing instruments and began to study the puzzle. Beside him Grace crossed her arms and fidgeted as the minutes went by, but she didn't say anything.

Grace's anger radiated out of her body like a blazing fire consuming everything in its path. Alex heard the intake of her breath and knew what that meant. He'd experienced enough of her lectures in the past to know. He dropped the pencil onto the desk and leaned back in the chair.

"Okay, let's have it."

She hesitated. "Have what?"

"The lecture you're about to deliver. What is it this time? I'm insensitive to your feelings, or I don't under-

stand you or your opinion is never important to me?
Which one is it? I've heard them all."

He turned to her, and his heart pricked at the tears
she tried unsuccessfully to blink from her eyes. Her
mouth opened as if she meant to speak, but she said
nothing. Her shoulders drooped, and her body appeared
to deflate. She didn't move but held her gaze steady on
him. Finally, she frowned and slowly reached across
until her hand rested on his arm.

"Was I really that awful, Alex? Did I make you feel
like I thought I was superior?"

The sudden shift in her mood startled him, and he
regretted the harsh tone he'd used with her. His skin
grew warm where she touched him, and he had to force
himself not to cover her hand with his. He swallowed
as he stared at her. "Sometimes."

A tear escaped the corner of her eye and trickled
down her cheek. "I'm so sorry. I didn't realize." She
closed her eyes and shook her head. Then she reopened
her eyes and looked at him with a sad expression that
stabbed at his heart. "I guess old habits are hard to
break. I admit when I turned toward you a few minutes ago I was going to let you know that I wasn't the
only one at fault when we broke up. We were young,
and we wanted different things. We gave up too easily."

Alex pulled his arm toward him, and her hand released him. He rubbed his eyes and shook his head.
"Yeah, but we had a lot going against us, Grace. You
wanted a life away from Memphis and I didn't. Besides
that, your family didn't like me." He sighed. "I guess
it turned out all right in the end."

"It will turn out all right only if we can forgive each

other and try to be friends again. Don't you want us to be able to be together without reliving all the hurts of the past?"

He didn't know how to answer her. He wished they could go back and capture the childhood friendship they'd had, but he didn't know if he could do that or not. However he felt, though, he had promised her father he would make sure nothing happened to her on her mission to find out the truth about Landon's death. But could his battered heart survive letting Grace back into his life? Alex and Grace together again. This time as friends. Nothing more.

Finally, he nodded. "I want to see if we can. I promise I'll do my part, and I won't bring up the past again."

She smiled, and the light from the room's crystal chandelier reflected in the tears standing in her eyes. "I won't, either. We'll start anew tomorrow, and we'll concentrate on finding the answer to Landon's death. Maybe by working together we can achieve some kind of truce between the two of us."

He squeezed her hand and smiled. "Maybe so." He picked up the puzzle from the desk and pushed to his feet. "I think I'd better go now. We both have a lot to think about. I'll finish the puzzle and come by the TV station tomorrow."

She smiled and stood beside him. "That sounds good. Make it after lunch if possible. The mornings are hectic."

"I have no idea how long this will take me, but I won't come in the morning."

"I'll see you to the door."

They walked from the room with Alex right behind

her. When Grace opened the front door, she smiled at him again. "Thank you for coming, Alex. You have eased my father's mind a lot. He's been so concerned that you wouldn't forgive him."

"I'm glad I came, too. I'd like to come see your father again sometime if he'd like."

"He would be thrilled. He gets very lonely."

Alex stepped outside and turned back to face Grace. "Then tell him I'll drop by from time to time to see how he's doing. Tell your mother thank you for the wonderful meal, and I'll see you tomorrow. Good night."

"Good night, Alex."

He walked to his car, which he'd parked in the circle driveway in front of the house, and got in. Grace stood in the doorway as he headed back to the main gate. Just before he got there, it opened, and he drove out onto the road. She must have opened it for him.

Alex settled back in his seat and glanced up at the bright Memphis skyline in the distance. He turned the car toward the city and smiled. All in all the evening had been a success, and he felt better than he had in a long time.

He patted the right side of his chest, and the puzzle paper inside his pocket rustled. Maybe this clue would give them some answers to Landon Mitchell's death. By tomorrow this time, he might be able to close a case that had been cold for twelve years. If they did solve the case, Alex had one regret—Landon's father wouldn't be there to know.

## Chapter Five

With the noon newscast completed, Grace hurried off the set toward her office. She had almost reached her destination when she realized she wasn't alone. She stopped and turned to face Todd, who had followed her.

She crossed her arms and arched an eyebrow. "Is there something I can do for you, Todd?"

"I've been concerned about your injury and wanted to ask how you're feeling." He smiled, and she wondered why his trademark grin never quite reached his eyes. Perhaps it was because she'd seen him practicing the expression in front of a mirror from time to time. She wasn't about to be fooled by his insincere interest in her well-being.

Grace pasted a smile on her face. "I'm almost as good as new, but thanks for asking."

She turned to leave, but he took a step closer. "Any leads in the investigation of your friend's death?"

She shook her head. "Nothing yet, but don't worry. If I learn anything, you'll be the *last* person I tell."

His smile disappeared, and anger flashed in his

eyes. "Don't get smart with me. I simply asked you a question."

"A question?" She frowned at him and took his measure. "I thought you might know the answer already. I have a feeling you're keeping a close watch on me."

His face turned red, and his eyes grew wide. "I—I don't know what you're talking about."

"Oh, come on, Todd. I know you'd like to get out of Memphis, and you'd do anything to make it happen, even snatch a story right out from under one of your colleagues. I've heard the stories about what you did to your last coanchor, and I don't intend to let you do that to me."

He shook his head. "I could care less about your story. I can find my own without any help from you." His angry voice echoed down the hall, and several cameramen who were standing at the other end turned and stared at them. He stepped closer and lowered his voice. "You're making a big mistake if you think you scare me. I intend to go somewhere else, and I won't allow you or anybody else to stop me."

She studied him for a moment before she spoke. "I assure you I won't stop you from going, but let this be a warning to you, Todd. You stay away from me and from my story. I'm going to be watching to make sure you do. If you want to get to the networks so badly, do it on your own. Don't use my work as your stepping stone."

Before he could reply, she whirled and stormed down the hallway. When she rounded the corner leading toward her office, she came to an abrupt halt. Alex, his back to her and with his cell phone to his ear, leaned against the wall across from her office door. She drank in the familiar sight. A smile tugged at her lips when she noticed his hair touching his collar in the back. How many times in the past had she reminded him it was time to get a haircut?

"I'll check in with you later, Brad," she heard him say, and she shook her head to rid it of those troubling thoughts from the past.

Grace took a deep breath and stepped closer. "Hello, Alex. I wondered when you would come by."

He straightened to his full height and turned to face her. He smiled as he slipped his phone in his pocket. "Hi, Grace," he said. "I arrived while you were doing the newscast. Some girl named Julie offered to let me sit in your office, but I told her I'd wait in the hall."

Grace rolled her eyes as she pushed the door open. "Julie is new here. We're having a time training her in proper office procedures. She's very naive." She grinned at him and waved him to a chair as she sat down in her desk chair. "Of course I wouldn't have minded you waiting in here."

"No problem." He pulled the puzzle out of his pocket. "I finished this while I was having my coffee this morning. I have the coordinates."

She reached across the desk. "May I see it?"

He hesitated a moment. "I suppose I'm hoping you'll give up this search." When she didn't respond, he sighed and handed her the puzzle. "I've written the coordinates at the bottom of the page."

She nodded and studied the completed puzzle. "I'm glad you like to do these. I never can get the numbers right. Are you sure this is correct?"

He nodded. "It has to be. All the lines across and all those going down have the numbers one through nine in them. You know you're wrong when you get to a point that some line has two of the same numbers in it. Then you've made a mistake. I did this very carefully, and there are no mistakes showing up."

"I'm not questioning you, Alex, but I've been doing a lot of thinking since I received that call and the puzzles started coming. Something popped into my mind this morning, and I wanted to ask your opinion."

"Okay, what is it?"

She took a deep breath. "Do you think Mr. Mitchell died in the fall from the bridge?"

"Of course he did. Nobody could have survived that fall."

"How can you be sure? You never recovered a body."

Alex shook his head. "Don't try to make this more complicated than it is. With the currents like they are in the river, his body is downstream somewhere. It may never be found. What made you start thinking about this anyway?"

"I think it's odd that a man called so soon after the newscast. What if it was Mr. Mitchell and he's the one sending all the clues?"

"It wasn't Mitchell. Harbor patrol combed the water around the bridge and along the banks for hours. If he had surfaced and come ashore, they would have seen him. He didn't survive the fall." He walked to the door and opened it. "Now let's go see what this next clue is going to tell us."

She started to protest, but she pursed her lips and nodded. Although she might wish Mr. Mitchell had survived that fall, Alex was right. It seemed highly unlikely. With a sigh, she reached into the drawer of her desk and pulled her purse out. "Then let's go."

He glanced at his watch. "I didn't realize the time. Would you like some lunch first?"

"That sounds good. Where would you like to go?"

"A new barbecue place opened a few blocks from here. Why don't we give it a try?"

She placed her purse strap over her shoulder and smiled. "Like we did every other barbecue place in the city? I don't think you'd ever get tired of eating it."

Alex chuckled as he walked over and held the door open for her. "You got that right. I guess you know me well."

Grace glanced up as she walked past and smiled. "I guess I do."

She expected him to frown at the teasing tone of her voice, but he didn't. Instead, he gave a small nod. "You've always known me better than anyone else."

She looked away from him and took a deep breath. For the first time in the past few days she felt Alex was more relaxed around her than he had been before. Perhaps dinner at her home last night and her father's apology had been what he needed to see it was possible for them to be friends again. She hoped so, because she liked that he was more like the old Alex. She only hoped they could continue this comfortable truce.

Alex frowned as he pulled into the parking lot at the entrance to the Wolf River Greenway and glanced over at Grace. "Are you sure you're following the coordinates correctly?"

She nodded. "Yes. The next clue has to be hidden somewhere along the greenway."

He came to a stop in one of parking places and

turned off the engine then turned toward her. "After what happened yesterday, there's no way we're going onto a path that runs through a forest and along the banks of the Wolf River. The guy who shot at us yesterday is probably out there somewhere waiting for us."

"I think you're right," she said. "What do you suggest we do?"

He pulled his cell phone out. "I'm going to call for some help. We can get some officers in there to search the forest. If they don't find anything, they can accompany us on the greenway when we go to find the spot. But we're not taking a step into that area before it's checked out first."

"That sounds good to me."

Alex made the call, and within minutes two squad cars pulled into the parking lot. Alex stepped out of the car and met them. They listened as he explained the situation and then headed onto the path that led down to the river. He watched them go before he climbed back in the car with Grace.

"Aren't you going with them?" she asked.

"No. I don't want to leave you alone. That guy would probably love to find you all alone sitting in a car in a parking lot. It's better that I stay behind and make sure nothing happens to you."

She smiled. "Thanks, Alex."

"No need to thank me. I really am a good cop, Grace."

Her cheeks flushed, and she glanced down at her clenched fists in her lap. "I know that."

He pulled his gaze away from her to look out the window. "The temperature is dropping outside. If you get too cold, I can start the car and turn the heat on."

She shook her head and pulled her coat tighter around her. "There's no need for that. How long do you think they'll be?"

"I don't know. The length of the greenway at this point is over a mile long. They'll have to search through the forest all along the path. It could take a while."

She yawned. "Then I think I'll close my eyes for a few minutes. I didn't sleep well last night."

"Go ahead. I'll wake you when they get back."

She adjusted the seat to lean back and snuggled down in it. Within minutes a soft snore rippled from her throat. Alex sat still as long as he could before he opened the door and stepped out into the parking lot.

He glanced at his watch and wondered where the officers were at that moment and if they had found anything. Even if they didn't, he wasn't sure he and Grace should follow through with the search for another clue. Every time he thought about the bullets that had flown past their heads the day before, he felt a moment of fear. It was astonishing that neither of them had been injured.

So far he had helped Grace survive two attempts on her life. All it would take for the killer to succeed would be for him to let his guard down for one second. He had to make sure he didn't do that.

He began to pace up and down beside the car. Each time he passed the window, he looked inside at Grace who appeared to be sleeping as if she didn't have a care in the world. He wished he could feel that way, but the promise he'd made her father weighed heavily on his mind.

An hour later he was still pacing when the officers

emerged from the greenway path. He stood still and waited as the officer in charge came toward him. "We didn't find anything, Detective. There wasn't a sign of anybody on the path or in the forest. We couldn't find any evidence that anyone had been there recently."

Alex breathed a sigh of relief. "That's good to know. As I told you, we have a note from a suspected killer. He claims he's left a clue for us in the woods. We need to find it, and I'd like for your men to accompany us in case he decides to show up while we're there."

The officer nodded. "We can do that."

Alex opened the car door, leaned in and shook Grace's shoulder. "Grace, wake up. The officers are back."

She bolted into a sitting position and wiped at her eyes. "Oh, I didn't mean to go to sleep. Did they find anything?"

"No, but they're going back with us. Are you ready?"

She nodded, stepped out of the car and pulled the GPS unit from her pocket. She looked around at the gathered officers and took a deep breath. "Well, let's go see what our friend has planned for us today."

Alex's heart thudded, and he fell into step with her. The officers fanned out on either side of them and behind as they headed for the path. Alex pulled his gun from the holster and bit down on his lip. They would soon know what Grace's mysterious caller had in store for them today.

Grace consulted the GPS coordinates as she, Alex, and the officers stepped onto the paved path that meandered along the banks of the Wolf River. Since she'd been back in Memphis, she'd enjoyed many weekend afternoons walking the pathway. Today was different, and it wasn't just the December chill in the air. The police officers who provided protection for them were a reminder of the danger involved in what they were about to do.

Out of the corner of her eye, she noticed Alex's gaze sweeping back and forth across the path and into the forest. He held his gun as if he was ready to fire at a moment's notice. They walked in silence for a few minutes before Alex spoke. "This is my first time along the greenway. It must be nice out here in the spring."

She glanced at him, but he was staring past her into the trees. "You don't have to try and keep me calm, Alex. I know we're in a dangerous position out in the open like this."

His face flushed, and he glanced at her. "No, I'm serious. I've never been out here before."

She laughed, and the tension in her body eased a bit. "You need to get out more often. You don't know what you're missing. I love walking along this path and looking at the river and the trees and plants all around. It makes me feel good, knowing this is a protected green area where I can enjoy what God has put in the world for us. By the time this project is finished, this path we're on is going to stretch for thirty miles all the way downtown from Germantown and Collierville."

One of the officers walking beside her spoke up. "She's right. You should get out here this spring and enjoy some of the activities."

Grace looked over her shoulder at all the officers and smiled. "Maybe all of you can join me some Saturday for a short hike along this trail."

After she spoke the words, she tensed. How would Alex react to her invitation? Would he think she wasn't taking today's mission seriously enough? To her relief, he smiled.

"I hope the next time we're not after some crazy guy who wants to shoot us."

"Me, too." She glanced down at the GPS unit. "Maybe we'll catch him before then, and he'll be safely behind bars."

No one spoke again as they continued walking along the pathway. After about a mile Grace stopped and pointed to the trees alongside the paved walkway. "It's in there."

Alex's gaze drifted over the densely covered area. "I'm glad the leaves are off. Maybe it won't be too difficult to find whatever's been left. Let's see what it is."

The police fanned out in a circle, and they all walked into the woods. They'd only been searching for a few minutes when Grace spotted a manila envelope. It stuck out from underneath a large rock that had been placed at the base of a tree. "I think I have something."

The officers formed a protective ring around Grace and continued scanning the forest as Alex trudged through the undergrowth, stopped beside her and glanced down. "He didn't hide this very well, did he?"

"No. He wanted to make sure we found it. Since there aren't any other rocks that size around, he must have moved this one from down near the river." She took a deep breath. "Let's see what it is."

She picked up the bubble-cushioned mailer that looked to be about six by nine inches and ripped the seal open. Then she stuck her hand inside and pulled out an object wrapped in a piece of paper.

"What's that?" Alex asked.

"I don't know." Grace frowned and unwrapped the object. A carved wooden wolf lay inside. She picked up the carving and turned it over and over as she studied it. Suddenly she winced. "Ouch!"

Alex stepped closer. "What's the matter?"

She shook her head. "I'm okay. There's a sharp edge on the wolf, and it pricked my finger."

He frowned. "Does it hurt?"

"No, but it startled me." She turned the carving around in her hand again, careful not to touch the edge, and then glanced at the paper it had been wrapped in. She swallowed hard at the words on the page. "He's left me another note. It says, 'Some ancient people thought the wolf represented danger. Landon found out it did. Are you next?'"

Alex raked his hand through his hair. "Okay, that's it. This guy is getting too vocal in his threats. You are getting out of this investigation right now before it gets more dangerous."

Grace glanced down at the wolf and the note again. "Don't be ridiculous. We must be getting closer, or he wouldn't feel the need to voice these threats."

Alex shook his head and glanced around the area. "We don't know if he's out there in the trees watching us or not. He could have you in the sights of a rifle right now." He grabbed her by the arm and pulled her toward the pathway as he called out to the officers. "We're leaving. Let's get out of here now."

Propelled by Alex's grip on her arm, Grace stumbled

forward as she stuck the note and the wolf in her coat pocket. Once on the pathway, Alex didn't slow down but kept a tight hold on her arm as they strode back toward the entrance. She glanced over her shoulder, and the officers hurried along the path behind them.

After about half a mile Grace winced at the numbing pain radiating through her trembling legs. What was Alex's hurry? Her chest heaved, and she panted for breath. "Alex, please slow down. You're walking too fast for me."

His gaze swept the pathway and the trees beside it. "We need to get out of here, Grace. There are too many places someone could be hiding. We'll slow down when we get to the parking lot."

She nodded and allowed him to pull her forward. By the time they'd gone five hundred feet farther her heart pounded so hard, she thought her chest might explode any minute. Her rubbery legs wanted to collapse, but she pushed on.

A sudden crushing pain gripped her chest, and she gasped for breath. A sound from somewhere in her head filled her, and she glanced toward the trees. She shook her head to clear away the dizziness and squinted at the image staring at her from between two trees. With every ounce of strength she could muster she pulled free of Alex. "Look who's here," she mumbled.

Alex jerked to a stop, whirled to face the trees, and pointed his gun in that direction. "Who is it?"

The other officers surrounded them within seconds. "What's going on?" she heard one say.

"Something's wrong with Grace," Alex said, but his voice seemed to be coming from far away.

She frowned at the gun in Alex's hand. There was no need for that. She glanced back at the familiar face in the trees staring at her, held out her hand and wiggled her fingers. "It's all right. You can come to me."

Alex turned back to her. "I don't see..." His eyebrows drew together as he scanned her face. "Grace, are you all right?"

"I'm fine." She looked up at Alex. "Why won't he come here?" She closed her eyes as another wave of dizziness swept over her. She reached for Alex, and he caught her in his arms when she toppled toward him.

"Grace, what's the matter?" He knelt down and cradled her in his arms. "You're not making any sense. Who did you see?"

She raised a shaking finger and pointed to the trees. "Snowball. I'll ride him home."

"The pony you had when you were a child?" Alex turned his head to stare in the direction she pointed, then back to her. "Where is he?"

"Right there," she gasped. "Don't you see him?"

"There's nothing there, Grace."

What was the matter with Alex? Didn't he recognize the pony they'd ridden together when they were children? She struggled to push to her feet, but Alex's strong arms held her still. "He's there. I want to ride him."

Her eyesight blurred, and she blinked to clear her vision. When she reopened her eyes, the pony had disappeared. She frowned and glanced up at a strange man who hovered over her. Several other faces looked down at her. "Wh-who are you?" she stammered.

"Grace, it's Alex. Don't you recognize me?"

She shook her head and tried to pull from this stranger's grasp. "Don't touch me," she screamed. "Alex, where are you?" she yelled.

"I'm right here, Grace."

She looked up into the face of the man who spoke, but she didn't know him. "Do you know Alex?"

"Grace, I'm Alex."

She saw his lips move, but the ringing in her ears drowned out his words. He leaned closer, and she tried to speak. Her breath hitched in her throat, and her words died on her lips.

The man moved slightly, and she saw a cell phone in his hand. With a sigh she surrendered to the darkness that crept over her.

Alex started to punch in 911 on his cell phone, but one of the other officers was already calling on his phone. Alex cradled Grace's limp body in his arms as another officer helped him to his feet. He glanced at the man on the phone. "Tell them to meet us at the parking lot. We're almost there."

He held her close as he ran down the path that led back to where he'd left his car. He heard the sirens just before he and the officers reached the entrance to the greenway and stumbled into the parking lot at the same moment the ambulance pulled to a stop.

The EMTs were out of the ambulance almost before they'd come to a stop, and Alex laid Grace on the gurney they pulled out. Alex stepped back and watched Grace's pale face as the two men began to check her vitals.

One of them glanced around at him. "Are you the officer who called this in?"

The man who'd called stepped forward. "No, I did."

The EMT turned his attention back to Alex. "Did anything unusual happen to cause her to faint?"

"No. We were on our way back to the parking lot when she collapsed. She started breathing heavily, and she became disoriented. She didn't recognize me and thought she saw a pony she had when she was a child."

The second EMT pulled the stethoscope he'd been using to check her heartbeat from his ears and glanced at his partner. "Heartbeat is weak and breathing is shallow. Let's get her on some oxygen and put her in the ambulance. We need to get to the E.R. right away."

Alex nodded. "I'll follow in my car." He turned to the officers who'd accompanied them on the greenway. "Thanks, guys. I appreciate all your help today. I need to go to the hospital."

The officer in charge nodded. "You go on. I've never seen anything like what happened to her out there. Let us know how she gets along."

"I will."

He cast one last look at Grace before he ran back to his car. Within minutes he was headed up the street. The ambulance's siren and the wail of the one on his unmarked police car split the afternoon air. Traffic pulled out of their way and allowed them to speed unchecked along the street.

Alex roared into the hospital parking lot and jumped from his car as soon as it came to a stop. He knew from experience he wouldn't be allowed through the bay where the EMTs took Grace, so he paused in the parking lot long enough to call his office and alert his partners, Brad and Seth, to what had happened before he ran toward the doors of the emergency room waiting area.

He rushed inside, came to a stop at the desk and held up his badge. "The EMTs just brought my friend Grace Kincaid in. I followed the ambulance here."

The receptionist peered over the rim of her glasses, which sat propped on her nose. "I'll let you know when there's any news."

He opened his mouth to protest, but he realized it would do no good. As difficult as it was going to be, he had to wait until the doctor had determined what had happened to Grace. He groaned and slunk off to find a seat in the crowded room.

He'd barely settled in his chair before he thought of Grace's parents. He'd promised them he would keep their daughter safe and he hadn't. The bad thing was that he had no idea what had happened to her. Had their mysterious caller with his GPS puzzles been able to cause Grace's collapse?

"Alex." The sound of his name being call jerked him from his thoughts, and he found Laura Austin, his partner Brad's wife and Grace's best friend, standing in front of him. He jumped to his feet, and she threw her arms around him. "I just finished a counseling session upstairs, and Brad called to tell me Grace has been brought in."

He released her, and they sat down together on the couch. "I'm glad he did. I didn't know if you were working here or at Cornerstone Clinic today. Thank you for coming down."

Laura smiled. "Where else would I be? I've always

been there when Grace has gotten into scrapes. But tell me what's happened. Brad said she's unconscious."

She listened as Alex related the events earlier on the greenway. When he got to the part about how she had become delusional and passed out, his voice grew husky. He swallowed before finishing his story. "I've been over everything that happened on the greenway, but I can't figure out what caused her attack. It was like some allergic reaction."

Laura pursed her mouth and frowned. "Could it have been something in the environment? A tree or plant?"

"I thought of that, but it's December. There's very little vegetation out there."

Laura thought for a moment. "Then did she touch anything?"

Alex shook his head. "Nothing but the…" He stopped in midsentence, and his eyes widened. "The wood carving!"

His loud words startled Laura, and she jumped. "What are you talking about?"

"The envelope contained a carving of a wolf and a note. She touched those. The carving had a sharp edge on it, and she pricked her finger with it. That has to be it!" He sprang from his seat. "They're still in her pocket. I need to tell the doctor to test them."

He took a step to go to the desk, but Laura grabbed his arm to stop him. "Wait, Alex. You can't go back there, but as a nurse, I can. I'll go tell the doctor. You sit tight, and I'll let you know what he says."

He nodded. "All right, but tell the doctor to be careful. He needs to wear gloves before handling those items."

"I'll tell him and be right back." Laura strode across

the room, stopped at the desk and spoke with the receptionist. She nodded and pushed a button, and the entrance to the treatment area opened.

Alex sat down and waited for Laura to return. It seemed like hours before he saw the door open again and Laura emerge. He was on his feet before she reached him. "How is she?"

"She's still unconscious."

"What did the doctor say when you told him about the note and the carving?"

"The doctor found both of them in Grace's pocket. He's sent them to the lab for testing. They should know something in a little while. In the meantime, we just have to wait."

He sank back on the couch and raised a shaking hand to wipe his forehead. "Waiting has always been hard for me to do, but I'm glad you're here."

She sighed, glanced at her watch and rose to her feet. "I wish I could stay, but I need to get back to work. I'll check with you later to see how Grace is doing. When she wakes up, tell her I was here."

He stood and gave her a kiss on the cheek. "Thanks for coming, Laura."

She smiled before she turned and walked down the hallway that led into the hospital proper. He stared after her for a moment and then stepped to the side of the room and pulled out his cell phone. There was no putting off the inevitable any longer. He had to call Grace's parents and tell them he hadn't been able to protect their daughter the way he'd promised.

# Chapter Six

Grace opened her eyes and frowned as she tried to determine where she was. She lay in a bed, but this wasn't the comfortable mattress she was so used to. She squinted at a small light shining through a cracked door that led into another room, a bathroom perhaps. A soft snore alerted her she wasn't alone, and she turned her head to look to her right.

In the darkened room she could make out the form of her mother in the chair next to the bed. She tried to raise her head, but it was no use. She slumped back, her head against the pillow and moaned.

Her mother jerked upright and was on her feet in one swift move. She leaned over the bed and gazed down at her. "Grace, are you awake?"

She licked at her dry lips and struggled to speak. "Wh-where am I?"

"You're in the hospital."

Grace closed her eyes and tried to remember what had happened. The greenway popped into her mind, and her eyes blinked open. "Alex?"

Her mother patted her arm. "Alex is fine. You collapsed while the two of you were with the police officers at the greenway. They called 911 and got you here in time. You're going to be fine."

A memory of running along the path returned, but nothing else. "Wh-where is Alex?"

"He called us after you were brought in, and your father and I came right away. When the doctors told us you were going to be all right, Alex took your father home so I could stay. He'll be by in the morning to see you."

She nodded and closed her eyes. She wanted to talk more, but she couldn't concentrate. Right now she wanted to go back to sleep. There would be time later to find out why she was in the hospital.

The next time Grace opened her eyes, the sun streamed through the windows. She turned her head toward where her mother had sat the last time she awoke and saw instead Alex reading a newspaper in a chair next to her bed.

He glanced up and saw her looking at him. "Good morning. So you're finally awake. I thought you were going to sleep all day."

She frowned. "What time is it?"

"It's nearly ten o'clock."

"Why aren't you at work?"

"I'll go in after lunch. I wanted to be with you when you woke up."

She looked around the room. "Where's my mother? She was here when I woke up before."

"I sent her home when I got here. She hadn't slept any, and I told her I'd stay with you."

"What about my father? Mother told me you took him home last night."

Alex nodded. "He didn't want to leave, but he was really tired. I took him home and got him settled in bed."

Grace's eyes grew wide. "You helped my father to bed?"

Alex's face flushed, and he nodded. "I was glad to do it. Your mother wanted to stay here, and I told her I'd make sure your father got to bed."

"Thank you for doing that." A sudden thought struck her. "But it was the maid's night off. Did he stay in the house alone?"

Alex shook his head. "No. I couldn't leave him alone. I stayed in the guest room and put the phone by his bed so he could call my cell phone during the night if he needed me."

Grace's mouth gaped open. "You stayed at our house with my father?"

"I did."

Tears filled Grace's eyes. "Thank you, Alex. That was very kind of you. Especially since you and my father haven't had a good relationship in the past."

Alex smiled at her. "When your father apologized, I knew I had to meet him halfway if we were ever to overcome the memories of the past. The more I'm around him, the more I can see his good qualities. I think we may end up being friends."

Grace smiled, too, and wiped at the corner of her eye. "Nothing would make me happier."

Alex cleared his throat and folded the newspaper he'd been holding when she woke up. "Laura's been here several times. She came in yesterday after we got here, and she dropped by this morning on her way to work."

"I hope she wasn't worried about me."

His eyes darkened, and his gaze lingered on her face. "We were all worried about you, Grace."

She tried to pull her gaze away from him, but she couldn't. "I'll call her later." Alex stared at her without speaking, and after a moment Grace cleared her throat and started to rise. "I need to get up."

Alex jumped to his feet and shook his head. "You can't get up until a nurse comes to help you. I'll call for one."

He grabbed the cord for the call button and punched it. "She's awake," he responded when the nurse's station answered.

Within seconds a nurse entered the room, stopped beside the bed and smiled. "It's good to see you awake. How are you feeling?"

Grace hesitated before she answered. "I'm not sure yet."

"Do you think you're strong enough to walk to the bathroom?"

"I think so."

The nurse turned to Alex. "If you'll excuse us for a moment, I'll help Miss Kincaid get freshened up a bit. I'll call you back in when we have her ready for breakfast."

Alex nodded. "I'll be outside."

When he'd exited the room, the nurse released the side rails of the bed and supported Grace as she sat up on the side of the bed. "How's that?"

A wave of dizziness swept over her, and she swayed. "I'll be okay in a moment."

"Take it easy. You've been through a lot."

Grace looked up at her and frowned. "What happened to me?"

"We can talk about that after you're feeling stronger. First, let's get you ready to visit with that handsome police detective. From what the other nurses tell me, he was a nervous wreck when you were brought in. He paced the waiting room floor for hours. It's plain to see how he feels about you."

Grace smiled and shook her head. "We're really good friends. We have been since we were children."

The nurse arched her eyebrows. "All I can say is I wish I had a friend who cared about me so much."

Grace laughed and allowed herself to be helped to her feet. Thirty minutes later with a clean hospital gown on and her breakfast tray in front of her Grace sat up in bed and smiled as Alex walked back into the room.

"I was beginning to wonder where you'd gone."

He grinned and slipped his cell phone in his pocket. "I was on the phone with Brad. He said Laura is worried sick about you."

Grace laid her fork on the tray and looked at Alex as he sat down in the chair next to the bed. "I've been trying to remember what happened. The last thing I remember is you pulling me along the path. I thought my lungs were going to explode. What happened?"

"You collapsed, and we called 911."

"I know that, but why did I faint?"

Alex shifted to the edge of his chair and stared at her. "Do you remember the wolf and the note?"

"Yes."

"And do you remember pricking your finger on a sharp edge?"

"Yes."

Alex inhaled a deep breath. "When the lab tested the wolf and the note, they found both of them were covered with cyanide. The poison was able to enter your system through the small nick on your finger, and your mysterious puzzle maker knew that's what would happen. If we hadn't gotten here in time, you might be dead now."

"Cyanide?" A shiver ran up her spine, and Grace flinched. "But I thought cyanide killed you right away."

"From what the doctor said, that only happens in the movies. It actually works much slower than chomping down on a capsule and dying instantly."

"Was I really in danger of dying?"

"You could have. The doctor told us cyanide poisoning can occur in different ways—by eating cyanide-laced food, inhaling cyanide gas or absorbing it through the skin. I wrote down what they gave you as an antidote." He pulled a piece of paper out of his pocket and glanced down at it. "They gave you sodium nitrite and sodium thiosulfate. You'll be fine in a few days. You just need to rest."

Grace rubbed her hand over her forehead. "I wish I could remember. I recall trying to keep up with you on the pathway, and I remember falling down. But nothing else." She glanced up at Alex. "Did I just faint?"

He fidgeted in his chair. "I thought you were conscious, but you were talking out of your head."

"What did I say?"

"You said you saw Snowball standing in the forest."

Her eyes grew wide. "Snowball? I thought I saw my pony?"

He chuckled. "Yeah. You said you wanted to ride him home."

"Did I say anything else?"

He hesitated a moment, then took a deep breath. "No, you lost consciousness. None of us could figure out what happened to you. It was really scary, Grace. Thank goodness we got you here in time."

"I remember being dizzy, and then I felt really frightened." She swallowed the fear that rose in her throat. "Alex, he's tried to kill me twice."

He looked at her without blinking. "I know. This has gotten out of hand, Grace. We can't let this happen again. He might be successful the next time."

"But what are we going to do? We can't let him scare us off."

He shook his head. "I don't know. I haven't figured it out yet, but I will. I've promised your parents I'll keep you safe, and I intend to keep that promise. For now, though, you need to rest and get well."

"You're right. I should have listened to you all along. Right now I'm so grateful to be alive, and I have you to thank for that. You've done what you promised."

He leaned over and covered her hand with his. "Don't worry, Grace. We're going to get this guy. We just have to go about it in a different way now."

She nodded and lay back on her pillow. Her heartbeat quickened at the thought of what might have happened if Alex and the other officers hadn't been with her yesterday. For some reason the person who had killed Landon had set his sights on her. She'd been fortunate to escape him twice, but she might not be able to a third time.

Perhaps she'd been wrong to push Alex into including her in this investigation. Now she had put him in the position of not only finding a killer but protecting her at the same time. Her stubborn determination to have her way in this investigation had put him in danger also, and she regretted that. She should have realized he was the trained police officer and listened to him, but she had pushed him into including her. And he had given in, just like he always had when they were children.

She glanced over at him sitting beside the bed. "I'm sorry, Alex."

He lowered the newspaper he was reading. "For what?"

"For insisting on being included in this investigation. I have put you in danger, and I'm truly sorry for that."

His Adam's apple bobbed up and down, and after a moment he spoke. "It's something I face every day, Grace. It's not your fault that somebody wants to kill you. I just want to keep you safe."

Tears filled her eyes, and she blinked. "Thank you. I know you'll do that."

She looked down at her hand on top of the blanket and stared at Landon's ring on her finger. Whoever had tried to kill her had kept that ring for twelve years. How she wished it could talk and tell her where it had been, but that was impossible. After a moment she turned over, pulled the covers up to her chin and closed her eyes. She needed to sleep. Maybe when she woke she wouldn't be haunted by the thought of some-one lurking in the shadows and planning his next at-tempt on her life.

Alex drank the last drops out of the soda can, tossed it into the waiting room trash can and glanced at his watch. The doctor had been in Grace's room for about fifteen minutes. What could be taking him so long?

Alex walked to the door and peered down the hall toward Grace's room. A nurse stepped out and walked back toward the nurse's station. He stopped her when she drew even with him. "Excuse me, but is the doc-tor still in Miss Kincaid's room?"

She nodded. "He is, but he'll be out in a few min-utes."

"Thank you." He smiled at her and watched as she continued to her destination. He was about to go back and sit down when his cell phone rang. Brad's number flashed on caller ID. He raised the phone to his ear. "Hey, Brad. What's up?"

"I thought you were coming to the office this af-ternoon."

Alex sighed and rubbed the back of his neck. "I had intended to, but I kept waiting for the doctor. I wanted to hear what he would say about Grace's condition."

"Has he come yet?"

"Yeah, he's in with her now. I'm waiting for him to leave. Then I'll probably come in."

"No need to, buddy. Everything's under control here. Stay with Grace as long as she needs you. I know it's hard for her parents to be there with her father's condition."

"He was here for a while last night, but I took him home."

Brad's startled gasp vibrated in Alex's ear. "Since when did you and Harrison Kincaid get so friendly? I thought the guy hated you."

Alex chuckled. "Not anymore. It seems the shooting has made a changed man out of him. He's turned his life over to God. In fact, he asked me to forgive him for the way he treated me when I was growing up."

"I never thought I'd hear that, but I'm glad he's changed. It's too bad it took him being shot to open his eyes to God's love for him."

"I guess you're right."

"When you see Grace, tell her Laura is coming back to the hospital when she gets off work. She wanted to stay this morning, but she had to get to work because they were short staffed at the clinic. She has some counseling sessions later at the hospital, so she's going to see Grace before her patients get there."

"I told her Laura had come by, so she's looking forward to seeing her."

"Well, they have been best friends since elementary school." Brad hesitated a moment. "Are things getting better between you and Grace?"

Alex sighed. "I think we're getting there. It's better than it has been."

"Good. Laura and I hate to think about our two best

friends at odds with each other. We're praying you and Grace can learn to at least be civil to each other."

"Thanks, Brad."

"Now if Laura had her way…" He paused for a moment. "Hey, I'm getting a call on another line. I'll check with you later."

Alex ended the call and stared at his phone for a moment. Brad didn't have to finish his sentence for him to know what he was about to say. Brad and Laura would be happy if he and Grace could get together again. They were his closest friends, too, but he couldn't make them understand it was too late for him and Grace. She had chosen another life instead of having one with him, and he was doing all right on his own.

Gritting his teeth, Alex whirled and stormed back into the waiting room. He strode toward the window, stopped in front of it and looked out at the parking lot. Snow had begun to fall, and he watched the swirling flakes fall to the ground.

Maybe they were going to have a white Christmas this year. When he and Grace were children, they'd wish every year that it would snow for the holidays, but Memphis had seen little snowfall during their childhood. The biggest one had been when they were ten years old. They'd built a snowman and placed one of her father's hats on its head. He smiled at the memory. Why did things like that keep popping into his head?

Before he could answer the question in his mind, he heard footsteps in the hall, and he turned to see the doctor walk past the waiting room. He needed to find out what the doctor had said. He strode down the hall to Grace's room and knocked before entering.

"Come in," she called out.

Her bed was positioned so that she was sitting upright, and she smiled when he walked in. His heart thudded at the thought that she'd almost died the day before. Having her back in his life might be difficult, but having her dead would be unbearable.

He returned the smile and sat down beside the bed. "What did the doctor say?"

"He wants me to stay another night, but he feels sure I can go home tomorrow."

Alex nodded. "I think that's wise."

"I also talked to my boss at the station. I have two weeks of vacation coming, and I'm going to take off until after Christmas. That should give us some time to figure out where we go from here in the investigation of Landon's death."

His eyes grew wide, and he jumped to his feet. "Whoa, there. What makes you think we go anywhere after what's happened?"

She sat up straighter and clenched her hands in her lap. "Because we haven't found the answer yet." She took a deep breath. "I've thought about this since I woke up. I have to admit I'm scared this guy will come after me again. I don't think I should go looking for any more of his clues, but we can't just drop the investigation."

Alex shook his head. "No, Grace. You've had two attempts on your life. You need to stay out of this. Let me handle it by myself."

"I know you're the trained police officer, and I'm just a nosy news reporter. But I can't give up." She held up her hand. "Look at that ring, Alex. Somebody killed

Landon and kept it for twelve years. I want to know who did that. Please don't shut me out. Let me help you with this case. I promise I'll do whatever you say."

He ran his hand through his hair and muttered under his breath. "Why are you so pigheaded? I'm only trying to protect you. I was scared to death yesterday that you were going to die before I could get help. I don't want to go through that again."

Tears pooled in her eyes, and she nodded. "I'm sorry you were scared, but I'm so thankful you were there. Please, Alex, help me find out the truth, and then I'll never ask you for anything again."

He looked at her for a moment, and he felt his resolve crumbling. He sighed in resignation. "Okay, but no more puzzles. This time we're doing it my way. We'll investigate with some good old-fashioned police work. Do you understand?"

She nodded, and the smile that lit her face sent a warm rush through his veins. "Yes, and I promise I'll listen to you."

His gaze drifted over her face, and his breath hitched in his throat when he spied the tiny scar at the edge of her hairline on the right side of her forehead. He reached over and let his finger trace the jagged line that had faded with time. "You'll listen to me like you did when I was teaching you to ride the bicycle you got for Christmas?"

She reached up, placed her finger on top of his, and looked into his eyes. "It wasn't your fault I had a wreck and cut my head. I should have listened to you and let you hold on to me until I learned to balance better."

"But your father blamed me, and I blamed myself, too."

"I never wanted you to do that." She smiled. "This scar is very special to me. Every time I look in the mirror to comb my hair, I see it and I think of you. It's helped me get through a lot of difficult times."

He pulled away from her, and she smiled. Then without saying another word, she lay back in bed and closed her eyes. He sat down in the chair beside her bed and picked up a magazine that lay on the bedside table. After a few minutes her breathing became steady, and he realized she had dropped off to sleep.

There was work to be done at the police station, but he couldn't bring himself to leave. He'd made a promise to her father that he would protect her, and he would do whatever it took to keep that promise. In the past three days she'd almost been killed twice, and he couldn't let that happen again. If their puzzle maker was determined to get to Grace, he was going to have to go through him first.

## Chapter Seven

Grace closed the high school annual she'd been looking at for the past hour, laid it on the den desk and glanced at her watch. This was her second day home from the hospital, and she'd been waiting for Alex to visit all morning. Now that it was midafternoon, she'd begun to wonder if he was coming at all.

He'd brought her home yesterday and had barely seen her settled before he rushed off to his office. But she really couldn't blame him. For the past few days he'd been at the hospital a good deal of the time, and his work had probably piled up while he'd been away.

She stood, walked to the window and pulled back the curtain. The snow that had fallen while she was in the hospital had melted, but the weather prediction called for more accumulation before Christmas, which was only a week and a half away.

The sound of someone entering the room caught her attention, and she turned to see Alex coming toward her. Tired lines creased his face, and his eyes looked as if he hadn't slept in days. She frowned. "I didn't hear you come in."

"Nancy let me in."

She took a step toward him. "You look tired. Are you all right?"

A small smile pulled at his lips, and he nodded. "It's been a hard day at work. My partner Seth and I have been working on a case with a retired police officer for a while now, and it seems to be going nowhere. Besides I haven't slept much the past few nights."

"Why not?"

"For one thing I've been trying to figure out where we go with the Mitchell case now, and the other problem is my father."

Grace's eyebrows knit. "What's wrong with your father?"

He looked down at his feet, and she recognized the mannerism he'd had ever since they were children. She knew he would take a breath, look up in a few seconds and proceed to tell her something she probably didn't want to hear. She braced herself for what he was about to say. "Since my father retired to Florida, he's been after me to come down there. The town where he lives is going to hire a new police chief, and he wants me to apply for the job. He's been calling me every day about it."

Grace couldn't control the gasp that escaped her throat. It was as if someone had thrown a glass of ice water in her face. "You aren't seriously considering it, are you?"

Alex shrugged. "You know how I feel about Memphis, but my father's getting older and he's not well.

I suppose I'm kind of in the same situation you were when you had to come back to Memphis because of your father's situation. Of course my dad's illness doesn't compare to what your father's going through, but he's my father. He needs me."

"I can understand that. Our parents took care of us when we were little. Now it seems it's our turn to help them. I'll be praying for you to make the right decision. When do you think you'll decide?"

"I told him I'd let him know at Christmas. He's coming here to spend it with me."

Grace smiled. "Then maybe I'll get to see him. I would like that."

Alex nodded. "Maybe so."

Grace took a deep breath and walked back to the desk where she'd placed the annuals she'd been studying before Alex arrived. She picked up one and opened it. "I found something I wanted to show you."

"What is it?" He walked over and peered down at the book she held.

She pointed to the three books on the desk and the one she held. "These are our high school annuals. I've been looking through them, and I've noticed something. In all the pictures of Landon in our freshman and sophomore years he looks like a happy boy. He's healthy-looking, and he's smiling in every picture. There are some action shots of him on the football field, and he's in a lot of pictures with groups of kids. He was one of the leaders in our geocache club during our sophomore year."

Alex nodded. "I remember how quick he was on the football field. Once he got started running toward the goal line, there was no stopping him. He was tough, and he could outrun anybody on the team. Coach thought Landon would get a scholarship to a major university."

Grace sank down in the desk chair and motioned for Alex to sit in the one beside her. "He had everything going for him. I don't understand what happened during our junior year that made his life start to fall apart."

She opened the annual from their junior year and pointed to his picture. "Look at his face. He had this cocky expression that he never had before. That's about the time he began to act like he was big man on campus. By the time we were seniors, he'd dropped out of the geocache club. He said he didn't have time for childish activities. He was into other things."

"Did he say what those other things were?"

Grace shook her head. "When I would ask, he'd just laugh and tell me I was better off not knowing. He dropped all his old friends, including me, quit the football team and took up with a whole new group of kids."

"I remember him quitting. Coach was fit to be tied, but Landon wouldn't change his mind. Do you know who his new friends were?"

"Yes. They were Jeremy Baker, Billy Warren, Sam Jefferson, Clay Mercer and Dustin Shelton."

Alex narrowed his eyes as if he was in deep thought. After a few moments, he nodded. "I remember them. They were a bunch of spoiled rich boys who drove the fastest cars and thought the rules didn't apply to them. Do you know where they are now?"

Grace grinned and laid the book on the desk. "No, but I know how we can find out."

"How?"

"I called our high school this morning and talked with the secretary. Did you know that Mr. Donner is still the principal there?"

He nodded. "Yeah, I see his name in the paper from time to time when the school makes the news."

"Well, we have an appointment to see him in…" She paused and glanced at her watch. "In about thirty minutes. I'm glad I thought about calling this morning. This is the last day before Christmas break, and the school will be closed for the next two and a half weeks."

"Do you think he might know where these guys are now?" Alex asked.

Grace rolled her eyes and groaned. "I can't imagine his not knowing. There probably isn't a school in the whole state that has an alumni association as active as the one at our old school. I suppose that's to be expected since it's a private school that receives a lot of their operating funds from donations. Mr. Donner has even hired an office worker who makes it a priority to keep an updated address list of former students and their families. They send out newsletters and requests for contributions to the school all the time." She paused and propped her hands on her hips. "Sometimes it seems like I get two letters a week wanting me to donate to some program at the school."

Alex chuckled and nodded. "Yeah, I get them, too. In fact, I mailed a check last week for the fund-raiser for some new computers in the technology department."

"I got that letter, too."

Alex glanced at his watch. "Well, if we're going,

we need to be on our way. Traffic may be heavy this time of day."

"My coat's in the hall closet. I'll get it."

He nodded and followed her from the room. When they reached the closet, she pulled the coat out, and he held it for her to slip her arms inside. Then he turned her to face him and pulled the coat tight around her. "It's cold outside today."

His fingers brushed her throat, and her pulse raced. "I know."

He stared at her for a moment, and his Adam's apple bobbed. Then he stepped back, cleared his throat and glanced over his shoulder. "Where are your parents?"

"They're upstairs. My father is taking a nap, and my mother is wrapping Christmas presents. She wants to get all of them under the tree tonight. And that reminds me, they said they'd like for you to stay for dinner."

He shook his head. "That's not necessary. I've already eaten here once this week."

She stopped and looked up at him. "It's an invitation, Alex. They appreciate what you did for us."

"I didn't do anything special."

"You called for an ambulance and carried me from the greenway, then you brought my father home and put him to bed. You also stayed the night so he wouldn't be alone. You did a lot."

"It was no more than any friend would have done."

"Then stay and let us show you how much we appreciate your friendship."

He seemed to consider the offer, and she held her breath, waiting for his answer. After a moment he nodded. "Okay, I'll stay for dinner."

Grace smiled and opened the door. "Good. Now let's go see if our former principal can help us locate Landon's friends. If we can find them, they may be able to answer a lot of questions about what made Landon change from the boy we'd known and why he had a wolf's head tattooed on his shoulder."

The school had changed very little since the last time Alex had been inside. The trophy case still hung on the wall in the spot where it had been when he was a student, and posters of club meetings and extracurricular activities dotted the walls.

He stopped in front of the trophy case and saw the gold-plated championship cup his football team had won his senior year. The memory of the night they became state champs still excited him after all these years. He knew the coach had retired some years ago, but he had no idea where most of his teammates were. He hadn't kept up with anyone after high school except Grace and Brad.

The door to the school office opened, and Grace stepped out into the hall. She walked over and stopped beside him. "The principal is on the phone. His secretary will call us when he's ready to see us." She didn't speak for a few minutes as she looked at the awards inside the case. "There's the state championship trophy from our senior year. Do you remember the night of the game?"

He straightened and grinned. "Yeah, I do. I couldn't believe we beat the top-ranked school, but we did. We all went to that hamburger place down the street to celebrate."

She laughed. "I was so proud of you because you'd been named Most Valuable Player for the game, but you shrugged it off like it was no big deal."

He grinned. "I thought it was more macho to pretend I didn't care. Of course I was proud." He looked at the trophy again. "Seeing it after all this time takes me back to our school days. I can't believe it's been twelve years since we graduated from high school."

She rolled her eyes. "I can. A lot has happened since then. I'm twelve years older, and I know I'm not that young girl anymore. I check the mirror every morning to see how many new wrinkles I have."

Alex laughed and cocked an eyebrow. "I don't think you have anything to worry about. You're prettier now than you were then."

She batted her eyelashes at him. "Thank you, kind sir. I needed that, especially after spending two days in the hospital."

The teasing tone of her voice made him smile. He was about to reply when the office door opened, and the secretary stuck her head out. "Mr. Donner is off the phone now. He said for you to come in."

They followed the young woman inside and to the door of Mr. Donner's private office. When he saw them, he rose from behind his desk and motioned for them to enter. "Grace Kincaid and Alex Crowne. It's good to see you."

"And you, too," Alex said as he reached out and shook the principal's hand. "Thank you for seeing us on such short notice."

He shook Grace's hand and motioned for them to

take two chairs in front of his desk. "How long has it been since you graduated? Eight years?"

Grace chuckled. "No, twelve."

Mr. Donner shook his head. "It can't have been that long. It seems like yesterday."

Alex settled back in his chair and let his gaze travel over the room. He smiled when he spied a framed picture on a shelf behind the principal's desk. It was a younger Mr. Donner standing in the parking lot beside a motorcycle he used to ride to school. He laughed and pointed to the picture. "I remember the day that was taken. Some of the guys on the football team were examining your bike when you came outside to go home. You asked one of the fellows to take your picture."

Mr. Donner smiled. "Yeah, I was proud of that bike."

Alex nodded. "We could tell. We thought it was really cool that our principal rode a motorcycle. Do you still ride?"

"I do. Not that bike of course. I gave it to my son when he got older and bought myself a bigger one. I ride in a club with a bunch of friends. It's my only hobby." He clasped his hands on top of his desk and leaned forward. "But I doubt if you came by to talk to me about my bike. Tell me what brings you back to school."

Alex cast one last glance at the picture before he looked back at Mr. Donner. "I don't know if you've heard or not, but I'm with the Memphis Police Department. I work on cold cases, and at present I'm investigating the death of Landon Mitchell who was thought to have committed suicide the year Grace and I were seniors."

Mr. Donner sat back, rested his elbows on the chair arms and tented his fingers in front of him. "I remember when that happened. It was a horrible thing." He glanced at Grace. "I saw your coverage about Landon's father and heard you say you would be trying to find out the truth. Are the two of you working together?"

Grace nodded. "We are."

Mr. Donner pursed his mouth as if in deep thought before he spoke. "I've always had my doubts about Landon's death. I thought the police ruled it a suicide too quickly. Have they reopened the case?"

"It was never officially closed even though they did recover his body and do an autopsy. The investigators thought it was suicide but the medical examiner couldn't make a definite ruling because of other injuries to the body, such as a head wound."

Mr. Donner frowned. "But couldn't that have been caused by the impact from the fall?"

"That's the problem," Alex said. "It might have been, and it might not have been. I hope this time we find the answer."

"What can I do to help?"

Alex settled back in his chair and took a deep breath. "If you heard Grace's report about Mr. Mitchell's death, then you know he thought his son was involved in some secret society here at the school and that they killed him. Have you ever suspected there might be a club that operates in the shadows out of the administration's sight?"

Mr. Donner thought for a moment before he shook his head. "Soon after I took this job, I heard rumors of such a group. I investigated it and never found anything that would make me think such a group existed."

Alex pursed his lips and thought about what the principal had said for a moment. "Would it surprise you to know such a group was talked about often in the locker room?"

The man's eyes grew wide and he nodded. "Really? I talked to students I knew to be trustworthy, and they all assured me no such group existed."

"It could have just been kids talking without any real knowledge of a secret society." He glanced at Grace. "But it's still difficult to understand why Landon would suddenly drop all his old friends and associate himself with a new group."

"Did he do that?" Mr. Donner asked.

Alex glanced at Grace. "Tell him about Landon's friends."

She scooted to the edge of her chair. "Landon and I dated up until our senior year when he suddenly broke up with me. He also dropped all his old friends and started hanging out with a new group. I lost track of them after high school, and we wondered if you had any information on where they are now."

"I try to keep up with our graduates for our alumni council." He turned to his computer. "Give me a name, and I'll look him up."

"The first one is Sam Jefferson," Grace said.

Mr. Donner smiled. "I don't have to look him up. Sam is a lawyer with offices downtown. He's done really well for himself. In fact, my wife and I have used him when we've needed legal advice."

Alex pulled a small notepad from his pocket and

wrote down Sam's information. "That's good to hear. What about Dustin Shelton?"

Mr. Donner sat back in his chair, a sad expression on his face. "I don't have to look him up, either. Dustin disappeared while on a trip to the Gulf Coast a few years after he graduated. I attended the memorial service his family had."

Alex relaxed his grip on the pen poised to write Dustin's address and stared at Mr. Donner. "I remember Dustin. He was in one of my classes. I'm sorry to hear that."

"Yes, it was very sad. His family has never recovered from not finding his body." He shifted in his chair. "Who's the next one, Grace?"

"Jeremy Baker."

"Um, I don't remember him, but I'm sure he's in the alumni database." He typed the name into the computer, and his eyebrows rose as the information came on the screen. "This is a coincidence."

Alex leaned forward. "What is?"

Mr. Donner looked up from the computer screen. "Jeremy died in California about five years ago." His forehead wrinkled, and he looked back to the screen. Suddenly he nodded. "I do remember something about this young man. I remember some of the teachers talking about a former student who was found shot to death in his apartment in California. The police thought he'd been killed in a home invasion."

Alex and Grace exchanged startled glances before he wrote the latest information down. Then he swallowed and turned back to Mr. Donner. "What about Clay Mercer?"

He smiled. "Oh, I see Clay from time to time, although he lives in Nashville now. He's a political advisor and works with the governor's office."

Alex scribbled on the notepad and nodded. "What about Billy Warren?"

"Billy Warren," Mr. Donner murmured as he typed in the name. "Here he is. Oh, no. He's dead also. He was killed in a car wreck in Colorado four years ago." He glanced from Alex to Grace. "Those were the boys Landon had started hanging out with?"

"Yes." Alex's stomach roiled from the thoughts racing through his head. Of the six boys who had been friends, four of them were dead. The odds against that happening must be astronomical. He closed the notepad and glanced back at Mr. Donner. "We really appreciate your time today, but I know you're ready to begin your Christmas vacation. We won't take up any more of your time. It's been great being back here."

The principal stood and held out his hand. "Don't you two stay away so long before you come back to visit. If I can help you any more, please let me know."

Alex shook his hand and then Grace stood and did the same. "Thanks, Mr. Donner. It's been great seeing you today."

"It's always good to see you, Grace. And by the way, you know our annual fund-raiser is coming up in February. It would be great if you could maybe play it up on your newscast after Christmas. Let your viewers know the school you attended needs the support of the community if we are to continue providing quality programs to our students."

Grace smiled. "I'll see what I can do, Mr. Donner."

She turned toward the door, and Alex followed her from the room. They were almost to the front door of the school when a voice rang out in the hallway. "Grace Kincaid! What are you doing here?"

They whirled to face the man coming toward them. "Mr. Caldwell!" Grace hurried to him, and he enveloped her in a big hug. She pulled back and studied him at arm's length. "It's so good to see you. I haven't seen you in years."

Alex walked to where the two stood and stuck out his hand. "Mr. Caldwell, I don't know whether you remember me or not. I'm Alex Crowne."

The man grabbed Alex's hand and pumped it up and down. "Of course I remember. Who could forget that winning touchdown pass you threw in the state championship your senior year?" He leaned closer to Grace conspiratorially and said in a loud whisper, "We haven't won a title since then."

Grace laughed and looped her arm through Mr. Caldwell's. "Alex, this is my favorite teacher from my high school years. This man turned me on to writing and made me want to be a journalist. I owe him so much."

Mr. Caldwell gazed down at her and patted her hand. "You owe me nothing. It was a pleasure to teach a student who hung on my every word. I worried all the time that I would give out some wrong information in class and you would correct me."

Grace shook her head. "I wouldn't have known if you had. I was too busy trying to be the perfect student in your class."

He nodded and glanced at Alex. "I don't think I ever had you in my class, Alex."

"No, I was sorry I never got you for a teacher. Grace talked about you all the time. I guess you knew Landon Mitchell well, too, since he was your student."

"I did."

"And he was a good student?"

"He…" Mr. Caldwell hesitated. "He was a good student until about halfway through his junior year. Then something happened to him. It was like he didn't have his mind on his studies, and his grades took a nosedive. I talked to him and to his father, but nothing I said helped. By the middle of his senior year, I was afraid he might not graduate."

"I know," Grace said. "I saw it happening, too, but I couldn't figure it out. Did you have any theories concerning this abrupt change in him?"

Mr. Caldwell looked over his shoulder as if to make sure no one could hear what he was about to say. Then he leaned closer. "Of course the first thing you think about is drugs. He had all the symptoms of drug use— failing grades, avoiding old friends, skipping school, getting in trouble all the time. And then I heard he was involved with some secret group here at the school."

Alex's eyes grew wide. "What secret group?"

"I don't know who was in the group, but some of the kids told me they all had wolves tattooed on their shoulders. I was afraid they were selling drugs, but Mr. Donner wouldn't listen to me."

Alex and Grace exchanged quick glances. "Did you tell Mr. Donner about what the kids were saying?"

"Yes, but he dismissed it and wouldn't investigate.

When I told him, he looked at me, laughed and said, 'Patrick, don't be ridiculous. There are no drugs in this school.' He doesn't want the school board to think there are any problems in this school, and he tries to keep quiet anything that might blemish the school's reputation and cut down on donations from alumni. He's been this way ever since he came here."

"So he buries his head in the sand and hopes things will work out?" Grace asked.

Mr. Caldwell nodded. "Yes. If he had taken my concerns seriously and allowed me to find out more, we might have prevented the problem we have now."

"And what kind of problem is that?" Alex asked.

"Drugs. Drugs are everywhere in this school, and the problem gets worse every day. The administration refuses to acknowledge it, and teachers can't fight it on their own. I'm thinking of retiring at the end of this year. I've already cut back to part-time, but I know it's time for me to do something else."

Grace's forehead wrinkled, and she grabbed Mr. Caldwell's arm. "What will you do?"

He shook his head. "I don't know, but I can't take much more of the atmosphere around here."

"I'm so sorry," Grace said. "The students are losing a great teacher."

Mr. Caldwell straightened to his full height. "My time here is drawing to a close. Somebody else is going to have to take up the fight." He glanced at his watch. "Oh, my. I didn't realize it's so late. I have some Christmas gifts to pick up on my way home. They're for some of the residents at a retirement home where I volunteer."

"That's a very nice thing for you to do," Grace said.

He shrugged and smiled. "I have no family, and neither do some of them. So we've become each other's family. I'll spend Christmas with them."

Grace grasped his hand once more. "You're a good man, Mr. Caldwell. It was great to see you again."

He smiled and took her hand with both of his. "It was good seeing you, Grace. Don't stay away so long again."

"I won't, and I hope you and your friends at the retirement home have a merry Christmas."

"I'm sure we will, and merry Christmas to both of you." Mr. Caldwell turned and hurried down the hall to the door that led to the faculty parking lot. When he exited, Grace turned to Alex. "Mr. Caldwell always seemed so sad when I was in his class. He talked about having no wife or children and how teaching was his life. Volunteering at a retirement home helps fill that void I suppose."

"I guess so," Alex replied.

She tilted her head and looked at him. "But his story is a bit different from Mr. Donner's. I wonder why the principal lied to us about never having heard about a secret group."

Alex pursed his lips and stared in the direction of the office. "I don't know, but he did give us some new information about Landon's friends. I think our next step should be to question Sam Jefferson. I'll call his office in the morning and get an appointment for us to see him. For now, let's go see what they're serving at the Kincaid house for dinner tonight."

"It sounds like you're becoming more comfortable

being around my family. I'm glad. I've wanted that for years."

Alex didn't say anything as she headed toward the door. Was he becoming more comfortable with her family? If he was, he needed to be careful. His experience with the Kincaids had only brought him heartache in the past, and it could happen again.

As much as he loved Memphis, maybe his father was right. That job in Florida might be just what he needed to start a new life. Just he and his father living where there was no cold weather and you could walk on the beach every day of the year. The more he thought about it, the more it appealed to him.

# *Chapter Eight*

The minute she and Alex walked through the door at the law offices of Jefferson, Brooks and Dunbar the next morning Grace knew their old schoolmate Sam had done all right for himself. The waiting area resonated with the unspoken message one needed a fat bank account to afford this firm's high retainers and huge billing hours.

Grace slowed her steps as she followed Alex into the room and let her gaze drift over the large, framed photographs of breathtaking scenes hanging on the walls. The huge pictures offered a panoramic view of some of the most famous places in the world, places she'd always wanted to visit. Leather couches and chairs with tables beside them were scattered across the area where several people who Grace assumed to be clients sat reading newspapers or magazines.

A huge Christmas tree, its white lights twinkling like tiny diamonds and ornaments dangling from every branch, took up a whole corner of the massive room. The halo of the angel at the top touched the ceiling, and packages wrapped in gold paper sat underneath. A cart next to the tree was loaded with coffee carafes, Christmas cookies, pastries and fruit.

The receptionist smiled at them as she and Alex approached her desk. "May I help you?"

Alex pulled out his badge and showed it to the young woman. "I'm Detective Crowne with the Memphis Police. This is Grace Kincaid from WKIZ. I called earlier this morning. Mr. Jefferson is expecting us."

The woman's smile grew larger. "Mr. Jefferson told me you were coming. He's with a client right now, but I'll let you know when he's available. In the meantime, help yourself to the food on the cart."

Alex nodded and headed to the coffee cart, but Grace stepped closer to the receptionist's desk. "I couldn't help but notice all these beautiful framed photographs on the wall. I'd love to have some for my home. Would you mind telling me where you bought them?"

The woman laughed and shook her head. "I'm afraid you can't buy them anywhere. They're all Mr. Jefferson's work."

"Really? Sam shot all those pictures?"

"Yes. He's quite the photographer, and he loves to travel. He took them all while he was on trips."

"I'll have to tell him how beautiful they are," Grace murmured. She glanced around at Alex who balanced a cup of coffee in one hand and a Christmas cookie with thick icing in the other as he eased onto a sofa.

He glanced up as she sat down beside him. "This cookie is good. Want one?"

She shook her head. "No, thanks."

"They have eggnog, too."

"I'll wait. It's almost lunchtime."

"I know, but I didn't have time for breakfast this morning. I need something to tide me over until we go to lunch."

His words left a question in her mind. Did he mean they would eat together or go their separate ways after seeing Sam? She directed her eyes to her hands clenched in her lap. "You've done so much for me over the past few days, I'd like to take you to lunch."

He washed a bite of cookie down with a swig of coffee and nodded. "Okay. Where would you like to go?"

She thought for a moment before she answered. "A new tea room just opened down on Madison. Laura and I had lunch there the other day, and the food was delicious. They have all kinds of salads and sandwiches."

He swallowed another sip of coffee. "Do they have barbecue?"

She frowned. "Barbecue? I don't think so."

"So they don't have *all kinds* of sandwiches. Just chick food that's on some kind of bread I can't pronounce and a veggie substitute inside instead of meat."

Her face grew warm, and she leaned closer. "Well, pardon me. I forgot you live and breathe barbecue. Tell me where you want to go, and I'll take you there."

He laughed, and several people in the waiting area turned to look at them. "I'm sorry, Grace. I couldn't resist teasing you a bit. You always wanted to introduce me to the culinary delights of Memphis as you called them, but I'm still a meat and potatoes kind of guy. And there's nothing better to me than Memphis barbecue."

She burst out laughing at the twinkle in his eye.

"I know, Alex, and I won't try to change you. Since I'm treating you, we'll go wherever you want. Where will it be?"

He studied her for a moment, then a slow smile spread across his face. "I think I'd like to try the tea room on Madison. Maybe it's time for some changes in my life."

His gaze caressed her face as it traveled from her eyes to her lips, where it lingered for a moment before he took a quick breath and settled back on the sofa. Grace eased back into the cushions, picked up a magazine from the table next to the couch and held it in front of her face. What had just happened between her and Alex? Just now they'd laughed and joked together as they had years ago. Was it possible they could become friends again?

Before she could dwell any longer on the relationship changes she and Alex appeared to be experiencing, the receptionist rose from her desk and motioned for them. "Mr. Jefferson will see you now."

Alex drained the last drop of coffee from his cup and rose to follow Grace. When they reached the desk, the young woman took the cup and set it on a tray beside the door before she led them down a long hallway. They stopped in front of a mahogany door, and she knocked.

"Come in." The muffled voice came from inside.

She opened the door, stepped aside and motioned for them to enter. Grace eased into the room with Alex right behind her. Sam Jefferson rose from the chair behind his desk and held out his hand. "Alex, Grace. It's good to see you again." He shook both their hands and motioned them to the chairs in front of his desk, then he sat down.

Alex propped his elbows on the arms of his chair and leaned forward. "Thanks for seeing us on such short notice, Sam. From the looks of people waiting, it must be a busy day around here."

Sam shook his head. "No more than usual. But I always have time for old friends. I don't think I've seen you since we graduated." He glanced at Grace. "Of course I see you on the news every day, but that's not the same. How have you been doing?"

Grace smiled. "I'm fine."

He leaned back in his chair. "And how's your father doing? I heard about the drive-by shooting. I hope he's recovered and doing all right."

"He lived, but he'll spend the rest of his life in a wheelchair. That's been difficult for him to accept, but I think he has now."

Sam's eyes grew wide. "I had no idea." He stared at her for a moment before he cleared his throat and turned to Alex. "And I read in the paper you're heading up a new unit at the police department with Brad Austin and another detective."

Alex nodded. "A Cold Case Unit. Seth Dawtry is the other officer who works with Brad and me. In fact, Grace and I are here today about a case the police have never closed."

"Oh? Which one?"

"Landon Mitchell's death."

Sam's face paled, and he clasped his hands on top of his desk. "I thought Landon's death was ruled a suicide."

Alex shook his head. "Suicide was suspected but never proved. If you saw Grace's coverage earlier this week, you know Landon's father jumped from the

Memphis-Arkansas Bridge. Before he did, he made some accusations we're looking into."

Sam shifted in his chair and narrowed his eyes. "What kind of accusations?"

"He said he suspected Landon was involved with a secret group of some kind before his death. Mr. Mitchell found lots of money hidden in his son's room, and he also saw a wolf tattooed on his shoulder." Alex paused and took a breath. "We thought you might know something about these things."

Sam regarded Alex with an aloof expression and shrugged. "Why would I know anything? I barely knew Landon."

Grace sat up straight and gasped. "Sam, how can you say that? Our senior year you were with him all the time."

Sam directed a frosty glare in her direction, and a shiver went up Grace's spine. "I had a lot of friends. Landon was one of them, but we didn't hang out together after school. In fact, I found him rather boring."

"So these other friends you had," Alex interrupted. "Would they have been Jeremy Baker, Billy Warren, Clay Mercer and Dustin Shelton?"

Sam picked up a pencil from the desk and began to roll it in his fingers. "Yes, they were friends of mine."

"Did you know that Jeremy, Billy and Dustin are all dead, too?"

"Yes. I was sad when I heard about each of them."

Alex leaned forward. "Don't you think it's strange that four boys you were friends with in school have all died."

Sam shook his head. "Not necessarily. Everybody dies, Alex. Some sooner than others."

"Do you know if any of them had a wolf tattooed on their shoulders?" Alex's stare didn't waver from Sam's face.

Sam didn't flinch but returned an icy glare. "I have no idea."

Alex let his gaze drop to Sam's shoulder. "What about you? Do you have a wolf tattooed on yours?"

Sam rose to his feet, tossed the pencil he held to the desk, and glanced at his watch. "I'm afraid I'm going to have to cut our visit short. I have paying clients waiting to see me."

Alex and Grace rose as Sam walked over to the door and opened it. "It was good seeing you two again. Maybe we'll meet at the next reunion of our graduating class."

Alex trailed Grace to the door and stopped in front of Sam. "I'm going to find out what happened to Landon, Sam. If you think of anything that might help, give me a call at the station."

"I will."

"Goodbye, Sam," Grace said as she and Alex walked from the office.

They had only taken a few steps when Sam's voice called out. "Oh, Alex."

They stopped and turned to face him. "Yes?" Alex said.

"For your information I've always been afraid of needles. I have no tattoo."

Before they could answer, he closed the door. They looked at the door then back to each other and walked from the office. They didn't speak until they'd climbed into Alex's car. Then Grace swiveled in her seat and faced him. "What did you make of our visit?"

Alex smiled and shook his head. "He knows something. He tried to hide it under his courtroom facade, but my question about the tattoo rattled him."

"What will we do now?"

"Let's give him a few days to stew over what we told him. Then we'll come back. In the meantime, how would you like to take a trip to Nashville to see Clay?"

"That sounds like a great idea. When do you want to go?"

"I don't know. With the holidays Clay may be back in Memphis. I'll check tomorrow and let you know." He turned the key in the ignition. "Now how about some lunch? I'm starved."

Grace laughed and nodded. "You're the chauffeur. Go wherever you like."

He grinned, and Grace's heart fluttered at the boyish teasing that sparkled in his eyes. From somewhere deep inside her a memory surfaced. She remembered how she used to run the tip of her index finger down his jawline, and how he would smile in contentment when she did. She couldn't move for a moment, and then she blinked and took a deep breath. She couldn't let herself think like that. Right now she needed to concentrate on finding the man whose attempts on her life had turned it into a living nightmare. Then she could go back to her peaceful life, and Alex could go to Florida.

Alex leaned back into the plush sofa cushions in the Kincaids' den and stretched his legs out in front of him. Dinner at the Kincaid house had been delicious as he'd known it would be, and conversation with Harrison had proved interesting. He couldn't believe he was actually beginning to like the man. Now as he waited for Grace to return from helping her mother put her father to bed he was glad for a few minutes alone to reflect on what was happening in his life.

A week ago he'd been content to go to work every day and search old files in the hopes some piece of overlooked information would leap off the page and send him in pursuit of someone who'd gotten away with murder years before. Then he'd been called to the bridge where a man was threatening suicide, and Grace had reentered his life.

Now he was beginning to feel comfortable around her again, and he couldn't let that happen. He didn't believe for one minute that she'd stay in Memphis if her father's condition improved. She'd be knocking at the networks' doors again to get her old job back, and he really couldn't blame her. She was the total package when it came to what the networks wanted in an anchor. She was beautiful, smart and had the ability to connect with viewers.

He jumped to his feet, strode to the window and looked outside. The question remained, what was he going to do? Did he really want to give up his job in Memphis to go to Florida? He really missed his father and would like to be with him again. He sighed and leaned against the window frame. It wouldn't hurt to apply for the job down there. There was no guarantee he'd get it. Perhaps he should apply and see what happened.

"What are you doing?" Grace's voice startled him, and he glanced over his shoulder to see her entering the room.

"Just looking outside. Did you get your father settled?"

She nodded. "He said to say good-night for him and tell you he was glad you came to dinner again. He's enjoying getting to know you."

"It's good to see this side of him, too." A glow lit her face, and he let his gaze drift over her. She'd never looked more beautiful. He swallowed and turned back to look outside. "The weatherman says we may get some more snow next week."

She eased up beside him and looked out into the night. "I hope so. Do you remember how we used to wish for snow at Christmas when we were children?"

They stood so close he could smell her perfume, which gave off a fruity fragrance. "I remember, but we're not children anymore, Grace."

A sad look flickered in her eyes. "No, we're not. I suppose going back to the school yesterday brought up a lot of old memories and a lot of unexplained reasons for why things turned out the way they did between us."

His heart pounded, and he shook his head. "Grace, please, I don't want to talk about this."

"There's something I want to ask you. Did you ever wish you had gotten in touch with me after we broke up?"

He nodded. "I did. But then I could ask you the same question. Did you wish you had called me?"

"Yes." The word was barely a whisper.

His eyebrows arched at her answer. What had made him wait so long? Pride? Anger? He had no answer, but it really didn't matter. There was no going back and making everything right again.

He sighed. "Well, neither of us did, and we both survived. I have a great job here in Memphis, and you went on to New York and built a great career in television as an investigative reporter and then a news anchor. I imagine when your father improves you'll be off to the networks to continue your career, and I'll be happy for you."

Her eyes filled with tears. "I don't know if—"

The ringing of his cell phone interrupted what she was about to say, and he pulled the phone from his pocket. He glanced at the caller ID and frowned. "It's our office phone." He connected the call. "Hello."

"Alex, it's Seth."

"Hey, man. Are you still at the office?"

"Yeah, I've been looking over the files from the Mitchell case."

"Did you find anything?"

"No, I called to tell you something else. I know when you called in this morning you said you and Grace were going downtown to some lawyer's office."

"Yes. Sam Jefferson's."

"I thought Jefferson was the guy's name."

Alex frowned and glanced at Grace. "What makes you ask about Sam?"

"One of the homicide detectives I used to work with dropped by the office a few minutes ago and told me they found Sam Jefferson's body earlier tonight in the parking lot at his office building. He said it looked like he'd been shot execution-style in the back of the head when he was getting in his car."

The breath exploded from Alex's body in a rush, and he clamped his hand over his eyes. "No, no. This can't be true."

"I'm afraid it is, buddy. Sorry I have to tell you."

Alex took a deep breath. "Don't worry about it." He pulled the phone away from his ear and looked at Grace. "The police found Sam Jefferson shot to death." Her mouth dropped open, and she sank onto the couch. Alex turned his attention back to Seth. "Are the police still at the scene?"

"I think the crime scene investigators are there now. The medical examiner has the body."

"Thanks for calling, Seth. I'll see you in the morning."

He ended the call and sat down beside Grace on the couch. "What happened?" she asked.

Alex related what Seth had told him and took a deep breath. "I need to make another call." He punched in the number he'd called so many times in his years on the force. Dr. Harvey answered on the first ring.

"Medical examiner's office. Dr. Harvey speaking."

"Dr. Harvey, this is Alex Crowne. I understand you've brought Sam Jefferson's body to your office."

"Yes, Alex, but I haven't done any work yet."

"I realize that, but there's something I'd like for you to check for me first. It may shed some light on a cold case I'm working."

"What is it?"

"Would you check the victim's shoulders and see if he has a wolf tattooed on either one?"

"Sure, Alex. Give me a minute."

Alex drummed his fingers on the sofa cushion as

he waited for Dr. Harvey to return. Within minutes his voice came over the phone. "Alex?"

"Yes?"

"I checked, and he does indeed have a wolf tattoo. Do you want me to take some pictures of it and email them to you?"

"I would appreciate it very much. Thanks, Doc."

"No problem."

Alex disconnected the call and nodded. "He has the same tattoo Landon had. I think Mr. Mitchell must have been right. Those boys became involved in some kind of secret society and used the wolf as its symbol. And now five of the six are dead. We need to get to Clay as soon as possible. He may be next on the killer's list."

"I think you're right," Grace said.

"Or…" Alex paused. "As the only survivor, he may be the killer who's trying to protect some secret."

Grace only nodded, but he could tell his words concerned her. She hadn't forgotten, and neither had he, that someone out there had also tried to kill her. It had to be tied into whatever Landon Mitchell and his friends had done twelve years ago. He hoped he could find the answer before someone else was silenced.

# *Chapter Nine*

In the early afternoon the next day, Alex and Grace sped along Interstate 40 on the three-hour drive from Memphis to Nashville. Neither had spoken for the past fifteen minutes, and Grace didn't think she could endure the silence much longer. She glanced at Alex out of the corner of her eye and saw the muscle in his jaw twitch, a sign he was in deep thought. What was going on in his head? Was he upset over Sam's death, or was it something else? Their interrupted conversation last night might be the reason for his silence.

She took a deep breath and swiveled in her seat to face him. "I'm surprised you were able to reach Clay. I thought surely he would already have left Nashville for the holidays."

Alex nodded. "I thought so, too. He said he and his wife are leaving later today for a skiing trip. They're spending the holidays in Germany."

"Probably in Garmisch. Our families used to see each other there on skiing vacations. His father and mine loved skiing the trails of the Zugspitzplatt. It's a beautiful place."

"I wouldn't know. I've never taken a ski trip. For that matter, I never learned to ski."

"It's not too late, you know. You can still learn."

He chuckled and shook his head. "Not on a policeman's salary. Can't afford it."

"Sure you can. There are a lot of places around that don't cost all that much. You could go there while you're saving up for a bigger trip later on."

He cast a sideways glance at her before he turned his attention back to the highway. "I don't think so. Besides, there aren't many ski resorts in Florida."

His words hit her like a punch in the stomach. She took a deep breath. "So you're really going to move."

He nodded. "I'm considering it. It makes sense. Even if I don't get the chief of police job, I'm sure I can get on with one of the law enforcement agencies down there, and I can take care of my father."

"I see. If that's what you want, I wish you well."

She closed her eyes and settled back in her seat. The sound of the tires on the pavement lulled her, and she began to nod. The next thing she knew, Alex was shaking her shoulder. "Wake up, Grace. We're at the restaurant where I told Clay we would meet him."

She sat up and rubbed her eyes. The afternoon sun had begun to sink into the west, and shadows stretched across the parking lot. Christmas lights around the roofline of the restaurant twinkled in the coming darkness.

She unbuckled her seat belt, pulled the sun visor down and looked in the mirror on the back. "The days are so short in winter. By five o'clock it'll be dark, and then we have the drive home."

"I may let you drive back to Memphis so I can sleep like you did on the way to Nashville."

She glanced around at him, and her heart thumped at his grin. "As long as you feed me, I can do that."

He surveyed the restaurant. "Clay mentioned dinner, but I don't know when he has to leave for the airport. If he can't stay, we'll eat anyway."

"I just hope he understands the urgency of what we have to ask him. We don't want him to end up like all his friends."

Alex held up a finger as if to caution her. "Unless he's the killer. Remember that, and watch his every move. Also remember I have no jurisdiction here. This is strictly a meeting to question him about what he knows. He's not required to answer anything I ask him."

She swallowed her fear. "Do you really think he could have been the one who tried to kill me?"

"I don't know. At this point I'd say with his connection to the other victims, we could consider him a person of interest."

Grace nodded and opened the car door. Together they walked to the front door and entered the restaurant. Soft Christmas music drifted through the interior, and a decorated tree graced one corner of the entry. A young woman dressed in a knee-length full black skirt and a white blouse with billowing sleeves buttoned at the wrists greeted them.

"Good evening. Welcome to Antonio's. Do you have a reservation?"

Alex nodded. "Yes. It's in Clay Mercer's name."

Her eyes lit in recognition, and she smiled. "Mr. Mercer's been here for a while. I'll show you to his table."

As they followed the hostess to the table, Grace let her gaze drift over the restaurant. Since it would be several hours before the dinner crowd arrived, there were only a few customers seated at the elegantly draped tables adorned with flickering candles. Waiters and waitresses in their black pants with matching vests and white shirts bustled about the room as they prepared for expected customers.

Grace caught sight of Clay halfway across the room, and he waved to them. The boy whose family had shared vacations with the Kincaids was hardly visible in the man with the receding hairline and expanding waistline. He staggered a bit as he rose and clasped her hand when she stopped beside the table.

"Grace Kincaid. I can't believe it's you. I haven't seen you in years." Clay's slurred words rolled from his mouth. The smell of alcohol on his breath let Grace know how Clay had spent his time waiting for them.

"It has been a long time, Clay." She shook his hand and then eased into the chair Alex held for her next to Clay. She cast a smile over her shoulder. "Thanks, Alex."

Clay's gaze drifted back to Alex, and he reached out and shook his hand. "And Alex. Good to see you, too. I don't think I've seen you since graduation."

"It has been a while."

Clay motioned for Alex to have a seat, then picked up his glass and swallowed what was left of his drink.

With a cocky smile he held up the empty glass. "Marjorie, darling, find out what my friends are drinking and bring me one of these."

Concern flickered in Marjorie's eyes, and she hesitated. "Mr. Mercer, you're already over your limit. Maybe you need to order something to eat."

His eyes narrowed, and his face flushed. "Don't tell me what I need. Just do what I say."

Marjorie's lips trembled, and she cast a quick look at Grace. "But Antonio said—"

Clay slammed the glass down on the table and glared at her. "I don't care what he said. I'm the customer, and I told you what I wanted."

Grace smiled reassuringly at Marjorie. "All I want to drink is a glass of water." She glanced up at Clay. "And I am a bit hungry. I'd really like to order. What about you, Alex?"

"Water's fine for me, too." He smiled at the hostess. "If you'll have the waiter come over, we'll order."

Marjorie cast a grateful smile in their direction and hurried away from the table. Clay shook his head and frowned as he sank back into his chair. "I keep telling Antonio he should get better help in here, but he won't listen to me."

Grace started to respond, but the waiter arrived at that moment to tell them the specials of the day. After ordering, Clay slumped back in his seat and looked from Grace to Alex. "Okay, so let's have it. I don't think a TV anchor and a police detective drove all the way from Memphis to Nashville just to have a reunion with a high school classmate. What do you two really want?"

Alex leaned forward and crossed his arms on top of the table. "We want to talk to you about Landon Mitchell."

Clay picked up his water glass and took a drink. When he set it back on the table, it wobbled, and he grabbed it to keep it from turning over. "Are you talking about the kid who committed suicide when we were in high school?"

"Yes."

Clay shrugged. "I don't know how I can help. I barely knew him."

Grace shook her head. "That's not true, Clay. You and Landon were inseparable our senior year. I saw the two of you together all the time."

"We were lab partners in chemistry class. We were only together to study." He reached for his glass again, and his hand shook.

Grace reached over and placed her hand on his arm. "Clay, Landon didn't take chemistry our senior year."

His face grew red, and he glared at her. "Yes, he did."

"No, he didn't. I know what his schedule was because it was just like mine. And he didn't take chemistry."

He shook free of her and shrugged. "Then maybe I'm mixed up. It must have been our junior year. Anyway, what does a twelve-year-old suicide have to do with me?"

Alex's stare bored into Clay. "It's strange, isn't it, that so many of the kids we graduated with are dead now."

"Wh-what do you mean?" Clay asked.

Alex pursed his lips as if in deep thought. "Well, there's Landon, of course, and Jeremy, Billy and Dustin. You remember all of them, don't you?"

Clay picked up his drink glass and frowned at the empty container. "Of course I remember them."

"And now Sam Jefferson."

Clay's mouth twitched, and he swallowed before he set the glass back on the table. "Sam's dead?"

Alex nodded. "Yes. He was murdered yesterday."

Grace had expected a violent reaction from Clay, but it didn't happen. Instead, he sat perfectly still. After a moment, he took a deep breath. "What do you really want from me, Alex?"

Alex leaned forward. "For starters, Clay, I'd like to know if you have a wolf tattooed on your shoulder."

He shook his head. "No, I don't."

"Landon did, and so did Sam."

Clay sighed. "I wouldn't know anything about that."

Alex didn't blink as he stared at Clay. "Would you be willing to prove it to me?"

Clay frowned and shook his head. "Why should I have to prove anything to you?"

"Because then we'll know you weren't part of the group that had the tattoos."

Clay pushed his chair back from the table and glanced at them. "You don't have any proof that I know anything about Landon's death or you'd have a warrant. Now why don't we agree to have dinner as three old friends and leave it at that?"

Alex shook his head. "Because right now the Memphis police are investigating Sam's murder. You're going to have to talk to them at some point. Why not do it now instead of later?"

Clay worried his lip and looked at Grace. "I'm really sorry about Sam. He was a good friend. It looks like I'm the only one of our group of friends left."

Grace nodded. "If you know anything that can help Alex find out who killed Sam, you need to tell him."

He shook his head. "I don't know anything about Sam's murder or what happened to the others." He glanced down at his glass again and sighed. "All this talk has made me thirsty. I sure could use another drink before dinner. I don't care what Marjorie and Antonio say." He rose and laid his napkin on the table. "I'm going to speak with the bartender. I'll be back in a minute."

Grace's gaze followed him as he strode across the dining room. When he disappeared into the bar area, she looked at Alex and frowned. "He seemed genuinely sorry about Sam's death. Do you think he could be the murderer?"

Alex shrugged. "I don't know. Maybe he'll say something else while we're eating that will shed some light on this case. I just hope the bartender doesn't give him another drink. His blood alcohol is probably already too high to drive."

Grace nodded and glanced around the room. Several tables had filled while they'd been talking with Clay. Her wandering gaze locked on a young couple a few tables away from them. A large Christmas shopping bag sat in the empty chair next to the woman, and she smiled as she pulled out a doll and passed it to the man. His eyes lit up, and he nodded and smiled as he examined the toy. Her heart lurched. They must be a married couple, and the woman had just purchased the doll for their daughter's Christmas present. How happy they looked.

She shifted her gaze to Alex and struggled to keep tears from filling her eyes. If things had worked out for them, she and Alex might very well be discussing Christmas presents for their children. Instead, all that drew them together this Christmas were some unsolved murders and attempts on her life.

"Excuse me." A voice interrupted her thoughts, and she glanced up to see Marjorie standing by their table. "Mr. Mercer asked me to give you a message."

Alex's gaze darted past her to the entrance to the bar. "Is there a problem?"

She nodded. "I'm afraid so. He asked me to tell you he received an urgent phone call and had to leave. Your dinner is paid for, and it will be here in a few minutes. He said for you to enjoy your time here and he'll phone you when he gets back from Germany."

Alex let out a long breath. "Thank you for telling us."

Grace waited for Marjorie to leave before she spoke. "Can you believe that?"

"I should have suspected he was up to something and gone with him." The look on his face reminded Grace of how Alex used to look when she beat him at one of the board games they loved. Amusement bubbled up in her. She pressed her hand against her mouth, but it was no use. A loud burst of laughter escaped her lips. He frowned. "What's the matter?"

She struggled to quiet down. "I was just thinking we

are pathetic. Here you are a police detective who deals with criminals all the time and I'm a journalist who interviews people from all walks of life. We're trained to tell when people are lying, and neither one of us tried to stop Clay from walking out of here."

He regarded her with a serious look for a moment, then his lips pulled into a grin. A sheepish expression covered his face. "You're right. We let him outsmart us. We'll have to be more careful in the future."

Her laughter died, and she crossed her arms on top of the table. "Do you think we'll get the chance to question him again?"

Alex nodded. "Oh, yeah. And the next time he won't get away so easily."

Two waiters appeared at their table just as he finished speaking. The smells from the covered plates they carried made Grace's stomach growl, and she pressed her hand to her abdomen. "Mmm, that smells good."

The waiters set the plates in front of them and removed their covers. "Is everything satisfactory?" one of them asked.

"Mine looks scrumptious," Grace said.

"And my steak is perfect," Alex added.

When the two men had left, Grace picked up her fork and knife and cut off a bite of chicken. Before she could raise it to her mouth, Alex spoke. "Grace?"

She halted, her fork in midair, and looked up at him. His gaze drifted over her face, and her skin tingled. "Yes?"

"I've enjoyed being with you these past few days."

She swallowed and nodded. "I've enjoyed it, too."

"I'm kind of glad Clay ran out on us. He's not here, and we're not at the table with your parents. Tonight we can just enjoy being together."

Before she could respond, he looked back at his plate and began to cut into his steak. She smiled and dropped her gaze back to her plate. Over the past few days she and Alex had become more comfortable around each other, and she was glad. Their friendship had been the best part of her childhood, and she hoped they could eventually reach the place where they could lay the bad memories of their adulthood to rest.

With a sigh she raised her fork to her lips and closed them around the bite of chicken.

Alex relaxed behind the wheel of the car and hummed along with the music of his favorite Memphis radio station as he cruised along Interstate 40. He glanced over at Grace sleeping soundly in the passenger seat and smiled.

It seemed so right to have her in the car with him. He'd been lonely since their breakup, and a day didn't go by without some memory of her popping into his head. Some days it might have been an angry thought, but most of the time it was about the good times they'd spent together, especially during their childhood.

She groaned in her sleep, and he jerked his head to glance at her. A look as if she were in pain flashed across her face, and she moaned again. "No, no."

He reached over and gave her a gentle shake. "Grace, are you all right?"

Her eyes blinked open. She looked at him with a wild-eyed stare and sat up straight in her seat. "Alex…"

"I'm here, Grace."

She turned her head from side to side as if to get her bearings and rubbed her hands over her eyes. She exhaled a deep breath. "Where are we?"

"Just outside of Memphis. You called out in your sleep."

She yawned and settled back in her seat. "I must have been dreaming. I don't know what it was, though."

"We should be at your house before too long. You can go right to bed."

She shook her head. "No, I'll have to wait up for my parents. They went to see the church's Christmas program tonight. In fact, they took our maid and cook with them, as well. There shouldn't be anybody at home when I get there."

"Then maybe I'd better stay until they get home."

She glanced at the clock on the car dashboard. "If you don't mind, I'd appreciate your doing that. I didn't think I'd ever be afraid to stay alone. I suppose those two attempts to kill me have changed my mind, but my parents should be home soon. I'm sorry to be such a nuisance."

He nodded and kept his attention directed to the traffic, which had increased since they got closer to the city. "You aren't a nuisance. You've been a lot braver than most people would have been in your situation. I'm glad to see that you're finally beginning to be cautious instead of charging in without thinking."

"Oh, is that what you think I do? Charge in without thinking?"

He chuckled. "I'd say that's right. Do you remember the time when we were about twelve years old and you decided you wanted a soft drink and there weren't any in the refrigerator in the kitchen?"

She laughed. "So I decided to borrow my mother's car and drive down to the convenience store and get some for you and me to drink."

"Yeah. I tried to talk you out of it, but you wouldn't listen."

"And you were afraid for me go alone," Grace continued, "so you jumped in the car with me so you could help me if anything happened."

By this time they were both laughing. Alex glanced at her. "And we didn't make it down the driveway before you hit a tree."

Grace lay back in the seat and shook her head. "I don't think I've ever seen my father so angry. I was grounded for weeks."

"As well you deserved to be." They rode in silence for a few minutes, each lost in their own thoughts, before Alex spoke again. "We have some great memories, Grace."

"Yes, we do," she whispered and turned to gaze out the window.

Thirty minutes later he pulled the car to a stop at the gate to Grace's house and typed in the code. The big iron gates opened, and he drove through the entrance to the walled Kincaid estate. He watched in the rearview mirror as the gates closed automatically behind him.

Beside him, Grace leaned forward in her seat and looked through the windshield. "That's strange."

"What is?"

She pointed toward the house. "Look. Every light in the house is on."

He stared straight ahead and frowned at the bright beams shining through every window. The house practically glowed it was so lit up. "Is that unusual?"

She nodded. "My parents are always after me to turn out a light when I leave a room to conserve energy. There's no way they would have left home with every bulb in the house burning."

"Are you sure? Maybe they wanted the outside Christmas decorations to show up."

She shook her head. "I know my parents. They would never have left all those lights on."

Alex pulled the car to a stop at the front of the house and got out. Grace jumped out and fumbled in her purse for her key as she ran toward the front steps. He raced around the front of the vehicle and caught her arm just as she started up the steps. "Wait, Grace. Let me go first."

She turned back to him, her eyes wide. "Why? Do you think something's wrong?"

He stepped in front of her and pulled his gun from the holster. "I don't know, but I need to check this out before we go bursting in there."

She gasped, and her hand covered her mouth. "Do you think someone could be in there?"

"Could be. Go ahead and unlock the door for me, but wait on the porch. I'll be back in a few minutes."

She nodded and started to stick the key in the door but turned back to him. "The door's open. It looks like somebody jimmied it."

He pulled her away from the door, reached for his cell phone and dialed 911. When the operator answered, he identified himself. "I need backup for a B and E at

3947 Tulip Grove Road. I'm entering the house now."
He glanced over his shoulder at Grace. "Drive my car
back to the gate and open it for the police. Don't come
inside the house until we've cleared it."

She nodded and backed away. He waited until she
drove down the driveway before he entered the house.
Holding the gun in front of him, he eased inside and
swept it back and forth as he surveyed the scene before
him. The home looked as if a whirlwind had ripped
through it. Sofas and chairs, their pillows cut open and
the stuffing pulled out, lay overturned amid upended
tables and shattered lamps. Picture frames with their
glass broken out hung at crooked angles on the wall.

In the den the Christmas tree lay on its side, its broken ornaments scattered across the floor. The Christmas presents had been opened, and the items that had
been inside littered the floor.

The sound of a police siren split the air, and he
pulled out his badge. He'd just arrived at the front door
when the first patrol car pulled to a stop. He held his
badge up as the officers jumped out of the cruiser. "I'm
Detective Alex Crowne. I've cleared the front rooms
downstairs, but I haven't been upstairs or checked the
back of the house."

Two more cars with Grace trailing behind rolled
to a stop, and officers rushed to the porch. The officer in charge nodded to Alex. "Thanks. We'll take it
from here."

Alex moved out of the way and met Grace at the bottom of the steps. "Was there anyone inside?"

"I didn't see anyone, but the officers are checking."
He took a deep breath. "Grace, it looks bad in there. It

looks like somebody took their time and moved from room to room trashing everything in their path."

Her eyes filled with tears, and she started toward the porch. He grabbed her arm and pulled her back. "You can't go in there yet. The police are still working, and you need to be prepared when you see it."

She turned back to him, and his heart thudded at the fear in her eyes. "It's the killer, isn't it? I've survived his attempts to kill me, so he wants to hurt me in another way by destroying my home. Why does he hate me so?"

"I don't know." A wail escaped her throat, and she covered her eyes with her hands as the tears rolled down her cheeks. Her shoulders shook, and before he realized what he was doing, he had wrapped his arms around her and pulled her close. She laid her head against his chest, and he tightened his arms. "Don't cry. It's going to be all right."

She pulled back and stared up into his eyes. "It's not going to be all right. I should have listened to you. You warned me about getting involved in Landon's death, and now I've brought more misery on my parents. They have enough to face with my father's condition. In the past week they've had to worry about me almost being killed twice, and now they're going to come back to a vandalized home. They don't deserve this."

She sagged against him, and her head dropped to his chest. He didn't know what to say that would comfort her. This latest development probably was related to the Mitchell case, but it also told him something else. Mr. Mitchell had been right about his son being murdered, and he and Grace must have gotten close to some answers. But if Landon's killer had come into the Kincaids' house, he had to know they wouldn't be home and he had to know how to access the property some way other than through the main gate.

Perhaps the killer knew more about the Kincaids than Alex had thought. He could have been watching them all along. He tightened his arms around Grace and looked out into the dark night. "Don't worry, Grace," he whispered. "I promise you we'll get this guy."

# Chapter Ten

An hour after coming home to the chaos inside the house, Grace stood on the front porch, two suitcases at her feet, and scanned the driveway leading from the now-open gate. Police cars, some with their blue lights still flashing, were parked up and down the driveway. From time to time she could hear voices inside the house and wondered if the officers had found any clues as to who had invaded their home.

The front door opened, and Alex stepped onto the porch. "I thought I'd check and see if your parents had gotten here yet."

She shook her head. "Mom called when they left the church to see if I'd gotten home, and I told her what had happened. They're on their way now."

He glanced down at the suitcases. "Were you able to find enough clothes for all of you to take with you?"

"Yes. There had been some left in the closets of the bedrooms, and I collected enough for overnight. I called the Peabody and reserved us a suite with two bedrooms, and I called the drugstore." Anger flowed through her, and she clenched her hands at her sides. "Why did he have to pour all my father's medications in the toilet and then not flush it? It was almost like a taunt to see his medicine in the water and know it was useless to help with pain if needed."

"I know. I've seen burglars and vandals do a lot of crazy things. It's hard to know the mindset of someone like that. What did the pharmacist say when you talked with him?"

Grace let out a long breath. "I explained the situation, and he said we could get enough medicine to get us through the night. We'll contact the doctor in the morning for new prescriptions."

"Good." Alex stared toward the gate as a vehicle turned into the driveway. "Is that your folks' van?"

"No, that's the WKIZ van."

He turned to her and frowned. "What's it doing here?"

"I called Derek, the cameraman that came to the bridge with me, and asked him to come over and bring a reporter."

"Why?"

Grace steeled herself for Alex's anger when she told him what she had planned. "I'm going to do a live feed on the ten o'clock news."

"You're what?" The words exploded out of Alex's mouth.

"I talked with the producer, and he okayed it. I'm going to let the person who did this know he can't scare me. We may not be able to prove it yet, but I know whoever did this killed Landon and a lot of other people."

Alex raked his hand through his hair. "Grace, I don't think—"

She reached out and grasped his arm. "Alex, this guy has killed people we went to school with, he's attempted to kill me and now he's violated the security of my home. Reporting is my job, and I have to cover this story."

After a moment he nodded, then directed his gaze back down the driveway where a second vehicle had just entered. "Tell that to your folks. Here they come." He picked up the suitcases and waited for her parents' van to come to a stop.

Grace walked down the steps with Alex behind her, motioned for Derek to park beside the house, and waited for her mother to stop next to her. She then opened the sliding door on the side and peered in at her father strapped in his wheelchair.

She reached in and grasped his outstretched hand. "The police haven't finished inside yet, so there's no need for you to come in. Go on to the Peabody, but don't forget the medicine at the drugstore. The pharmacist said he'd have it at the drive-through. I'll meet you at the hotel when I can leave here."

Her father shook his head. "I don't want you driving downtown alone."

Alex shoved the two bags into the van and glanced at Grace. "Don't worry, sir. I'll drive Grace down there and see that she's settled."

Grace frowned. "Alex, that's not—"

He held up his hand to stop her. "I insist. No discussion needed."

Her parents exchanged quick glances, and a smile

pulled at her father's lips. "Thanks, Alex. It seems like I'm thanking you a lot lately for taking care of my daughter." His gaze drifted to the house. "For years I worked day and night to buy the things I thought would make my family happy. Now I realize those were just possessions. There's nothing in that house that can even start to compare with the safety of my wife and daughter. I wish I had learned that lesson sooner."

Grace patted his hand and smiled. "Don't think about that now, Dad. You go with Mother, and I'll see the two of you later."

She and Alex watched as her mother turned the van around and drove back toward the gate. When the van turned onto the road leading toward the city, Alex looked at her and shook his head. "I still can't believe how much your father has changed. He's not the same man I knew."

"I know. That's what happens when God takes over in someone's life. He becomes a new person."

"I've heard that, but I never thought it possible. Now I've seen it with my own eyes. It makes me wish I could be more like your father."

She smiled up at him. "You can, Alex. All you have to do is open up your heart to God."

He shrugged. "I'll think about it." He glanced past her and frowned. "Here comes the cameraman. It's not too late to change your mind."

She turned to smile at Derek, but her mouth opened in surprise at the sight of Julie Colter walking with him. They came to a stop beside her, and she glanced from one to the other. "Julie, what a surprise. I didn't expect to see you."

Julie bit down on her lip and glanced up at Derek. "Well, you see…" She hesitated and turned to Derek.

Derek shifted the camera he was carrying in his arms and smiled at Julie "She's going to do your interview."

Grace's eyes grew wide. "Wh-what?"

Derek nodded. "Julie's been talking to me at the station, and she's not cut out for what management has her doing. They told her she'd get a chance to prove herself with some public interest stories. So far they haven't followed through on their promise. How about it, Grace? Let's give her a chance."

Grace blinked and searched her mind for something to say. Did she really want klutzy Julie to do this interview? Since the girl had arrived at the station, she'd made so many mistakes the station manager was about to fire her.

Before she could reply to Derek's question, Julie lifted her chin and took a deep breath. "I know I've made some mistakes, Miss Kincaid, but nobody has ever really given me any guidance. I've tried to do what I thought the manager wanted, but I haven't seemed to please him. I have a degree in journalism, and I worked at my college's TV station as a reporter. In fact, I won some awards, but he won't give me an assignment. Derek is trying to help me out. I'd be forever grateful if you would, too."

Grace cast a helpless glance at Alex who shrugged and then to Derek before she locked gazes with Julie. "But this is a live feed into the news which is in progress right now. There'll be no do-overs, and we can't correct any mistakes we make. Do you understand?"

Julie nodded, and the plea that sparkled in her eyes reminded Grace of her own hunger for a first chance to do an on-camera interview. She'd been fortunate, though. There were many people who'd helped her, including Richard Champion. Without their support she wouldn't be a news anchor today.

Had she paid their support forward and helped another wannabe reporter? The answer made her cringe. She couldn't recall one single person she'd helped. Instead of thanking God for all the blessings He'd showered on her, she'd spent years dwelling on the bad things that had happened in her life—her breakup with Alex, Richard's unfaithfulness and her father's attack. It was time for a change in her life.

Some things like her misguided infatuation with Richard and her father's injuries couldn't be changed, and she and Alex might never recapture their childhood friendship, but she could still be happy. She could start right now by helping a young reporter get her first story.

She smiled at Julie. "I think Derek had a good idea, Julie. Let's do an interview that will get you noticed."

Julie glanced at Derek, and the look that passed between them reminded her of the way she and Alex used to look at each other. Out of the corner of her eye she saw Alex watching them also. A smile crooked his mouth, and tears filled her eyes. It was the same way he'd smiled at her when they were children and he approved of something she'd done. But they weren't children anymore.

She took a deep breath and motioned for Derek and Julie to follow her into the house.

\* \* \*

Alex stood inside the Kincaids' den near the door and watched Julie discussing the upcoming interview with Grace. He remembered the day he'd gone to the TV station and how Grace had complained about the girl's incompetence. Minutes ago she'd agreed to let Julie interview her on a live feed.

He smiled and let his gaze travel over Grace who had always held everyone, herself included, to the highest standards when reporting the news. Why would she allow an unproven reporter to interview her on a breaking story? The answer came to him almost before the question had flashed in his mind. It was because of the path Grace's life had taken in her new relationship with God. Like her parents, her eyes had been opened to the needs in others, and she was different in many ways than she'd been before. He couldn't deny he liked the new Grace much better than the one he'd known all his life.

In an effort to bring his thoughts back to the matter at hand, he turned his attention to Julie who was bustling about the room like a director getting ready to stage a play. Her commanding professional attitude indicated she hadn't wasted her time at the station. She'd been watching, and she'd been learning. He hoped she could please Grace, who at the moment appeared to be following Julie's instructions to stand in the middle of the broken ornaments littering the floor from the fallen Christmas tree.

Julie turned to Derek for their last sound check. When they'd finished, he held up three fingers and mouthed the countdown to her. Julie looked into the camera with a no-nonsense expression on her face.

"This is Julie Colter coming to you live from the home of WKIZ news anchor Grace Kincaid. As much as I wish this was a social visit, I'm here tonight with Grace to discuss the vandalism of her beautiful home." She paused as the camera swept the room. "As you can see, some unknown person or persons entered the home while the family was away and left a trail of destruction throughout the entire house. Police are on the scene as we speak, and one of my sources tells me evidence has been recovered that may lead to an arrest." She paused and faced Grace. "This must have been a terrible shock when you arrived home tonight. What was your reaction when you walked in to find your home had been invaded?"

Alex couldn't take his eyes off Grace as she proceeded to relate the shock of walking in to find nearly everything in the house destroyed. With sympathy flickering in her eyes, Julie hung on every word Grace spoke.

Grace paused and then addressed the camera. "I'm sure anyone who has come home to find their home burglarized knows how violated I'm feeling right now. We read about these things happening or we see it on the news, but somehow we never think we'll be the victim of a crime. Yet it happens all the time."

Julie nodded. "You're right. According to statistics, a burglary happens every fourteen seconds, and the number is rising every year. We all are potential victims." She turned back to Grace. "One of the deterrents to home invasion is a security system. Does your home have one?"

"Yes, but unfortunately it wasn't working. Either my parents forgot to turn it on when they left or the burglar disabled it. If my parents did forget, we'll have to make sure they don't again."

"And speaking of your parents," Julie continued, "I know they aren't here right now. How are they holding up? Your father especially. We were all saddened when he was gunned down in a drive-by shooting earlier this year."

"They're doing all right. My father is strong, and he'll get through this. Whoever shot him may have taken the use of his legs away, but it's made a stronger man out of him. I'm very proud of him."

"That's good to hear. Grace, we only have a minute left, and I understand you'd like to make a statement to our viewers."

Grace smiled. "I would. As many of you know, a few days ago I reported the death of Timothy Mitchell, who jumped from the Memphis-Arkansas Bridge. He was the father of one of my high school friends who was thought to have committed suicide twelve years ago. Thanks to the help of Detective Alex Crowne, I have been able to investigate Mr. Mitchell's belief that his son was murdered. Our findings suggest he may have been right. In pursuing this case, however, I've been shot at, poisoned by a cyanide-laced note and now my home has been vandalized."

"Excuse me, Grace," Julie interrupted. "Are you saying you believe Landon Mitchell was indeed murdered and his killer is responsible for the acts of violence you've suffered since you broke the story of his father's plunge from the Memphis-Arkansas Bridge?"

"I am. In fact, I'm convinced of it." Grace glanced over at him, and Alex smiled. Then she continued. "So, I want to take this opportunity to let the murderer, who thinks he can intimidate me, know his attempts to stop the search for the truth haven't worked. The police are on this case and before too long I expect they'll have the answer to who murdered Landon Mitchell and at least four other people. You can't stay hidden forever."

Julie frowned and leaned closer to Grace. "Those are brave words, Grace, and I'm sure our viewers wish you well in your search. Is there anything the public can do to help?"

"Yes, there is." She paused and took a breath. "One of you viewing this report may have information about the deaths of Landon Mitchell or Sam Jefferson, or about a secret high school club whose members were tattooed with a wolf. If you do, get in touch with me. You can leave a message on my voice mail at the station or you can email me at my address on the station's website."

Julie turned and looked at Derek as he zoomed in on her for a close-up. "Grace needs your help. If you have information, get in touch with her. In the meantime, keep watching this station for the latest developments in the investigation. This is Julie Colter for WKIZ news, live at the home of Grace Kincaid."

Derek signaled that the camera was off, and Julie let out a long breath. Grace smiled and patted her on the back. "Great job, Julie. I think you're right. Your talents are wasted working as a glorified gopher. When I come back to work, I'll talk to the manager about making you my assistant. Would you like that?"

Julie's eyes grew wide. "Oh, Miss Kincaid, it would be like a dream come true."

"Then that's what I'll do. Now I think I'd better check with Detective Crowne and see if I need to stay here any longer."

Derek nodded and grasped Julie's arm. "We'll get out of your way, Grace. I hope to see you back at work soon."

"I'll be back after Christmas."

Alex straightened from leaning against the wall as Grace walked toward him and smiled. "Good job on the interview. If our guy saw it, he's probably trying to decide what he can do next to make our lives miserable." He let his gaze drift over her face. "I don't want anything to happen to you."

"I don't either, but we can't let him control us much longer." She propped her hands on hips and glanced around the room. "Do you think Clay could have had time to drive from Nashville and do this?"

"I don't know, but I doubt it. He looked more scared than angry, but that doesn't mean he couldn't be involved. He could have made a quick telephone call and set this in motion." He sighed and rubbed his hand over his eyes. "Every way I turn with this case new questions pop up, and I have this thought niggling in my head that I've forgotten something."

"But you can't figure out what it is?"

He shook his head. "It's like it's just out of reach of my memory, and I know it's something important. I'm missing something, but I don't know what."

She yawned. "Don't worry. You'll remember."

"I hope so." He sighed and glanced over his shoulder. "There's no need for us to stay here any longer. The officers can take it from here. Let's get you down to the Peabody, and then I'll go home and get some sleep. Maybe tomorrow will bring some new leads in the case."

"I sure hope so. I'll get my bag and be back in a minute."

He stood still and watched as she left the room. It had been a long day, and he was ready to get some rest. He hoped he could sleep. If only he could get this thought out of his mind that he knew something that could bring this case to a close right now. It was something someone had said. Not recently, but a long time ago. Something he should have remembered. But what was it?

After a minute, he exhaled and shook his head. There was no use racking his brain tonight. Maybe tomorrow he could remember what he needed to know.

## Chapter Eleven

Grace swallowed the last bite of her omelet and picked up her coffee cup. Breakfast had always been one of her favorite meals, and nothing could be better than being served in the dining room of the Peabody Hotel. Her parents were having a quiet morning with room service, but she'd wanted to mingle with other guests and enjoy the beautiful Christmas decorations that had turned the hotel into a wonderland.

She'd attended many private parties at the Peabody and had dined here several times with friends, but this was the first time she'd ever spent the night in the elegant hotel. The visit would have been very exciting if it weren't for the reason she and her parents had become guests. Her forehead wrinkled as she recalled the events of the night before. When she'd checked on her parents earlier, her father had mentioned they needed to contact their insurance company, and she needed to take care of that right away.

She pulled her cell phone from her purse and was about to dial the number when she looked up and spied

Alex walking in the door. Her pulse quickened at the sight of him. She'd always thought him handsome, but somehow this morning his presence set her heart to beating faster.

He stopped at the table and dropped into the chair across from her. "Sorry to be so late. I took advantage of it being Saturday. Since I didn't have to go to work, I slept in longer than usual."

"Do you want something to eat?"

He shook his head. "I ate before I left home, but I could use some coffee."

As if she'd heard the request, a waitress stopped beside the table. "Coffee, sir?"

He smiled. "Yes, please."

Grace waited until the woman had poured the coffee before she leaned closer. "How's the case you're helping Seth with coming along?"

"We're at a standstill, but it's a case that goes back a lot further that Landon's. We may never get the answer to that one."

Grace closed her eyes and shuddered. "It's horrible for families not to have answers. I hope we can find some about all the deaths of our classmates."

"Me, too." He looked down at the cell phone she still held. "Have you checked to see if anyone left you an email or a voice mail?"

"No, I was about to call the insurance company, but I think I'll check voice mail first."

Grace punched in the number and drummed her fingers on the table as she listened to the messages. From time to time she knit her eyebrows and shook her head.

Every crazy in Memphis must have left a message for her, and they all claimed to know the killer's name.

She was about to give up when she clasped the phone tighter and sat up in her chair. "Hello, Grace, this is Sharon Warren," a woman's voice said. "I was Sharon Ashley when we attended school together, and I married Billy Warren. I'm in Memphis visiting my family for Christmas, and I saw your interview on television last night. I think we need to get together. I know some things that might help you with your case. You can reach me at 555-2721."

Alex set his cup down and frowned. "What is it?"

"I had a message from Billy Warren's widow. She wants to meet with me. She says she knows something that may help the case."

An excited look flashed on Alex's face. "When?"

"I have to call her." Grace punched in the number and waited for someone to answer.

A woman's voice answered. "Hello."

"This is Grace Kincaid calling for Sharon Warren."

"Grace, this is Sharon. Thank you for returning my call."

"No, it's I who need to thank you. I'm very much interested in talking with you. When can we meet?"

Sharon hesitated a moment. "I'm at my parents' home, and we're leaving to take my daughter to Disneyworld this afternoon. It's her Christmas present. Would it be possible for us to meet now?"

"Yes, I can do that. Tell me where."

"Why don't you come here? My parents have taken my daughter to the mall to get some last-minute items for the trip and won't be back for a while."

"We can do that." She pulled the phone away from her ear and whispered to Alex. "Do you have time to meet with Sharon?" He nodded, and she spoke into the phone. "Alex Crowne with the Memphis Police will be with me. It's been a long time since I was at your parents' home. What's the address?"

Alex pulled a pen and a small notepad from his shirt pocket and slid them across the table to her. Grace mouthed a thank-you and wrote down the address as Sharon recited it to her. "And one more thing, Grace," Sharon said, "don't tell anyone else I'm in town. I still don't feel safe when I come back to Memphis."

"Okay. We'll keep this to ourselves, and we'll leave right now. We should be there in about thirty minutes."

"I'll see you then."

Grace ended the call and placed the phone in her purse. "Sharon doesn't want anyone to know she's in town. She sounded scared. Maybe this is the tip we've been looking for."

"I hope so."

Thirty minutes later they pulled to a stop in front of the address Sharon had given her. Grace stared at the rambling house with the circle driveway and re- membered high school parties she'd attended here. "I haven't been to this house since we graduated."

Alex turned off the ignition and opened the car door. "I didn't know you and Sharon were friends."

Grace climbed out and looked over the car's roof at him. "We weren't close friends. Our families were members at the same country club, and I was always invited to Sharon's parties. It's strange, though, I hadn't even thought of her since I heard Billy was dead. I don't know why I didn't."

Alex rubbed his neck and frowned. "I know what you mean. I've still got this feeling that I've forgotten something."

Grace walked around the car, and they climbed the steps to the front porch. "I'm sure it will come to you."

Before they could ring the bell, Sharon opened the door. Even though Grace hadn't seen her in years, she still recognized the girl she'd known growing up. She had matured, and her once-blond hair was darker than Grace remembered. But the blue eyes still crinkled at the corners when she smiled.

She reached out and grabbed Grace's hand in both of hers. "Grace, it's so good to see you."

Then she turned to Alex and shook his hand. "And Alex Crowne. You're still as good-looking as ever. Come in."

Alex's face flushed, and he grinned. "Thanks, Sharon. I didn't know if you'd remember me or not."

"Of course I remember you. Who could forget the guy who helped us win the state football championship?"

Alex's smile grew larger. "That was a long time ago."

Sharon rolled her eyes. "Don't remind me." She held the door for them to enter the house and led them to a study in the rear of the residence. When they entered the room, she closed the door. "I thought we'd talk in here since this is more private. Some of the household staff might pop into an open room while we're talking, but they won't open a closed door."

Grace sat down on a sofa and waited for Alex and Sharon to take their seats before she shifted to the edge of the cushions. "I was excited to hear from you. What is it you think might help us?"

Sharon took a deep breath. "As you know, Billy and I dated through high school. Everything went well until about midway through our junior year. Something happened to change Billy. He became surly, his grades dropped and he cut school all the time. I was so concerned I went to his parents."

"Had they noticed the change in him?" Alex asked.

"Yes, but they had no idea what was going on. Then when Landon died, it got worse. Billy became paranoid and said he was going to be the next to die. His parents were afraid he'd commit suicide, too, so they placed him in an institution."

A gasp escaped Grace's throat. "I'd forgotten Billy wasn't there to walk through graduation with us."

"No, he was off in another state undergoing treatment for a mental collapse. In the fall I started college at Rhodes here in Memphis, but I loved Billy, and I went with his parents to see him often. It was two years before he was able to leave the facility, but he said he couldn't live in Memphis anymore. His father had a business out in Colorado, so he gave Billy a job there. By the time I finished college, he seemed like the old Billy, and we were married."

Grace counted up the years in her head. "So you must have been married about four years before he died."

Sharon nodded. "I found out after we were married he wasn't the old Billy. He hardly slept at night. When he did, he'd wake up shouting all kinds of things."

Alex frowned. "What would he say?"

"He'd say things like 'I'm next' or 'Don't kill me.'"

Alex leaned forward. "Did you ask him about this?"

"I did over and over. Finally, one night he broke down and told me that during our junior year in high school, he and Landon, Clay, Jeremy, Sam and Dustin had gotten some fake IDs and gone to a club in one of the seamier sides of the city. They were looking for some excitement in their lives, and they found it. Billy said the guys who hung out there were like characters you'd see in a gangster movie, but they were real. Billy and his friends wanted to be a part of that macho lifestyle, and before long they were pedaling drugs for their new friends. They made a lot of money selling to kids at school, and then they branched out with college kids."

Grace's mouth gaped open, and she turned to stare at Alex. "They were drug dealers. That explains the money Mr. Mitchell found in Landon's room."

Sharon nodded. "Things were going great for them. They were making money, hanging out with drug lords and thinking of themselves as smarter than the cops who were trying to get drugs off the streets. Then they began to get email messages from someone who warned them not to sell drugs to this one guy. Of course they ignored them. They thought they were untouchable. One day Landon emailed the others to tell them he'd found out who was sending the messages. He said he'd let them know that night. Instead, his car was found on the bridge."

"So he never told them who it was?"

"No, but the messages continued. The person who sent the messages said he had killed Landon, and each one of them would meet the same fate if they sold this man's son any more drugs. They wanted to go to the police, but they were scared. The last thing they wanted was for their parents to find out what they'd done. So they told their suppliers they were through selling, which didn't sit well with them. For weeks they were afraid they were going to die in a drive-by shooting, but the emails stopped."

"What happened next?" Alex asked.

"Billy had his breakdown and entered the hospital, and the others got their parents to send them somewhere for the summer before college in the fall. Dustin went to the Gulf Coast where he disappeared. By the time school started, the police had busted the drug ring, and their suppliers were in jail. They thought they were safe...that is until the letters began to arrive a year or so later."

Grace leaned forward. "What did they say this time?"

"They said the boy they'd been warned about selling drugs to had died of an overdose, and it was their fault because they'd gotten him hooked. They were warned to watch their backs because the Wolf Pack was about to pay for what they did."

"Wolf Pack?" Grace and Alex spoke at the same time.

"That's what the boys called themselves. They had a wolf's head tattooed on their shoulders."

Alex stared at Sharon. "Why didn't you go to the police with this?"

"Because Billy made me promise not to. He said if anything happened to him, I was to keep quiet. He didn't want me or our daughter harmed. A week later he died when his Jeep crashed through a guardrail and ended up at the bottom of a Colorado ravine. The police suspected his brakes might have been tampered with, but they couldn't prove it. I was scared, and I kept quiet." Tears sparkled in her eyes. "But when I saw Grace on television last night, I knew I had to come forward. This killer has to pay for what he's done."

Grace reached over and grasped Sharon's hand. "I'm glad you called. What you've told us lets us know that Landon was indeed murdered, and it looks like the others were, too. Did Billy tell you the name of the boy who died?"

She shook her head and wiped at her eye. "No."

"Did he mention anything that might give us a lead about where to start looking for someone who'd want to avenge his death?"

"No, he didn't…" She paused, and her eyes grew large. "He did say the guy was a college student, but they weren't the ones who sold him his first drugs. He'd started using when he was in high school. He mentioned that the first time they sold this guy drugs he was stoned out of his head and sitting on a motorcycle in a parking lot. Sam had been trying to get his dad to buy him one like it, and he kept asking questions about the bike. The guy mumbled something about it not being his but his father's."

"Is there anything else you can tell us?" Alex asked.

She shook her head. "I can't think of anything else."

Alex let out a big breath and rose. "You've been very helpful, Sharon. I hope you and your family have a great time at Disneyworld. Maybe by the time you get back, we'll have all this sorted out."

She stood and looked from one to the other. "I know

Billy did some bad things, but he was really sorry about it later. It robbed him of his life, and our daughter will never know her father."

Grace hugged her and smiled. "Thank you, Sharon. If we catch this guy, it will be because of your help."

She gave a small shake of her head and led them back through the house. "If I had done it earlier, Sam might still be alive."

When they were back in the car, Grace swiveled in her seat and faced Alex. "Are you thinking what I'm thinking? Mr. Donner rides a motorcycle."

He nodded. "That he gave to his son. But there are still some unanswered questions. I'm going to the station to search the police records for all the deaths by drug overdoses in the years following our high school graduation. When I get the names, I'll check each one out."

"But even if you have all the names, how will you be able to tell which one is connected to the boys from our school?"

"We know the kid who died was in college, so I'll pull out the ones that fit the age. Then I'll trace the families and talk with each one of them."

"That may take a long time."

He smiled and turned the ignition. "This is the way cases are solved, Grace. We follow up one lead at a time, no matter where it takes us. Sometimes it leads nowhere, and other times we find answers. There's still something I'm missing, and I'm not going to rest until I find out what it is. I'll take you back to the hotel first."

"All right. I told Mom I'd go shopping with her to buy replacement presents for the ones destroyed last night. We also have an appointment to stop by our decorator's office to discuss getting the house cleaned out and buying new furniture."

"What's your Dad going to do?"

"He'll stay at the hotel."

"Alone? What if he needs something?"

"That concerns me, too, but he assured Mom this morning he'd be all right."

"What if..." Alex hesitated as if he wasn't sure what he was going to say. "What if I stayed with him?"

Her mouth dropped open, and she stared at him. "You'd stay with my father? What about going to your office to check those records?"

He waved his hand in dismissal. "I can go later after you and your mother get back."

"No, I couldn't ask you to do that," Grace protested.

"Really I don't mind. I'd feel better knowing he wasn't alone."

Grace could hardly believe Alex had volunteered to stay with her father, especially with the history between the two. She blinked back tears and squeezed Alex's arm. "Thank you. It means so much to me that you'd offer to stay. Even though it looks like the suite may be home for us for a while, he still hasn't learned to navigate well in his new surroundings."

Alex glanced down at her hand on his arm and cleared his throat. "No problem. I'm glad to do it." He pulled free of her and reached for his seat belt. "So is your family planning to spend Christmas there?"

She sighed and buckled her seat belt. "It's not about the house where you spend Christmas, Alex. It's about being with the people you love. By the way, that reminds me. When will your father arrive for the holidays?"

"He's not coming. I talked with him this morning, and he's not feeling well. I'll probably leave Christmas Eve and drive down there."

"That's only a few days away. Will you be back for New Year's?"

"I don't think so. I've already put in for some vacation time. I'll probably stay a few weeks."

She hoped her face didn't convey the disappointment she felt knowing Alex would be gone all through the holidays. But if he decided to stay in Florida, he'd be gone for good. She forced a smile to her lips. "I know your father will be glad to see you."

He nodded and put the car in gear. He didn't speak as they drove back to the hotel, but Grace glanced at him every once in a while. The muscle in his jaw twitched, and she knew he was deep in thought. Whether it was about the killer they were after or his sudden decision to drive to Florida, she didn't know. Whatever it was, she wondered how much longer Alex would be in Memphis.

Alex still found it hard to believe he could feel so relaxed with Grace's father, the man he had feared most of his life. Now as he sat in the hotel suite and chatted with Harrison Kincaid he saw nothing in his demeanor that even resembled the arrogant bank president of a few years ago.

Mr. Kincaid took a sip of his coffee and set the cup and saucer on the tray of his wheelchair. "Thanks for sticking around to keep me company while Grace and

her mother are shopping. They don't want the vandalism of our house to ruin our Christmas. I'm sure when
they come back they'll have a tree as well as bags filled
with all kinds of ornaments and presents to replace the
ones damaged last night."

Alex smiled. "I was glad to stay." He let his gaze
drift over the room. "This suite is very comfortable.
Grace said you'll probably spend Christmas here at
the hotel."

Mr. Kincaid nodded. "Of course we'd prefer to be in
our home, but we're thankful we can be together. Why
don't you join us for Christmas dinner? We'd love to
have you with us."

"Thanks, but I'm going to Florida to see my dad."

"I'm sure he'll be glad to see you. Tell him I said
hello."

"I'll do that. My father asks about you every time
we talk. He always enjoyed taking care of the gardens
at your house."

"He always did a good job. I hope you'll tell him
I'm sorry for the way I acted about him bringing you
along all the time."

"I'll tell him." Alex hesitated a moment. "About
that… I still find it hard to believe how different you
are now. I've heard people talk about how God can
change your life, but I never saw it until now."

Mr. Kincaid nodded. "I suppose some people would
think I should be angry because I'm unable to walk and
confined to this wheelchair, but the truth is I'm happier than I've ever been. When I turned my life over
to God, He filled me with peace and the greatest love
I've ever known. If He can do it for me, He can do it for

anybody." He pointed to his useless legs. "Don't mis-understand me, Alex. It's not easy, but I find myself able to cope with my disability because I trust God to make me content in my situation."

Alex's brow wrinkled, and he shifted to the edge of his seat. "But how can you trust something you can't see?"

"It comes from faith, Alex. It's a feeling inside that lets you know you're not alone, that you'll never be alone again. I have to admit some days I feel sorry for myself, then it's like a small voice whispers in my head and tells me I'm not alone. When I feel like I've gone as far as I can go, I turn it over to Him, and He gives me the strength to carry on. He can do it for you, too."

Alex shook his head. "I don't know."

Mr. Kincaid smiled. "Think about what I've said, and maybe we can talk about it again sometime. If you change your mind about going to Florida, then join us." He took a deep breath and pointed to a manila folder on his wheelchair tray. "Now if you don't mind, I have some work to do."

"I didn't realize you were still working," Alex said.

"I do a lot of work for the bank from home. These are some loan applications I want to study."

Alex chuckled. "I'm glad it's you and not me mak-ing those decisions. It would be hard for me to turn down anybody for a loan."

Mr. Kincaid nodded. "It is. There have been people I knew and respected that I had to say no to because they couldn't afford to repay the money. I wouldn't have done them any favors if I had led them deeper into debt. Unfortunately they didn't always see it that way. I've had some really angry customers over the years." He glanced back down at the folder. "But that's all in the past. I think I'll go in the bedroom to work on these. There are soft drinks in the refrigerator. Help yourself and turn on the TV."

"I will, and I'll be right here if you need anything." Alex rose to his feet and watched Mr. Kincaid guide his wheelchair toward the bedroom. Just before he reached the bedroom door, Alex called out to him, "I enjoyed talking with you. I'll think about what you said."

Grace's father turned his chair around and smiled at Alex. "I hope you will." He swallowed, and his Adam's apple bobbed up and down. "I have many regrets, Alex, but my biggest one is that I interfered in your and Grace's relationship. If it wasn't for me, you two might be married, and I would be a grandfather. I don't know if I'll ever get that chance now. She'll never love anyone else the way she loved you."

"Mr. Kincaid, it wasn't…"

He held up his hand. "I know it wasn't entirely my fault, but I was determined to break you two up. Now I have no idea why. I didn't realize until I was shot how much I loved Grace's mother. I wasted a lot of years when we could have been happy." He paused and took a deep breath. "In spite of everything that's happened this past week, Grace has been happier than she has in years because you're back with her. She told me you might move to Florida, but I know she doesn't want that. I think you have to decide what you want. I've been praying you will discover what our family knows now—it's never too late for love."

Alex stood in stunned silence as Mr. Kincaid disappeared into the bedroom. He wanted to run into the room and tell Grace's father he wasn't to blame for their breakup. Alex could blame no one but himself. He and Grace could have worked out some sort of compromise if they had tried. Instead, he had declared that if she loved him, she'd give up her dreams, and she'd turned the same argument around on him.

It made him sad now to think how he had decided Grace was only concerned with her own needs and that he could never trust her to care about his. Then when she became engaged to Richard Champion, he'd known he'd been right. Why hadn't he gone to her and insisted they work out their problems instead of letting years pass while resentment and anger build up in both of them?

For the past week they'd struggled to regain the trust they once had in each other, and they'd made progress. Even though she'd said she wanted his friendship, her father had hinted she still loved him. Was he ready to risk his heart again, or would it be best to walk away while he still could?

He sank down on the sofa and covered his face with his hands. He had no idea what to do.

# Chapter Twelve

Grace frowned and glanced at the clock on the bedside table. It was nearly eleven o'clock, and Alex hadn't
phoned. When she and her mother had gotten back
from shopping, he'd made his excuses and rushed off.
She'd expected to hear from him by now to let her
know if he'd found anything in the police records that
might help solve their case.

Her parents had gone to bed early in the adjoining
bedroom after dinner, and she'd rattled around the suite
trying to entertain herself while she waited for a call
from Alex. She picked up her cell phone for the third
time to call him. Before she could punch in his number,
she shook her head and laid it back on the table. He'd
call when he had any information for her.

Thirty minutes later when he still hadn't called, she
gave up and got ready for bed. She'd just gotten her
gown and robe on when the phone rang. Her excitement over Alex finally calling died when a number she
didn't recognize popped up on caller ID. She connected
the call and raised the phone to her ear.

"Hello."

"Good evening, Grace. Did you have a good visit with Sharon Warren today?"

Her breath hitched in her throat, and she clutched the phone tighter. "H-how did you—"

"Know you saw Sharon?" her anonymous caller finished for her. "I know everything you've done for days. You'd think two people trained as a news investigator and a police officer would realize when they were being followed. You and Alex Crowne are pathetic."

She narrowed her eyes and gritted her teeth. "What do you want?"

"I want to tell you who killed Landon."

"And Sam, Dustin, Billy and Jeremy, too? You took care of the Wolf Pack, didn't you?"

A chuckle came over the phone, and a chill went up her spine. "So you think you know the whole story, but you haven't arrived at the full truth yet. Do you want to know?"

"Yes, what is it?"

"Don't be so eager, Grace. I'm not going to tell you over the phone, but I'm sure you're suspicious of meeting me."

Grace gave a snort of disgust. "I've tried doing things your way. Once I was shot at, and the next time I was poisoned."

"There'll be nothing like that this time. I'm leaving town in a few minutes, but I've left you something."

"What is it?"

He sighed. "I'm tired, Grace. I've stalked the Wolf Pack for years, and I'm ready to finish my quest. In fact, I'm sitting on board a plane right now bound for Germany. I hope to meet up with Clay there. But don't get any ideas. We are taxiing to the runway and will be in the air before you can alert the police to my plan."

Grace sucked in her breath. "You won't get away with killing Clay. The police will notify the German police, and they'll stop you."

He laughed. "Maybe they will, but I doubt it. All kinds of accidents can happen on a ski trail. Afterward, I plan to disappear, and you'll never hear from me again. So I've left you something to remember me by."

"What is it?"

"I've made a video of my confession. When you see it, you'll know who I am and why I've done what I did."

"Where's this video?"

"It's in an appropriate place. I've left it underneath the entrance to the Memphis-Arkansas Bridge."

"Why there?"

He laughed again. "I thought since your interest in the Wolf Pack started on the bridge, it would be a good place for you to learn the truth. The video is easy to find. Leave your car at the E. H. Crump Park visitors' area and walk up the grassy rise toward the entrance to the bridge. At the top of the rise, walk down the slope toward the river, and you'll find the DVD in a box on the bank that runs underneath the bridge. Do you understand?"

"Yes, but how do I know I can trust you?"

"I suppose you'll have to decide. We're in line for takeoff right now, and I'm going to have to stow my cell phone. By the time you get to the bridge I should be safely away from the city. Goodbye, Grace."

Before she could say another word, the call disconnected. She stared at the phone, undecided what she should do. Alex would know. She punched in his number and waited as the phone rang. When it went to voice mail, she blurted out her message. "I just had a call from the killer. He's on a plane for Germany, and he's left me a recording of his confession. I'm going to find the video, Alex. If you get this message, meet me at the E. H. Crump Park near the entrance to the bridge."

She disconnected the call, tossed her phone on the table and ran to the closet. Within minutes she was dressed and ready to leave. She debated whether or not to leave a message for her parents but decided against it. She would be back before they woke.

Grabbing her purse, she hurried out the door and down to the parking garage where she'd left her mother's van earlier. She unlocked the car, jumped in and turned the ignition. She glanced at the menu panel on the dash and frowned when the Bluetooth didn't connect with her cell phone in her purse. With a groan she smacked the steering wheel with her hand. The phone wasn't in her purse. It was still lying in her hotel room. Why had she run out of the suite without picking up her phone?

Ignoring the urge to leave the phone behind, she leaned forward to turn off the ignition but froze when something round and cold touched the back of her neck. Only the barrel of a gun could feel like that. "Hello, Grace," a soft voice purred from the backseat. "I've been waiting."

She closed her eyes and berated herself. How could she have been so gullible? The answer popped into her head. She'd let the story become so personal that she'd lost her objectivity. She'd been quick to believe a killer, and now it might cost her dearly. "I thought you were on a plane."

"I lied."

Grace's heart thumped wildly, and she struggled to breathe. "Wh-what do you want?"

"I thought I'd ride with you to the bridge."

She clasped her hands in her lap and tried not to move. "How did you get inside this car?"

The sound of jingling keys echoed in her ear, and she cast a sideways glance at her mother's extra set of keys. "I found these when I was at your house last night. I must say they came in quite handy."

She straightened in her seat and lifted her chin. "So what do you have planned next for me?"

He gave a sharp gasp. "I want to tell you the truth. I thought we could all do it at the bridge. I'm sure you phoned Alex, and he'll be along shortly. Just the three of us at the bridge where it all started, but only one of us will walk away tonight. After you two are out of the way, your father will be next, then I'll get to Clay. That part wasn't a lie. I think he's about to have a skiing accident. As much as he drinks it won't come as a surprise to anyone."

He laughed when he'd finished speaking, and the hatred in his voice made her skin prickle. "You're despicable. Why would you want to kill my father?" She almost spat the words at him.

"You'll find out in good time, Grace. Now drive. We don't want to keep Alex waiting."

She shook her head. "Not yet. Not until I know who you are."

"Then turn around and see."

She took a deep breath, looked over her shoulder and gasped at the familiar face smiling at her from the backseat.

* * *

Alex walked back into his office from his trip to the break room, opened the tab on the soft drink can he'd purchased and dropped down in his desk chair. He took a long drink and set the can aside before he turned his computer on and berated himself for not getting to the office earlier.

Grace and her mother had returned exactly when they said they would, and he'd begged off staying for dinner so he could go to his office. The truth was, however, he wanted to put some space between himself and Grace. After the conversation with her father, he felt the need to ponder everything that had happened in the past week.

So instead of going to his office, he'd driven home, fixed something to eat and paced through his apartment for hours trying to decide what he wanted. Now at his office with the clock inching toward midnight, he was no closer to an answer than he'd been earlier.

He sighed, took one more sip from the soft drink and turned back to the computer. Looking through the records of several years for some unknown person might be a hopeless task, but he did have a few leads that might prove helpful.

He pulled a legal pad out of his desk and wrote Randal Donner at the top of the page. Underneath he began to write the things he knew about his former principal. (1) Rides motorcycles (2) Father of a son (3) Gave son his motorcycle and bought himself a bigger one (4) Denied drug use in school (5) Denied knowledge of a secret society.

Alex looked over the list, turned the page and started a new list under the heading Facts About The Killer.

(1) Rides a motorcycle (2) Had a son who died of an overdose (3) Gave his son a motorcycle (4) Killed the boys who sold his son drugs.

When he'd finished, he laid both lists side by side. The two lists appeared very much alike. However, he didn't know if Mr. Donner's son had died, but he knew who would. He pulled his cell phone from his pocket and punched in Brad's number.

He answered after two rings. "Hello."

"Brad, it's Alex. I'm at the office working on something, and I wanted to run a few things past you."

"Alex, do you know what time it is? It's nearly midnight. What are you doing there so late?"

"It's this case about the kids at our high school. I feel like I'm so close, but there's something I'm missing. I thought I'd bounce some things off you."

Brad sighed. "Man, you need to get a life. You can't let work rule you. Take it from an old married man. You need a wife."

Alex snorted. "I'll think about that. In the meantime, I wanted to ask you about Mr. Donner."

"Our high school principal?"

"Yeah. What do you know about him?"

"Hmm, well, he's been at the school for years, and from what I hear, he's done a good job."

"Did you know he's in a motorcycle club?"

"Yes. It's a group of professional people who do charity rides for different organizations. They also do some mission work."

Alex's eyebrows arched. "What kind of mission work?"

"They go to motorcycle rallies and set up a tent where

they speak to people about God's love. They've become well-known across the southeast for their work at events."

"Very interesting. And what about Mr. Donner's son?"

"Which one?"

"He has more than one?"

"There are three. The oldest is a doctor in Nashville, the middle one is a teacher at the University of Tennessee and the youngest one is in college."

Alex's phone beeped, and he pulled it away from his ear to stare at the screen. A message popped up that he had an incoming call from Grace. He'd return the call when he finished talking to Brad. He pulled the phone back to his ear.

"So, did Mr. Donner have a son who died?"

Brad was quiet for a moment before he answered. "No, I don't think so. Not unless he died in infancy. My parents have known his family for years, and they never mentioned a child dying."

"This son would have been college-aged."

"Then, no," Brad said. "I know he didn't have one die at that age."

Alex exhaled a long breath and drew a big X through the page where he'd written the things he knew about Mr. Donner. "Well, that eliminates him as a suspect. My guy's son bought drugs from Landon and his friends, and he rode his dad's motorcycle. The son died of a drug overdose when he was college age. I guess I'll have to keep looking."

"Wait a minute, Alex. You say this guy's son died of a drug overdose?"

"Yes."

"Have you thought of Mr. Caldwell?"

Alex bolted upright in his seat. "What?"

"He had a son who died of an overdose. His body was found in an alley near the downtown area about two years after we graduated from high school. Don't you remember us talking about it? We were in college, and a guy we graduated with came by our table in the cafeteria and told us Mr. Caldwell's son had died of an overdose. He remarked how surprised he was because none of the students even knew he had a son. The boy had grown up with his mother in Chicago. Evidently he got into drugs, and she couldn't handle him anymore. So when he started college, she sent him to live with his dad."

Alex hit his palm on his desk and groaned. "I knew there was something I had forgotten. This is it. When Grace and I went to the school the other day, we talked to him, and he mentioned he had no family. Grace later told me she always felt sorry for him because he didn't have a wife and children. Thanks, Brad. You've given me the answers I needed."

"One more thing," Brad interrupted. "Mr. Caldwell also rides a motorcycle. In fact, he's in the club with Mr. Donner."

Alex clenched his fist and pulled it down in a victory salute. "Yes, this is what I needed. I need to find Mr. Caldwell's son's death record now. Maybe by Monday morning I'll have enough evidence to take it to the D.A. By the way, do you know his son's first name?"

"I think it was Dennis, but he went by Denny."

"Thanks, buddy. I owe you for this one. I'll see you Monday."

"See you then."

Alex disconnected the call and turned to the computer

screen. Within minutes he'd found the death certificate of Dennis Caldwell. The death was ruled a drug overdose, and the next of kin listed the name Patrick Caldwell.

Alex sat back in his chair and smiled. Ever since he started in law enforcement, he had a deep desire to bring closure to a victim's family. Now with his job in the Cold Case Unit, he was able to do that. In Landon's case, however, it was too late for his father, but Grace would be happy.

At the thought of Grace, he remembered her call. He needed to let her know what had happened, but she might already be in bed. He picked up his phone and noticed she'd left a message when she called, maybe to tell him good-night. Smiling, he retrieved the message, but his smile disappeared as he listened to what she was saying. His hand began to shake, and he groaned aloud.

"No!" he screamed when the message ended.

He willed his shaking fingers to punch in her number and waited for her to answer. When it went to voice mail, he yelled into the phone. "Grace, the killer is Patrick Caldwell. Do not trust him. I am on my way to the bridge. I hope you get this message."

When he'd hung up, he looked back at her message. It had been sent twenty minutes ago. The Peabody wasn't too far from the entrance to the bridge, and she had a head start on him.

Shoving the phone in his pocket, he ran from the building, jumped in his car and roared off to the park where Grace had told him to meet her. He hoped he wouldn't be too late.

## Chapter Thirteen

Grace pulled the van to a stop in the parking lot where Mr. Caldwell had directed her. She then turned off the ignition and sat back in her seat. "What now?"

"Give me the keys," he said. She passed the key ring to him and locked gazes with him in the rearview mirror. He opened the back door, stepped out and motioned for her to do the same. When she stood on the ground beside him, he pointed toward the grassy rise that led to the side of the bridge. "Now walk up that way."

She turned around, and he stuck the gun in her back as they began their ascent toward the bridge. "You can't get away with this, you know. Alex will track you down and see that you go to jail."

"Don't waste your breath, Grace. Alex should have kept his nose out of this, and he would have been all right. Now he knows too much, so I have to get rid of him, too."

"How do you think you can escape? The police patrol this area all the time. Gunshots would bring them on the double. Then how are you going to get away?"

He chuckled. "I already have my escape plan. I stopped by here earlier and left my motorcycle underneath the bridge before I called for a cab to take me to the Peabody. I'll be out of here before anybody knows what's happened. Now get moving."

She walked a few more steps before she stopped and glanced over her shoulder. "But I don't understand. What is your connection to the Wolf Pack?"

"It's simple. They killed my son."

Her eyes grew wide. "You had a son?"

"Yes. His mother and I divorced before he was born, and she kept him in Chicago and away from me for years. When she finally sent him to me, he was a nineteen-year-old drug addict. I tried everything to help him, but it was no use."

"So your son was the one who died from the drug overdose?"

"Yes. I tried to keep an eye on him, but he hooked up with Landon and his friends right away. They were only too glad to sell him what he wanted."

"And you blame them for his death?"

"Partly, but I also blame the dealers in Chicago who got him started—there was someone else to blame, too."

"Who?"

"Your father. I could have saved my son if it hadn't been for him."

Grace's mouth dropped open, and she stared at him as if he'd lost his mind. "How on earth is my father involved in this?"

"When Denny got so bad, I knew he had to go into rehab, but I didn't have the money to put him where he'd get the best help. I went to your father at the bank and begged him." He hesitated, and his features dissolved into that of a madman. "I begged him," he yelled, "to give me a loan so I could put Denny in rehab. And do you know what your father did?"

"N-no."

"He turned me down without a second thought. I pleaded and told him it was a matter of life and death, but he called the guards in and had me removed from his office. When they were dragging me out of there, I told him he'd be sorry. And he was, when I put him in that wheelchair."

Grace's legs wobbled, and she struggled to stand. "You shot my father?"

He laughed. "Yes, and when I saw you on television talking about Landon's father dying at the bridge, I knew I could hurt him even more if I killed you." He eased closer and grabbed her arm. "So you see this past week, it's been all about killing you." He put the gun to her head. "And that's what I'm about to do."

"Hold it right there, Caldwell. I have a gun pointed at your back." Alex's voice sent a shock wave of relief flowing through her. She'd known he would come. Before she could move, Mr. Caldwell grabbed her around the waist, whirled around, and held her in front of him with one arm while the other held the gun to her head.

"Hello, Alex. I wondered when you would get here. As you can see, we're at a standoff right now. You may shoot me, but you can't stop me from killing Grace. Now back off, or she's a dead woman."

Alex looked at her from perhaps ten feet away, and Grace held her breath. She sensed the hesitation in

Alex, and she screamed at him. "Shoot him, Alex, before he kills us both."

Alex moved a step closer, his gun pointed at Mr. Caldwell. Suddenly, a police officer emerged from the darkness beside Alex, a gun in his hand. "What's going on here?"

Alex glanced over at him, but before he could say anything two shots rang out. Alex and the officer both hit the ground.

"No," Grace screamed and struggled to free herself.

Mr. Caldwell's grip tightened, and he laughed. "I should have told Alex I've been trained in how to handle a gun."

A surge of energy rushed through her body, and she slipped one arm free from the vise he held her in. Raising her hand, she gouged at his eye and then dug her fingernails into the side of his face and pulled downward.

He screamed in pain, grabbed at his face, and released her. She drew her foot back and kicked him in the knee with all the force she could manage. He started to point the gun at her, and she kicked him in the other knee. He sank to the ground. "You'll pay for that," he yelled.

Grace longed to go to Alex and make sure he was alive, but there was no time for that now. In case he and the policeman were still alive, she needed to get Mr. Caldwell away from them before he finished the job.

She turned and ran toward the bridge and onto the walkway headed toward Arkansas. She'd only gone a few feet when she realized her mistake. She should be running back toward the streets of Memphis. There she could find hiding places and elude capture until she could get some help.

She turned to head back the way she'd come, and then she heard the engine of a motorcycle crank. Before she had time to process what that meant, the bike roared to life, and she heard it coming up the bank toward the bridge.

Mr. Caldwell stopped the motorcycle at the entry to the walkway and let the motor idle. He smiled and called out to her. "There's no escaping me, Grace."

The lights on the bridge lit the Memphis sky, and she realized she would be visible to any passing car. She glanced helplessly around, but there wasn't a single vehicle in sight. He revved the engine again, and she swallowed her fear. Slowly, the motorcycle glided onto the walkway and stopped. Breathing a prayer, Grace turned and ran toward the Arkansas side of the river.

Alex opened his eyes and saw the sky. The stars twinkled, and a peaceful feeling filled him. He blinked and tried to remember what had happened. The heavens appeared lit with a bright light, and he looked around to see where it came from. His gaze came to a stop on the lights outlining the bridge span between Memphis and Arkansas.

He tried to move, but a pain in his left shoulder ricocheted through his body. He gasped and grabbed at the spot where the pain seemed concentrated. A sticky substance covered his fingers. Blood. He shook his head to clear it, and the memory of Patrick Caldwell holding Grace in front of him and firing at him and another officer who had appeared out of nowhere flashed in his mind.

He pushed into a sitting position and closed his eyes to ward off the dizziness that had everything in his vision spinning out of control. After a moment his head cleared, and he opened his eyes and looked around. Where were Grace and Caldwell? From somewhere near the bridge an engine cranked, and a motorcycle roared out from underneath the abutment. He caught sight of Patrick Caldwell on the bike as it skidded across the dew-covered grass and sped up the embankment to the bridge walkway where it came to a stop.

Alex patted the grass with his right hand until he touched his gun. He picked it up and pushed to his feet. From somewhere in the darkness a woman's soft cries drifted on the night air. Grace? Where was she? On the walkway?

He pushed to his feet and clenched his teeth to keep from crying out at the pain in his shoulder. Patrick Caldwell's voice rang out from the top of the hill. "There's no escaping me, Grace."

Alex took a deep breath and willed his legs to move. With his left arm dangling at his side and his gun clutched in the other, he staggered up the hill. Perspiration popped out on his forehead even though the night air was cold. Halfway there he stumbled but regained his footing.

The engine revved again, and Alex staggered on. Grace must have gotten away from Caldwell, and he was the only one who could help her. Something warm trickled down his arm and dripped from his hand to the ground. He'd seen gunshot victims before, and he knew he was losing too much blood. His body screamed he didn't have the strength to go on.

Then words Grace's father had spoken welled up inside him as if he stood there on the banks of the Mississippi River with him. *When I feel like I've gone as far as I can go, I turn it over to Him, and He gives me the strength to carry on. He can do it for you, too, Alex.*

Alex looked up at the stars again. *God,* he prayed, *help me save Grace. She's the only woman I'll ever love.*

The motorcycle eased onto the walkway, and with renewed strength Alex charged up the embankment. He arrived at the end of the walkway just as Caldwell accelerated and headed down the concrete path. In the distance Alex saw Grace running in the opposite direction.

Taking a deep breath, Alex steadied his arm, aimed at the rear tire of the motorcycle and fired. The back tire of the motorcycle exploded in a blast that split the night air, and the bike skidded. Pieces of rubber flew into the air as the motorcycle crashed into one side of the walkway, veered across to the other side and hit the opposite wall. Caldwell struggled for control, but it was no use. The bike careened once more from side to side and jumped the barrier that separated the walkway from the highway.

The motorcycle landed on its side in the middle of the highway and skidded across the asphalt with Caldwell pinned underneath. Sparks like those from a Roman candle shot up from the pavement as the metal scraped the surface and the bike slid to a stop.

Alex climbed the barrier and stumbled across the

road to where Caldwell lay unconscious. Behind him Grace's voice called out from somewhere down the walkway. "Alex, are you all right?"

She leaped over the barrier and reached him just as he sank to his knees. He laid his gun on the pavement, pulled his cell phone from his pocket and handed it to her. "Call 911. Tell them two officers and a suspect are down at the bridge. We need help right away. We have no way to stop traffic."

Grace nodded and grabbed the phone from his hand. He heard her speaking, but he couldn't concentrate on what she was saying. He slumped to the pavement and closed his eyes. All he wanted was to sleep, but he needed to stay awake until the EMTs arrived.

He licked his lips and swallowed. "Grace," he whispered.

She dropped to her knees beside him and grabbed his hand. "Help is on the way. Stay with me, Alex. Talk to me."

He stared up at her and tried to focus his eyes. "Are you all right?"

"I'm fine. Thanks to you."

"We're in the middle of the bridge. Watch for cars."

She clasped his hand tighter. "Don't worry about anything right now. I told the 911 operator. She's getting word to the Arkansas Highway Patrol to shut off that end of the bridge." She glanced past him and smiled as a siren wailed. "And here come our guys now."

A vehicle screeched to a stop near him, and then the sound of voices filled the quiet night. Alex closed his eyes and thought of the mighty river flowing so far below them. The muddy water stopped for no one, and it felt as if he floated with it. He reached for Grace's hand and let the darkness carry him away.

Grace glanced at the clock on the wall as she paced the hospital waiting room. It was 3:00 a.m. Alex had gone into surgery two hours ago, and she hadn't heard a word.

The room and hallway looked like a constantly shifting sea of blue from the uniformed, on-duty police officers who arrived and then departed after checking on two of their own who had been shot. As Grace let her gaze travel over the assembled officers, she realized how fortunate Alex was to belong to such a brotherhood.

The sound of the elevator opening in the hall caught her attention, and she looked out the door to see Police Chief Watson striding toward them. Captain Wilson, the officer who'd been at the bridge the morning Mr. Mitchell died, rose from the sofa where he was sitting and met the chief at the door.

"Evening, sir," he said.

The chief nodded. "More like good morning, I'd say. How's Detective Crowne?"

"He's in surgery, sir. The bullet hit an artery, and he lost a lot of blood. The EMTs said he was fortunate he got to a hospital so quickly."

"Good, good. And the other officer. How is he?"

"Patrolman Grayson suffered a head wound, but the doctors are optimistic. He's still in surgery, too."

"And the suspect? What's his condition?"

"Mr. Caldwell has a broken leg, a broken arm and

multiple contusions. He's in surgery down on the orthopedic floor. I have officers waiting there for him to come out of surgery."

"Have the families been notified?"

Captain Wilson nodded. "Patrolman Grayson's parents are on their way from Nashville where they live. I've talked to Detective Crowne's father in Florida, but his friend Miss Grace Kincaid is here."

"It seems like you have everything under control, Captain. Good work." He turned and smiled at Grace. "I understand you and Detective Crowne have had an interesting night. Not only have you solved a twelve-year-old cold case, but you've captured the killer of four other people and the man who shot your father. Would you like to tell me about it?"

"I'd be happy to." Grace walked to a sofa, and the Chief followed. When they were seated, she related the events that began the year she and Alex were in high school and ended in the middle of the Memphis-Arkansas Bridge that night. When she finished, she clasped her hands in her lap and glanced toward the door. "Now I wish someone would come tell me how Alex is doing."

The elevator opened again, and Brad and Laura Austin rushed into the room. Grace ran to Laura and embraced her. "We came as soon as we heard. How's Alex?"

Grace pulled back from Laura and looked from one to the other. Their faces mirrored the fear in her heart. She'd held her feelings at bay ever since she'd arrived at the hospital, but with the arrival of her and Alex's two best friends her resolve flew out the window. She put one arm around Laura's waist and one around Brad's and dissolved into tears. They pulled her close and let her cry for several minutes before Brad pulled loose and led her to the couch.

She sank onto the hard cushions, and Laura sat down beside her. Brad stood in front of them. "Would you like something to eat or drink? Some coffee maybe?"

Grace shook her head. "No, thank you. I just want to know how Alex is." She looked from Brad to Laura. "I thought we were both going to die on that bridge tonight, and all I could think about was how we'd wasted so many years when we could have been happy." She burst out crying again.

Laura put her arm around Grace's shoulders and smiled. "It's not too late. You and Alex can still have a life together if you love each other."

Grace looked up, her vision blurred by her tears. "That's just it. I love him so much, but I have no idea how he feels about me. He still blames me for our breakup, and now he wants to move to Florida. What will I do if he leaves?"

Brad's eyes grew wide. "Move to Florida? He hasn't said anything to me about it."

Grace sniffed and wiped at her eyes. "Well, he has to me. He knows I love him, but it's like he wants to punish me and get as far away from me as he can."

Laura placed a hand on each of Grace's shoulders and looked into her eyes. "And just how does he know you love him? Have you told him so?"

"Well, no, but I've tried to show him with my actions."

Brad squatted down in front of Grace and smiled.

"I think you and Alex have a communication problem. When you see him, tell him how you feel. Give him a chance to tell you his feelings. You and Alex have driven Laura and me crazy for years. We're ready for you two to decide if you belong together or not."

Laura laughed. "He's right, Grace. God has given you another chance with Alex. Don't ignore it because of what you think he feels. Find out."

Grace reached out and clasped Laura's hand, then Brad's. "I'm so thankful God gave me friends like you. I remember when you were going through all your problems, and look at you now. You're happy…"

"And we're going to have a baby," Laura interrupted.

"What?" Grace squealed. "Why haven't you told me?"

Laura smiled. "We just found out, and you've been busy the past few days."

Grace hugged her friend again. "Oh, I'm so happy for you and Brad. I knew you two were meant to be together."

"Just like you and Alex are," Laura said.

Before Grace could respond, she glanced up at the doctor walking into the room. She jumped to her feet, and all the police officers moved in to hear what he had to say. He approached Grace.

"Miss Kincaid, I believe you're the one who came in with the patient."

"Yes, doctor. How is he?"

"He's in recovery and doing well. He lost a lot of blood, but we were able to repair the damage. If all goes well, he should be able to leave the hospital in a few days."

A sigh of relief went up from the assembled officers, and they smiled and patted each other on the back. "We're all relieved to hear that, Doctor," Chief Watson said. "Detective Crowne is a valuable member of our force. Thank you for taking care of him."

The doctor nodded. "It was my pleasure." He turned to Grace. "The patient is awake and is asking to see you. Do you want to go in?"

"Oh, yes. I need to see him."

The doctor smiled. "I thought you might like that. Come with me. I'll take you back."

At the door Grace turned and smiled at Laura, who gave her a thumbs-up. She returned the gesture and followed the doctor down the hall. A few hours ago she had climbed over a barrier on the Memphis-Arkansas Bridge and feared Alex would die before she had a chance to tell him she loved him.

But he wasn't going to die. Not tonight. And God had given her this time to make things right between them. And that's what she intended to do.

# Chapter Fourteen

Grace stopped at the entrance to the cubicle where Alex lay and took a deep breath. Her gaze scanned the tubes and machines hooked to his body, and her heart lurched. Had the doctor been honest with her about Alex's condition?

She spied a nurse coming down the hall and stopped her. "Excuse me. I wondered about all the tubes attached to Alex Crowne."

The nurse smiled. "That's standard after surgery. Don't worry. We'll probably disconnect some of them by the time he gets to his room."

Grace sighed in relief. "That makes me feel better. Is he awake?"

"He's been going in and out. You can have a seat in there and wait. The effects of the anesthetic should wear off soon."

"Thank you."

Grace stepped back into the room and walked to the bed. Alex's hand lay out from under the sheet, and she covered it with hers. She threaded her fingers between his and remembered how holding his hand had always made her feel so safe. She hoped he could feel the same from her now.

His eyelashes fluttered, and his eyes blinked open. He stared upward for a moment but then turned his head to face her. "Grace." Her name sounded almost like a croak coming from his lips.

She smiled and bent over him. "I'm here."

His gaze took in her face. "Are you all right?"

"I am because of you. I don't know how you were able to walk up to the bridge. I thought Mr. Caldwell had killed you." A tear rolled out of her eye, and Alex reached up with his free hand and wiped it away.

"I knew I had to get to you before he killed you."

She frowned. "But how could you walk? The EMTs were astonished that you could go that distance when you had lost so much blood."

"It was something your father said to me that got me there. He told me when he didn't think he could go any further, he asked God to take over, and He gave him the strength he needed. God did that for me, too."

She smiled and squeezed his hand tighter. "He'll be so glad to know that."

"Over the past week I've come to realize what a wonderful man your father is. I look forward to getting to know him even better."

Her eyes grew wide. "Oh, that reminds me. You don't know why Mr. Caldwell decided to add me to his list of victims."

He listened as she related what her old teacher had told her in the van. When she'd finished, he shook his head. "Your father told me there were people he'd been unable to approve loans for who hated him. I never thought any of them could be the murderer in our case."

Grace closed her eyes for a moment and shook her head. "It's just all so unbelievable, but we did it, Alex. We found out the truth about Landon's death just like we promised his father we would."

Her hand still covered his, and he tightened his grip as he glanced down at their intertwined fingers. "We did. Now what are you going to do with Landon's ring?"

She pulled free of him and held her hand up. The tiny birthstones in the ring sparkled, and she looked at it for a moment before she slipped it from her finger and dropped it in her purse. "This ring belongs in the past like so many things in my life do. I feel like I've helped an old friend by finding out the truth about his death, although I found out some things I was sorry to know. Now I can let that part of my life go."

"We did what we promised Mr. Mitchell. I wish he was here today to know about it," Alex whispered.

She took a deep breath and straightened her shoulders. "I do, too, but enough talk about sad things. We need to be happy. You're going to be all right, and there are some things about our past that we need to get settled."

"I think so, too, but first I have a question. Has anybody called my father?"

"Captain Wilson called him when he called Patrolman Grayson's parents. And by the way, that young patrolman is going to be okay, too."

"Good. So would you mind if I called my father

before we talk about whatever it is you have on your mind? I want him to know I'm okay."

Grace nodded and reached for his cell phone, which lay on the bedside table. "Want me to connect it for you?"

He shook his head. "I have him on speed dial. I'll do it."

She handed him the phone and sat down in the chair beside his bed. He put the phone to his ear and waited for his father to answer. It only took a moment.

"Hi, Dad," he said. "I'm in recovery and wanted you to know I'm okay."

He nodded while he listened, and Grace gazed at his profile. Even with all the tubes and machines as well as a five o'clock shadow, she didn't think he'd ever looked so handsome. Her heart swelled with love for him. Now if only he could feel the same about her.

"Yeah, it looks like I won't be able to make it for Christmas."

Grace's heartbeat quickened. Maybe he wanted to spend it with her.

"I doubt if the doctor will want me to travel that soon," he continued. "I may have to postpone the trip for a few weeks, but I'm still coming."

Grace swallowed her disappointment. So his plans for going to Florida were still in place, which meant he still wanted the job there. She brushed at a tear in the corner of her eye.

"But when I come, I'm going to bring someone with me—my fiancée." He turned to look at her. "Do you think you can get some time off to go visit my father?"

All she could do was stare in dumbfounded disbelief and nod. Alex laughed and winked at her before he turned his attention back to his father. "Yeah, it's Grace. Who else would it be? I'll call you later today and let you know how I'm feeling. Bye, Dad. I love you."

He ended the call and handed her the phone. "Dad said to tell you hi."

She frowned, shook her head, and placed his cell phone back on the table. Then she rose to her feet and stared at him. "What just happened here?"

"You mean the part about you being my fiancée?"

"Yes, where did that come from?"

He reached for her hand and laced their fingers together. "When I woke up on that riverbank and thought Patrick Caldwell was going to kill you, I regretted every minute that we'd been apart. I knew if God let us live, I was going to spend the rest of my life making it up to you for being such a jealous guy and ruining our chance at happiness years ago." He paused and pulled her closer. "I've never quit loving you, Grace. Please let me show you how much."

"B-but you told your father we were engaged, and you didn't even know if I love you or not."

"Yes, I do."

She smiled at him. "And how do you know?"

His eyes sparkled. "Because there's been a bond between us since we were ten years old. It grew deeper as we got older. I've never loved anybody else, and I never will. We've wasted enough years when we should have been together. If you'll marry me, I'll do everything in my power to make you happy. I'll leave Memphis if you want to go back to the networks. My life is meaningless if you're not in it. How about it, Grace? Will you spend the rest of your life with me?"

Tears filled her eyes. "I've loved you for as long as I can remember. I don't want anybody else but you." She leaned closer and squeezed his hand. "But I don't want the networks. I want to live our life together here where we met and grew up. All I want is you."

"Then marry me," he whispered. "I don't ever want to be away from you again."

"Neither do I. Yes, I'll marry you."

He released her hand, grasped the back of her neck and pulled her head down until their lips touched. "I love you, Grace Kincaid," he whispered.

"And I love you, Alex Crowne," she answered.

She pressed her lips to his, and her heart soared. The love they shared had never died, and she could hardly wait to begin their new life together.

Alex sat down on the sofa in the Kincaids' hotel suite, stretched his legs out in front of him and closed his eyes. He didn't know when he'd ever spent a better Christmas Day. The dinner prepared by the hotel staff had been delicious, but the best part of the meal had been Grace and her parents. The only thing that could have made it better would have been to have his father with them, but he would be here soon.

His father had decided that moving to Florida hadn't been the best choice for him. He'd missed the life he'd known in Memphis, but he'd especially missed being with his son. Now with Alex and Grace getting married, he wanted to be nearby in case there were grandchildren in his future.

The cushion next to him dipped, and he opened his eyes to see Grace sitting beside him. She had her arm on the back of the couch and one leg curled underneath her. She scooted closer and smiled. "What are you thinking about?"

"My dad. I'm glad he's moving back. With him nearby, I can keep a close watch on his health."

"We both will," Grace said as she leaned back into the cushions. "Did you get enough to eat?"

He groaned. "I'm stuffed more than the turkey was, but I think I'll be hungry again by nighttime." She laughed, reached over and trailed the tip of her forefinger down his jawline. He closed his eyes at the pleasure that raced through him. "I always liked it when you did that."

"And I always liked it, too." She leaned closer and brushed her lips across his. "It's almost been a perfect day, hasn't it?"

He nodded. "It has. Now all that's left to do is open the presents. I can hardly wait to see what you got me."

She laughed and arched her eyebrows. "If I'd had more time to shop, I could have gotten something better. But all my time these past few days has been spent playing nurse to a grumpy patient."

"And you've done a mighty good job, ma'am. I may decide to keep you around for quite a while."

She laughed and swatted his leg as the bedroom door opened and her father's wheelchair rolled into the room. Her mother followed behind. "It sounds like everybody in here has the Christmas spirit," Mr. Kincaid said as he came to a stop. "I move that we keep the festivities going by opening presents."

Grace clapped her hands and smiled. "And I second the motion. All in favor say aye."

All four yelled their response at the same time. Mr. Kincaid smiled at his daughter. "Grace, do you want to do the honors and pass out the gifts?"

Fifteen minutes later Christmas paper and ribbons littered the floor. Grace jumped up and ran to give her parents each a kiss. "Thank you for everything you gave me. I love the clothes, and the jewelry will set each outfit off."

Alex held up his present. "Mr. Kincaid, I can't believe this. A private suite with catering and a server for the remainder of the Memphis Grizzlies' season? This is too much."

Mr. Kincaid waved his hand in dismissal. "Not at all. If you decide you like having the suite, I'll get one for the whole season next year. I do have to warn you, though, that Grace would rather go to a play at the Orpheum than see a basketball game. I thought if you didn't mind, I might go with you sometime."

Alex's throat closed up, and tears stung his eyes. He'd never thought to see the day when Grace's father would tolerate his presence, much less want to hang out with him at a ball game. It only reaffirmed what he was just beginning to understand—with God nothing was impossible.

"Thank you, sir. I'd like that a lot." He took a deep breath and rose to his feet. "Now there's something I'd like to do." He looked at Grace. "Please come sit down."

She looked at her mother and laughed. "This sounds interesting."

She sat down on the couch, and he turned to face her parents. "As you know, things happened rather quickly over the past two weeks. When I woke up in the hospital, all I could think about was how much I loved Grace and how much time we'd wasted being apart. When she came to see me in recovery, I'm afraid I didn't give her a very romantic proposal. In fact, I informed her we were getting married."

Her parents smiled, and her father shook his head. "That's all right. We're glad you're both safe and weren't hurt."

"I am, too, but I really feel like I should have talked with both of you before we started making plans. I really want to be a part of this family, and I want to make sure you want that, too."

Her father nodded. "You needn't worry, Alex. We couldn't be happier to have you for a son."

"Thank you, sir." He reached in his pocket with his good arm, pulled out a ring box, and knelt in front of Grace. He opened it and looked up at her. "Grace Kincaid, I love you with all my heart. Please marry me and make me the happiest man on earth."

Tears filled her eyes, and she looked at the ring, then back at him. "It's a beautiful ring. And nothing would make me happier than to be your wife."

Smiling, he pulled the ring from the box and slipped it on her finger. "Now it's official. I don't want that ring to ever come off your finger."

"It won't," she whispered and leaned forward to kiss him.

They pulled apart, but Alex didn't want to move. It had been so long since he was this happy he wanted to keep looking at her and soak up every inch of the woman he'd loved since he was ten years old. After a moment her father's discreet cough caught his attention, and he rose.

"Have you two decided when you want to have the wedding?" her father asked.

Alex shook his head. "I don't know. We haven't had a chance to talk about where we're going to live. I don't think my apartment's big enough. Grace couldn't get all her clothes in the tiny closet."

Her mother laughed and nodded. "She'll need some room, that's for sure."

Grace frowned. "We also have to think about you two. Who will help you at night, Mother, if I'm not there?"

Her father shook his head. "You're not to worry about me. I'm going to hire a personal assistant as soon as we get back in the house. We'll make it fine, and I don't want you to start married life with your parents. So I decided to do something about it."

Grace stared at her father. "What have you done?"

He picked up an envelope from the tray of his wheelchair and held it out. "This is for you and Alex with love from your mother and me."

Alex looked at Grace, and she shrugged. She took the envelope from her father, and Alex looked over her shoulder as she unfolded the papers inside. His eyes grew wide, and he shook his head in disbelief. "Mr. Kincaid, this is too much."

"No, it's not, Alex. You saved my daughter's life and helped bring the man who put me in this wheelchair to justice. I can never repay you for all you've done for me."

"But a house? You want to give us a house?"

Grace's father laughed. "It's only a starter house. You can sell it later on and move into a larger one when you decide to bless us with grandchildren. I spent a lot of years working for the money I accumulated. Now I want my family to enjoy it. The house belongs to you and Grace."

Tears ran down Grace's face. She ran to her parents and embraced them. "Thank you, Mom and Dad. I don't know what to say."

Her mother kissed her on the cheek. "Just be happy, darling. That's all we want for you."

"I will."

"Now," her father said, "if all the gifts are distributed, I think I'll take a nap." He looked at his wife. "Want to join me?"

She cast a glance at Grace and Alex. "I think these two might like to have some time alone."

When her parents had disappeared into the bedroom, Alex put his arms around Grace and pulled her to him. "I think your father had a good idea about leaving us alone. What would you like to do?"

Before she could answer, her cell phone rang. She pulled it from her pocket and smiled. "It's Derek from the station. I guess he's calling to wish us merry Christmas." She pressed the phone to her ear. "Hello, Derek. Are you having a good Christmas?"

She listened for a moment, and her smile grew larger. "Spending it with Julie? You don't say. It sounds like things are going well for you."

She walked to the window and looked out as she continued to listen. "That's the best news I've had in a long time. Thanks for calling to let me know. I'm looking forward to getting back to work, and tell Julie I'll be in touch in a few days. Bye, Derek."

She hung up but didn't turn away from the window right away. Alex frowned and took a step toward her. "Is everything okay?"

She looked over her shoulder and smiled. "This was already the best Christmas ever, but it just got a lot sweeter."

"How's that?"

"Derek called to tell me Todd has gotten a job as anchor at a Los Angeles television station. He's leaving after the first of the year."

He laughed. "So you got your wish."

She turned around and held out her hand. "But I got another one, too."

He walked to her and put his arm around her. "What's the second one?"

She pointed to the window. "Look outside, Alex. It's snowing. After all these years we finally got our wish for a white Christmas."

He looked out the window at the snowflakes drifting to the ground. Already a blanket of snow had covered the street. The memories of Christmases past and wishes made floated through his mind. He remembered the innocent children they'd been and the angry adults they'd become.

Outside the snow continued to fall as it covered everything and made a new world in the street below. That's what the love he and Grace had for each other was going to do. With God's help, their love would wipe away the hurts of the past and create a new life for them together.

Alex tightened his arm around her waist and pulled her close. She snuggled against him as they gazed out the window at the falling snow. Contentment like he'd never known welled up in him. Smiling, she turned to face him, and he brushed the hair away from her face and kissed the scar on her forehead from so many years ago. "I love you, Grace," he whispered. "This is the perfect ending for a perfect day."

\* \* \* \* \*

Dear Reader,

I hope you enjoyed reading Alex and Grace's story. When I first began to write this book, it was hard to imagine how two people who'd been childhood friends could wind up as angry adults. Then I realized jealousy, anger and imagined betrayal can sever the tightest of bonds. As I wrote their perilous journey toward the truth, I wanted them to learn what I've known for many years—God's love can sustain us in our darkest hours. It is my prayer that if you haven't found the strength that comes with knowing God's love, you'll tune your heart to His voice. Then you'll know, like Alex and Grace, that He can fill you with peace and give your life new meaning. He's waiting to hear from you.

*Sandra Robbins*

WE HOPE YOU
ENJOYED THIS

# LOVE INSPIRED® SUSPENSE BOOK.

Discover more **heart-pounding** romances of **danger** and **faith** from the Love Inspired Suspense series.

Be sure to look for all six Love Inspired Suspense books every month.

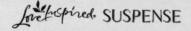 SUSPENSE

www.LoveInspired.com

Canyon Air Force Base was silent. Houses shuttered, lights off. Streets quiet. Just the way it should be in the darkest hours of the morning. Captain Justin Blackwood didn't let the quiet make him complacent. Seven months ago, an enemy had infiltrated the base. Boyd Sullivan, aka the Red Rose Killer—a man who'd murdered five people in his hometown before he'd been caught—had escaped from prison and continued his crime spree, murdering several more people and wreaking havoc on the base.

"What are your thoughts, Captain?" Captain Gretchen Hill asked as he sped through the quiet community.

"I don't think we're going to find him at the house," he responded. "But when it comes to Boyd Sullivan, I believe in checking out every lead."

"The witness reported lights? She didn't actually see Boyd?"

"She didn't see him, but the family who lived in the house left for a new post two days ago. Lots of moving trucks and activity. She's worried Sullivan might have noticed and decided to squat in the empty property."

"Based on how easily Boyd has slipped through our fingers these past few months, I'd say he's too smart to squat in base housing," Gretchen said.

"I agree," Justin responded. He'd been surprised at how much he enjoyed working with Gretchen. He'd expected her presence to feel like a burden, one more person to worry about and protect. But she had razor-sharp intellect and a calm, focused demeanor that had been an asset to the team.

"Even if he decided to spend a few nights in an empty house, why turn on lights?"

"If he's there, he wants us to know it," Justin responded. It was the only explanation that made sense. And it was the kind of game Sullivan liked to play—taunting his intended victims, letting them know that he was closing in.

He needed to be stopped.

Tonight.

For the sake of the people on base and for his daughter Portia's sake.

*Don't miss*
Valiant Defender *by Shirlee McCoy,*
*available November 2018 wherever*
Love Inspired® Suspense *books and ebooks are sold.*

www.LoveInspired.com

# *Love Inspired*®

## Save $1.00

on the purchase of any
Love Inspired® or Love Inspired®
Suspense book.

Available wherever books are sold,
including most bookstores, supermarkets,
drugstores and discount stores.

---

## Save $1.00

on the purchase of any Love Inspired® or
Love Inspired® Suspense book.

Coupon valid until April 30, 2019. Redeemable at participating retail outlets in the
U.S. and Canada only. Limit one coupon per customer.

52616033

5 65373 00076 2    (8100)0 12391

® and ™ are trademarks owned and used by the trademark owner and/or its licensee.

© 2018 Harlequin Enterprises Limited

LICOUP44816